Praise for *The Good Journey*

"The author writes with her driving energy, subtle humor and wonderful nuances woven among the characters. The book is part history, part romance and part mystery. It's absorbing and a wonderful read."
—Diane Hartman, *The Denver Post*

"[This] ambitiously researched, gracefully narrated first novel . . . traces an exciting time during the Black Hawk Wars of the mid-nineteenth century on the Missouri prairie. . . . Characters are fleshed out to the smallest detail. . . . Gilchrist has managed to create a work that is both historically riveting in the manner of eighteenth-century captivity narratives and as deft in the depiction of a beleaguered marriage as C. S. Godshalk's *Kalimantaan*."
—*Publishers Weekly*

"Micaela Gilchrist is an extraordinary writer. From the first page of the book, she sweeps you off your feet and plants you firmly on the frontier. It is clear that she has done intensive research and she uses it in her keen descriptions, her brilliant use of language and her finely drawn characters. She breathes life into every person and place and puts the reader smack in the middle of history. Bravo!"
—Janet Wallach, author of *Desert Queen*

"Top-notch fiction. A graceful novel based on the real-life letters of Mary Bullitt and the military writings of her husband, General Henry Atkinson, from the Black Hawk Wars of nineteenth-century Missouri."
—Tom Walker, *The Denver Post* Books Editor

"Unlike the typical one-dimensional portrayals of Native American and white-settler relationships, Gilchrist weaves a colorful tapestry of the rivalry between the General and Black Hawk, chief of the Suak nation."
—Deborah Peterson, *St. Louis Post-Dispatch*

"A sweeping and powerful story."
—Pamela Thompson-Kirk, *Lincoln Journal Star*

"*The Good Journey* marks the writing debut of Micaela Gilchrist, and she has done a spectacular job. Gilchrist has deftly woven a narrative that, while fictitious, wholly transports readers into situations of danger, romance, mystery and intrigue. Gilchrist's strength lies in her ability to paint an even, nuanced portrait of Mary, not only as intelligent and poised in her social sphere but also as inexperienced and stubborn as she moves with her husband toward the new, untamed West. . . . Cleanly illustrates the intricacies of war."

—Nathan Tsoi, staff writer, *Military Lifestyle Magazine*

"Much of what the American West was, *The Good Journey* is. In this historical novel, first-time author Micaela Gilchrist uses an authentic voice to present a vibrant portrait of western life in the 1820s and 1830s. Fact and fiction are entwined so expertly in the book that readers will want to tease out the two, if only to gain a better understanding of the time period and its people."

—Anne Owens, Gateway Heritage, Missouri Historical Society

Micaela Gilchrist

The Good Journey

A Novel

Scribner Paperback Fiction

Published by Simon & Schuster

New York   London   Toronto   Sydney   Singapore

For Scott

SCRIBNER PAPERBACK FICTION
Simon & Schuster, Inc.
Rockefeller Center
1230 Avenue of the Americas
New York, NY 10020

First Scribner Paperback Fiction edition 2002

For information about special discounts for bulk purchases,
please contact Simon & Schuster Special Sales:
1-800-465-6798 or business@simonandschuster.com

Designed by Karolina Harris
Map by Jeffrey Ward

Manufactured in the United States of America

1   3   5   7   9   10   8   6   4   2

Library of Congress Cataloging-in-Publication data is available.

ISBN 0-684-87143-2
0-7432-2377-2 (Pbk)

A Note Before You Begin the Journey

✲ Do you ever wonder how writers of historical fiction pick their subjects? Or why they were inspired by a particular project? A series of accidental discoveries and coincidences compelled me to begin work on *The Good Journey.* This book and my life as a writer began after I read letters written by an aristocratic Southern woman named Mary Bullitt Atkinson one hundred thirty-five years ago. In the spring of 1997, I found a disintegrating paperback titled *General Henry Atkinson: A Western Military Career.* The book moldered in an old bookstore located in a nineteenth-century warehouse—the sort of bookstore with ladders reaching into the gloom of the ceiling, invisible rats scuffling over the pipes and the pipes leaking on the customers.

I sank into an old armchair and flipped disinterestedly through the pages. Of course I'd heard about General Henry Atkinson, the most powerful military commander on the western frontier in the 1820s and 1830s. Yes, I'd passed many hours exploring the reconstructed fort he built in 1819 and walking the roads rutted with wheel tracks left a century and a half ago by the quartermaster's wagons. But Dr. Roger Nichol's military study brought to light a fact I had not considered.

The General had married, after a long bachelorhood, a young woman who used her influence and her connections to accomplish things the General could not. For example, when the Senate contemplated promoting the General, his enemies circulated ugly rumors about his health in Washington. Mary Bullitt Atkinson prevailed upon her twin brother Alexander Bullitt, part owner and editor of the *New Orleans Picayune,* to sway Southern opinion in the General's favor. Bullitt, at Mary's behest, denounced the anonymous letter writers in the Senate as "vile slanderers and midnight assassins who set forth lies then hid themselves in the dark . . ." Dr. Nichols described Mary as having "railed" against her husband's detractors for spreading "the most shameful and outrageous lies."

I like a woman who isn't afraid to rail now and again.

A few days after buying the book, I called the author, Dr. Nichols, professor of history at the University of Arizona at Tucson, and asked him what he knew about Mary Bullitt Atkinson, whom he'd mentioned twice in his military study. After several subsequent discussions and an exchange of letters, Dr. Nichols volunteered to share copies of Mary Bullitt's correspondence.

They arrived at my home in the Rocky Mountains one day in June 1997.

Mary Bullitt Atkinson's letters—vibrant, witty, mournful, expressive missives brimming with a living presence—captivated me. Through those letters, she described the violence, sensuality and exhilaration of nineteenth-century life in St. Louis at a time of incredible social and political upheaval. Every Sunday evening in the library of her home in Jefferson Barracks, Missouri, Mary Bullitt Atkinson wrote to her brother-in-law, Lieutenant Thomas Alexander. Lieutenant Alexander had been widowed in 1835 when Mary's nineteen-year-old sister, Anne Bullitt Alexander, died during childbirth less than a year after her marriage to the lieutenant. Shortly after his wife's death, Lieutenant Alexander was assigned to frontier duty.

His military friends informed Mary that Alexander was depressed and self-destructive. Mary was determined that her brother-in-law would not believe himself abandoned by his Bullitt relatives even when he found himself stationed hundreds of miles away in the Florida mangroves or the Kansas flatlands. She hoped to sustain him by sharing her perceptions of daily life in St. Louis in the 1830s and 1840s.

Each letter opened with *My dear Brother,* followed by lengthy, almost journalistic, reports of the events of the day. Mary wrote of the arrival in St. Louis of Robert E. Lee, a handsome young civil engineer struggling to reopen the Mississippi river channel, in danger of silting shut. The artist George Caitlin pestered her with questions about Black Hawk before painting the war leader's portrait. Zachary Taylor conversed with her about children and gardening as he dined at her table.

Lieutenant Alexander read these letters on troop transport steamers, under the miserable sag of rain-soaked canvas tents in Florida, while traversing the South Platte, and in camp at Cerro Gordo, Mexico. The young officer rolled Mary's letters into his knapsack, bundled them in his footlocker, tied them with fraying pieces of hemp and thrust them into his saddlebags, accumulating dozens of them over the years as he rose through the ranks of the army's officer corps. After Lieutenant Alexander's death, Mary's letters were entrusted to her grandchildren and thereafter were preserved by her descendants.

I was most intrigued by Mary Bullitt's plaintive recitations of a war that threatened to destroy her marriage and the lives of everyone she loved. I could hear her voice as she called through the wooded hills above the Mississippi for her children. I could see her at work in her garden, her face shaded by the weave of her straw hat. She came to live in our home, a gracious presence, a vivacious woman eager to reveal the tale of her loves and her losses. I felt I had no choice but to write Mary's story. So I quit my job. I let the children and dogs run wild and started writing *The Good Journey*.

Which brings us to the next question readers always ask: Where is the line between historical fact and fiction in this book?

With a few exceptions, all of the characters in this novel are historical persons and their actions are based on their correspondence. I spent five wonderful years reading the personal papers of the people in this novel. If Mary or General Atkinson mentioned someone in their correspondence, I sought out that person's papers at historical repositories to see if they perchance mentioned the Atkinsons to develop a complete view of the times. It's exciting work if you can get it, making the acquaintance of our nineteenth-century predecessors.

The major plot turns in this novel are also based in fact and historical truth—to the extent there is such a thing. The few histories written about the Black Hawk War were penned by participants in the battle and were self-aggrandizing because most of the militia historians were running for political office: 1832 was an election year. The histories written in the twentieth century espoused hard-line political agendas; some read like Native American history written by John Wayne, others were so steeped in the militant mood of the 1970s that the pages reeked of peyote. Even so, I was grateful to these historians, because they gave me a scaffolding—albeit a rickety one—from which to begin.

As a novelist, I could venture into places where historians could not go and I could take the reader with me. We could meet in the General's tent before battle, and I could whisper to the reader to take notice of the color of the General's cheek as he raged against his political enemy Lewis Cass. Quietly, discreetly, you and I could tiptoe into the General's bedchamber and breathe in the smell of the soap lather on the cloth as his widow bathes his body for burial. My job as the novelist is to be your guide through the territory, rending open a vanished world so that for a few hours at least, you can inhabit the commanding general's house on the banks of the Mississippi river in the early part of the nineteenth century.

Mary Bullitt Atkinson and I invite you to journey into another time and another place, where—as Mary observes—"the most reckless desires of men are manifest." I can't help but feel that Mary's desire to enlighten, educate and amuse, ever reminding a young army lieutenant that he was beloved, somehow crossed the centuries through a series of coincidences and happenstances to reach you. I hope this story of Mary Atkinson's life and times and her indomitable spirit will inspire and delight you.

Prologue

Jefferson Barracks, Missouri, June 16, 1842

W E buried him this morning, but the shock of his death pulls me back through the decades where I wander unbidden through every moment of the years we spent together on the banks of the Mississippi river. I see the prairie swept purple with coneflower, I find myself upon the soft grass of the peninsula, and it is difficult to pull myself back to my duties, to my son and to this place. The house is dark, but for the taper light, and the quiet is broken by the dispirited groan of his spaniel, who looks to me for reassurance I cannot offer. How is it possible that my love is not sleeping in the next room? I rise to search for him but find only a cold silence over our bed.

After the funeral service, the widow James pressed a speckled hand against my cheek and whispered to me, "Now he is gone, you must pacify yourself with living as though your footsteps have never marked the earth." Her words have wisped around in my mind since she said them, slighting words, and if this is Mrs. James's way of comforting the grieving, she can keep her comfort. My sorrow is born of my wound, for with his death, my soul has been halved.

On spring evenings such as this, we would walk together through the hickory grove and talk for hours of the people and the times we had known together. He would take me in his arms, but look wistfully past me at the river, toward the north, and he would say to me, "I believe the work of the living is the retelling of memory. A thread not to be broken." And knowing what he said to be true, I awoke this morning, having slept beside him one last time. I looked down upon his silent countenance and dreaded the task before me.

I would have to begin the work of remembering.

But when I try to impose order on my memories, I cannot find sequence, nor am I able to prompt a beginning. Even now, I begin to drift back, but only to the evening before this one, when I undressed him and bathed him. He lay so quietly, his lips parted and his head tossed back. His coat smelled of bran, there were marks where the dust had been beaten from the seams. I forced the brass buttons through their grommets, and the wool placket felt thick in my hands. When I peeled it back, the sight of his broadcloth shirt bearing the marks of the iron made me believe he would wake to me. A dead man would not worry whether his shirt was neatly ironed.

"Wake up, Henry. You always were a promiscuous napper. Wake up, now."

Something crisped when I opened his coat. I was watchful of him as I slipped my fingers into the pocket and removed the piece of foolscap, creased into fours. I pressed my nose to his dark hair as I unfolded the paper. The letter was penned in his hand—cruel slashes over the *t*'s, bold down strokes, neat spacing. It was dated June 11, 1842. There was no salutation.

> I received your message and was both shocked and perplexed by it. As for myself, that memory haunts me—indeed it has shaped my years in aspects I have yet to comprehend. But this explains why I was never asked questions that I would have welcomed and perceived as natural, yet I too am guilty of reticence, for I never volunteered a single word. I am glad you have told me. How could you question whether I would come to you? Ever I shall come to you, know that I shall always honor a request from you. In youth and dotage we have shared that which no

And there the letter ended. I let it flutter onto my lap and opened the buttons of his shirt. I sat beside him on our bed with my hand to his breast, regarding those written words once again and then the broad bones of his face. My stomach soured and churned. Though I sat awhile, and tried to trick the knot of his letter apart, the skeins remained tangled. This was the way of him, to leave me mired in place under the burden of his deceptions, committed with honorable intentions, of course.

I picked the letter from my lap and placed it under his hand in the hope a revelatory dream would come to me. It would be a dream wherein I would forgive him his trespasses, and the General, finding comfort in death, would finally speak the truth to me. Wouldn't I be foolish to wait for such a thing? I've always known that it was my charge to venture forth as a self-possessed woman and seek the truth for myself. Until I did, years ago, I had become adept at subsisting on his assurances.

Ever I shall come to you . . . who had inspired my husband to pen words resonating of such urgency and discretion? It could be a letter to anyone. Anyone at all. But not to me. In all the years of our marriage, he never spoke so floridly to me. I snatched the letter out from under his hand, crumpled it, then tossed it upon the chest of drawers.

The General's limbs were corded from a hard life, and few would have guessed him to be fifty-nine. I cupped the arches of his bare feet in my hands and watched the water sparkle as it dripped from his heels.

I took great care not to touch his toes.

My servants touched the toes of the dead to keep them from turning ghostly. I wanted the General to come back and haunt me. I cradled the hope of it. I lay beside him after he died, not feeling a bit of peculiarity in it for he was my husband, gone a little bit chilly is all. In the night, I kissed his face, and his skin felt like cooled paraffin against my lips.

"It is safe now to talk of it, Henry, you can tell me now. There is no one here but the two of us. You can tell me everything, and I shall not reproach you."

The hair of his chest was dark and curly with a few gray strands. I squeezed the rag into the basin, soaped the rag with my own lavender soap, not the laundry soap made of lye and ashes. The water left a silty line in the hollow of his ribs. My breath caused the brown air to dance about me as I pulled the brush through his hair. Then I scraped the flesh from under his fingernails. With small, even steps, I crossed to the bed stand and burned the tiny mound of it in the taper flare.

With a fresh cloth and salt water, I cleaned blood having the texture of coffee grounds from the General's teeth, patting his lips to let him know I had finished. And when he was free of his clothing, I let him lie there a while, as if he were napping on a heavy July afternoon, sleeping with no hope of a cool breeze. Innocent and naked. I saved the Spanish milled coins until the moment the soldiers put him into the box, and that was the worst of it; placing death weights on his beautiful eyes. But, I would not let the camp surgeon knot a winding sheet about his limbs. My husband lived freely on this vast Western landscape. How then, could I allow them to re-strain him for all eternity?

The General has been gone two days from me. I held him as he passed, rather selfishly, I suppose, I wanted him to speak of our recent reconcilia-tion, I wanted him to tell me that I had always been vital to him. But that was not his way. He stared off as his breath became shallow, and he thought instead of his place in the next world. "Beyond forgiveness," he murmured, and then . . . he slipped off so quietly, I asked after him . . . "Husband?"

Late last evening, the Sauk, Winnebago and Maha Peoples settled in the center of the barracks esplanade to set up their tipis. The wind blew the sound of clattering lodge poles through my open window, I could hear the Indians speaking to one another as they prepared to make their last visit to the General. And this morning, citizens of St. Louis chartered the steamer *Lebanon,* then disembarked at the landing, a grim cloud lofting and rippling up the hillside. There were politicians and matrons, shopkeepers and a volunteer force of militia from outlying counties, half drunk at midmorning from their breakfast of crackers and whiskey, all filled up with false sentiment for a general they did not know.

Those militiamen did not know my husband, nor would he have cared to make their acquaintance. The General learned during the wars of the thirties that having the militia along on campaign would surely doom the effort. They were dirty and unkempt. I know he would have despised the look of them. But the regular troops had been ordered to Florida to fight the Seminole, so the barracks were deserted, and my husband deserved an honor guard, even a pitiable one. In his last year, my husband was a general without troops.

As the Reverend Hedges read the service, my veil formed a shield around me, dropping to my toes so I appeared as a sniffling black bell jar to the other mourners. It wasn't that I wanted the privacy to cry, such a thing hasn't been possible since he left me. Crying seemed too small a grace to the worst event of my life. Now and then, the crowd would shift under the long winds blowing up from the river and right themselves when a scuddering cloud crossed the sun.

The regimental band played "Roslin Castle," a dirge the General disliked, then the militiamen shrieked, causing everyone to jump, shouted a lament and poured bottles of mash in the dirt mounded round the grave. They sang a ragged a cappella version of "Mo Ghile Mear," "Our Hero," then fell to weeping upon one another. I know my husband would have been bemused by the exertion of this false grief on his account.

I closed my eyes and imagined him near me, sheltering me with his arm, and I wondered what was left for me beyond his memory. I was discouraged by what I conjured, for the years to come were entirely too dark to be seen through. I felt vanquished, I believed I could tolerate no more of this ceremony. But then I was distracted from my reverie by the sight of the General's bay.

Now, as I simply couldn't fathom the General flourishing in the afterlife without his horse, I had asked a Maha warrior to perform a ritual common to his people at the burial ceremony. Billy, our groom, led the General's horse around to stand before the assembly. The warrior stepped forward, said something none of us understood, then wrapped a hemp loop around the animal's neck and strangled it with grace and ease.

A horrified gasp went up from the crowd, and the militia aimed their Harper's Ferry rifles at the Indians standing opposite me. I jumped before their guns, explaining that this honor had been performed at my request. While the crowd settled, I overheard ugly mention of the red men who had come to pay their respects.

The grave looked a slack mouth under the toe of my boot, asking questions none of us dared answer. I leaned forward, pinioned by Senator Benton on my left and Colonel Stephen Kearny on my right. They held tight to me as if I were a bedlamite contemplating escape. My veiled glance sent the mourners to panicked searching of the horizon. When I leveled my gaze upon them, they hurriedly looked away from me. I knew what they thought; they feared my reason had once again slipped under a cloud. Have you seen the Mad Widow Atkinson? they would ask one another. *Avoir le diable au corps.* A pity. The senator and the colonel tensed, silently willing me to forgo grievous outpouring. They had borne witness at the last burial. Ten years had elapsed, and I hoped they had forgotten what was past, but apparently, they had not.

Senator Benton offered his arm, and we led the cortege to the regimental dining hall for a breakfast, but I do not remember most of what transpired this morning. It was a blur of half-wept condolences and somber greetings. Numbly, I watched the crowd mill about like so many black beetles, emitting a low humming sound. In the corner, watchful and silent, were the Indians, all of them dressed in their best ceremonial wear.

And that is when I saw Bright Sun, rising gracefully with a nod to her companions. My hand flew reflexively to my bodice in a protective gesture, and I peered sidelong at her, under my lashes.

Bright Sun was dressed after the manner of Indian women who live along the rivers, in a red skirt, a calico blouse and, despite the heat, a Hudson Bay three-point blanket over her left shoulder. But she was distinguished by the red star upon her forehead, the "mark of honor" denoting her status as daughter of a war chief. Throughout the morning, we caught the glance of one another, and each of us intuited an unspoken curiosity about the other. It has always been this way between us, scrutinizing, but pretending disinterest. Of course, I knew *who* she was. Bright Sun was a translator for the Sauk and Fox tribes. But I have never, in sixteen years of sightings, chance meetings and surprising arrivals, been able to discern *what* she was to my husband.

In late afternoon, the crowd thinned and I took my leave with Colonel Kearny. The silence was thick after the noise of the hall. I was glad for his company but eager to rest, for I was deeply wearied by my sorrow. When I stepped onto the sagging porch of our log house, I glanced over my shoulder and saw a tribal contingent coming toward us. Bright Sun followed a respectful distance behind the warriors, clasping her hands to her waist. Her head was slightly bowed, and her skirts blew elliptically over the grass as she strode along with that vexingly confident posture of hers.

Colonel Kearny opened the door and motioned me across the threshold. I looked back once again at the approaching group.

"The Sauk men go first."

"What?" Kearny asked with a worried look at me.

"I once told the General that I disliked their practice of making the women walk behind the men until he explained that the warriors clear the path of danger for their women."

"Uh-huh. Now, Mary, don't allow company to wear you out. You're not in a form to entertain, so I'll tell Nicholas to urge them along after they've made their condolences."

"Thank you, Colonel, that's very kind of you."

"I'll be leaving now, but you let me know if there is anything you need. May I write to your ma or to your brothers and sisters? They're all in Europe, aren't they?"

"Yes."

"A shame they're so far away at a time like this."

"I'll get along."

"You ask my wife or myself for anything you might need. Don't be proud."

"I'll be fine. You'd best head back to the landing before it gets any darker. I wouldn't want you to miss the steamer. Give my regards to Mrs. Kearny." He placed a chaste kiss on my forehead, then took his leave.

It was much too hot for a fire this afternoon, but Nicholas built one of pine, which I object to mightily, for nothing pops more violently than pine, and I feared the plank floors would catch fire once again. And it would be terribly inconsiderate of me to burn the commanding officer's house just when I am required to turn it over to Colonel Stephen Kearny and his wife.

The Kearnys had not hurried me to vacate, but I sensed their eagerness to "ascend to the throne" and did not begrudge them their happiness. Oh, well, perhaps I did just a bit. It was painful to see my husband's heir apparent, a man very much like the General, preparing to assume command of the Ninth District. This was the cruel truth of military life; a fortnight previous my husband controlled all of the American West. Now that he had died, my son and I were to be tossed out of the only home we have known these past sixteen years.

I walked through our bedroom and opened the wardrobe. The General's uniforms and breeches hung from hooks, his boots were lined up neatly on the bottom shelf as if awaiting marching orders. But I was not prepared for the clean scent of him wafting from his clothing. I turned quickly, expecting to see him quietly about some task in the room with me, expecting him to grin and shrug and assure me that the past few days had been a terrible misunderstanding.

"Henry?" I said aloud, then bent in pain at my folly. When my eyes began to sting, I drew a breath and straightened my back. Though I had been an old bride of twenty-two, I was now a young widow of thirty-seven. A wiser woman, perhaps, would see balance in such a thing. The mirror over the chest of drawers showed me my decay. Well, I must be honest; I was widely considered a beauteous woman and vainly pleased by the popular opinion. I owned a thick mass of dark brown hair and had an oval shape to my face and, when I was nineteen, Thomas Sully of Philadelphia painted my portrait, sipping his Frontignan whilst paraphrasing Herrick. The artist flitted and dabbled, saying, "Mary, oh Mary, I'll kiss the threshold of thy door."

When he went so far as quoting "Upon Julia's Breasts," and rather brashly substituting my name for Julia's, I harrumphed him and marched out of the drawing room. But now, my mourning weeds were a drain to color, my blue eyes were mostly red and my dark hair had been flattened by the weight of my bonnet. "You brazen out the day, Mary Bullitt Atkinson," I said to my reflection.

Having chastised myself, I removed a dimity bag from the top drawer and took my journal into the library. I intended to scribble every bit of spurious gossip I'd heard over the past year to distract myself and thereby waste the hours until dawn. But when I took my seat, I saw the General's letter neatly arranged on the desk blotter. Doubtless, Nicholas had saved it. I crumpled it again and made to toss it into the fire but did not. I dropped it, and chin in hand, puzzled at it. *Ever I shall come to you . . .*

I hunched over the journal the General had given me so many years ago, a palm-sized book, bound in calfskin, edged in gold leaf. The nib of my quill made scritching noises as I wrote.

Nicholas, a graying and cranky servant who had come West with me years ago from Kentucky, entered the library with a worried glance and stood silently, waiting for me to acknowledge him.

"They here," he said, finally.

"Please direct them in."

I rose and smoothed my black skirt, pulled the floor-length black veil over my head so that I presented a ghoulish figure. My mind spiraled with anxiety and odd fixations on inconsequential things, an attempt, I know, to control some aspect of my life, any little thing at all. I despaired at the nettles that snaked hairy stalks up through the floor. Those weeds were defiantly rooted, as if telling me I was an intruder on the tallgrass prairie. For sixteen years I suffered every hardship a woman could know, and now I had discovered weeds in my library floor.

I bent to pick the artemisia, and the room was filled with an odor like that of juniper. This is what happened when a house was built of green cottonwood. It warped and withered, and there was not enough lime in the whole of the river country to point the gaps. Over the years, Mama had crusaded the cause of the mercantile class from a distance, had shipped me seventeenth-century French antiques, paintings of Huguenot ancestors, then paid a local seamstress to drape the windows in crimson damask, but still, artemisia grew up wild through my floor.

"Ma'am, the—" Nicholas patted the air with a worried look and searched for something to call the group, then said, "The chiefs is here. And Miss Me'um'bane the Bright Sun, ma'am."

I glanced up to see a dozen plainsmen enter quietly, then stand in a line while Bright Sun, a small-boned woman, hid behind them. She stepped cautiously away from the hearth. I tossed my veil over my head to get a better look at her. I knew her to be about thirty-three years old.

"Yes, I'd stay away from the fire too, if I were you. Strouding easily catches a spark and you'd torch right up and there wouldn't be a thing I could do to save you."

Bright Sun did not respond but cast her gaze upon my feet. What she found so fascinating there, I did not know, nor did I care. She looked away, not because she was shy or retiring, nor was she intimidated by me. Bright Sun believed avoiding my eyes was the polite thing, under the circumstances. I was not so polite. I feigned a smile to study her. She looked away from my scrutiny, muttering *"wado 'becnede,"* words that I had heard many times these years passing. It meant one who stares, but I could not help my-self.

Bright Sun had black hair, broad cheekbones underlayed by a nervous pink bloom and hazel eyes, uptilted and large. The many winters she had quartered within the smoky haze of wickiups and wind lodges had weathered her beyond her years. Her face bore the mysterious impress of several races. She adjusted her blanket and surveyed the room. Despite the crowd of humanity, none of us said a word. They were waiting for me to speak. And so I did. "Thank you for attending today, it would have made the General so happy to know you have come one last time," I said.

Blank stares and blinking.

"Miss Bright Sun, will you translate for us, please?"

I waved her through, and she looked over her shoulder to where she had just been. One of the warriors said something. Bright Sun cleared her throat and spoke, "An'geda said he is happy to meet the General's woman and he knew General Atkinson was going to die because he dreamt of him with snakes creeping into his nose and ears."

I was not quite sure how to respond to this, so I smiled and bowed a little and said thank you. The chief spoke again, and Bright Sun began, "And you may sleep at the *hu'thuga* with the Burnt Leg People whenever you come north once again on the river."

"How nice. Thank you, An'geda. I shall certainly consider your invitation the next time I come to the territories."

And they turned and filed out as silently as they had entered.

Nicholas and I exchanged baffled shrugs.

I watched my visitors drift away over the grass. When they reached the twilit shade of the oak trees, Bright Sun said good-bye to the chiefs and warriors. She paused uncertainly, glancing up the hill at our family burial ground, then down across the green lawn to the river.

She lifted her skirts and dashed up the hill toward the General's grave.

I felt a jealous catch in my breast and decided to follow her. I stepped out from under the black locust trees the General had planted after I had given birth to our third child. I strode over the grassy hill flowering with copper mallow. The twilight was green, the air was cool, and I held my breath when I saw Bright Sun stop before my husband's new bed. Her visit seemed an affront to the intimacy of the setting. I considered setting up a shout to order her away, but I was curious so instead I waited in the shadow of the tree.

Bright Sun knelt, fumbled at her waist pouch, removed a pair of scissors and cut a hank of her blue-black hair. After lofting it to the wind like a small flag, she plunged the whole handful into the dirt and anchored it there with a little mound. Then she removed a few slender, sharp twigs from her waist pouch and thrust them into her forearms. Blood rilled down her hands into the soil.

Who did she think she was, to mourn the General as if he were *her* husband? I balled my fists and clenched my jaw. I turned away for an instant to gather my wits, then coerced myself into a false calm by reminding myself that once, long ago, Bright Sun tendered a generous favor to me at a time when she knew great suffering. Besides, in the days to come, many strangers were going to knock on my door as I packed up my belongings and prepared to return home to Louisville. They too would ask to visit my husband's grave. Should I excoriate every mourner who dared appear at my door? Talk would ripple through the camp and the city entire that Mary Bullitt Atkinson's reason had once again taken flight. And I did not want to travel *that* road again.

"Miss Bright Sun?" I ventured, stepping out from under the tree.

She turned a peppery look upon me, as if I were the interloper upon my own family burial ground. When I said nothing further, she plucked a willow needle from above her wrist and tossed it into the dirt, then offered without meeting my eyes, "I promised Black Hawk and the others I would come."

Black Hawk.

Even now, I see Black Hawk's apparition, and familiar resentments roil out of my heart. I hear the trade bells jingling along Black Hawk's snakeskin armbands as he stands in the willow thicket behind my house, his eyes boring at me through the darkness. From the day I first met my husband, Black Hawk's specter hovered over us.

"How could you possibly have promised Black Hawk . . . ?"

But Bright Sun continued as if I had not spoken at all, "My people—the Sauk, the Yellow Earth People—asked me to burn a fire for four nights to light his way. The General is uncertain, he waits here. He is reluctant to go on. And I wanted to come, after what he did for me . . . and my daughter. In a way, he was ours too. The General belonged to us in the seasons of war."

Her smug, proprietary tone infuriated me. So I asked, "The willow sprigs. Do they hurt?"

She shrugged and touched a curling spray of leaves splattered with her blood. "Willow is only for warriors who are greatly respected."

"I'm not leaving the General here, you know. You may pretend he was yours for as long as you wish, but I'm taking my husband—and my other loved ones—home with me, back to Louisville, as soon as I can arrange passage. I won't leave them in this wretched place."

With a nod, I folded my arms about me and left Bright Sun at the grave. As I walked away, I wanted to create an impression of dignity, but my toe caught a compass-plant root and I stumbled, then blushed at my clumsiness. The cottonwood trees whispered above my head, and the weeds released their musky summer odors underfoot. *Henry,* I thought, *how could you have allowed a visit from her, of all people . . . and at a time like this.*

I entered through the back ell, let the door slam, poured myself a bumper of brandy, then slumped in the General's chair in our library. Dust swirled up from the floor on a column of bronze light, yellowing about me like muddy rivers in the springtime. I brought the glass to my lips and regarded the General's portrait, filling the wall opposite.

He returned my scrutiny with cunning disdain. The portrait was commissioned by his men, the Sixth Infantry, after the Black Hawk War. The General cut an imposing figure. He had dark wavy hair and sideburns that fringed around his jaw. His chin was cleft, his nose perfectly straight, his Scottish complexion ruddy. His shoulders were broad, and he was above medium height, but not so tall as Uncle William or the other Clark men. He presented the traditional stance of handsome men, confident he would obtain whatever he pursued. His white trousers were tucked into his boots. He never wore the plumed chapeau that was part of a General's uniform in the army of this new republic. The General could do as he wished. For twenty-three years he commanded all of the Western Frontier, from Canada to the Red River.

His eyes were portrayed as suspicious under heavy lids. In life, his eyes were intensely blue, vivid with thought and speculation; his were the eyes of a man born of the Enlightenment. The first time ever we locked eyes, I curled my toes, my face colored like a majolica poppy; neither modesty nor false delicacy could compel me to look away from him. He captured my reasoning and my heart in that moment; I felt myself being studied for distinct purposes by his scientific eye. By his pagan eye.

When I was eight years old, my Calvinist governess pinned a drawing of a solitary eye over the nursery hearth. Black tangs radiated from a jet circle at its center; this was the eye of a goat or a reptile. The governess wagged her finger at me, "I know your type, Miss Mary. You are a voluptuary. When you are tempted to give way to your true nature, look up into the eye of God and remember he hates your kind. You must submit humbly until the hour of your death and hope against reason for redemption."

That night, I crept into the dark nursery as the moon haze drifted through the windows, illuminating the eye of God. I removed my nightdress and danced naked before Him, thinking that if I was lost to heaven, I may as well entertain the Lord as I descended the circles of hell, one by one.

I have always been enraptured by the forbidden and unknowable.

From the moment the General took my hand in his, I was captivated by what I could neither discern nor fathom in him. At our wedding, I heard murmuring about the difference of twenty-two years in our ages, about the fineness and surety of an accomplished man being ruler of his domain with a rich and comely young wife at his side. They could not guess at the hours when I ruled, the days when I was sovereign, the months when I governed.

I drained my glass and poured myself another, turning slowly to find him watching me. His father's scabbard was slung low over his left hip, gloves covered the broad spans of his hands. I let the liquor swirl over my tongue as the slanting light glinted around us. He was trapped in the room with me, he was a hant locked into a temple of memory where I was the sole congregant.

Sixteen years ago, when I followed the General away, I had known him for only three days. I reconciled myself then to sleeping with a gentlemanly stranger. How could I have known that years later a stranger would die in my arms?

Perhaps in death I shall know thee.

I

❧ THERE is no place more unforgiving or colder than a Louisville church on the first Sunday after Christmas, I thought as I navigated my way to our family pew. Despite the clutter of bodies, the air was glacial perfection, and with each passing moment, my hands and feet became more blockish and icy. Surely this was what was meant by mortification of the flesh. I grimaced at the Reverend Shaw, who said there was no contradiction to be found in the biblical entreaty to render unto Caesar. I could have cared less what Caesar was or was not owed, because the winter sun through the window burned a nick upon the back of my neck.

My neck was on fire and my feet were numb with cold. They would find me dead in my place after service, with a scalded neck and blue, frostbitten feet. I slumped in the pew, away from the light, and poked the leather cover of my psalmbook with a gloved finger. That winter, I was twenty-two and discomfited at having been forced to attend service. Mama rapped me sharply with her Bible. I gasped and bent over, complaining of a fainting spell. The odor of wood oil filled my nostrils. I peered around Ma and caught the gaze of a brigadier general grinning from the pew directly across the aisle. He leaned over his knees with his hands upon his white breeches, mocking my discomfort.

I stared at the General in a way that I hoped made him feel much reduced in rank. I quirked a brow, which he mistook for encouragement, because he tickled the air with his fingers. I lifted my chin to let him know I disapproved, but he seemed pleased by my lofty pretense. He looked pointedly at the door and then at me. Forty, I estimated, about the same age as my pa, and he died of the afflictions of age in the spring of last year. This General was dark haired; he had a proud and stern countenance and remarkable blue eyes.

I was intrigued by his bad behavior and felt an odd prickling on the surface of my forearms when he regarded me as if determining my worth. My seventeen-year-old sister, the precocious Eloise, a child prone to homely outbursts about the mischief in her heart, squirmed about as the General smiled at her. At the tap of Eloise's fingers upon my skirt, I tipped my ear to catch her whispers.

"He is as proud as a prince and he's staring so lasciviously. What kind of a man stares so in church?"

I wiggled my fingers and blew upon them. "Glance away, Eloise, do not meet his gaze; you should elevate your thoughts and disregard that gentleman. And you hush up. Mama's going to beat me like a stray dog if I let you whisper at me through service."

"Mary, I was wrong. That is no stare; that rises to a leer. He is at least as old as Papa, and military men are poor, even the generals."

"Eloise, look at my neck. Am I getting a blister on my neck from sunburn?"

She wrinkled her nose and examined me. "No, but you have farmer wrinkles there. Looks to me as if you've passed summers tethered to the hemp-break wheels at Oxmoor. Mary! *Will* you focus on the matter at hand? I was talking to you about that general over there who wants you. Listen to me!" Eloise rubbed her hands over mine. "I was at General Cadwallader's last evening for the musicale, and by the bye, Lizzie Griffin played the harp so ploddingly you would have thought her loaded up to her ears with laudanum. All Lizzie could talk about last night was your admirer, that ruddy-faced general across the aisle. She said he's come from St. Louis, and though he spends his days at the Western Department headquarters, he spends his nights searching for a bride. The General has declared himself ready for sons. Now he goes in search of their mother. The rumor is, several belles have set their caps for him."

"I hope he finds a respectable old widow. They could spoon castor oil into one another and commiserate about the gout."

"Lizzie says you're in view of his sparking." I ignored that comment. It was too dreadful to contemplate. Eloise blathered on: "It was Uncle William Clark who is guilty of arranging this. He thinks you're hopeless, Mary. He told me so, over supper yesterday. Just you watch, that general will force an introduction to Ma after service. Indeed, I'll wager Mama expects such a thing. Surely Uncle William has talked to her. It's a conspiracy to deprive you of your freedom. They're going to toss the yoke of subjugation about your shoulders and force you to give birth to furry little babies that look just like that general."

Mama swooped over me in a rustle of organdy, sending her anise-scented breath my way. She put her lips to my ear and whispered, "Mary, take one peek over the aisle at the handsome general and smile fetchingly."

I puckered my chin and rubbed my cold fingers upon it, because it pleasantly resembled a peach pit. "Fetchingly, Mama? What's your idea of 'fetchingly'?"

"Like this," Eloise simpered, rattling her eyelashes and rounding her lips into a coo.

I squinted at the General. By this time, he was brashly ignoring the sermon altogether and had turned sideways on the bench to stare boldly at me with an amused expression. The General had a disconcerting manner of looking at a woman. In the dark confines of my black satin slippers, I curled my toes.

Eloise leaned back and looked around behind my head. "It's not as though the General's hands are bluish and shaky. He's not drooling, and I don't see a walking stick. He appears vigorous. Maybe you could get one baby out of him before he dies."

Mama lifted the flat of her hand and walloped me.

"Mama, I did not come to church to harvest bruises!"

"I told you to smile *once* at that general, Mary, not babble to Eloise all through service. Now, you girls be reverent, mind your prayers and your manners. And don't look at that general anymore. One glance is enough, or you'll appear too eager. Honestly, sometimes I feel I've failed utterly. I'm raising up a litter of Hottentots."

Of course, lingering in the air at all times was Mama's disappointment in me. Mama was a Gwathmey, one of the *Grand English Gwathmeys* of the Virginia tidewater. She was all sangfroid, stepping elegantly through her days as if expecting courtiers to assemble and pay homage. I suppose I am more like my father.

Pa's family, the Louisville Bullitts, were originally the French Huguenot Bouilits, a name that meant to seethe or boil, a fairly apt description of my temperament. He raged through his years, accumulating land, cash and human beings, then died of an apoplectic fit with his face swimming in a bowl of two o'clock burgoo. When I was seventeen, Pa spent a summer's income upon my coming-out ball. He had a garden of white flowers shipped from

Louisiana, hired an orchestra and imported a gown of Flemish lace from Antwerp, then hosted a grand dinner for two hundred people.

"Why not just tether me and expose my bosom like a mulatto slave on the auction block?" I railed as I was pulled from my room. "Why not strip me down to my stays and let the boys see the goods?"

"Some might not like the look of your ass, and then where would you be?" Pa snorted as he arm-yanked me down the staircase.

The year I met the General, I had just celebrated my birthday and was a *very* naïve twenty-two-year-old, gone socially stale by Louisville's courtship standards. You see, I was widely perceived as being difficult. Mama had told me to select a man in my youth when I was freshest and allow him to guide me as nature had directed.

"You are a ripe and fruitful olive, Mary. You must learn to accept your vocation."

I waited for Mama to tell me what my vocation must be, but the wretched truth was that my belly was my future, and what future is that? She told me that my highest aspiration must be to bear children. To ensure my obedience, my parents sent me away to the Ursuline Convent in New Orleans on my fifteenth birthday. How I loathed the scorch of that city. Why, I felt as if I had been espaliered like a peach tree, forced to bloom in a climate where I could never flourish unless restrained. The Ursulines made an expert button polisher of me. I was forever getting into trouble for refusing to do as I was told. My punishment was to launder the chemises and polish the buttons of the whole convent with Spanish whiting until my fingers cracked and bled. In my third year, when I was eighteen, I was sent home midterm with a letter pinned to my frock-apron.

Dear Monsieur Bullitt,
Mary inspires the other girls to heresy and temporal revelry. We would rather she inflicted her obstinacy elsewhere.
Sincerely, Mother Froissart.
P.S. A generous donation *will not* work this time.

Mama had sobbed distressingly for a fortnight.

"If even the Romanists can't tame our girl, no one will; she is lost, O Lord, she is lost forever to the Kingdom. Maybe we could try giving her to the Baptists. I understand they are much less convivial than we Episcopalians."

Pa's jowls flapped as he paced the floor. "Pah! She's rotted clean through. Jaysus would get back up on his cross if he were married to her, so you may as well begin your search now for some sucker who is more patient than the Almighty."

Apparently, the patient sucker charged with my redemption was sitting across the aisle from me in the blue uniform of the United States Army. When the service ended, I rose stiffly from the pew and found my dress clinging immodestly to my legs. As I fluffed my petticoats, I peered up to see the General reveling in my discomfort. His eyes were full of wicked sparkle that I did not appreciate one little bit. And after service, my family shivered together upon the limestone steps while we waited for our carriage to be brought around. I huddled with Eloise, bouncing from one foot to another and hissing at our driver, *"Hurry, hurry."* Mama conversed with the reverend. While the children giggled and tumbled like marbles in the snow, Eloise pointed frantically at the vestry, warning me that the General was coming in our direction.

The Reverend Shaw gently steered Mama around to greet the General.

"Mrs. Bullitt, may I present General Henry Atkinson, recently arrived from St. Louis, and working temporarily at the Western Department headquarters here in Louisville."

"Oh, yes. I understand you are a good friend of Uncle William's?"

"Yes, we consult one another several times a week as he manages Indian affairs for Missouri, and I am required to keep the peace along the frontier."

"That's rather a large job, I'd imagine," Ma said as she hooked a strand of hair into the ruched lining of her bonnet.

"Aye, but requiring more patience than anything else."

"General, you must come to visit. On the morrow, perhaps?" Ma smiled pointedly at me.

As Ma and the reverend talked, the General lit his pipe and stared a proprietary stare at me. And though I hated to admit it, I found him handsome. His white trousers were tucked into his shiny black boots. Despite the cold, he wore no cape, and he unbuttoned his blue uniform coat and summed me up. I let my eyes wander and found myself looking at his hands. He had removed his gloves, and I stared at his broad palms and the fine, dark hair on his long fingers. What was it Lizzie Griffin said about a man's fingers? My eyes drifted to the General's white breeches.

Mama coughed, then pinched me on the upper arm.

The General narrowed his gaze with a small, secretive grin at me. Fearing he could read my mind, I quickly averted my glance to the snow under my slippers.

"Tomorrow, then, Miss Bullitt?" the General asked.

I shrugged my response, and he smiled once again.

Ma bowed her head as if the Holy Ghost had anointed her. The drivers pulled the two barouches to the curb, and all thirteen of us shuffled in, sat atop one another, poking and knobbing until we were situated to bear the short ride home. I tried to calm the shrews running wild through my belly as I took a last look at the General.

"He is a bit insouciant, but this is to be expected." Ma gave me a blithe pat upon the hand, then pulled the shade.

On the morning the General came to call, he tied his horse to the iron hitching post by the stone steps. The General strolled through the house with his hands clasped firmly behind his back, looking directly ahead as if the walls were invisible and he was keeping watch over something on a distant horizon. He made no comment on the furnishings or frippery. I admired this about him; it raised him in my estimation.

The General found the great hall crowded with my little brothers and sisters, who thundered up the stairs, slid down the balustrade, then started over again, hollering all the while. They glared at him as if he were something vile that had slithered up from the falls. He glared back, and they were duly cowed. Mama danced down the stairs with a regal swishing noise, one hand lifting the skirts of her aubergine gown, the other waving a welcome to the General. But her greeting was interrupted by footfalls upon the threshold of the front entrance, followed by Uncle William Clark's voice sounding sharply and urgently.

Eloise clutched at me with a worried look. "What do you suppose they're about?"

"Miss Eloise, we must investigate," I whispered.

It was easy to dash about undetected in our house. Pa had built the limestone thing as a monument to himself. I called it "the old sepulcher," which infuriated Mama. Visitors wandered through the rooms, gaping at the black walnut floors so polished they appeared as dark water underfoot, at the lofty ceilings, the tiger-maple and rosewood marquetry, the sixteenth-century Italian furniture, Flemish tapestries and hand-painted wallpapers. There were portraits of dead Bullitts, Gwathmeys and Clarks in every hall.

But Eloise and I were still in dressing robes with our hair floating behind us. To be seen in sleeping clothes and naked feet by men, worse yet, by a man who had come to court, was an act of unpardonable lewdness, punishable by a whipping. Thrilled by the promise of intrigue and our own brashness, we crept hand in hand toward the library, listening to the General and Uncle William Clark bark at one another. Having had his hopes for the governorship of Missouri dashed, Uncle served as the Superintendent of Indian Affairs, and the General enforced federal regulations pertaining to the Indians on the frontier. That was all I understood of their lives. Mama said Uncle and the General were fast friends.

Eloise squared her shoulders against the wall as if someone were pressing a musket to her heart. She lifted her chin and stared at the ceiling. I thought her posture rather too dramatic. I crouched low, hugging my knees as I strained to hear what they were saying.

Uncle was agitated. He paced back and forth, popping his fist into his palm to emphasize his points: "I shall thrust a wedge into the heart of that tribe, that's what. Split 'em in two. I will make it clear to the Sauk Nation that I will not negotiate with that scrawny little bastard Black Hawk."

I peeked round the pilaster to see Uncle making throttling motions with his hands.

The General lit his pipe and spoke calmly. "Who will you negotiate with? Certainly, Keokuk can not be trusted. I will not put my faith in a man who steals annuities from his own people, keeps a harem and dresses like a dandy."

Fishing his snuff box from his pocket, Uncle William Clark said, "I'll pay him enough that he can be trusted. And incidentally, old friend, half of all of my troubles I attribute to you. What the hell did you do to Black Hawk to make him want to kill you and every white soul on the frontier? He hates both your innards and your out-ards."

The General clenched the silver stem of his pipe between his teeth and tented his fingers. "That's a small matter, greatly exaggerated."

"Don't scoop that fuggin' balderdash at me, Henry. Speak the truth, damn you."

When the General maintained his silence, flicking an ash away from his sleeve, Uncle William raged, "I have a right to know, don't I? What the fug did you do to him? Sleep with his wife? Gig the family dog? Or did you gig his wife and sleep with his dog?"

The General smirked. Uncle pointed a warning finger at him. "Tell me, you sonofabitch."

"Well, if you're going to get into a dudgeon about it. It began in the winter of 1814, on the shores of Lake Champlain, when I was a young captain leading a company of men through the woods in a snowfall. We knew the British lines were somewhere to the north of us, and we feared stumbling into them. As twilight descended, we were too far from the barracks and had to make camp, but we could not build fires for fear of alerting the British to our position. My men glanced fearfully about at each snap of twig and birdcall. We could always see the British coming because of their garish costume. We could hear them coming because they announced themselves with bagpipes. It was the Sauk we feared. They were invisible warriors in the woods. And the light was so gray . . . well . . . I had picked where we were going to bivouac, and the men had begun to settle when the air was cut by eerie war whoops. My men slipped their bayonets onto their muskets, poured powder and balls and affixed their flints with clumsy fingers. And we waited. The outlines of the trees were blurred by the snow, and the growing darkness, yet we sensed movement toward us. My men held their fire until the first of the Sauk were clearly visible, creeping through the underbrush. We fired; the woods lit up with powder blast. Because of the smoke, I could not see anything. The Sauk came out of the darkness, running with their axes held high.

"A slight-made young warrior, bald except for his vermilion roach, came at me with his knife in one hand, an axe in the other. He was no more than seventeen. He cut the outside of my thigh, and we struggled in the snow and the muck. I was much taller and heavier than he, but when I rolled atop him, he tried to drub me with his axe. I cut him. With his own knife. I cut the vein on the side of his throat.

"All around me, I heard men go down, bludgeoned, stabbed . . . when the Sauk took scalps, it sounded like the rending of fabric. In the distance, I could hear the British setting up their artillery. They must have intended to blow the forest into slivers with their six-pound guns, because this was a dense wood and they were long yards away from us. There was a moment when I paused and squinted through the snow and darkness, looking about for ways to help my men. I heard a cry of anguish. A Sauk warrior leapt before me. Despite the cold, he wore only a breechclout and moccasins, his thin and narrow body bore not a bit of fat. He crouched, staring at the dead boy behind me.

"The gash on my leg flowed blood like a creek after the spring thaw, and I felt weak. I held my pistol before me, but my hands were clumsy from the cold and they slipped all over the butt. I couldn't get a grip on it. I dropped it behind me and yanked my saber from its scabbard. We circled for a few minutes, then the Sauk leapt upon me the way a cougar jumps an elk on a game trail. I couldn't believe his speed. He was going to kill me very quickly. With every bit of strength I could muster, I got to my feet, but he was right on me again. He had the advantage over me.

"But then something happened that saved my life; I am convinced of it. The British opened fire with their big guns. The concussive blast was so great that the Sauk warrior was thrown off of me, and in the smoke and confusion, I saw my men running. I looked up and there had to have been a whole regiment of British coming across the creek. I took advantage of the smoke cover, grabbed my pistol out of the snow and joined my men. I glanced back at the Sauk warrior, and he was crouched over the dead boy, howling out his pain and despair. I tell you, that was bad to see. But the second time I looked back, the Sauk was staring at me, and seeing me look at him, he raised his hand and made a slicing motion across his throat, then across his own scalp to let me know what he thought of me."

"That was Black Hawk?" Uncle William asked, pouring himself a dram of bourbon.

"That was Black Hawk." The General studied the ceiling of the library as if it were a map to the promised land. Uncle pinched, then snorted the snuff from an onyx vial. From my vantage point, his snuff box looked like a black plum in his hand. He said, "Black Hawk is a pompous little scaramouche with aspirations to be the next Tecumseh. But he is too fuggin' shortsighted ever to unite the Lake Nations."

"Agh, Clark, but if he ever does . . . if Black Hawk ever unites the Lake tribes . . . my men will be outnumbered six to one. Say good-bye to every white soul on the frontier. And I don't think he's stupid or shortsighted."

"General, you seem awfully generously disposed toward the little savage, given he wants to slit you nose to nuts. What is it that grips you? Guilt?"

The General's boots pressed dents into the leather of the ottoman.

Uncle ran his hands through his long gray hair with its few coppery strands and blurted, "I don't care a shat about that little momma-sucker. I'll starve him out. Starve him!" The General squinted up at Uncle through a blue cloud of pipe smoke.

"MARY BULLITT! You are en déshabillé!"

I flinched, squeezed my eyes shut and then rose up to accept my punishment. It was Mama. Her pretty face was mottled red with fury as she yanked me and Eloise by our collars and shook us hard. Uncle and the General stepped into the hallway, but I had been struck all of a heap by the General's bloody story of Black Hawk. I mulled over the idea of Black Hawk's vengeance, told in half measures, while everyone chattered around me. If I had the wisdom of a few more years, I would have known that the General had omitted whole chapters from his account. But at the time, I goggled at him, as stunned as a duck in a thunderstorm.

The General shook his head as if we had offended his delicate sensibilities. "Sir," I began, meeting his eye because I wanted to quiz him, but Uncle

William interrupted, teasing me as if I were a child. It was his custom, after all.

"You, Miss Mary, do I see your feet?"

I tucked my bare feet under my robe as best as I was able. "Uncle, I can see your feet too."

"Yes, Miss Mary, but I'm wearing shoes."

"Yes, Uncle, but they're ugly shoes."

The General knit his brow and looked at my mama, who dipped a little, apologizing, "General, ordinarily Mary is the embodiment of piety, purity, submissiveness and—"

Uncle William clapped a hand over his mouth, laughing at Mama's bald lie. Eloise hawed like an old mule suffering the lung rot, and Mama triggered a wallop upside the back of her head that left her tingly for weeks.

I called out over the banister as Mama dragged me up the stairs, "After all these years passing, Black Hawk doesn't remember who you are, does he, General?" When I peeked back over my shoulder, a smile played over the General's lips, and right there, before everyone, before Mama and Uncle William, *he winked at me!*

Eloise gasped at his audacity, "Mama, that general winked at Mary!"

"Dahlia, put Mary in her rose gown of India mull, it makes her appear demure. No woman, even Mary, can look rebellious in pink."

"He winked at me, Mama. I think he's dissipated. Miss Mary Wollstonecraft says only corrupt men wink."

Dahlia tied my waist tapers, as Mama violently jerked my hair up atop my head, and with her teeth clenched, growled at me, "Do not mention *that woman's* name in my house. She is immoral and she is dangerous." Mama continued her hopeful preparations. She turned me in rough circles, lifted my top lip with her small finger and rubbed at the space between my teeth with her fingernail, muttering, "At least your front teeth are still fine and white." She gripped my wrist and pointed a warning finger at Eloise. "You stay right there, young lady, don't you interfere. Mary, repeat after me— piety, purity, submissiveness and domesticity."

"Piety . . ." I sighed, as Mama hauled me down the staircase, depositing me before the library entrance. I drifted sullenly through the door and glanced around for Uncle William, but apparently he had left us. The General bowed, then pressed the knuckles of my hand to his lips *and held it there.* I rolled my eyes at the ceiling and let him nibble at me as long as it pleased him.

"Tasty, isn't it, General?" I said.

He laughed and gave my arm a playful jiggle before releasing it. "Tasty like a stewed ham hock, Miss Bullitt."

"Not a very auspicious beginning, sir—likening me to a pig, that is."

"Mary Bullitt!" Mama exclaimed, shoving me down onto a chaise. The General postured upon Pa's favorite chair as the high-yellow kitchen maid brought a tray of tea and gâteaux. I wondered which of the General's legs had been cut by the Sauk warrior's knife while Mama engaged him in breathless conversation. He watched her red silk handkerchief flutter against her breast. She confessed her relief at having a Southern gentleman in her parlor as opposed to that vicious freshet of Yankees who'd crowded the house of late.

"It is one thing to have Yankee officers coming to court, it is quite another to consider that your grandchild might be one of them," Ma said.

"Yes, yes indeed, Mrs. Bullitt." The General glanced pointedly at my hips as if to assess my breeding capability.

I cringed. The man just arrived and Mama had him filling my belly with children. The window admitted a wan breeze and I turned to welcome it. Dahlia, my waiting maid, sat upon the rug before the door. The General and I shared a skeptical look as Dahlia touched her fingers to her head scarf and loosed a small cough to let Mama know she had arrived.

"Oh, General," Mama said, "that is Dahlia. She will matron the two of you, for today is my receiving day, and I must take calls from the ladies of Louisville. You will, I hope, understand?"

The General bid her good day. Mama banged the latch into the jamb with the finality of the undertaker pulling shut the doors of a family mausoleum. Dahlia cast a sleepy glance at us, waved a little wave, yawned, then slumped over in a deep sleep on the rug.

We scrutinized one another for as long as it pleased us. The General had a fan of lines at the corners of his blue eyes and a sprinkle of gray in his hair. I thought he was a stark representation of prime on the cusp of decay. I could hear all of Louisville gossiping now: *Have you heard about Mary Ann Bullitt and her dignified old General?* Ugh. I made fists and pressed my knuckles into the chaise's brocade until a red imprint bloomed on my skin.

It was time someone said something.

"Are you enjoying your visit to Louisville, General?"

"Yes. Are you looking forward to the spring cotillion season, Miss Bullitt?"

"No. I despise cotillions."

"I understand entirely."

"How nice to be understood."

He rubbed a hand over his face to steady his expression. "I must go now," he said, rising with great dignity from his chair as if he expected me to salute him. His dismay was obvious when I jumped up gleefully, with a clap of my hands.

"General, may I give you directions to Lizzie Griffin's house? I've heard she finds you quite interesting."

"I do not reciprocate that sentiment, Miss Bullitt."

"That's unfortunate for me, isn't it?" I muttered, putting a hand to the globe and giving it a spin. The General paused a moment, then looked at the ceiling as if contemplating his next action.

I said hopefully, "Now that we're alone, you should know I'm rotted clean through. You can leave and I'll tell Mama I was horrible to you and she'll believe me. You've lingered longer than most of my suitors."

"Sit down, Miss Bullitt, right here."

He pointed at the ottoman and waited for me to obey him.

"Why? Because that's a lower position than you have? So I can gaze up admiringly at you? No, General, I think I'll sit on the table. Then I'll be higher up than you."

"Suit yourself, young lady."

"And so I shall." I tossed the books off the drum table beside his chair, planted myself and held the globe as if it were an infant.

"Miss Bullitt, I want you to share with me your opinion of the world and how you see your place in it."

I blinked at him. No grown man had ever asked me such a question before. It gave me reason to consider that the General might not be so decrepit after all. He waited patiently for my response, cupping his chin in one hand, focusing on my face an unblinking gaze that wandered now and again from my throat to my knees. Oh, he was brash. I paused dramatically, looked about for something clever to say, and finding nothing inspirational in the cavernous emptiness of my head, said, "I think the world in general and Louisville in particular is being ruined by civilization. Why, they're paving the streets of this city with cobbles—"

"*No!*" He interrupted with mock incredulity and slapped a hand to his jaw.

I began to recount the depredations of encroaching civilization for him. "I hear tell there's an ordinance being bandied to stop the boys from fighting before the grog houses; what, I ask you, will they do to occupy their time now? There are too many churches being built in Louisville and too many ministers moving in to fill the pulpits. There are rules everywhere governing everyone, as if we wanted rules at all. The city and all of the Kentucky people in it are going to be ruined by gentility, and I'll be destroyed right along with them."

The General circled around behind me where I sat and leaned over me. His hand closed over mine and he lifted my forefinger, then laid it on the globe over the township of St. Louis. A darkling sensation went all through me. I had never before experienced such an intimate connection with the body of a grown man. I could feel the rough wool of his coat against my bare arms as he pressed against me, and when he leaned forward so that I could feel his breath upon my neck, I nearly went limp against him. Though convention told me to be outraged by his breach of decorum, I was paralyzed with enjoyment. Indeed, I rehearsed womanly outrage in my mind, but I didn't feel it and feared a display would ring false.

He returned to his chair.

"Miss Bullitt, you ever been to the Indian country?"

"No, sir."

"Why not?"

"Why would I go to the Indian country? Who's there besides Black Hawk? And you'd better kill him before he kills you. To my way of thinking, you've got to turn the Old Testament upside down. None of this eye for an eye business. You've got to steal away the other fellow's eyes before he takes yours. What do you think of that?"

He took my hand once again, I felt the corners of my mouth lifting in a traitorous smile. His breath smelled like almonds. "Black Hawk poses no danger; he's an old man. He must be nearing fifty winters now."

I narrowed my eyes and yanked free of him.

"You've got to be nearing fifty winters too, so you're not a danger to me."

The General cast a sly look at me, then put his hands on the toes of my slippers. I could feel the heat of his hands through the silk, and I leaned over him. The color rose on his cheeks when I came very close and whispered, "You're not telling the truth about that Indian who wants to kill you. I can sniff out fibbing, and you're fibbing to me now, General. You often fib to women, don't you?"

"I only fib to the wicked ones." His eyes twinkled at me.

I nudged at his shoulder, ruffling the fringe of his epaulet, and said, "Tell me about the frontier. What does St. Louis look like? I hear they call it Little Rome because it's crowded with the popish French. Is that true?"

As he was unduly proud of himself, I expected the hearty budget of bragging tales customary to military men. But when the General began to talk in his North Carolina drawl of what it meant to live in a place where there were no cities, in a place beyond the telling of rules, where the most reckless desires of men were manifest, I closed my eyes and allowed him to lull me across time and space to places I had never seen. He talked and talked for nearly two hours, but he said nothing more of Black Hawk.

When I asked him once again about Black Hawk, he demurred, "Not yet, Miss Bullitt. You are far too accustomed to receiving whatever you wish."

"General, you are far too accustomed to giving out what no one wants."

The General smiled at me and rose from the chair. With a quick motion, he gripped my wrist, then brought my fingertips to his lips. I resisted the urge to rub them back and forth to feel the texture of his mouth.

"Then it's decided. You'll do fine," he said, his look sweeping me from head to toe.

"I'll what?"

"Mind what I say."

A derisive glottal noise erupted out of me, and he dropped my hand as if I had the scrofula.

"What was that noise that just came out of you, Miss Bullitt?"

"A stomach disturbance."

He regarded me doubtfully, then stepped around Dahlia, who still slept on the floor. I trotted along after him like an amiable puppy.

"Now, Mary, I must go play brag with General Gaines," he said, turning to face me. "Shall I see you tomorrow, then?" He winked and touched his fingertips to his brow in a sort of casual salute.

Before I could give my answer, Mama scrambled down the steps and, with a conciliatory smile to the General, yanked me by the pelerine, back into the house, all the while scolding me for running out-of-doors after a suitor as if I were some overeager hill cracker in heat.

On the second day the General laid siege to our household, a steady rain warped the wood floors until opening doors traced perfect arcs through the beeswax finish. I lay abed and watched a dreary light filter through the window as a servant brought my breakfast of biscuits and milk. By eight, I'd been corseted, at half past I accompanied Ma to the storeroom. Ma did not release the keys to her stores to anyone as our family's livelihood depended upon her careful management of the preserves, dry goods and medicines.

"Mama? About this General . . . I think you should know, he vexes me terribly."

Ma reviewed her list and squinted at the low state of copper polish, then muttered something about all of us being about to die from verdigris poisoning.

"What don't you like about him, Mary?"

Ma removed a barlow knife from her pocket, peeled away the brown wrapper from the nine-pound loaf of sugar and took a chunk out of the white brick for Dahlia.

"He's too old."

"The General is the perfect age for marrying. You aren't suited to marry a boy. What else?"

"He has a rotten temperament, Mama. He's obdurate. He bosses me around."

When Ma finally began to speak, her voice sounded, as always, like a low hymn with distinct rhythms. "Mary, I observed the two of you together for a few moments. It struck me that between your mulishness and his pride flourishes paradise."

"Paradise?"

Mama sighed. "Yes, well to the devil, an inferno is paradise. See here, Mary, the two of you relish this sparking and circling. After you marry, and this man *will* offer marriage, you'll take turns dethroning one another. He'll lord it over you for a time until you tire of it, then you'll usurp him in a brief but thrilling revolution until he hobbles you once again. And so on. When the General talks to you, does his conversation interest you?"

"He told me an Indian wants to kill him."

Mama ignored this. "Is the General kind?"

"No, I fear he is the sort who will apply stripes to me before bedtime."

Mama scrutinized her candle inventory.

"Now you're being silly. I happen to know he is a gentleman of the highest order, stern perhaps, accustomed to deference from all living things, but still and all, truly gentle in his manner and desirous of pleasing you. No, I can guess a man's proclivities at the outset and this one is kindhearted. And for some reason, he is the only man come a-courting who doesn't think you're a harpy. Dahlia and Hannah, you may go."

Mama waited until they were down the stairs before she spoke.

"Let us have an understanding between us, Mary, and I say this with all solemnity—I would never force you into marriage."

"You wouldn't?"

"No, I wouldn't. And if I truly believed you'd be happy to live out your days in this house as a maiden lady, then I would tell you so now. I would love your company forever. But, Mary, I am asking you to consider, for the first time in your life, that you have a very difficult nature. You would be miserable if you were married to some bird-hearted crumpet of a boy. The General is a good match for you; he could show you so much of the world, and in a way you'd like to see it."

"Why can't I see the world by myself, Ma? Why do I need him?"

"You don't *need* him. But neither are you suited to . . . to a life of celibacy, Mary."

"Oh my God, I can't believe you just said that."

"Do *not* blaspheme in my presence! Part of your dislike of the General is prompted by the stew of emotions he boils up in you. There is a very heady current between the two of you when you are together; I sense it and you need to recognize that he understands it. You're misinterpreting what your heart tells you. He's the first man you've met who won't grovel for you. Virtue in a woman is a good thing except when it's . . . well, *antique,* my dear. Then it changes into something, ah, something much less appealing. For once in your life, think about your actions before you turn him away for good. You consider my words before he comes to call today and try to behave. The last thing you want is to regret sending away the one man who could make you happy."

I took my leave of Ma to greet Mister Rammey, who had come to give me lessons in Italian song. At ten I played the harp for an hour, all the while considering Ma's words. I dined on turkey galantine at two with my lady cousins, Louisiana, Octavia and Celeste, but the memory of my last encounter with the General scratched around in my head like a caged squirrel. At three, I reviewed the calling cards we'd received that day, taking them from the gold-plated receiver, a shallow bowl uplifted by a full-breasted goddess who appeared blissful in her duties as she stood on her pediment. For a long while, I sat miserably on the staircase, stared up at the clerestory windows above the doors and grumped about my future. What if nothing ever changed for me? My days were something like living inside a field glass, it seemed each was a view to the last, one telescoping upon the other, the same narrow view recurring over and again with maddening clarity.

That night, a bath was drawn for me in my bedroom. I immersed myself into the tepid water and examined the red marks left on my breasts and ribs by the whale-bone corset stays. As I bathed, I traced each angry indentation with a wet finger, hoping to translate the secret cursive of the lines, the code of duty and obligation written into my skin by the Louisville society that had governed me since birth. Maybe Mama was just plain wrong about me. Maybe I was meant to make a life for myself. I would read all of the books I'd hesitated starting, I would ride out and explore reaches of Kentucky I had not seen. A lifetime of self-indulgent spinsterly pursuits awaited me— such was the future I yearned for, wasn't it? The fulsome and independent life of an aged maiden lady. Mary Ann Bullitt: spinster. I liked the sound of it. And it made me perfectly miserable because I wanted my journey. I wanted to see the gold and russet prairies of autumn, and I wanted to cross the same mountains Uncle William Clark and his Corps of Discovery had crossed in the winters after I was born.

When I was young, Uncle William would tell me how he had planned the arrival of the Corps of Discovery at the Pacific Ocean to coincide with my birthday. For the men of the corps arrived on the western shore in December of 1805, and my uncle was so joyous, that he carved his name and mine into an alder tree overlooking the great waters. He would say to me, "Mary, on that day, despite my jubilance at what we had discovered, I was troubled by the idea that you and everyone I loved back home were celebrating your second birthday. I could not bring you a gift, so I carved your name into a tree in the wilderness."

And then Uncle William would sigh and say, "I apologize, Niece."

And knowing how the story ended, I would pretend concern and touch my hands to his cheeks and plead, "Why do you apologize, Uncle?"

"Without your knowledge or permission, Mary, I gave you then, to the West. You were married to the West when you were only two years old."

I stepped from the tub and pulled the pins from my hair. I watched the dark length of it fall to the white curve of my calves, then stared at myself in the mirror. With arms outstretched, I turned barefoot circles upon the old Turkish carpet until my hair lifted and splayed like wings searching for loft over the windy savanna and the spreading dark rivers of the West.

2

Louisville, Kentucky, January 1826

✣ I MARRIED the General because he wound springs in me that were likely to uncoil without warning and that is the whole truth of the matter. When he called upon me on January 5, 1826, at four o'clock, the household recognized that finally I was being courted by a man intent to propose. This was no skittish boy caller arriving with a pride of ten others, blushing and making frivolous jokes. We sat together silently in the library, listening to our tea cups rattle upon the saucers. His face was weather stained, and he would startle me with intense looks, as if a cloud were passing over him, as if he sought dispensation of something only I could grant him. I had never been in a room with a man who changed my perception of time and caused me to glance up and down nervously, as in the moments before a storm breaks and the sky dissolves overhead. I stared at the dark sprouts of fine hair on the backs of his fingers.

He took my free hand in his and said earnestly, "Miss Bullitt, Louisville is bound to make you feel like a bee in a bottle."

"Like a trapped and dying insect, you mean?"

"Yes. You're a strong-blooded woman. You need your journey. Your ancestors set out when they were about your age to carve civilization into the wilderness. Why, your uncle William Clark set out to see the whole of the continent, your uncle George Rogers Clark mapped the old Northwest, chased the British from the territories and fought Indians. Even your ma left behind the comfortable Gwathmey plantation on the tidewater to join your pa in building his mercantile business in the wilds of Kentucky. But here you are, up to your withers in calling cards, perishing of frivolity."

He must have sensed the turmoil I was suffering, for when he looked at me, his expression reflected such gentle perception of who I was, that a tremor rippled all through me. I was overcome with an impulse to throw my arms about him. In a subtle way, I think, I gnashed my teeth to suppress the urge to bite him on the earlobe. And I unsettled him by regarding him without blinking.

He said in the courteous tone one expects from the haberdasher, "Would you consider an offer of marriage?"

I put my cup down and looked him in the eye with firmness and resolve. "How old are you anyhow, General?"

"How *old* am I? Are you wearing your best Kentucky manners, Miss Bullitt?"

The General knew it was rude to accuse anyone of having Kentucky manners.

"Ordinarily, sir, I have the finest manners in Kentucky, but something about you doesn't inspire me to use them."

"How old do you *think* I am, Miss Bullitt?"

"Seventy-three."

"I am forty-four."

"Lord. A man of Revolutionary memory."

He rolled his eyes and pulled a gold pocket watch from his coat, then popped the lid and hummed to himself. I half rose up and tried to peek at the watch face, but he drew it back with an insufferably superior glance at me.

"Why are you staring at your watch, General?"

"Because, Miss Bullitt, I have never until this moment proposed marriage to a woman, though many would clamor to have me. And I had been told by your admirers that you were bold and impulsive and daring, but two minutes have elapsed since I have offered you eternal bliss as my bride, yet you hesitate. Why would that be? Have I been misled?"

"You must admit there is a considerable difference in our ages, sir. Though you appear vigorous now, I fear I shall soon be spooning beef tea into you before a sunny window."

He yawned and said, "Three minutes. Dare you to marry me."

"Dare? You're daring me to marry you? Put the watch away, I find this wretchedly disingenuous of you."

"See here, Miss Bullitt, when I grow feeble, you can push me off a cliff into the river."

"I don't know you, General. Aside from Uncle William, no one in our family knows you. How can I go off and marry a man I don't know?"

"Read the papers; I'm famous. President Monroe calls me by my first name. President Adams calls me by my last. Vice President Calhoun calls me a name I can't repeat in your presence. Four minutes."

"Stop timing me, you lunatic."

"We're nearing five minutes, Miss Bullitt, and then my offer expires."

"You annoy me, General. You're a gnat in the nostril. A flea in the ear."

The General sighed and leveled his gaze upon me. "You're not annoyed, Miss Bullitt, you're dithered senseless with attraction for my person."

"I can dither myself senseless, thank you very much."

"Not too often, I hope; a body can go insane from such a thing."

"There are worse fates. Such as—"

"Such as?"

"Such as being pinned under an amorous cadaver."

"Miss Bullitt, you're exactly what I want. And I'm exactly what you need; now give me your answer, or I'll leave you forever in peace as the cantankerous spinster of Louisville. Will you marry me, then?"

I stood uncertainly, clasping my hands as he began to whistle tunelessly.

"Five seconds left to decide."

"Oh, all right, I shall marry you. I've never been proposed to under such duress."

He clapped the lid of his watch shut triumphantly and smirked, "Could you depart Louisville on Twelfth Day?"

"General, that's tomorrow!"

"She can read a calendar too! Ah, the brilliance of the ruling class. Why, Miss Bullitt, you are truly remarkable." He sucked in his cheeks as if biting them from the insides, his nostrils flared and he lofted his brows roguishly at me. "You haven't answered me, Miss Bullitt, time escapes us. I see no reason for conventional delay as I have decided upon you, and you clearly cannot go another day without falling helplessly into my arms in a swoon. So to preserve your reputation, let's get married tomorrow, and then I shall make you happier than you've ever been. I've noticed a little petting turns you docile."

With this he leapt up crisply, and I cast a glouty look at him, "I suppose tomorrow is fine."

"Then come here and let me teach you how to kiss."

I held him off at arm's length with both hands, for I was smarting from his comment about my willingness to be petted, and I objected, "I am not kissing you until we are married. You are much too pleased with yourself, sir."

The next day, on the morning of my wedding, Twelfth Day of 1826, Mama told two of our servants, Nicholas and Dahlia, that they were going to follow me to my new home in St. Louis. Having heard all sorts of Indian-horror tales and believing they would be killed by red men upon arriving in Missouri, they asked if they might be permitted to celebrate with loved ones before their departure. "I am soon to meet the King of Friday," Nicholas said mournfully to Mama, who gave her consent to their funeral party.

Eloise and I looped our arms around each other's waists and peered onto the back piazza through an open window in our music room to watch them rehearse at death. A gray light filled the windows. Our house was two city squares distant from the levee, and the river was clenched in a mist of its own making. A cord of cloud held to Jefferson Street like skin over the spine of a giant, and the sun showed itself in the milky light.

It was a perfect day for a wake, less so for a wedding. Eloise paced the floor, jumping skittishly when the Negroes smashed plates on the cobbles. They marched in circles around Nicholas and Dahlia, who feigned the long sleep, clasping wands of dried angelica to their breasts.

An eerie wail cut the fog, and Eloise blurted, "Oh, how I wish they wouldn't do that. It jangles my nerves. And besides, who ever heard of a wake for the living? They've been sobbing and dancing since dawn. Look at the torches flaring out there. Mama's letting them drink New Orleans taife. They'll murder us in our sleep. Then they'll run about with our heads on pikes and dance a jig on our entrails. Squish, squish, your spleen will stick to their boot heels. Dahlia and Nicholas would sooner kill you than be ex-iled to St. Louis. How can you do this to me? To all of us? What are you thinking, going off and marrying this . . . this elderly soldier?"

"The General's forty-four, Eloise, that's hardly elderly."

"He must care very little for you to carry you off to hell. Listen to those Negroes wailing and lamenting. How long can they go on like this?"

"All day and probably into the night. And St. Louis is not hell. The Gen-eral told me there are several churches, four newspapers, a library associa-tion—"

"Five thousand taverns, Frenchmen piss in the street and the Indians burn white people, then toss their bodies into the river. What happens when you find yourself taken hostage by Indians, then being passed over the prairie from wigwam to wigwam? Mary Bullitt. Wife to every red man."

I snorted derisively at her. "Pity the red men. Who told you of such a thing?"

"Lizzie Griffin."

"Wishful thinking. Now I know how she thrills herself to sleep."

A muffled chorus swelled in the mist. The servants sang out their grief:

O Mary don't you weep, don't you mourn
Pharaoh's army got drownded
O Mary don't you weep.
Sister, what do you want to stay here for?
Dis old world is no place to live.

Eloise put her face near to mine, "Hear that? They're singing for you! *Don't you weep, Mary.* They're likening you to dead, just as they're mourning Dahlia and Nicholas for dead."

"Eloise, they're singing about Mother Mary and how all of us white sinners are going to fall down before God just like Pharaoh's army drowned in the sea. How many times have you heard that song? Are you telling me each time you've heard it, you thought they were singing to me?"

"Nicholas and Dahlia don't want to go with you. They know about Black Hawk. They heard what happened on the Cuivre River. When he proposed, did the General tell you anything of the dead in Missouri? Did he tell you how the bodies were mutilated?"

"We prefer talk of putrefaction and disfiguring afflictions. What is in your mind, Eloise? I am not being courted by a ghoul."

She snorted. "Don't speak too soon, Sister, a man so old could hop the twig before tea. Did he mention that Black Hawk, that Indian we overheard about? The one who wants to kill him?"

I clasped my hands together and whimpered in falsetto, "General, why does an Indian want to launch you into eternity?"

"Mary, this night, you're goin' to let him play between your feet, but you haven't asked him if that Indian is goin' to come after you too? Are you being foolish?" Eloise was spiraling herself into a tempest. She said, "The Negroes *know* what happened at Cuivre."

"How can they know if you and I don't know?"

"The Negroes always know," Eloise said in a stage whisper that made me cackle.

She paused mournfully, then laced her fingers about my neck and buried her face in my shoulder. Eloise was my dearest friend, and the worst of this marrying business was having to begin a new life without her. I promised to write to her everything about my days, I rubbed circles between her shoulders and told her the General would buy passage on the steamer for all of them to come and stay with us in St. Louis. She lifted her wet face and renewed her protests. "Mama asked the General if she could write news of the wedding to his family. He told her such a thing was not necessary, as if he had no family at all. When she asked him for his invitation list, it was all officers and War Department officials. It's unnatural the way he won't speak of his family. None of our people except for Uncle William know him. And remember how Mama warned us off bachelors over forty? Remember what she said?"

"They prefer the company of hairless boys?"

Eloise howled merrily, "That's why he didn't kiss you last night. You'll be a virgin forever!"

A servant hollered that Mama wanted us in my bedroom right this instant or she'd crush us like butterflies at the wheel. We linked arms and sprinted up the stairs. Hannah and Dexter teetered into the room with pails of warm water and sloshed them into the tub. Mama clapped her hands and ordered, "Mary, disrobe. A wedding justifies a bath. Hannah will be back shortly to dress you. Guests are arriving, and I haven't dressed yet. Eloise, you jump in after, and hurry it along. Don't dawdle and don't look at yourself."

"That's right, Mama, I just can't keep my hands off me!" Eloise laughed, flopped on the bed and clutched a pillow to her breast.

Mama distrusted my habit of frequent bathing, preferring to apply heliotrope toilet water to her person throughout the day. Bathing, Mama said, gave occasion to self-pollution, and I knew her to dip into waters once a month only. As for me, I could not bear to stink. I bathed every few days, which inspired Mama to give me long talks about permanent blindness. Mama darted about in the bedroom, as graying strands fell from the tuck of her chignon. She was the same age as the General, but worn from bearing thirteen children. Her waist had gone thick, her breasts hung low and all of her back teeth were missing, causing her cheeks to hollow prettily. Eloise lay on the bed, clutching my linens under her chin.

When Mama left us alone for a moment, Eloise said to me, "You must write me immediately and let me know how it feels when he sticks it in you. Lizzie Griffin says it hurts terribly."

"Oh? How would she know?"

"She knows more than either of us. I'll wager Mama has told you nothing."

"Well, Lu, I'm not thinking of it."

I snatched my chemise from her and held it before me, studying myself in the mirror.

"You're thinking of it, Mary. It's the only thing you've thought of since rising."

I ignored her and let the chemise drop. I looked at my profile. I favored my mother's family, the tall English Clarks and Gwathmeys. My face was a long oval and my nose fine and narrow, I had large blue eyes and a strong, dark brow. I was tall and slender, and the boys of Louisville called me the Bullitt Beauty.

"Mary, why? Just give me one reason why you are marrying this man."

"He smells better than any man I have ever met."

Eloise paused significantly, then recited in sonorous tones, *"Officers are also particularly attentive to their persons, fond of dancing, crowded rooms, adventures and ridicule."*

"Oh, stop quoting *her* will you? What will you do when faced with your own conflicts, Eloise? Let her book fall open and point at the page, then augur the truth from a random passage?"

"Why not? People do it with the Bible."

I pinched her cheek affectionately. "You bony little humanist."

Eloise jumped before me, noosing my hair about my neck. "I ought to strangle you for leaving me. What happened to our plans? All of those nights we nearly burned ourselves to death in bed, huddled with a candle under the duvet while we secretly read *A Vindication of the Rights of Women?* I thought we were going to be happy spinsters forever. I thought we were going to found the Wollstonecraft School for Rational Girls. Now, you throw it all off, and for what?"

"Eloise, even Miss Wollstonecraft married eventually. If we don't, we'll be stuck in Louisville forever and become pitiable objects of contempt to all who know us. On our receiving day, people will shuffle reluctantly through our door, then hurry away because the Bullitt spinsters smell of camphor and loneliness. We'll grow dark lip shadows and titter inappropriately at men passing by us on the street. Is that what you want for yourself? For me?"

Eloise pursed her lips and frowned. "Oh, I s'pose you're right about that. Are you in love with him, Mary?"

"I don't *love* him. I want to taste his spit. I want to see him without his clothes."

"You're marrying for impure motives."

"Yes. I can think of none better. Except this. When he called upon me, he asked me this question: 'Miss Bullitt, what do you think of the world and your place in it?' And given he had the perspicacity to ask that question, I—"

"You're going to throw your dress over your head for him. You disappoint me."

"Oh, Eloise, there's more. He reads *books*. Real books, by Burke, Hume and Locke. He's invented navigation equipment, and the President asked him to lead those expeditions into the territories. He's the least boring man who has come to call upon me."

"That's mighty high praise, Sister."

My dressing robe warmed on the fender before the hearth. I wrapped it about me, then crawled back into my bed, "Eloise, you can nap with me."

"How can you sleep? You're getting married."

"I have plenty of time to sleep, come lie beside me."

She threw her leg over me to hold me down on the bed as she thrashed at me with a pillow. I laughed, and withy tendrils flew about my face. Mama swished back into the room with an armload of gownage, jerked me from the bed, raked my chemise to the floor, then barked directions at Hannah. I stared blankly at my reflection as Eloise sermonized: "This sickens me. You don't even know this man. This is like a cold arrangement between the Hanoverians and the Stuarts. It is vile and European. You'll see, Mary. The General will throw you away if you don't produce a son within the year."

"Then I'll hole up here with my screaming baby girls. They'll chase after you with green horrors leaking from their noses, howling, 'Auntie Eloise, change our cloths!'"

Hannah dashed about with a red scarf wrapped about her head, distracted by the death celebration below. She briskly slapped pearl powder all over my body, and I coughed. She piled my hair atop my head and dripped sugar water all over it. Hannah laced me into my stays and rolled lisle stockings over my knee. I tied my own slipper ribbons.

Eloise sat on the edge of the bed, tugging at the calfskin cover over my psalmbook until she had successfully loosed it. She tossed the psalms onto the floor and shoved another book into the cover, then threw that into my lap.

"What is this, Eloise?" I asked her.

"Your psalmbook."

Mama burst into the room, shoved me down on the bed and began chattering breathlessly at me. Though it appeared she wanted to be tender, for I was leaving her house forever, Mama was short of time, and guests had begun to arrive. She reminded me of an angry squirrel clacking at a hound dog, "Mary, never call your husband by his first name, it's so white-folksy-trashy."

A perfunctory pat on the hand and a peck on the cheek. Huff, huff.

"And initially, the carnal connection hurts, but thereafter it will probably become your most favorite pastime. There isn't much to explain. You've seen horses and dogs?"

I nodded, fiddling with the combs in my hair. "And cats in estrus."

"Well then, you understand more than I did when I married. Oh dear, it's time to have this wedding. Stand up, please."

Now, weddings in the twenties were simple ceremonies. There were no candles, flowers, music or bridal white. Most assuredly, kissing before God was not approved, indeed, I knew no bride of my time to have been married in a church. With hands cold as January ice, a stomach burbling distress and a heart pounding for reprieve, I was hauled into the library, where officers formed a blue phalanx and ladies sat quietly in pale gowns, staring expectantly at me as if awaiting the rapture. The General rose from his chair. He did not take my hand or offer a gentle greeting, but looked over my head and then popped the lid of his watch. He maintained a sober phiz as if he had come to treat with a foreign nation.

"Eloise, I fear I shall vomit," I whispered.

"Well, don't."

Reverend Shaw adjusted his white collar, fluffed his black robe, fumbled with his book, then pointed to the places where we were to stand. As Eloise was too young to witness for me, my cousin Octavia did the honors. I clutched at my psalmbook as if it were driftwood and I were lost at sea. My mouth was dry and my palms were moist. Octavia stood on my right, the General on my left and his officer bearing witness beside him. I looked at the General; here was a man who had grown fond of solitude, keeping great distances between himself and the messy distraction of women and families. Why had he thrown over his independence now? Why had I, for that matter? I stole another glance at him. The General was immaculately groomed, a virtue that I found daunting, because it hinted of cruelty. Exactitude and cruelty. The reverend began speaking the familiar words.

Someone behind me coughed, and I turned, startled by it.

I stared dim eyed at the frost ferns sporing over the huge windows. I had been oddly nonchalant about this whole affair until I entered the library and saw the General, and at that moment, the gravity of the whole enterprise struck me, and my senses cottoned over, my vision blurred, my hearing left me. Suddenly, I wanted nothing more than to pass my life in Mama's house, hollering at the servants for applying too much wax to the furniture. But there was no turning back now, as Reverend Shaw was about to pronounce us man and rib. Once again, my impulsiveness had caused a world of trouble.

Octavia poked me. "Cousin, give him your hand."

"Who?" I asked, looking around.

"Me," the General whispered brusquely. He grasped my hand, which palsied so violently that he clamped my whole arm under his, squeezing my palm tightly to slide the plain band over my finger. There were more words said, and the reverend raised his brows at me.

The room behind us was silent.

Ice tapped at the window like a visitor begging admittance. The clock ticked. The fire popped and sent an orange shower of sparks onto the puncheon and a woman squealed gleefully.

The reverend sighed and clutched my shoulder, then gave me a little shake.

"Miss Bullitt, for the third time, please listen, then repeat after me."

"Oh all right, then."

The thing was done.

Though it is now the vogue for a groom to surprise his bride with a kiss after the ceremony, in 1826, for a respectable man to do such a thing to a lady, particularly his wife, would have raised an uproar. The General and I turned awkwardly, side by side, facing the crowded room. We did not touch or look at one another. The guests behaved as was expected, the more demonstrative of them smiled, but everyone else regarded us as placidly as milk cows watching jaybirds on a fence rail. I wriggled my nose, furrowed my brow, then shrugged at the guests as if to ask, *What is it you people want from us?*

Mama rose and chirped, "Supper waits!"

Everyone rose up at once, murmuring congratulations. They greeted us with the dumbest statements. "A fine union of good families"—that garnered a worried look from me. How did they know if the General's family was good? General Edmund Gaines suckled my fingers as a smoky cataract of hair spilled over his forehead. He stared raptly at my breasts like a nursing infant, then said to my husband, "Fresh and pretty." I was cheek-pecked by a brace of aunts, and my hand was lipped by a score of officers who said, "Congratulations, ma'am," then glanced nervously at the General and dashed from the room. A blond major slugged the General's arm jovially, then coughed. "I hear old Black Hawk left you a wedding present on the Cuivre, eh?" he said.

The General scowled at the major until he trailed away sullenly. I watched them all go until we were left alone in the room. I dared not look at the General for fear I would blurt that I had just committed the heaviest mistake of my life. So I asked, "When do we leave?"

"The coach comes at seven o'clock. We have a few hours yet. With all the mayhem on the Cuivre, I hope you understand . . ."

I was so overcome with doubt at what I had done, I desired immediately to know what it was about the scent of him that had driven me to marriage. I leaned forward, closed my eyes and sniffed. Almonds. Soap. And a distinctive man smell.

The General put his hands upon my waist, and I felt myself turn scarlet as I stared down at them. He pressed firmly against my creaking stays, and I caught my breath as he put his lips to the soft inner wrist under the hem of my glove. He studied me for my reaction, lowering his face to mine so that I felt the curly hair at his temple tickling my cheek.

"What are you sniffing at, Mary?"

"You."

"What a little fox you are."

"Don't liken me to animals. It's coarse."

"It's not as though I called you a distempered stoat. And we are being waited upon. We must go or we will be thought inconsiderate."

I took his arm, and we followed the others to the dining room. We were placed opposite one another at the long dining table. Uncle William Clark sat beside the General. Uncle quaffed Madeira and laughed uproariously until his face was so flushed that his white pustule scars maculed brightly over his cheeks. His thinning hair, mostly gray, with traces of red, drooped over his ears, and he monopolized the General with a discussion of serious subjects.

I could not hear most of what was said but for this brief exchange: "Black Hawk argues that the men who signed the 1804 treaty were drunk at the time and were not authorized by the tribe to cede their lands. He says that the entire tribe must consent to the sale to make it lawful."

The General answered, "It doesn't matter what he thinks."

Our guests chattered gaily and loudly, some offered stories of their own weddings. I looked at the General only once. He poked at his turbot thoughtfully, a dark expression furrowing his brow as he listened to Uncle. I was glad I did not have to speak to him. I looked down the table and smiled at my mama who motioned at the silver trays covering the table, her lips forming the words, *"Eat something, dear."* The board groaned under seventy-nine dishes, as it was the custom of the time to put every course, including entremets and four removes for the potages, on the table all at once. We supped for four hours, drank through nearly twenty bottles of wine, and finished with pies, cheesecakes and liqueurs.

Uncle lifted his glass to us. He was a broad and jovial presence in the shadow-fretted room. The fire popped and the candles guttered. The silver covers on the dishes speared reflections at the ceiling, a queer scattered light cast dark hollows where Uncle's eyes should have been, the tapers glowed up under chins with macabre effect until all of my familiars seemed haunting relics of a life that was escaping me. It was a most disconcerting moment wherein I demonstrated a complete absence of grace, opening and closing my mouth wordlessly like a trout being thrust into a creel.

But then a beef-lard candle sparked high from its own grease. Mama's table cover began to burn. Whoosh! The taper flared over the blancmange and red partridges fumet. My aunts shrieked, and my uncles leapt into gallant action, batting at the flames with their frock coats and dinner napkins and handkerchiefs. The fire was subdued, and everyone took their seats with jittery laughter about our collective heroism.

Nearly departed Nicholas tottered drunkenly into the dining room, bobbled at half tilt, then announced that the accommodation coach had arrived. The General glanced sharply at the servant and then at me. He dropped a forkful of gooseberry pie onto his plate, rose up with dignity, then declared it was time we leave for our new home.

A bitter fright took hold of me as I looked first at Mama and then Eloise, waiting for them to shout, *"Surprise, Mary, you're not really married after all. Get you to bed and rest up, now!"*

But instead, Mama's eyes filled with tears. Both she and Eloise cried out and scampered round the table to embrace me, sobbing until my shoulders were soaking wet. I stared at the General, who was saying good-bye to the guests and at the same time supervising the loading of our trunks. Someone threw a cape over me. Mama clapped my bonnet upon my head, and it felt like an iron pot. There was a scrambling of relations shouting farewell and good luck. Eloise tugged my gloves over my knuckles, and the General shuffled beside me, his gray great cape swinging over his black boots. The servants wept and shouted good-bye to Dahlia, who sobbed out the door and into the night. The Negroes loosed a final howl of misery on behalf of their doomed kin, then retired contentedly to their beds.

The little ones scrambled to love me good-bye, overcome by a contagious sobbing that afflicted them one and all. The grown guests, being well into their cups, shouted sloppy felicitations. Those far in the back waggled their hands in the air. Uncle kissed Mama on the forehead and promised he would look after me.

Eloise grinned mischievously, tugged my psalmbook from my cape pocket, then giggled. "Look what you married over!" She removed the cover, and I saw that she had substituted *A Vindication* for my psalms. Then she kissed me on both cheeks and said melodramatically, "I've underlined our favorite passages. Seek the nobler field, Sister!" Then, cupping her hand around my ear, she whispered, "And write to me what it feels like, everything he does to you."

The General slipped his hands under my elbows, steered me out the door and down the steps. I stepped onto the narrow pedal-up, but when I peered into the coach, I stopped in puzzlement and glanced over my shoulder at him. He said, "The straw is mounded high to keep you warm. Step into it, find your seat, then cover yourself over with it."

It scratched my legs. The coach was uncomfortable, the seats were not tufted morocco like Mama's barouche and the bench was hard. I shifted about as if I were shaking spiders from my petticoats. The General blew silver clouds of breath into the dark air. He leaned over me, and looking over my shoulder, reached under the straw, then ran his hands along my thighs. I gasped in shock and leapt up so that I was pressed awkwardly against him, but he only laughed in response and pushed me gently back onto the seat, for he had found the lap strap and he tied it about my waist.

"Calm yourself, Miss Bullitt. This coach yaws like a shallop on the sea. Hickory Cee-springs, you know. You may get sick to your stomach."

Trying to recover my composure, I blurted, "So that's how passengers count the hours."

He leveled a keen eye on me, then shouted after Uncle, "Clark! We'd best be going if we're to be at the inn by midnight."

Uncle trotted jauntily from the house bearing an enormous hamper Mama had thrust into his arms. He crouched into the coach, slid onto the bench across from us, tossing straw in the air like a gleeful child. His liquored breath filled the air. The General rapped on the roof and the coach lurched forward. I crouched low in the seat, gripping the wing cushion as I was knocked into him. I murmured an apology.

But the General noticed not at all. He said, "Clark, open that basket and see if Mrs. Bullitt has packed ardent spirits for us." Uncle flipped the wooden lid of the hamper and poked about blindly for a while. He fondled the provender and praised his discoveries. "Ah, succulent Bayonne ham; oh, a rich wheel of cheese; um, beaten biscuits; oh yes, that heavenly gooseberry pie, uh . . . what are these beauties I hear clinking? But of course."

It was a moonless night, and a limb-bending snow fell upon the trees. The carriage rocked us side to side like a mother soothing an infant. I peered out the fogged windows at the houses we passed. They were taper-lit yellow, nested upon snowy lawns. Uncle thrust a goblet brimming with

Jurançon into my hand. I sipped as we passed out of Louisville and I sipped as we crossed into dark woods, where I heard distant rivers rushing. The world turned soft and warm about me. I let my cheek rest against the General's cape. Uncle talked, and the General said barely a word, but now and again, I felt him squeeze my hand. Then, when my glass was half empty—indeed, when my head felt like glass—I interrupted Uncle and turned to the General, whose face I could not see at all. But I could feel his breath upon my nose and chin when I looked up at him. There was an awkward silence. The wine had warmed my blood, and I lifted my face so close to his that I felt my lips brush the beard stubble on his chin.

"Miss Bullitt . . ." he began.

"Hah!" Uncle shouted, refilling our glasses, "can't call her that anymore. Mary, insist he call you Mrs. Atkinson. What was it that Eloise was hollering as we all skipped out? 'Exact respect from your husband.' Agh, Henry, before I forget, when we arrive home, I'll send an express to Keokuk and his council, and tell them to leave Black Hawk behind. I'll make it official. We won't negotiate with the Sauk if it means negotiating with Black Hawk."

I brought my knees up and plucked at straw that had needled through my petticoats. I must have been whittled, because I mischievously flicked at the buttons on his uniform, but this garnered no response from the General.

"Twelve years is an awfully long time to nurse a hatred, isn't it?" I asked as I dumped straw out of my slipper then rapped it against the door.

The General unclasped his cape at the throat, tipped his head back and made as if to nap. "Not a long time for Black Hawk. When Zebulon Pike traveled to Saukenuk—"

"To what?" I interrupted him.

"Black Hawk and the Sauk people live in Saukenuk. That is the name of their village. It is located at the confluence of the Mississippi and Rock Rivers; a four-day trip downriver by canoe to St. Louis. When Pike went up there after the last war, Black Hawk attacked his boats and sent a message that until he has avenged his son's death at my hand, there will never be peace between the Americans and the Sauk people. That is the way of things, but you have no cause for fear. You'll be well and duly protected. I assure you, no one will trouble you. There is no safer place than a camp of seven hundred armed men."

The General drank deeply from his glass.

Uncle clinked the bottle neck against the General's goblet as he filled it again. "Say, Mary, you should see the new house your husband has built for you on the prettiest hill in the whole of the camp."

I strained to see the General's face. Tiny bumps rose all over my skin. The General covered my hand with his, and a heavy silence fell over us. So Black Hawk knew where and how to find the General. That meant Black Hawk knew where to find *me*. I suddenly understood that my new husband's tale of vengeance formed the basis for the first bargain I'd made in my adult life. It seemed such a cruel blow to realize that in marrying the General, I had unwittingly contracted a lifelong union with his deadly apparition, Black Hawk. Henceforward, whatever the season or venue, Black Hawk would follow me where I ventured, just as he followed the General.

Snow crunched under the wheels and wind buffeted the carriage and I allowed my cheek to rest again against the General's cape. He put his hand over my face, and the warmth and nearness of him comforted me, but one thought troubled the pitching and sinking rhythm of my drowsing mind. On this sleet-riddled night, I was going where the earth was broken from the knowable. And I had bound up my future with a man whose life was mostly behind him.

3

The National Road, January 1826

Upon awakening, I thought I was sleepwalking in the realm of dream, so weird did it seem to be on a midnight road and not in my own bed. My eyes felt gritty as I rubbed at them. Very soon thereafter, I once again fell to sleep, but I awoke by degrees. By the quality of the light and the depth of the shadows under the shifting clouds, I guessed it to be somewhere in the small hours. My insides leapt with the flustering realization that I was not at home. I closed my eyes, then opened them quickly in the manner of a woman deceiving herself. This cannot be. Where am I and who in the world is *he?* I thought as I looked up at the General. He faced into his moonlit reflection in the glass, and finding his countenance inscrutable, I stared too.

That, I thought as I looked at the General's profile, is a very large chin. I tried to divine a truth about his character from that chin, but nothing came to me. The General exhaled and stretched his legs, crossing his feet at the ankles and looping his hands behind his head. Then he glinted at me. It was a small, caretaking sort of glint. A passing glint, like patting your pocket to reassure yourself something you've put there hasn't fallen out. Uncle William slept with his head against the hood, his mouth slack, his lower teeth in plain sight. I hoped I hadn't slept with my mouth open. Seeing me awake, the General nodded at Uncle and grinned. "Unlike your uncle, you do not give your tongue so much air when you sleep."

I turned aside to whisper, "He is our favorite uncle, but he suffers the blues now and again since Aunt Julia and his children died. Aunt Harriet watches over him, but Mama worries that he is growing more melancholy every year."

The General regarded Uncle and whispered back, "We reconcile ourselves, all of us, to what we've lost. Your uncle is entitled to his melancholy. He doesn't indulge himself, but he has a right to remember."

"Yes, you're right, I suppose I'd think less of him if he wasn't blue now and again."

For a long moment, the General seemed to indulge his own melancholy, but just as quickly shook it off. He leaned closer to me and began in a teasing voice, "I met your uncle in 1819 as I was preparing to go into the Indian country, up the Missouri River to keep the Arikara from closing the rivers to the fur traders, to push the British out of the territories."

"Yes, I recall. I read about that in the *Intelligencer.* I heard about the Crow. About how they tried to steal your guns. What did you do to them?"

"Now why is it, Miss Bullitt, that I think your next question is going to be, did you shoot anybody?"

"I am not so callow, General. But your expedition did make for great reading by the fire." I tried not to appear too admiring or too eager when I lifted my face to him. "But . . . did you? Shoot anybody?"

He scratched his sideburns, and they rasped under his nails. "Why is it women love hearing about bloodshed?"

"I do not. And it is indelicate of you to suggest it."

"I wasn't the one who brought up shooting people. You do that, you know. I've noticed you suggest the illicit, then act appalled when I answer you directly. That's a fine trick. But I am not fooled by you as I saw your nature clearly the instant we met."

I rolled my eyes, scooted away from him and looked out the window. But he continued, "Your uncle said to me, 'Mary Bullitt is the great-granddaughter of Huguenots, so her heart is heretical. She is the niece of Fletcher Christian, so mutiny is in her soul. She is a descendant of Patrick Henry, and every one of her bones is marrowed with revolution. You court her at your own risk. She will throw you into a ferment.' I said, 'Clark, what would her address be?'"

The carriage careened, and I slid helplessly into him, and he into the wing cushions. I thought we would upend like an egg crate. The General put his arms around me with more urgency than was warranted. When the carriage leveled out, he did not release me. The shadows in the carriage wove a tension through the darkness. Under our cover of straw, I could feel the bones of his legs pressed up firmly against mine—his preference, as there was room for him to be away from me. At that moment, I knew a dark wish, and when I looked up at him, it was apparent he did too. I occupied myself with speculation and wondering. We riveted upon one another but did not dare to do more, as Uncle slumbered tenuously and so close. Reluctantly, he pulled away from me but kept his hand upon my forearm.

I asked, "Your mother and father? When shall I meet them?"

"They have passed over."

"Oh. Oh, I am sorry." But he waved my sympathy away and peered out the window.

The sky was burdened with low-slung clouds that obscured a watery moon. We were in a wood. Though I looked first at whence we had come, then toward where we would go, I could see nothing but the white ribbon of the road disappearing in both directions. He said, "I wish we could hire a sleigh. If this snow gets much deeper, the hubs will sink and we will founder."

Our journey from Louisville to St. Louis would take twenty hours if the team of four horses was changed off frequently and kept to a pace of twelve miles per hour. Of course, with this snow, we couldn't go that fast. The General had arranged for a new team and driver to meet us at intervals. We would travel straight through the second night. Barring accidents and breakdowns, and providing the roads hadn't reduced to gumbo, we would arrive at our new home early the morning after this.

The driver rapped on the coach roof with his whip handle. Without a word of explanation, the General ducked out of the carriage and assisted me down.

Kicking a shower of straw before me, I ricketed sleepily onto the road and then said, "Why have we stopped before a stable?"

To which Uncle William replied wearily, "Lord, Mary, this is an inn, where the rest of the world catches respite."

I turned back to the coach, then made as if to climb in.

"Then I shall forgo respite and keep to the coach."

But the General hooked my arm and dragged me after him. A harsh wind pelted us with drifted snow at the horizontal, and I turned away from it. Uncle knocked upon the door. The snow melted into my slippers, clasped icy bracelets around my shins, and I felt moisture between my toes. I peered ahead into the brushy darkness of gnarled post oaks and skeletal undergrowth. A hiss sounded, and snow slid from the branches overhead, dropping in pillows about me. I leaned into the General's cape and pressed my face between his shoulder bones for warmth.

The door creaked open.

I peered around to have a look and instantly regretted my curiosity.

The innkeeper was a bulky she-muskrat hunched in the snow. As she looked at me, she poked her finger into her mouth to unlatch her two upper teeth from her two lower. I knew from her scrutiny that she was determining whether or not I was a slattern. All of her was the color of milk, from her white hair hanging in elf locks to her lunar-pale skin and the cambric of her dress. She stank of underarms and cider. When she spoke, her voice came from her nose.

"You be wantin'?"

"Madam, have you any beds?" Uncle William inquired.

She stepped into the road, surveyed both Uncle and the General, then came round to have another look at me. The stench of her caused me to press my face fully into the General's back, and I breathed wool fibers into my nose. Uncle tipped his head so as to make his neck pop. The General turned, offended by her manner. I turned with him, in shuffly little steps as he kept a wary eye upon the innkeeper.

She said, "It's nearing dawn, but you'll pay the full price in specie. I don't take no paper money here, most specially not St. Louis paper."

The General muttered something faintly derogatory that I could not hear.

The innkeeper lifted her lip at the General in warning, grumbling about sunshine soldiers, and lumbered before us without a backward glance. The General took my hand and cautiously poked his head into the darkness, gingerly crossing over as if he expected the floor to drop away from under his boot heels. Before the ruddy embers of the fire, I saw men strewn in rows and a lot of dogs. Both exhaled malodorous vapors, wheezed gas and talked to themselves in slumber. The air over this concert of animal noises was soft and stale.

The General kept my hand in a bulldog grip as we followed the shadowy forms of the innkeeper and Uncle.

"And what have we here? A woman in disarray upon the stair!" Uncle said.

"Shut the fug oop," someone on the floor snarled at him.

The General muttered warnings all the way up until, finally, we reached a landing not much bigger than the inside of a musty wardrobe. The four of us crowded there. The innkeeper heaved at the door, and upon entering hollered, "You, Emmet! Out of the bed, we got quality folks paying specie for it."

She stomped to a three-legged table, sparked flint to tinder and lit the single candle. A corpulent man, dressed in soiled trousers, heavy boots and an unbuttoned shirt innocent of washing, rose up congenially from the bed, said, "Good Evening," then stumbled past us down the stairs. The innkeeper waved grandly at a caving mattress of indeterminate color and said, "'Ere's plenty room . . . sleep as drunk lords. Slosh jar under the table."

Uncle shoved her out the door, then latched it behind her. He removed his frock coat, then nodded at the sagging mattress, "Mary, please, you and the General sleep there."

"Oh no. I'll be flea-jumped. I would sooner sleep upon the floor than upon a mattress that has never been scalded."

Uncle looked around the room doubtfully, then said, "I wish she had taken the candle with her."

I turned circles to have a look about, but could see nothing other than that we were locked into a poorly chinked ashwood casket. Aside from the tiny bed table and the bed itself, the room was bereft of furnishings. Snow blew in between the logs and drifted in perfect little white triangles. Spiderwebs drooped from the ceiling like seining nets. I glanced at Uncle, who snapped his great cape over the floor, settled himself and reposed contentedly before the bed table. He laced his fingers over his heart like the happy dead.

"Good night, children."

I heard a snort from him and knew him to be sleeping.

The General frowned at the room, then shook his head at me as if he were ashamed. I shrugged with a wistful expression. I didn't want him to think that one night of discomfort would cause me to dissolve. So I pointed at the floor and said brightly, "Here?"

He removed his cape and tossed it on the floor beside the bed on the side opposite Uncle. He took great care to smooth it out, then removed my cape from my shoulders and rolled it into a sort of long pillow. With dignified comportment, he said softly, "This is most disappointing. As much to me as to you. I had hoped . . ."

"Yes. So had I."

"You had?" He looked surprised.

"Well, of course. Why would I not?" I scratched at my neck and stared at the floor.

He offered in a boyishly eager way, "We will be home the morning after this."

"Yes."

The General nodded as if all doubt between us had been put to rest, but I kept a wary eye upon him. He began undressing, intent upon the small details of himself.

The taper light rendered him an interesting study in bachelor ritual. He untied his cravat and rolled it over the first two fingers of his left hand, then placed it carefully into the inside pocket of his uniform coat. The collar of his shirt stood high over his jaw. He opened it at the neck, watching each button slip through its grommet. The shirt flapped as he sat on the floor and removed his boots, carefully arranging them side by each, flicking away offending streaks of melted snow with his thumb and forefinger. His belly creased when he bent over, and I tried to see his body through the shadows. He cleared his throat as he rolled his sleeves over his elbows in neat folds and loosened the knot of the waist strap that held his white trousers up.

I stood on my tiptoes with my eyes straining downward, to no avail.

He yawned, then sat with his arms about his knees, arranging his socks just so. I stepped briskly away from the little pallet and turned a futile circle in search of a reason not to lie upon it. He tried to smile reassuringly but only looked tired.

"Come rest."

He patted the cape and waited.

The boards cut into my knees as I knelt, then lowered myself onto my side. Turning my face cautiously, I found him gazing at me from under the heavy lid of his eye. I could feel his breath upon my cheek and I believed something was about to happen. He slid a look under the bed at Uncle, who was snoring. He sighed and, propping himself up on one elbow, said, "You're not going to sleep tonight, are you?"

"No."

I felt his mouth close to my ear, and I squeezed my eyes shut, then drew my knees up.

"Did you sleep well on the steamer when you traveled with your parents, back East?"

"Yes."

"Then imagine for a moment that you are on a steamer packet, one of those luxury boats, a side-wheeler like the *Cleopatra,* or perhaps the *Alton.* And as you stand on the pilot's deck, the paddles thrum against the current, and sometimes, the hull is scratched by the bony fingers of snags and sawyers reaching out of the dark water. You are traveling north upon the Mississippi. The shore passes you by, green and lush and deep. There you see the great herds of buffalo descending into the water, and gray wolves waiting to snatch the young red calves, or one of the cows, with a deep red wound on her flanks—"

"From Indian arrows?"

"Uh, in my story, it's from rutting, the bulls bite the cows in their enthusiasm."

I laughed and jabbed at his chest with my fingers, but the warmth of his skin unsettled me in a fierce way, and I brought my hand back to the safe place under my ear. He continued, "The Mississippi River forks in the Indian territories where it is joined by a broad and shallow stream called the Rivière de la Roche. The Rock River. Here the land swells up to gentle bluffs. In the center of this river is a limestone island that flowers bright yellow with puccoon in the spring. And on this island, from the beginning of time, has lived an enormous bird. A great bird as white as a summer cloud, with wings that span the breadth of the Mississippi when he takes flight. When the children fetching up crawfish out of the Rock River look up at him, they see that old white bird blocking out the sun."

I peered skeptically at him. "Is this a true story?"

"Of course it's true; the native peoples have always known of this spirit bird. It nests in the great caves on the island, and when it flies over the people who live near, they are granted peace and wealth and good fortune in the hunt, and all of their children live many winters, to become gray-haired and wise. The Sauk people do not walk upon the island, but they paddle up to the great bird's cave in their canoes and leave him peace offerings, then take their leave quietly. The spirit bird dislikes noise and intrusion. He isn't much for human talking."

"What happens when the bird dies?"

"The Sauk believe that if the bird goes away, so will their hold upon the land. But they will have lived as an honorable people. They will have made the good journey through this life."

"Oh, that is the saddest story," I said, my lids drooping heavily. "How can a journey be a good one if they lose everything they love?"

And that is all I remember of his story, for though I was on thorns, I was overcome with fatigue, and soon I slept.

As I fell off, I thought I heard him say, "You are too sharp a temptation, Mary Bullitt."

I could feel the currents of the Mississippi lulling me to sleep. But then, I gasped out of slumber and stared into the darkness about me. My limbs were immobile because the General was lying almost completely over me, speaking to his nocturnal phantoms. He was so heavy that I could not breathe, and my hipbones were crushed to the floor under his thigh.

"General?" I whispered, and as I did so, he pressed his mouth to my cheek. He spoke gibberish, quickly, softly, as if sharing confidences. I attempted translation, but got no closer than something akin to oh me, comb me, oh me, nick oh me.

Until he said, "Give us a kiss in our favorite place. Oh me. Nick oh me."

I filled my lungs and thrust him off me, and the back of his head plunked on the floor, but still he slept soundly with his arms outflung. I hoarded the pillow he'd made of my cape under my ear, then fell back to dreaming as the wind scraped at the log walls.

At dawn, the General moaned himself awake, then sat up and dressed. He picked at the corner of his eye and bent into his boots, facing away from me. My neck hurt, my shoulders hurt and my limbs felt leaden. As he tied his cravat, he looked me over genially, with his mouth in a twist. He reached out his forefinger, then ran it along the side of my face and said, "You've a brand from the planking on your cheek."

"Yes, well, you talk in your sleep."

He shrugged my comment away, but I persisted.

"By the bye, where is your favorite place, General? Washington City?"

The General turned purple as a damson plum. Without responding to me, he crossed the room, kicked gently at the bottom of Uncle's boots and said, "Clark. We'll be leaving now."

"Who do you talk to in your dreams?" I peered up at him suspiciously.

"Never you mind. Stay behind me and try not to walk on people as you go."

As the three of us departed, the stairs creaked underfoot. A little man honked openmouthed with his face in the lap of a corn-colored woman. She slept with her skirt hiked up over her thighs and one flaccid breast exposed. The General stared fixedly at her, and stopped only when he was in danger of tripping and looking foolish. We lifted the latchstring and opened the door as quietly as we were able, then dashed out into the snowfall.

Our coach was pulled round, the horses whickered, and the snow plumed up around their hooves. Nicholas and Dahlia huddled together under a buffalo robe on the rumble seat. Another day of traveling had come to light as we lurched down the road. Having passed out of the woods, we crossed onto country cut by limestone cliffs and rocky outcroppings. I kept my face to the glass, drawing spiral patterns into the window fog with my forefinger. A herd of pronghorn, standing into the wind, lifted their bulging gaze to us, leapt vertically, then dashed across the field as if they were all of one body and not twenty.

The General broke off his conversation with Uncle for a moment and, following my gaze, bent to me then said, "Pronghorn follow a female leader to safety when they are threatened."

Uncle interjected with more talk about the Sauk problem. I found my uncle's presence increasingly trying. He was so much more familiar with the General than I. They conversed constantly, leaving no space for me. When I asked a question of the General, Uncle answered it. When the General began to address me, Uncle interrupted with a change of subject. The General did not seem to mind, but I did.

I watched a red-tail hawk circle above a snowfield momentarily illuminated by a break in the clouds. It left an imprint of contours in my mind even when I closed my eyes. At some points in the soft inner elbow of an inlet of the Mississippi, I saw winter-bleached scouring rush and heavy brown cobs of cattail splitting to January seed. The river ate at its own banks. Young trees crooked as if saying good-bye before taking their swim. After hours of bone-wearying travel northward, late that second day, we came upon a small cabin. I pushed my way out before the others and had a look around.

The cabin was situated in a swale cleared of cottonwood. Even through the snow, I could see horsetail and slough grass poking up like fingers of the dead protesting burial. Despite the brightness of the setting, I recognized this as a malarial floodplain and wondered why a man would put his family in such peril. Our driver, Nicholas and Dahlia, stayed near the coach and were watchful of us as we set forth to see if we could arrange supper. But as we neared the door, I happened to glance to my left, and there was the sad proof of a bad decision; three small graves, affixed with posts bearing names I could not see.

"Where are you going?" the General called after me as I trod to the little graveyard, kicking up snow before me.

"I must read their names," I said.

I stooped and squinted, tilting my head aside but saw only ages carved into the redbud: BOY ONE YEAR, GIRL AGED TEN, BOY AGED SIX. I glanced around to make sure the General would not see me, then I made the sign of the cross over myself. It was a habit I had contracted at the convent, and the motion of it put me at my ease. There wasn't, in my mind, anything troubling about borrowing this small motion of the hand from the Romanists. I viewed it as an earthly signal of respect that the departed would surely recognize and appreciate.

Uncle came up behind me.

"I cannot see a stone or post without wondering at the soul what's passed along. Rousseau was all wrong about the country, you know. The deeper into the prairie you go, the sicker and thinner the children become. You'll see the rosiest children in the cities of the East."

I knew he was thinking of his lost children, and his lost Julia. I was about to console him when we were distracted by a commotion twenty rods to the back of the house.

There, a herd of barefoot children swirled around a mulberry tree, shouting encouragement to one another. All of them had been shorn, even the girls, so their heads looked like spiky blooms of allium. The younger ones were dressed in old flour sacks with arm holes cut through, tied at the throat with a drawstring. Mongrels blotched at their heels, grinning and snapping. A shift in their movements allowed me to see what they were about.

They were having a gander-pull.

A large white goose was tied by his legs, upside down, crying piteously as the children jerked violently at his head, trying to separate the gander's neck from the rest of him. A little girl, whom I guessed to be no more than three, joyfully squeezed her hands around the gander's throat, lifted her feet from the ground, then tried to swing back and forth. The gander's bawling diminished to a whimper. He had been trussed for defeat, and his inverted wings were spotted with his own droppings.

I ran at the children, startling them so they stopped momentarily.

The eldest boy sneered at me. "What are you lookin' at?"

I bowed over him with my hands on my hips, "I'm trying to decide which of you is going to need the doctor first."

But the General pushed me aside, removed a knife from his belt, cut the gander free, then laid him upon the stump and cut his head off. The children raised their fists as they circled round the General, baying dissent. The gander's body shuddered, then dropped to the ground. The dogs jostled to lap at the stump as the children turned their attention to the General.

"Looka that knife!" the eldest boy crowed as the General wiped the blade in the snow. This boy had flat eyes, like those of a small-mouth bass, and at that moment, I knew him to be locked into malevolent ignorance that a lifetime of learning and compassion could not penetrate. The boy came near to the General, then stood obligingly still, like one receiving honors from the schoolmaster.

"My name is Reason," the child said as the General dried the blade on the tail of the boy's checked cotton shirt. Reason's brothers and sisters looked upon him reverently.

"Reason?" I asked, glancing down at the goose blood trickling through the snow.

"Reason. Mama said there was never a good one for me coming to be."

The three of us exchanged a look, but if Reason was seeking our sympathy, he had failed utterly. The General sheathed the knife, then patted his pockets for his pipe and tobacco. Uncle looked about the homestead with the jaded eye of a true frontiersman. I tried to extricate myself from the children's curiosity. The little girl who had used the gander's neck as a pulley picked at the scabs about her mouth, then strummed her fingers over my gown.

"Why are there sores all over your mouth?" I asked.

She glanced away shyly, but her older sister answered, "That's 'cause she sucks her bonnet strings. An' Mama dips 'em in vinegar and cayenne pepper to get her to quit. But she ain't quit."

The girls squatted on their haunches as they fingered the silk rosettes on my hem with goose-shat stained fingers. I was grateful when a woman's voice cut through the discord. She was quite obviously peeved at us, but spoke first to Uncle William. People always addressed him first. It was one of the disadvantages of being the tallest in an assembly. The woman bowed to Uncle with her hands locked before her bodice.

She was in her late twenties, broad shouldered and axe hipped, with a rounded belly showing under the gathers of her stained skirt that led me to reason she was either pregnant or so worn from it she was permanently fulled out. Her hair was the plain ashen color that is really no color at all. But though her mouth fell in a little as she was lacking teeth, I guessed she had been pretty once, in a soft way.

"I had thought to keep them amused with a-pulling for an hour or so. I can't get my tatting and mending done with them underfoot, and in the winter, there ain't so many chores. All the same, you've saved me the cutting of that gander's head and I am grateful. This here is my oldest boy and his name is Reason. Now, Reason, you hang him up, and when he's all drained out, the girls will see to plucking him."

The woman was attired in the same checked cotton worn by the older children, and each member of the family seemed a variation on the other, with wide faces, the common brown hair and greenish eyes. She introduced each of them airily, and we learned them to have been named for whatever was on her mind at the moment of their birth.

"This here is Pie, 'cause I was hungry for pie; that is Pink, because that's what color she was when she was born; she's Bird, 'cause—"

Uncle was enthused by this game and interrupted with his guess, "Because you saw a bird when she was born!"

"No, I was boiling up a bird for supper. This boy's called Trivet, the other's Prosperous, 'cause I hope he will be one day; she's named Wedding, 'cause that's where we was supposed to be when she was born, never having had the benefit of having words said over us; ah . . . that's Trip, 'cause I fell over a swage block and out he popped a scant moment later; the girl, she's named Cordite, and the baby inside the house is Spurge."

I stood on tiptoe, cupped my hands around my mouth and whispered to the General, "Isn't spurge a noxious weed?"

"They're all noxious weeds."

"Madam, you have been blessed," Uncle said solemnly.

"Oh, I don't know 'bout that. My old man? He grabs me by the ankles, says 'Make a wish, darlin,' and the next spring out pops one more child."

The General took my arm, but I hesitated. "Now what?" he asked, studying the doleful expression on my face. I hissed, "I don't want to go in. I'll wager she stuffed her grandparents and hung them over the mantel."

"You ought to find that reassuring. It would mean there's no room for you there."

The children taggled after us as the woman urged us before the fire. Inside the cabin, a few windows, narrow to keep out Indian arrows and bullets, admitted a feeble light from under the eaves. There was one room offset by a frost-walled ell crowded with cots. In the corner, an infant slept in the bottom drawer of a chest. We crossed a tamped dirt floor that had been burnt then flooded till it shone like glass. A millet broom in the corner bore proof of the woman's diligent attentiveness to her housekeeping. She told us her name was Miriam, that she and her husband had come to live here when Missouri was still a territory, as speculators had pushed up the prices so high elsewhere, they could not afford to buy land in a civilized place.

When Uncle introduced himself and us, Miriam blushed. "My husband did not vote for you to be governor, Mr. Clark. No one here in these parts did, you know. It was on account of how you love them Indians. As you might well understand, the last thing we can find it in our hearts to love is Indians."

The General and Uncle exchanged a humorous glance as I took my place upon the bench. The General lied, "I didn't vote for Mr. Clark, either. He's a rascal if there ever was one." Uncle shrugged affably and tugged the earlobe of the little girl standing closest to him. As the room was very dark, Miriam lit a pitch-pine knot in a tin tray, sending up the odor of burning resin. I put my hand atop the bristly head of the youngest child.

"Did you cut their hair to protect against nits?"

Miriam spooned yellow soup from a kettle into one large wooden bowl. "That's on account of me trying to protect their scalps. What Osage would want those homely scalps, I tell you what? Don't the lot of 'em look like little voles with the mange?" She laughed and waved a spurtle in the air. "Some soldiers goin' east to Louisville stopped here for supper. They said there is plenty of dead white people rotting on the Cuivre. They said that the Sauk, and most particularly . . . ah, what is his name?" Miriam held the bowl aloft as if waiting to catch her recollection with it. Then she brightened, "Black Bird . . . no! Black Hawk, that's it."

"What were the soldiers' names?" the General asked.

"Goodness, I have no idea of their names, but they did tell me they got this news of what happened down at the Cuivre from settlers who'd come runnin' to St. Louis for safety." Miriam shook her head hopelessly as she dug about in a drawer. The children leaned forward eagerly when her voice hardened with gossipry. "They said Mrs. Ramsay, who was quick with child, was milking her cow when it happened. She was pulled into the house by Mr. Ramsay, who had just the one leg. Their three pretty little children had been playing about. The Ramsays had to stand there and watch while Black Hawk hacked the children to bits. Then Black Hawk shot and killed Mr. Ramsay, and Mrs. Ramsay, he mangled her so badly she was not expected to live."

I blinked glazey eyed at Miriam, though the children delighted in this tale as if they were hearing about Jack chopping the beanstalk in advance of the giant. Having silently determined that these stories were bad for my constitution, Uncle turned the conversation. "Say, madam, what crops do you have luck with here?"

As if she had not heard Uncle William at all, Miriam made a circling motion above her head, crafting a halo for herself as she put the bowl in the center of the table. "That's the part they favor for scalps. Leaving a bloody patch like a little red toque atop the head. And the one dead Indian they found at the Cuivre River? They put him atop a dead white man to show as how even in death, the Sauk are victorious. That angered me much as anything. Thank the Lord my husband is a captain in the local militia. It's a good militia too. They call themselves the Wolf-Lick Rifles."

Miriam went on, "All of us can shoot, even the little girls. Say, shall I put up a bowl for the driver and your two servants outside there?"

"Please," the General said.

I popped a piece of ashcake into my mouth and peered sidelong at

Miriam. The boy-child Reason stared raptly at the General, trying to gain his attention. Finally, Reason blurted, "You know how you kilt that gander? I know a feller who can take a chicken's head off but leave it living. Leave it living and drop bugs down its gullet. Down its meat trap. It's true. That chicken? He lived for fifty days without a head. No. No. That chicken lived for ninety days."

The General looked skeptically at the boy and said, "Is that so?"

The boy squinched up his face at the General. "You wear that blue coat. That mean you likes killin', ain't it?"

But the General was not ready to accord the boy the privilege of a conversation. He muttered, "Not particularly."

Reason turned his face away by a quarter and eyed the General suspiciously. "That don't add. I like killin' well enough. I could be a so-jer one day soon. Mebbe I could be your so-jer. What is your name?"

"General."

"No, I mean your first name?"

"General."

The children tittered, and Reason cultivated an instant need to impress the General, "I got a pistol in my boot. Wanna see it?"

"No, I do not." The General sighed.

Miriam continued upon the subject of Indian rumors and alarms. "Them soldiers said Black Hawk killed all of those people on the Cuivre because he wanted the protection of the United States. I ask you what? Is it protection Black Hawk wants? From the soldiers? How so? They said to me, if Indians kill white people it means they got the stuff for bargaining with the army. Indians will force the army to give 'em all manner of gewgahs to stop 'em aforehand from killing decent white people. It's bribery, ain't it? Pure and simple, bribery. Explain that to me, will you? Which one of you is gonna give Black Hawk money and gewgahs for not killing white people?"

The General and Uncle politely ignored Miriam's questions. The children grinned at their mother, seeing in her the wisdom of the ages. With her fists balled upon her sturdy hips, Miriam looked the image of the good pioneer woman. She placed one large spoon before the General. He lifted it, and while the rest of us looked on, took a sip.

"Miriam? What sort of soup is this?" I asked.

"Owl," she said. "Reason shot him."

Once again, the General touched his spoon into the yellow murk. Onions, turnips and potatoes floated alongside dark wedges of owl meat. The children watched him ravenously, and it was then I realized that Miriam expected all of us to share the one spoon and to eat out of the communal bowl. But Reason was too hungry to wait for the General to relinquish the spoon to him.

"All best to you, and don't take this wrong, General, but I ain't waiting no more." The boy cupped his hand and dipped it up to the wrist into our dinner. His brothers and sisters crowded around the General and plunged in with slurping noises like water sluicing through a hand pump. Trivet, however, tasted a bit he didn't like and spit it back into the trough. At the sight of a dozen dirty hands swishing in the trough, the General winced, patted his stomach and declared himself full.

"Mrs. Atkinson, do come dine with the children. The soup is lovely."

"Thank you, General, but I wouldn't want to deprive them of their supper."

Miriam held her plain round face in her hands and inquired after news from Louisville, and we obliged her as best we could. Before nightfall, we took our leave and continued down the road as Miriam watched us from the doorway, surrounded by her children.

The General motioned me to the window of the carriage with a crook of his finger. I leaned beside him and followed his gaze to the trees behind the house.

"Look at that, will you? Twelve cottonwoods. One for each apostle. And the last on the end is charred from a fire, and that I should call Judas Iscariot."

I sat very close to my new husband until the homestead disappeared in the distance. Then, I put my arm across his chest and slept leaning against him, but I dreamt of the owl Reason had killed. I saw his heavy body skimming low over the house, I thought of that noble bird, navigating by intuition, before the bullet found him.

4

Jefferson Barracks, Missouri, January 1826

AT three o'clock in the morning, the driver hollered that we had arrived at the General's camp, the headquarters of the Army of the Frontier. The General's knees cracked as he rose up from the bench at the angle of a jack-knife half open. I banged my heels through the scanty remains of the straw to cure my feet of the stinging numbness. When at last I could feel them, I leapt out into the darkness, eager to see my new home. It was so cold that my eyes watered. We had stopped on a promontory in the midst of white bluffs that rolled away to the north. The snow changed underfoot, sculpted constantly into new forms. On every distant hill, I could make out the tents of the various regiments, pitched in orderly formation, snapping under the wind. Wood smoke from distant fires curled into the sky. The hills dropped off sharply to the Mississippi River, which I could not see from this vantage point.

"But . . . where is St. Louis?" I asked the General as he stepped into the blue light. The deep lines of his face stood out in bold relief. He turned away from me. Nicholas threw our trunks into the snow, and Dahlia lumbered down behind him.

"I will see you tomorrow," the General said to Uncle, who grunted and slumped into sleep as the coach rolled away.

"Where is St. Louis?" I asked again as he exhaled and squared his shoulders.

The General lifted his left arm. "That way."

I looked in that direction but saw only more hills rolling away. The four of us stood in a dismal little line and stared at the simple log house. It had a decided backwoods shrug.

"Such nice quarters for Nicholas and Dahlia," I declared, stomping my feet.

The General coughed, then bent to me. "This is the house I built for *you*. Their quarters are out back." Then he said to them, "You've earned your rest, you two. Go on and sleep now."

Nicholas and Dahlia deposited the trunk they carried in the hallway of my new home, then marched out the back door. The General walked ahead of me onto the porch. I followed him, thinking, Goodness, for a man who has given his life over to soldiering, you certainly are sensitive to innocent error. He held his arm out with courtly exaggeration and waited for me to slip mine through it. The iron hinges on the door creaked as we stepped over the threshold.

"It is precisely as I imagined it would be."

"That's not true. You imagined a grand stone house like your pa's."

He stopped before a console in the hallway and lit a candle. I glanced about.

"Did you build this?"

"I had help. We worked on it Sundays."

I knew he was watching me, so I expressed my enthusiasm. There were four simple rooms, each twelve by twelve, centered by the hallway. I walked through tentatively, inspecting the house floor to ceiling, touching latches, poking at the chinking, making inane observations. All the same, he seemed pleased, and my initial offense was forgotten. He said the iron battens were a gift from Colonel Zachary Taylor at Fort Armstrong, that Lieutenants Albert Sidney Johnston and Robert Anderson had done the masonry work, that he and Major Stephen Kearny hewed the logs. I took comfort that he had friends willing to supply that kind of help. It said something about him.

As the door on my immediate right was shut, I began my inspection with a shift to my left, entering a dark room shelved completely around and filled with books. At the moment I saw them, lined colorfully and neatly along the walls, I realized I had not lost all of the comforts of home. The General walked around the room lighting candles. I crouched to read the titles of the periodicals stacked on a low shelf: *Edinburgh Magazine, New London Monthly Review,* an agricultural journal, *American Repository* and *Gentlemen's Magazine.* He stored the books on the upper shelves, so I began pulling volumes. "Plutarch's *Lives* and . . . what's this? I've never heard of this. Boccaccio's *Decameron?*"

I frowned and held it up toward him.

"Give that to me. That's not proper subject matter for a lady."

"Well, now I'm intrigued." I turned away from him and opened the book but found it was in Italian, which I couldn't read. Flipping pages rapidly, I stopped at a simple ink sketch of two little naked people embracing upon a bed. They looked so happy. I heard the General's footfalls behind me, and fearing he would snatch the book away, I quickly flipped the pages to another sketch, this of a monk—he was naked too, but I knew it to be a monk because of his tonsure—with his mouth pressed between the legs of a woman who clasped her hands prayerfully.

Well, I'd never seen anything like *that* before.

"My God! What kind of a person would own such a book?" I turned swiftly to find the General just a hair's breadth away from me and slammed the book shut.

He laughed. "Didn't I warn you? Now, what have you seen that has riled you so?"

"As if I would tell you, of all people."

The General tried to reach behind me for the book, but I held it firmly. For a moment, he paused, poking his tongue into his cheek and smiling down on me. I faltered. I stepped back from him, but he slipped his arm about my waist and pulled me against him so that I could feel the buttons on his coat. My belly roiled up, and my shoulders felt weak. The warmth and pressure of his hands through my dress unsettled me in the best of ways. I dropped the book, grateful for the masking effect of my bonnet. I stared awkwardly at my feet, felt his legs against mine and reflexively brought my hands up against his forearms as he untied my bonnet strings, brushing his fingers against my throat. When I felt his touch, I reached up and shoved the bonnet gracelessly off my head, letting it plop on the floor. I remember that I stared at his mouth and brought my hand up to his face at the exact moment that a strange male voice sounded through the room as loudly as if the speaker were standing between us.

"Yah, haw, Reynolds. You got an arse like a circus horse."

We both startled, came apart, then looked at the hall from whence came the voice. It said, "By the bowels of Christ, I said, move it!"

"Does someone live with you?" I asked the General. He crossed the room and removed a Hawken rifle from the gun cabinet, loaded it, then said over his shoulder to me, "Wait right here. Don't follow after."

Of course, I followed after.

Cautiously, he pushed open the bedroom door, and we were met by the sight of two middle-aged, frock-coated men, asleep, huddled together upon *our* bed. The General gripped the nearest one by the collar and tossed him roughly to the floor, but the second leapt up with his hands wiggling surrender, and the General hollered, "What the hell is the meaning of this? Cass! Reynolds! Get outta my goddamned bedroom!"

"Waal! Where else we gonna sleep? It's cold out there, and the door was open!" With the odd perspicacity one possesses in moments of crisis and deep fatigue, I noted details of their appearances. I would, one day, be introduced to John Reynolds, a tobacco-colored man, a magistrate from Galena, Illinois, who hoped to be the governor of Illinois. The heavyset man was Lewis Cass, governor of the Michigan Territory, and later Secretary of War under President Jackson.

If I had the benefit of foresight, I would have stolen my husband's rifle, shot Cass dead on the spot and cried self-defense. I would have crowned them both with any available object and dumped their bodies into the well. And myself and all the country would have enjoyed a peaceable existence in the coming years. But even now, I know that killing them would not stop the course of events they put into motion by the unthinking act of sleeping upon our marriage bed. So began everything.

The bellicose Mr. Cass was dressed in a green coat. His straggly black hair was combed after the fashion of a Roman senator around his long face. Though he was by that time a teetotaler, his nose told me he had once liked bourbon. A goiter bulged above his cravat, and his front teeth were darkly spotted with decay.

"Don't you go handlin' me," Cass burbled, as he rolled onto his back. He swept at his knees as if the immaculate floor could have done his trousers damage.

John Reynolds's hair was white, his coarse features unlit by compassion. His eyes bagged from neuralgia. Reynolds commenced a harangue against the General, a loud litany of the injustices done him by aborigines of the soil, as he referred to the Sauk peoples. The General shoved him toward the hallway. "Out with you, my wife requires her rest."

"*Your wife!* Hah! The old bachelor finally got himself caught? Surely there is a cold wind blowing through hell this day." Reynolds cast a mocking look upon me.

The General pushed him again. "So, some Indian vealed your calf, is that right, Reynolds?" And the General wheeled them both out, then shut the door. For a moment, I allowed the silence of the room to have me. After two days and two nights shifting side to side, jolting up and down over the roads, I reveled in the stillness. I removed my cape and my gloves. There was a window above the narrow bed, a new chest of drawers, a wardrobe along one wall and a cold fireplace, swept free of ashes, on another.

It struck me, as I surveyed this room, that the General had prepared it before leaving in the hope of returning with a wife. It looked as though he had taken great care to arrange small items. There was a pearl-handled pier glass and an atomizer upon the chest next to the dry basin. The basin was new and unscratched. In it was one folded small cloth and an expensive piece of French milled soap. I touched it with a fingertip, then looked down at the chest of drawers. I tugged at a brass pull and found the drawers empty, but covered over with lavender paper for linens. It made me like him a little more, to think he would try to guess at practical things.

I peered into the wardrobe, and with a cautionary glance over my shoulder toward the door, I touched his uniform coat hanging upon the hook and fingered the eagles on the buttons. A pair of boots stood neatly below. I crouched and slid the small bottom drawer out and saw his folded stockings and linens. My cheeks flushed at the idea of intimacies, but I scolded myself for being so silly.

I unpinned my hair and rolled my neck to be free of the weight of it piled high. I slipped out of my shoes and unlaced the back of my dress, then covered myself over with a brown woolen standard army issue blanket that smelled of strange bodies. I collapsed facedown, and I slept immediately, not caring to worry over the commotion outside my door. The hollering of the politicians had burgeoned up and was rolling along momentously.

I did not care. It had been two nights since I had slept on a bed, and I did not care. When I awoke, I knew I would have to comply with a universe of tenets that my meticulous new husband had forged to keep an orderly bead upon me—and himself—and the idea of us together.

Before I sank into sleep, I thought—but could have been mistaken—I thought I heard the door creak open whilst the male voices argued in the next room. I thought I felt the bed sink as the General sat beside me, and I thought I heard him murmur kind words. I felt his hands upon my chemise, but I do not know if this is true or only my dreaming. Later still, I drifted up from waves of sleep, having dreamt of being submerged in treadling water of the Mississippi, caught upon the knuckle of a cottonwood and left to bob in the current. I wondered if my soul could find its way free of the river.

❧ IN my new house, which felt nothing at all like *mine,* Governor Lewis Cass and John Reynolds circled like pickets about the General. I came to recognize a pattern in the General's way of keeping a distance between himself and those who sought to avail themselves of him, including me. He did this by looking above, not into, the faces of the politicians; he did this in my presence by maintaining an elaborate courtesy that conquered every attempt to approach him on equal footing.

Having been crowded from the only room in the house that I really liked, I stood upon a slat of morning light in the hall and watched the General pace across the library floor. With a quarter nod, the General would bend away a little as the politicians looked at him. John Reynolds followed after, sometimes squatting to peer up at the General, who would merely turn again and pat his uniform coat for his pipe. He pretended to forget the men were in the room with him as he filled the bowl with tobacco.

Lewis Cass dabbed a white glob of spittle upon his lower lip with a black handkerchief. Cass teetered back by littles, rubbed his belly, then announced, "I got the *mal de vache* from eating too much buffalo. I tell you, General, we put for your quarters a fortnight in passing, and the eating was dismal. We brought down the patriarch of the prairie and found ourselves grinding forever to get him into swallowing condition. All of this hardship we endured, and for no other reason than to offer you militia help."

With the stem of his pipe clenched between his teeth, the General lifted the tongs from their stand by the hearth and rearranged the logs there. "And here you are. Punctual as death."

Cass grabbed the poker, then parried at the logs. "Because, General, it all comes down to horses. Don't it?"

"If I need horses, I can requisition them."

"But how quickly? And from whom, for the numbers you'll need? You can't chase Indians across the plains with foot soldiers."

It was obvious that the truth of this remark stung the General. Every week for seven years, he said, he had written urgent letters to congressmen and War Department officials in Washington City. Long, patient letters explaining the necessity of a regiment of mounted dragoons for the Army of the Frontier. The letters could be summarized this way: *An Indian on horseback moves faster than a foot soldier.* The General turned away from the politicians with a lazy shrug that belied his mood. Even from this distance, I could see his jaw tensing as he said, "I have sent Kearny with a company of dragoons to investigate. Calling out the militia at this juncture is unnecessary."

"The militia could—" Cass began, but the General cut him off.

"The militia can't ride and they can't shoot. And you are their officers only until they decide otherwise. How do you expect to maintain discipline when *they* elect *you* to be their officers? A politician can't lead his constituents into battle and expect them to follow orders. They'll throw him over and desert the moment the campaign becomes difficult. Leave the militia to their plows."

Reynolds's eyes flicked from Cass to the General. When a silence fell over them, Reynolds marched to and fro like the slop-footed country rube he was.

"There's talk against you, General. They say you're afraid to chase Black Hawk. Some reason you like the comforts of St. Louis too much and don't know nothing about Indian fightin'. Others claim you is some kind of Indian lover 'cause you spent so much time up north with 'em. Me? I figure you're just biding your time. But I'll tell you, my men are eager to come down here and burn every Sauk village from the Kaskaskia to the Skunk River. We could solve your problems for you."

The General sparked the steel to light his pipe, then looked at Reynolds as if he were an insect that found its way into his coffee. He leaned menacingly in to the magistrate. "If your militia touches the bristle on the ass of any dog in those peaceable villages, I will evict from the territories every white squatter and trespassing lead miner from here to Galena. Then we'll see how quickly you're elected governor, *Mister Reynolds*. Do we understand one another?"

"What are you afraid of, General?"

"You're the one who should be afraid, Mr. Reynolds. I have kept the peace for seven years, but if the militia provoke the Sauk, there'll be six thousand Indians vying to hang you from a shamble by your weaver's weights, and there won't be a goddamned thing I can do to save you. Or myself for that matter."

Reynolds wheedled like a schoolboy who'd been shoved to the ground once too often. "It's the fuggin' English who's behind this—again—isn't it ,General? I saw what they did in the last war with Black Hawk's help, and by God, the English are probably giving Black Hawk guns and powder and horses again, don't you know. Am I right? Is it the English again?"

"The Hudson Bay men are, for the most part, keeping to Canada. They haven't proved a problem since '16," the General said.

Cass scowled at the General, tucked his thumbs into his waistcoat, then intoned with oily agreeability, "What is it you're recommending, General?"

"Let my men come back with their report. If Black Hawk is responsible, your constituents will have their hostages."

There was a lull in the conversation while Reynolds poured himself a tumbler of rum, even though it was still early morning. I poked my head around the door, hoping to catch the General's attention, but his back was turned to me. I was reluctant to interrupt this meeting but even more reluctant to introduce myself into the room and thereafter be forced into discourse with the General's two little swains.

So I walked a few paces down the hall and inspected the other two rooms of the house. There was one room with a trundle bed, which would presumably be a nursery, and a dining room furnished with a long, pine table and rush-bottom chairs. When the river broke, I would urge Mama to send my furniture and belongings. I made nesting plans like a wren with a beak full of rye straw. I would put this here and that there. And so on. As I decorated in my head, the back door flew open.

I turned and saw my young cousin, Second Lieutenant Philip St. George Cooke. He entered carrying a fistful of letters he'd come to deliver to the General. Delighted at seeing a relative in this distant exile, I jumped into his arms and kissed his cheek. Now, before I departed St. Louis, Mama had told me he was assigned here at Jefferson Barracks, but all the same, I was surprised at the sight of him. Philip was nineteen the year I arrived in Missouri, and being a recent graduate of West Point, he had come to the frontier with romantic notions of finding his personal glory in soldiering.

From my earliest remembrance, Philip had passed summers with us at the White Sulphur Springs in Virginia. At fourteen, he began writing poetry that inspired ripping howls of laughter from me and my sisters. Philip looked like the charcoal sketch of idealized manhood on the cover of penny sheet music. He was six feet four inches tall, narrow-hipped and slender-boned, with dark auburn hair, dark arching brows and the reddest lips I had ever seen on a man. Unfortunately, they covered teeth skewed as broken fence slats.

I forgot the General and the territorial politicians. As Philip twirled about with me, laughing, and calling out as he did in the old days when we passed the summers together at the White Sulphur,

"Miss Mary! What are you doin' here?"

"Oh, Philip, I got myself married to that General in there. The tall one. The *old* one."

Philip looked taken aback. He grimaced into the library, then whispered to me, "Hm. We thought the General'd gone ossified. Most longtime bachelors aren't good for much more than taking care of themselves. Huh. The General married you. Of all people."

"What do you mean, *me* of all people?"

"Mary, the General thrives on order and discipline. You're an unruly weed what found its way into his shorn and dusty garden to my way of thinking." Philip clapped a mocking hand over his heart and lifted his gaze heavenward. "Mary has slain St. George and married a dragon."

"You're pretty, but I don't go in for marrying my cousins. What do you think of it here, Philip?"

"I fear I am becoming more worldly than Mama would ever want to know. All the honest women here are French, you know. All of 'em. And they're too . . . *actressy* for my tastes."

"Tell me every rotten thing you've done."

Philip stepped back at this, as if I'd waved a roach under his nose. He looked pointedly over my head. I turned to see the General glowering at him, with a hand out for the letters Philip held. As he read them over, I introduced Philip as my cousin and briefly described how our affection for one another grew out of the summers we passed together at the White Sulphur Springs.

I could see that the politicians had put the General in a bad humor. He fairly bristled. I should, at that moment, have excused myself from his presence. But I was regrettably unschooled in reading him. The General ignored me, except for lifting a surly brow. He continued to study the letters until I touched his sleeve and said, "I was thinking Cousin Philip could escort me to St. Louis . . ."

"Absolutely not," the General said, raising his hand in the air dismissively.

Philip glanced at me, then spoke in a voice an octave deeper than I'd ever heard before, "But sir, I shall go armed, and as it is midweek, I cannot imagine—"

"I am not interested in what you imagine, Mister Cooke." Turning his attention to me, the General said, "Mrs. Atkinson, this is not Louisville. These rough-stock men of the fur trade who frequent St. Louis neither know nor care who you are."

"So I am to be kept in this house?" I said, keenly aware of Philip's discomfort.

The General blew air out his nose, and appeared to give this some thought. Through the open door to the library, I saw Lewis Cass purse his rubbery lips as he listened carefully to us. Indeed, the politicians strained to hear us disagree like the accomplished keyhole peepers they were. Philip stepped away from us to the front door, his hands clasped behind his back, and pretended to study the hinges. The General said, "The streets of St. Louis can be a violent place."

"Are they truly? Then perhaps I ought to return to Louisville."

My voice sounded brittle, and I instantly regretted having challenged him, but I was too proud to withdraw. No one needed to tell me I had violated one of his cardinal rules: *Thou shalt not contradict the General before his men.* The matter was made worse by my having done this before politicians who accused him of cowardice. Philip looked down in embarrassment, and made as if to stare into his empty portfolio.

The General reacted decisively, hauling me into the bedroom after the manner of one shaking a misbehaving puppy by the scruff. He seemed to be made all of sinews, a burled mass of callus and gristle in blue wool. He leaned into me to give me what for, and I steadied myself against the wardrobe. Mindful of those listening in the next room, the General spoke in tones low and firm. His voice would have soothed an infant had his words not been viciously barbed.

"Mrs. Atkinson, when I give you a directive, when I tell you to do something, when I make a request of you, I expect you to obey me. My demands are not a subject for you to accept or reject based upon some rule of law fashioned in the eccentric universe of Mary Bullitt. As my wife, I expect you to do as I say, happily, with a full measure of confidence that you are fulfilling your singular purpose on this earth, and that is to make my life more pleasurable. Now, do you understand me?"

That was when I knew that our argument had nothing to do with St. Louis and safety. When the General was angry he was something frightening to see. I wanted to cant my fists and box his ears, but such brashness could have ended in my untimely demise. So I said, with a bitter edge to my voice, "I understand."

He stepped away suspiciously and looked around as if I'd hidden an assassin under the bed. "You do?"

"I understand completely." But I thought, *Well, it appears you shall be quite as horrid as all of the other husbands I've seen women dragging along through their lives.*

He rested his hands upon his hips, nodded his satisfaction. "There now, isn't it best when everyone keeps to their respective places? Because I was thinking of making out a list, you know. A list of everything you should and shouldn't do. After all, my men have von Steuben's Blue Book and Nesmith's manual to guide them, why shouldn't you have a code of conduct? A long list that you would keep to remind yourself of how to behave in this new place. I think I shall write something up for you."

A long list? Little wonder the General hadn't married a St. Louis lady. They all probably *knew* about him. I cleared my throat and held my handkerchief protectively before my face.

"You do that. And I'll read your list first thing after I return from St. Louis with Philip."

I waited for him to correct me, to remind me that I wasn't going anywhere near St. Louis. But the ordinarily astute General's thinking was muddled by a lack of sleep and the dual distractions of vociferous politicians and a rebellious wife. He pulled a small bag from the chest of drawers and emptied four Spanish milled coins into my hand. I regarded the coins, then him. He said, "St. Louis has no currency of its own. The merchants accept guineas, doubloons, johannes . . . amongst others, so if this isn't enough, you'll have to set up accounts in my name."

Desirous of proving I would not be a financial burden to him, and thereby unwittingly flouting the General's second cardinal rule—*Thou shalt not discuss money with the General*—I returned the coins to him and said proudly, "I have my own money."

Had I known then what I understand of him now, I would have realized how he perceived this as a personal affront. His youthful poverty caused him to anticipate slights from me that never materialized. The General opened my fingers and pressed the coins into my palm. I glanced up at his dark and furzy sideburns and saw angry streaks of color upon his cheeks.

Startled at his mood, and misunderstanding the source of his anger, I tried to pull my hand away, but he held it easily. Then he said so quietly that despite our closeness I had to strain to hear him, "Mrs. Atkinson, you no longer have money of your own. Anything and everything you possessed before our marriage is now mine. You own nothing of value. Henceforth, I shall determine *when* and *if* you require money."

"Why are you so angry?"

"I am not angry."

"You're sore as a boil!"

"You will lower your voice." The General regarded me icily, and I was afraid of him.

"I will not. I think you are inspired by hurting me and I don't want to be around you anymore. You will take your hands from me."

The General turned a look on me that radiated disdain. He flattened his lips into a sharp line and looked down upon me reprovingly. He bowed the smallest bow imaginable and said under his breath, "It was not my intent to be cruel to you. I have never been cruel to a lady."

"You're being barbarous. You're cruel and you like it well enough. I wonder that you don't have yellow-haired maidens buried under these floor-boards."

I stomped the floor with my heel as if this proved my assertion. Now even as I said this, I wished to take back the sting of my words. His nostrils flared, and he moved his hand through the air as if fantasizing about slapping me. He said, "I've heard enough from you."

He kept a hurtful grip upon me as I tried to writhe away from him. The muscles of my neck were wound so tightly that I felt my head shivering imperceptibly back and forth as if I were saying *no*. At that moment, I saw him as a federal repository of petty snits and umbrages. I know he reciprocated my sentiments. I disliked him. He disliked me too, for his own reasons, in addition to which I had introduced chaos into his orderly existence. With cold force, the General directed me back to the hallway, then, in full view of my cousin, in manner calculated to humiliate me, he pressed his lips to my temple. Philip averted his glance from the General with disgust. He had doubtless heard everything and probably sensed even more.

"Mister Cooke, what arms have you?"

"The Harper's Ferry pistol, sir."

"A most excellent paperweight. Take your Hawken."

"Yes, sir."

The General said quietly, "And do not let her out of your sight. I rely upon you to protect what is mine." Then he left us. He shut us off, closing the door of the library behind him.

5

St. Louis, Missouri, January 1826

✼ THE General's carriage rolled through the old French Quarter of St. Louis upon a street so narrow that, should I stick my arm out the window, I could touch the buildings that leaned overhead like stiff awns of muhly grass. Carriages had to proceed single file, as there was no room for traffic abreast. I weltered in fury over my predicament. Being woefully ignorant about my new husband and men generally—moreover, being self-pitying—I had concluded that our marriage had collapsed. The General was horrid. I would have my marriage annulled and, Mama notwithstanding, I would, after all, seek out a bird-hearted crumpet of a boy. Our chaste union of three days had come to an ignominious conclusion. So be it.

"Look at your face, Mary," Philip said, squinting at me. "It's gone all sour. What are you thinking about?"

Not trusting myself to talk, I brushed away his comments and scrutinized St. Louis. The houses were plastered in soft colors, and the red mansard roofs reflected the sunlight. They crouched forward, like dowagers over teacups with a horn to the ear, asking "What was that you said?" Almost every house had two or three balconies from which the Creole women called to one another and chatted amicably. Their servants swept snow from the porches onto the street. Some of the houses were enclosed by *pieux de bout*, whitewashed mulberry pickets. Brightly painted flower boxes bowed under each window. Despite the dreary weather, the street was crowded and we made slow progress.

"Ugh, Philip, what is that odor?"

Philip lifted his chin. "Chouteau's warehouse . . . where the pelts and hides are kept. I suppose I didn't much notice it, being winter and all."

"It is the breath of this city, that's what it is."

The noise from the street was so great that Philip and I had to holler at one another. I looked through the window at a murk of ankle-deep manure on the roads. We stopped for sheep, cattle and pigs milling under the crooks of inept boys. Indians strolled the buckling brick walks. Some of them had trade muskets bandoleered over their shoulders, and they sported every form of dress and adornment from capotes and blue frock coats to deerskin and trade blankets. There were very few Americans, and those I saw were men in Kentucky leatherns, fur hats and buffalo robes. We followed barouches carrying French ladies who wore enormous white hats blooming with silk flowers and ribbons.

For the whole of the journey, Philip had tried to cheer me with an earnest dissertation on the virtues of the General. I mused, as Philip spoke, upon overland escape and upon annulment, and tried to anticipate the disappointment on Mama's face when she saw me standing bedraggled on her doorstep. Philip leaned over his knees and sermonized, "Of all the generals I've ever met, he is the most cultivated. Do you know he loves music? Really, he is our beau ideal of the perfect soldier. He is always writing for raises for his men and personally seeing to land warrants. And even though some of the old-school officers relish the European punishments. The General? Once I saw the General drum out a fifteen-year veteran for slicing off a boy's ears. The General won't let the veterans slit noses for desertion either. Sure, the General approves the laying of stripes for discipline, they all do—"

"The General has his soldiers whipped," I repeated flatly.

"W-Well, they all have men whipped, Mary, if the men have misbehaved. All of the officers do."

I curled my lip at him. "I think that is despicable."

Philip folded his arms over his chest and scrutinized me. "There are plenty of women who'd like to be the General's wife."

I did not deem *that* worthy of response. I tugged at my gloves and avoided his gaze. Philip leaned back against the seat and began lecturing me in a dismal tone about the great changes a woman could wreak upon the world if only she were a model of constancy and fortitude. I cut him off. "Philip, it is a cruel thing for men to make women their moral constabulary. I, for one, have no desire to pull gin glass and playing cards out of the General's hand, nor do I want to urge him to church or cure him of cursing. What do I have to gain?"

"Women bear the impress of the divine. The influence of a pious woman over the world could be enormous."

"May you suffer marriage to such a woman."

"I wouldn't expect you to understand, Mary."

"I don't want to understand, Philip, not if it requires me to change the habits of a man who has been a bachelor longer than I've been alive on this earth." I saw a general store between Turnbull's Books and Jaccard's Jewelers. "Ask the driver to stop, will you? I must buy some paper. I shall write to Mama. And to her lawyer."

We alighted before the general store and awaited a clearing on the brick walk. We waited rather a long while, then Philip fairly tossed me out of the coach, pushing me through the crowd while saying, "You can't wait for people here, Mary. They'll never give over to you."

Philip opened the door and held it for me. A trade bell jingled as we entered. I glanced up at shelves that seemed to go two stories high to a dark ceiling. The store's unpolished walnut floor was divided into islands of shelving overloaded with blankets, pelts, crates of brown eggs, boxes of green bottles containing chemicals for which I could see no practical use. Above my head were spools of grosgrain ribbon and bolts of polished cotton, buckram for stiffening and yellow nankeen for servants' clothing. I ran a finger over jars of horehound and peppermint candy. Philip tapped his feet impatiently until the shopkeeper appeared.

The shopkeeper was a thin-boned man with long brown hair that fell in waves down his back, and though he wasn't much older than thirty, he had a slight stoop to his shoulders. He smiled at us, pushed his iron-framed spectacles up the bridge of his nose and ran a hand over his ears to smooth his hair. There was a wen upon his neck, large and smooth as a yellow pebble. He touched at it with his fingertips, then pressed his hands to the counter. The shopkeeper was dressed in gray work coveralls, and looking us over once, apologized, saying he had been uncrating merchandise that had covered him with sawdust.

I wiggled a peppermint from the jar, and said to him, "I should like to open an account."

"But of course, and the gentleman's name would be?" He raised his brows expectantly at Philip.

"General Atkinson."

"Oh, certainly. And your name, miss?"

"*Mrs.* Atkinson."

"My apologies, of course, I misspoke."

I sincerely doubted this. I stood on tiptoe and tried to peek into the shopkeeper's ledger. "Are there other accounts open here under the General's name?" I asked.

"No," the shopkeeper replied, shutting the book with a solicitous smile that convinced me he lied. "*Mrs.* Atkinson, I shall be in the back room, you holler now when you're ready."

"Thank you."

I stooped in a little enclosure of shelving that came to my shoulder when I was standing, but which concealed me completely when I bent to examine layers of foolscap stacked neatly to my left. Before me was the beadboard bottom of the high and wicketed counter, behind me, one of two store windows. I ran a finger down the white stratum of paper and felt a little better about things. It was cozy in this little corner of the world. From here I could not see the other side of the store, the door or the window on the opposite side of the aisle. I enjoyed the pleasure of my small sanctuary as I rifled through the paper, while Philip shuffled behind me.

"Just pick out a quire, will you? Why are you being so particular, Mary?"

I ran my hand into the center of a stack of linen. I raised a sheet, then held it to my nose and looked wistfully over the edge of it at him. "This paper is all I have left to connect me to Mama and to my family."

Philip gazed out the window and said to the glass, "The General will send for your sisters and Ma when the river breaks, Mary. And when you get lonely for Louisville you can talk to me." The ladies passing by on the walk outside simpered at him, but Philip was oblivious to them. "Mary, would you mind if I jaunted next door to Turnbull's? I hear Cooper has a new book I'd like very much . . ."

"Oh, by all means, Philip, do go; I'm ruminating here." But Philip stayed put, and I feared he would pester me as I counted. I said, "Go, go. I'll wait here for you."

The small bell on the door handle jingled as Philip left.

The trade bell jingled again as customers entered. I did not see the new arrivals for I crouched contentedly in my spot, carefully arranging each sheet I pulled forth. I stacked the pieces one by one, intending to purchase several quires. When I'd finished, I'd fickle over the quills in that redware jar until my heart was content with each nib and plume. Anything to avoid thinking about returning to the General's house. I half listened to the shopkeeper's tenor pitch as he spoke to customers I could not see. I selected sheets of foolscap, fifteen, sixteen, seventeen, no . . . not seventeen, a flaw in the grain of seventeen, so let's put that one back on the shelf. There. There was my seventeen. Eighteen, nineteen, twenty.

The shopkeeper scolded his customers. "That last bunch of wolf pelts wasn't what you promised. They were mangy, the lot of them. Poor and all holey. Now you've gone two years in arrears on your debt to me. I can't give you no more credit. So there'll be no money today. Get out. Both of you get out."

Silence.

"I said go," the shopkeeper repeated. There was a tremor to his voice.

Rather absently, I wondered if the shopkeeper had gone loony and was speaking to himself. I touched the edges of the paper to even the pile. The shopkeeper cleared his throat. "Give me what you owe—"And I heard him give a wheezy chuckle. "Or her. For partial payment of this week's debts, I'll take her. Into the back room. Won't be much longer than a few minutes. What do you care? Bet you lend her out all the time to trappers and soldiers. Ain't that what all of you do? Give away your wives and daughters to anyone who comes along and for what? I won't hurt her. Won't do nothing that ain't probably already been done to her."

Or her? The skin atop my head suddenly felt tight as a cap.

There was no answer.

"Look here. She is real young. What? Thirteen, mebbe? Pretty hair too. So I tell you what, bring her by every week, Sat'dy night, fetch her up Sun'dy mornin', and I'll see your debt is paid in full."

The quiet was thick. I felt the hairs on my neck bristle and knew then that the shopkeeper believed me to have left the store with Philip. I must stand up, I told myself, but cowardice and a feeling of imminent danger kept me down. In my hiding place, I tensed, ducking my head as I continued my silent count. Something terrible was about to happen. I could feel it as surely as when the sky turned green over Louisville in the summer months, when the wind hollowed out like the breath of the penitent dying. Still I counted paper, noiselessly, to keep my mind orderly. I knew that if I rose up, I would never see the end of this day. I began a new quire, stacking it silently next to the last pile. Two. Three.

The gritty sound of feet sliding through the counter gate was followed by a young girl's light voice pleading something in protest, in a language I did not know. I pressed my forehead against the beadboard. Fetally curled and balancing on my toes, I felt the vibration of a body slamming on the other side of the beadboard. I heard a heaving breath, a pant and a groan.

Someone was lying on the counter above my head. I panicked, wondering if I could be seen. No one knows I am here, I assured myself, staring at the dirty boards under my feet, feeling my eyes about to pop from fright. I knew that just a few inches away, on the shopkeeper's high counter directly above me, someone was being brutalized.

The girl cried out again. I heard another man's voice, an enraged shout, sharp as a coyote bark, and then . . . a noise that was soft and harsh all at once. I had heard it before, and I recognized it. It was the sound of a butcher knife cutting into meat but scraping bone. A blade wedged in bone. I heard a gargling, then the sound of air escaping lips.

That is when the blood began dropping from the counter above my head like warm July rain from the eaves. I felt it dripping into my hair, down my neck, sliding onto my back and pooling where my corset caught it between my shoulder blades. It runneled down the side of my face. It smelled like metal and salt and eggs. Seven pages. Eight. Nine. Ten. It felt viscous between my fingers. My dress stuck to me where it soaked through. Eleven.

The floor under my feet leapt in sympathy as a heavy weight fell inside the counter just opposite me. Then the bell on the door tinkled, and with shaky relief, I realized the unseen customers were leaving.

I exhaled.

And lifting my face to the window that fronted the street, I caught the eye of the Indian who had just left the shop with his daughter. He paused, and we locked eyes.

The bell tinkled again.

I felt, though I did not hear, the footfalls of a man coming up behind me. I felt him lift me by the collar and turn me over easily. My chest was thrust up and my neck dangled my head back onto the high counter and my ankles locked together, and my fear was so great that I was paralyzed except . . . except that having had my hands shackled by a rosary three-thousand one-hundred and sixty-eight times in my youth, I found myself making the sign of the cross as a final, desperate, but wholly reflexive act, while I stared into the Indian's black eyes.

He laid me directly into a reservoir of blood, and I felt it go through my gown. It was still warm. I was a perfect example of irrelevant fastidiousness. Here I was, about to be slaughtered, but I was most bothered that I was lying in someone else's blood. And as I lay there, I gaped at my assailant's ears, for they had been pierced from curve to curve and run through with small trade buckles; the sort colonials put atop their shoes. *You have buckles in your ears,* I wanted to say, but his knife glittered at my throat, and instead, I heard myself talking to him, reciting something familiar. I stared into his eyes as I spoke, thinking if he was going to kill me, I was going to watch him do it and not end my life blind.

"*. . . full of grace, the . . .*"

He licked his lips, furrowed his brow, lowered his face until I could discern every crease and dot under his nose. The backs of my heels banged against the beadboard. He wore a rope of sweetgrass about his throat, and the anise scent of it so reminded me of Mama's breath, that I nearly cried of homesickness. Every hair on his head had been plucked out except for a black scalp lock.

He had no eyebrows.

I could see my fearful countenance reflected in his black eyes. He held my image inside him, but it did not prompt him to cultivate mercy for me. There was no regard for my person reflected there at all. I felt him lying atop me to hold me steady, then I saw two desiccated cardinals bobbing at his shoulders, looking at me with empty sockets. The Indian watched my hands curiously as I made the sign of the cross three, perhaps four times. The doing of it gave me comfort as I prepared for the inevitability of death. I talked at him because I wanted him to know that he was killing a sentient being, like him. He cocked his head at the crossing motion of my hand, let his knife move away from my throat and asked, "Blackrobe?"

"*. . . art thou amongst women and blessed . . .*"

"Blackrobe?"

"What?" My eyes shifted frightfully over the sharp cheekbones as he came closer yet.

"Père de Smet? Blackrobe?" The Indian poked my chest roughly with one finger, tapped my belly, tapped my forehead, then each of my shoulders.

"Yes. Blackrobe," I said, and my voice quavered.

"Blackrobe."

Then he dropped me. I bent forward, wincing at the young Indian girl standing across from me. Her tunic had been ripped completely away from her breasts. She covered herself with a black-and-brown striped trade blanket she had taken from a display by the door. She had a cut upon her cheek that she did not try to stanch. I guessed her to be no more than twelve or, perhaps, thirteen. The girl's legs were spindling, and the man's cheeks were hollowed with hunger. He pressed his face to the window and took the girl's hand in his. As they ran from the store, the trade bell jingled merrily with their exit. They sprinted down the street, the girl clutching the blanket at her throat, her black braid flying behind her.

"Twelve," I said aloud. I sidled away from the counter's edge where the blood kept up a steady drip and sat with my legs straight out before me.

The bell jingled again.

Doubtless, the Indian had changed his mind and had come back to kill me. Having now lost all of my courage, I decided to die blind after all. I squeezed my eyes shut.

"Mary!" Philip cried. "Who has killed you?"

I opened my eyes and tried to stand. "I am not dead."

"But all this blood! You are wounded and will probably soon die. So sit, Cousin." He opened the door, peering around for help. "Cousin, is there some prayer I ought to be saying for you about now? Because I will if it will give you comfort in your final moments. What do you want me to tell your mama? How about Eloise?"

"Tell Eloise she was right about everything."

Philip patted my cheek. Seeing the blood transfer to himself, he wiped it in streaks over his coat. "I'm going to miss you, Mary."

"Philip, I am not going to die. I am not wounded. I am not hurt. I want to go home. Take me back to the General's house. I want to wash this off of me." When I tried to wipe my face, I merely succeeded in smearing the blood around. I pointed at the high counter and said, "You'd better look and see if that shopkeeper is dead back there, Philip."

Philip propped himself and peered over to the other side and shook his head.

"Lord, Mary. His head has been nearly cut off."

Philip gazed in abject fascination at the dead. As for me, I harbored no sympathy for the shopkeeper. His dying made me sad in the way of the triumphant living, secretly relieved that they'll soon be away from their sorrow. Philip wrapped me in blankets and shoved me out the door, where passersby pointed at me and exclaimed at the awful vision I presented. I stumbled up the pedal, but the smell of the rancid lard blacking on the carriage hood made me sick. I opened the outer door, hung my head and threw up into the street. A watery effusion came stringing out of me, and the sight of it caused me to retch again.

Philip hollered at several Negroes to fetch up Sheriff Hammond and Deputy Mull, telling them to track the Indian who had murdered the shopkeeper. Soon, whole families of pedestrians dashed into the store to have a sportive look at the corpse. Inspired by the grisly scene, two children skipped onto the walk, then enacted a mock skirmish. Neither of them wanted to be the Indian, so they went back into the store to admire the victim. I pleaded with Philip to take me home.

"Should I take you to Uncle William's? His house is right down the street."

"I want to go home."

Philip yelled at the driver to make for the General's house posthaste. I do not recall the trip back to the house except for how the blood dried upon me. It stiffened over my fingers and itched upon my back. I rubbed at it, but it flaked like decaying brick all over the floor of the carriage. Nor do I recall stepping from the carriage and entering the house upon Philip's arm. Fortunately, the politicians had left. Philip urged Nicholas to ride to the camp of the Sixth Infantry where he would find the General meeting with his staff officers.

With trembling hands, Philip escorted me to the bedroom and sat me upon the bed. He removed a black phial from his pocket, poured brown drops into a tumbler of water, held the glass aloft, then swirled it until he was satisfied. Philip put the glass to my lips. At his behest, I quaffed the mixture dutifully. It caused a bitter crinkling in my tongue, and only then did I ask what I had swallowed.

"Tincture of laudanum."

"Philip! How could you have done that to me? Now I'll go all raccoon eyed."

"You are going to have a nervous fever. A terrible nervous fever from which you may never recover. The tincture will calm your nerves."

"That's utter nonsense, I've never had a nervous fever in my life. But now you've gone and poisoned me. It's only fair you drink some too. Go on, give yourself at least as much as you gave me."

Ever the obliging gentleman, Philip made a tincture for himself. I watched the lump of his throat bob up and down as he swallowed.

"Do you feel anything?" I asked. Philip responded by gripping his forehead and stumbling out of the room. I, too, had lost a degree of control over myself. It was as if a gypsy healer thrust her hand through the back of my neck and squeezed the base of my skull.

Dahlia entered cautiously, carrying a pail of snow that melted down to nothing at all. Dahlia had a spray of freckles over her nose and eyes shaped like a cat's. Her hair I had never seen, for she wore a white or yellow turban. Lifting me from where I slumped before the fire, she guided me gently into the copper tub that looked like an enormous teacup without the handle. I sat in a few inches of tepid water, shaking from cold and shock. Bits of humanity slid off me and floated in greasy pink swirls atop the water. Finding myself sitting in a gruesome soup and thoroughly repulsed by the sight, I leapt out of it. I splashed water all over the floor. Dahlia fussed and dropped towels about me.

Naked but for the old brown blanket that I held around me, I crouched before the hearth, unable to contemplate anything but the fire. When I closed my eyes, I found myself once again under the store counter. The full realization of what I had experienced began resolving itself, and I felt sick. My shivering ruled me, and my teeth chattered. Exasperated with me, Dahlia threw up her hands and said, "She won't get in it 'cause she say it smell like him."

"Then get her more water," the General said.

I jumped at the sound of his voice and wondered if I had gone shattery. As the laudanum began its work, I wanted to sleep, but fear kept me alert. I huddled inches from the firelight. I was so cold. The side of me nearest the fire was hot, but the other side of me was cold. I felt the General squat before me and chanced a look up at him.

I asked, "Aren't you goin' to lord over me for my error?"

"There now. No cause for that," he murmured.

The General ordered the servants to bring clean blankets and he covered me with them. Dahlia put the full basin and a cloth before the fire where I had sprung forth roots. Hulking down before me, the General removed his coat and rolled up his sleeves, dipped the cloth, then squeezed it out.

"Mary, I'm going to wash some of this off of you. Will you let me do that?"

I nodded at him, and he began washing my face. The water looked like plum mash when he finished. I glinted up at him, waiting for him to begin scolding me. Every tiny aspect of the General's countenance jumped to prominence; a series of parallel lines upon the bridge of his nose, a spot of ink upon his left earlobe, the dark shade of his beard stubble returning at day's end. He scrutinized my face, then picked something from my hair. He lifted his palm.

"Now, give me your hand."

He washed each finger, then my palms and wrists, and my arms up to the elbow. I do not know how long we knelt silently together in that room, but it grew dark before Dahlia brought in the second round of bathwater. At the General's direction, they drew the curtains and lit candles, then, with baleful looks, left us alone in the room. He pulled the blanket from my shoulders. It was a testament to my shocky condition that I did not worry over his perceptions. However, I did hear myself burble, "Miss . . . Miss Wollstone . . . Miss . . . Wollst . . ."

"What?" The General leaned forward and winced at me.

"Miss . . . that other Mary says, women ought to wash and dress alone . . ."

"Yes, well, you've gone plain incompetent. Let me help you in."

I sat in the water, and the warmth of it shook free all of the emotions I'd tamped down those four days passing. I could not pull myself out of the general store, nor could I shake the memory of the Indian child standing before me, wrapped in her blanket. I was mortally confused, more so than I had even been in my life. I wanted things to be clear and easily resolved in my mind, but everything had gone muddled. I kept seeing the shopkeeper, then the Indian holding me over the counter as if I were a rabbit he was preparing to butcher for dinner.

Like everyone else from an Eastern city, I had been taught that there were two kinds of Indians: the good ones like Pocahontas, who were spiritually superior to us, and the bad ones who killed white people for the joy of it. I tried to fit the Indian at the store into one of those two categories. Failing this, I covered my eyes with the heels of my palms until I saw galaxies. After a long silence I mumbled, "That Indian in the general store . . ."

"He's in the city jail with his daughter. Sheriff Hammond caught them both running up Rue d'Eglises." He looked down at me as I babbled out my account of the murder with my eyes half closed. The General sat aside the tub, in a quandary. I saw what it was that I had longed to possess of him when he had come to court me. There was a shine of gentle intelligence about him when he wasn't being irascible. He closed his hands over mine. His eyes riveted on my face at first, but then they began to wander. He seemed not to know what to do, so he unwrapped the soap on the dresser and dipped the cloth into the bathwater.

"What does it all mean?" I asked.

The General exhaled. "The Indian is a Sauk. His name is Ice on Wings. He is one of Black Hawk's lieutenants, and I can tell you that, ordinarily, he is known as a good man. He was desperate for credits owed him by that shopkeeper because he and his family are near starving. But he wasn't willing to pay the shopkeeper's price. That much you know."

"What will happen to him?"

"Hard to say. St. Louis is Sheriff Hammond's jurisdiction. Ice on Wings could be hanged in his cell before dawn."

"But he didn't want to kill me. I don't believe he did. Have you ever surprised a dog, seen it jump and snarl, then once it realized you're not a threat, back away? It was like that with Ice on Wings."

"Don't flatter yourself, Mary. And don't impose romantic Eastern ideals about 'nature's noblemen' on the native peoples either. It isn't wise and it isn't true. Back East, city folks say that Indians are so *spiritual*. Or they say, they're so *savage*. Neither is true. Both are true."

"He didn't kill me and he could have. I think he was more startled."

"From the account you shared, he spared you only because he believed you were somehow connected to the Jesuit missionaries, of whom the Sauk are inordinately fond."

"Are the Sauk Catholic?"

"No, they just have good memories of the Jesuits. That's all. He spared you out of a flashing moment of sentiment."

The General squeezed out the cloth. He moved the cloth over my arms as if he were preoccupied, but I observed the ruddy color of his face and the changing climate of his mood. Being made keenly aware of his intense focus, I slipped deeper into the water in an attempt to conceal myself, with little effect. I wanted to touch his face, but I only succeeded in knocking the soap from his fingers. When he fetched it out of the water, I caught his free hand and brought his fingers to my lower lip. He lifted his brows in surprise, but his eyes were fierce with emotion. I said, "I can't feel your hand upon me at all . . . I have gone numb."

The side of his mouth tipped up, and he said, "Fortunately for me, I can feel you. How much laudanum did that idiot Cooke give you?"

"Well . . . the room is spinning."

He lifted my ankle and took a goodly long while to work his way up my leg. I watched his hand slip around my knee, then atop my thigh, but by then, the laudanum had put me at complete remove. The room seemed to pulse with color, and I pressed my hands to my temples. My eyelids felt enormous. I watched the General's hands and I heard myself say to him, "This isn't fair, you seeing me first. If you were being fair, you'd disrobe so I could have a look."

He laughed and rubbed the soap over the cloth. I wiped a bubble of soap from the corner of my mouth and pointed accusingly at him. "Don't laugh at me. You are exceptious. I'm not sure I like you."

"That's twice you've lied to me in two days, Mary Bullitt. You like fighting with me well enough. And I think you find me irresistible."

"I do not."

"You do so."

He came up behind me, shoved me forward in the tub, lifted my hair and scrubbed at my back as if it were a washboard. When he had finished soaping me, he poured fresh water over me, and again through my hair, and scrubbed at my scalp with the bar of French milled from the basin. Then he held up a towel and said, "Get out."

I put my hands to the side of the tub and tried to rise up, but the ceiling suddenly fell down and smashed me, and the water held me tightly as if I were drowning in plaster. My voice sounded hollow and far away. "I can't."

"What do you mean, you can't?"

"I can't stand up at all. My feet are gone. They're gone."

"Christ. I'm going to kick his skinny West Point ass."

"Look at that. My legs are growing together."

He tossed the rag into the basin, then muttered something about me being troublesome. I laid my head back and saw his face directly above mine. He patted my cheek briskly and said, "Don't fall asleep yet. I'm going to lift you out of the tub. On the count of three. Mary? Hold tight to my neck."

"As if I'd consider holding tight to anything else." Up I flew, but my limbs felt as dead as if I'd been in my narrow house under six feet of holy dirt for a century.

"Now I'm soaked through," he grumbled as he lifted me out. I shimmied into my bulky nightdress and watched him fuss over the water on the floor. In despair over everything, I fell over and found my face locked into the pillow.

Unable to find my way out of its feathered deeps, I heard myself speaking aloud to him things I would ordinarily never say: "You despise me. After what you said to me today, it's all come clear to me."

"Nonsense, Mary." There was a lengthy pause, and he declared, "I don't know you well enough to despise you."

"Oh . . ." I wailed pathetically, facedown in the pillow. I felt myself suffocating. I tried to breathe but kept sucking in a mouthful of feathers and linen.

"Now what?"

"I can't breathe. Roll me over."

He obliged me, laughing to himself, and then he pressed his lips to my temple. I clasped his face in my hands and struggled to keep my eyes open. I had begun to drowse when the bed sank and he slipped under the blanket beside me. I rested my forehead against his shoulder and felt myself succumb to the luxuriant quiet of the room and the sentinel peace of his presence. I was tired of fighting with him. It seemed whenever we were together, we stirred up conflict the way children cause chiggers to fuzz up out of bluegrass. I wanted to show him we could care for one another. I thought of what Mama had said about the General and me being married to one another. It seemed so long ago that she had warned me against mulishness and pride. I felt myself falling into a black slumber. Marriage was an exhausting endeavor. As we fell into our first peaceful sleep together, the black rattle pod under our window whispered like a crone plying her trade at augury in the snowy darkness.

6

Jefferson Barracks, Missouri, January 1826

AT four in the morning, bugles all over the camp sounded reveille, causing me to jump straight out of bed and onto my feet. Dogs bayed against the bugles, and the windows shook when the drums banged out morning roll. I turned circles in sleepy confusion. There seemed to be hundreds of male voices filling the room, all of them shouting, Here! Here! It must have been some trick of the landscape and a tranquil dawn that made their voices carry the distance. I awoke convinced that I had been poisoned. My head throbbed, my vision was blurry and I felt sick at my stomach. "Hush now. Go away," I said to no one in particular.

Dahlia informed me the General had risen an hour earlier, and breakfast was being served. After dressing hurriedly and splashing my face in an attempt to overcome the dissipated expression of one who'd passed the night in an opium den, I followed the scent of coffee.

A half-dozen officers sat around my breakfast table. I covered my eyes with my hand and wobbled from a late-welling bud of laudanum left over in my system. The field and staff officers of the General's Sixth Infantry hunched around the table, plying a good knife and fork. They scraped their pewter plates clean of ham steak, slides of apple duff, beaten biscuits, bacon, flapjacks, eggs and red potatoes. They'd thoughtfully left one chair vacant. As I entered, they rose, and the General made proud introductions.

I tried my best, but their titles were murky business. Lieutenants should be addressed as Mister, and some of them had brevet ranks, which complicated matters further. I gave up and called everyone Mister until directed otherwise. As it was too early for me to feign politeness, I blinked at them and asked, "Isn't there a regimental mess hall for this sort of thing?"

The General smirked at me over his coffee. "Yes, but the men grew fond of your house in advance of your arrival, Mrs. Atkinson."

"I am grateful to those of you who helped the General build it. Thank you. All right, then. You may leave now. Good-bye." I flapped my hands at them, but they thought I was joking and laughed at me. Indeed, as I took my seat, they resumed their meeting, speaking to one another with urgent conviviality.

Lieutenant Albert Sidney Johnston, the General's aide-de-camp, said that his scouting party had followed Black Hawk to the sugaring grounds above the Henderson River. Johnston was a heavily muscled young man with a broad, handsome face and a gap between his big front teeth. When Cousin Philip asked why the scouting party hadn't apprehended Black Hawk, the other men looked at him as if he were mentally disordered. Johnston waved a forkful of ham steak at Philip and drawled, "Ah . . . that would be because there were six of us and seven hundred of them. You go on up there, Cooke, and rope him all by your own self."

Lieutenant Robert Anderson chided, "That's right, Philip, you go on up to the butcher shop first, will you? Make it easy on the rest of us."

Johnston interrupted their laughing and asked the General, "Sir, has there been any word from Kearny and his dragoons on the Cuivre?"

"Kearny has gathered statements from eyewitnesses and a few fur trappers with a one-winter trading house who had stopped over at the Cuivre for a rest when the attack occurred." All of the men leaned over the table, waiting for details, but the General looked pointedly at me as he said, "That is all I am willing to discuss. Mrs. Atkinson is going to William Clark's today to visit with her family. Mister Cooke? You're serving escort to Mrs. Atkinson today. And I don't appreciate your poisoning her drinking water with opium. It may be the custom in Virginia to go about crapulous, but this is not Virginia."

The other men watched this scene with derisive enjoyment, but I felt sorry for Philip. How humiliating it must have been for him to be relegated to hen duty. I said nothing at that breakfast, but watched them all chattering at one another as if I wasn't there. For once, I was grateful to be ignored. I pressed my fingertips to the balls of my closed eyes and made faces as I stared down at my lap. I pinched my forehead, cheeks and lips, testing for atrophy.

The General and I set off for St. Louis as the camp bugles began playing "Molly Put the Kettle On," signaling breakfast for the regiments. I wished we had a day to stay put and perhaps have a civil conversation, but such was not to be. The sky was torpid under a tide of glaring gray clouds that hurt my eyes.

The General explained that he would see me safely to Uncle William's, and thereafter attend a meeting at the Planters' House with Senator Benton. Philip rode behind us like a disgraced squire, with the General's horse in tow. When our carriage pulled between the two stone posts that marked the entrance to the camp, an explosion sounded just to the north.

I jumped up and asked, "What was that?"

The General settled spectacles over his nose, then opened a portfolio in his lap. "That is a four-pound gun. They fire it to signal my leaving and my arrival. You'll grow accustomed to it. Now, about our plans for the day . . . I should like to pass the evening with you. It is time we became acquainted. We'll begin by taking dinner at our home. I will fetch you up around noon, and the rest of the day shall be ours."

He put a severe look on me as if daring me to retort, but I think he was simply fearful we had orbited out of the ordinary. I was not fooled by his stern expression. He looked plain nervous as he asked this of me. Understanding his import most clearly, I nodded my assent. I stared at the little beaded reticule in my lap. After this, the General shuffled through stacks of papers he had pulled from an old leather envelope tied with string. He reviewed maps and tables of figures. I splintered a look on him, "What . . . ?" I began, but my voice faded away.

"Yes?"

"I guess what I am trying to ask you is how do you think we ought to go forward? Given everything."

The General looked side to side and squinted at me as if I were up to a trick. "Mary, I don't know what you are trying to say."

"These four days are close to being the worst of my life, and I am curious as to whether you could say the same."

"That is because you haven't had much of a life thus far." Then he returned his attention to his papers. I was disappointed and nervous all at once. I slid my hand over the document and forced him to meet my eyes. "You must have considered that we are not compatible? When you were holding forth in our bedroom before I went to St. Louis, I was quite convinced I never wanted to see you again."

The General had taken offense at my words. He tipped his chin to the left and looked away from me. I said, "Surely you were deeply unhappy too? With me?"

"It was an unpleasant start. We have remedied that. At least, I thought we had." He inhaled, and said in a voice that was falsely even, "But if you wish to return home, I shall not stop you." There was a disgruntled silence. If he wanted me to leave, I would, and not altogether unhappily. I was both fearful and eager, because I wanted this settled. Done. He was wound so tight, I half expected him to fray at the edges from the exertion of suppressing his emotions. My words came out sounding small and brittle: "Do you want me to leave?"

He did not answer me. I observed a minute downward tug in the corners of his mouth that I would not have noticed four days ago. If I left him, everyone he knew would think him a failure. They would think me a failure too, but I was accustomed to the cordial detestation of the pious; why, Mama said I cultivated it. But the General had not the cushioning benefit of family name and independent wealth to bolster him up. The General was self-made. He was careful of his reputation. And if I left him within the first week of marriage, he would be held up to ridicule. The first humble thought of my life germinated in the arrogant climate of my head, shot up, fragile and greenish white. I didn't want him to suffer the harsh opinion of small people. I waited for his answer with a pained expression.

"No," he said and turned a document over, then pointed at a column of numbers.

"No?"

"No," he said again. "No."

Our carriage came to a stop at William Clark's house on the southeast corner of Maine and Vine. When Billy, the groom, hopped from his seat and held open our door as he had been trained to do, the General barked at him, "Close it!"

Billy said, "Hew!" And slammed the door shut, leaving us sitting inside the carriage under an awkward silence. When the General had secured his feelings sufficiently so that he felt he would not betray them, he crossed to my side and took my hands in his. Having negotiated a peace, we shared the first speaking look of our marriage. He peered around the broad brim of my bonnet and put a finger to the rim of it. "How can you wear this thing? Isn't it like wearing horse blinders?"

I drew myself up and said, "It's very fashionable, and very new. Mama had it sent from New York." He thumped the brim with his thumb and forefinger.

I said, "Don't do that. I don't like it."

"I don't like this bonnet, Mrs. Atkinson. I can't kiss you when you're wearing it."

I shot him a challenging look and felt my cheeks color. I must have been transparent to him, having such bold feelings and all of them conflicting. I untied the stupid bonnet and tossed it across the carriage. Quick as a copperhead, he took my face in his hands, brushed his lips against my cheek and put his mouth upon mine in a way that I had never known before. He kissed me as if he had all the time in the world, as if he were sharing his best-kept secret with me. But then, too soon, he pulled away and leapt out the door, waiting to assist me down.

I took a deep breath, poked my head out the carriage, looked about furtively and said to him, "Come back here and do that again."

He wore that superior look. He folded his arms over his chest and said primly, "No. I'm saving myself."

Then he briskly turned aside and exclaimed, "By God, Miss Bright Sun! That you, old girl?"

Despite the General's greeting, there was nothing old about Miss Bright Sun. Bright Sun was dismayingly attractive and confident. She spoke an exotic patois that made her seem even prettier. I kept a keen eye upon the two of them, and I didn't like what I saw.

"I have come for Clark's council with Keokuk and the Peace Band. Why are you here?"

"Mrs. Atkinson is here to visit her Aunt Harriet. I didn't know Clark was meeting with Keokuk today."

Bright Sun's forehead was finely patterned with a small red circle radiating seven points. Her long black hair was pulled back in a single plait wrapped around with scarlet beads that tinkled whenever she lifted her shoulders. Bright Sun wore a blue calico shirt, covered over with a raccoon pelt. Her skirt was a square of black broadcloth, held up about her hips with a black leather strap, but I could see her leggings beneath it.

Taking my hand in his, the General escorted me up the brick walk to Uncle's house. The bricks were pebbled with snow that had turned to bubbly ice. I held tight to the General's arm for my own safety and to let Bright Sun know what I was about. Because I disliked her on sight, I smiled warmly at Miss Bright Sun—so warmly my face hurt. I was following Mama's example here. A well-born lady does not engage in arguments, scenes or demonstrations. She remains serene in adversity and allows everyone else to make a jackass of themselves.

I felt my renewed affection for the General ebbing with alarming speed as he chatted happily with the young Indian woman. The instant I began to trust him, he hailed an old paramour. Miss Bright Sun approached the General on the other side so closely that her arm touched his. This seemed very inappropriate to me.

Shoring me up beside him, he announced cheerfully to her, "Miss Bright Sun, this is my new wife. This is Mrs. General Atkinson."

Miss Bright Sun took on an unabashedly hostile expression at the General's announcement. She drew herself up, let her head fall back a bit and stared down her nose at me as if I weren't good enough for the General. He cleared his throat and said, "Yes, well. I thought you would like to know." Miss Bright Sun nodded cursorily. Then her mood shifted and she announced out of the blue, "Black Hawk is not here. He and Singing Bird went to the sugaring grounds."

"And you're not going with? What is winter for, if not sugaring?"

Everything he said to Bright Sun sounded like innuendo. She tilted her head prettily, causing her earrings to jingle. I was excluded from this conversation, something Bright Sun enjoyed immensely.

The General, who seemed relieved that the worst was over, smiled at her and teased, "When are you going to take a husband, Miss Bright Sun?"

Bright Sun tossed her head so that her black plait fell over her shoulder. She caressed the beads ornamenting her hair as she looked up from under her lashes at the General. "I live in Black Hawk's wickiup. He hunts for me."

"And yet you linger in St. Louis with Keokuk. How curious. Is he the one, perhaps?"

"Keokuk has six wives now. That is a crowded wickiup."

The General smiled knowingly, then politely waved her before him, saying, "We had best be getting along. I have a meeting in town." But Bright Sun had other ideas. She thrust her hand around the General's free arm and announced, "I am with child."

The General's face flushed a dark red. Bright Sun looked directly at me. My heart jolted about in my chest, yet I kept my composure and scrutinized them both, hoping for some explanation other than the one forming in my head. I suppressed the urge to garrote Bright Sun with the silk rope of the reticule around my wrist. I crossed my left ankle over my right to quash my impulse to kick her. I bit my lips. I waited and I hoped that Bright Sun would say, *Why, Mr. Indian-Thus-and-So is the daddy.*

But my husband clasped his hands behind his back, bowed forward a little, then spoke with deliberate care, "What can I do to assist you?"

"Black Hawk will look after me." She said this like a bratty child playing one feuding parent against another. She knew Black Hawk's name would have an effect upon the General's mood. He looked sidelong at me, warily, as if fearing to give away too much.

The General had a theory of his own. He asked hopefully, "Is the father Knows the Land?" She twirled her plait and rocked side to side as if she were daydreaming. He glanced at Bright Sun, then at me, and closed the conversation definitively, saying, "We do not need to discuss this here and now."

Bright Sun said with a sharp-eyed glance at me, "I do not have a place to sleep tonight." Then she lifted her skirt coquettishly to reveal a slim coppery ankle and sodden moccasins "My moccasins have frozen to my feet so that I must soak them in warm water to remove them. If I tried now, my skin would come off."

This incited a worrisome compassion in the General. His eyes worked the horizon as he considered rescuing her. I wagered he loved the role of rescuer, it seemed to suit him. He could make an appearance, do a good deed and return to bachelordom before sunset. I glared poisonously at him. I was prepared to walk home to Louisville tonight if he offered that woman shelter. The General bent forward a little, then raised his finger as if to lecture Bright Sun.

But Bright Sun stepped blithely away from him and lifted her face to the sky as if this were a balmy spring day rather than one dreary and cold. Her dainty little hands flurried about. Anticipating his scolding, she said to the General, "Eh, you worry too much, Worry, worry, worry, *Zha'becka.*"

She said the last word as if it were an insult. And then she added, "Red Hair and Keokuk wait for me. They cannot speak unless I am there . . . Besides, I cannot sleep in your house, Zha'becka. I know how you are. That little snoring noise you make."

Bright Sun turned on her heel and marched toward Uncle William's council house. Her moccasins made a soft padding noise upon the snow and ice. There was a suggestive wiggle to her hips, but I was mildly gratified when the General did not watch them. Rather, he looked down at his feet and shook his head, then muttered something to himself.

"Is she the woman you talk to in your sleep?"

The General squeezed his eyes shut tightly and rubbed his palms over his forehead and down his cheeks. He sighed. "What makes you think I talk to a woman?"

"I'd say we're both in deep waters if you're talking to a man about your 'favorite place.'"

"Look here, Mary, Bright Sun is a talented translator. She speaks and reads English, French, Sauk and Winnebago. I must admit her writing is awfully poor . . ."

"Talented? I'll wager you do find her talented."

"Oh, stop it, Mary. She traveled in an official capacity with my regiment when I took the first expedition up the Missouri River in 1819. She was very young, and to protect her from some of the men, who became dangerously lonely, she slept on the floor of the cabin I shared with another officer. That's how she knows I snore. Wait, now. You're jealous aren't you?"

"No."

"You are."

"I am not jealous."

"Nonsense, you're all spoony-eyed, Mrs. Atkinson."

"You know, sir, I begin to like you, and then almost as quickly, I find that I don't."

He grinned proudly as if he were all in love with himself. I yanked my arm away from him and strode off alone, speculating upon what he meant by protecting Bright Sun from other men. Keeping her to himself, in all likelihood. I had heard Uncle William's bawdy tales of the Corps of Discovery in the Mandan camps. Why should the General's experiences on expedition have been any different? Why should I care at this point? Because the General might have a little son or daughter next autumn, and what had once been a love affair now bloomed into a shadowy form of frontier marriage right before my eyes.

The General took my arm playfully and put his lips to my ear. "Mrs. Atkinson, I would be sore oppressed if you were to miss our dinner."

"I was under the impression you'd been recently fed."

"Not recently." He grinned roguishly, looking into my eyes for some reassurance that I wasn't miffed about Bright Sun's news. I had to stand there and be humiliated while the General was being so fat-witted and full of himself. Still and all, my desire to have a normal married life with him took hold of me. I told myself that this was part of the humble sprouting that had transpired moments earlier in the carriage. I was not comfortable with humility, indeed, humility swam around like the bilious fever in the environs of my skull. *Fever and chills.*

All right then, perhaps it wasn't humility at all, but pride that compelled me to calm myself. That, and a heavy measure of unladylike competitiveness. How many boys in Louisville did I know who had sired children out of wedlock? Plenty. And I did not know that the General was the father of this child, did I?

Now I sounded like my mother, making excuses to comfort myself into blind acceptance of something I didn't want to own. My insides felt rough as a nutmeg grater, but for the sake of appearances, I allowed him to hold my arm as we rounded the corner and approached the entrance to the council house.

The Clark house was a large, two-story brick one upon a lawn that sloped nobly to the river. Uncle's council room was a wing he had built onto the south side of his house. After years of seeing every Hepplewhite chair in her drawing room filled up with Indians, Aunt Harriet had told Uncle to build himself a man-house for entertaining his native guests.

A dozen Sauk men waited in orderly fashion for Philip to admit them to that south wing. They left slushy footprints, peeked curiously into Aunt Harriet's windows, snapped twigs from her dogwood shrubs and poked them into their mouths. Turning to Cousin Philip, who was standing sentry, the General said rather too harshly, "You stand your post at that front door. Don't go leaving it for any bookstore that might intrigue you."

The Sauk contingent seemed quite friendly and greeted the General, calling him Zha'becka.

"What does it mean?" I whispered to the General as I stomped the snow from my feet.

"I don't have time to explain, Mary, I must meet with the quartermaster and some others. Now listen to me. These councils are routine matters . . . so routine that your Aunt Harriet and your little cousins are accustomed to seeing all sorts of Indians running through the house. It would be an excellent introduction to the administrative side of things for you to observe a council now. I'll be back to fetch you up by noon." He hesitated and looked down at me.

"Keep your tongue behind the fence of your teeth. Don't go starting a war." He looked at his watch, then snapped the gold lid shut. It clicked like a knife upon marble, signaling the end of this conversation. At the General's behest, I quickly informed Uncle William of the truth behind the shopkeeper's murder, as I believed the truth to be. I told the story of Ice on Wings and his daughter with much flourish, appropriate gravity and emphasis supplied to Ice on Wing's act of mercy in sparing my life. I expected Uncle to leap to his feet, righteously indignant over the shopkeeper's attempted rape of a child.

"I regret you have had these troubles, Niece," Uncle responded, as if I had just told him I had a violent cold. "Aunt Harriet is doing petit point in the drawing room . . ."

"Uncle? Did you hear anything I just said?"

"An Indian did *not* kill you. You bought a quire of paper. Would you like bergamot tea?"

"No. No, I do not want tea. I want justice for Ice on Wings." I said this last bit with my arm uplifted like a crusader at Jerusalem. I imagined I looked quite impressive.

"I'd rather find you a cup of tea." Uncle stared implacably at me.

"Do you mind if I watch this council? There's nothing I'd like better."

"All right, Mary. But don't say anything, hey?"

"Why does everyone think I'm going to start a fight?"

"Do as your uncle says and keep your silence," the General said as he took his leave. I watched him go a little wistfully, but he left me behind without a backward glance, as if he had just made a routine delivery.

Uncle sat at the table, chin in hand. He had tied back his long hair, more gray than red now, with a green ribbon, and he wore a charcoal frock coat that was smudged with ash on the lapels. The deep acne scars on his cheeks stood out in bold relief. His face looked yellow and harsh under this light.

"Our friends have come, Mary. Why don't you have a seat?"

Uncle rose wearily and greeted each warrior by name.

I stared at the dozen Sauk warriors standing in mute composure before the long table at the far end of the room. There was no sound at all, but for a small cough from Bright Sun. She held the treaty aloft so that the candlelight filtered through it, then put her finger to each line as she read the terms. The Sauk men waited for her, as did Uncle William. I sat against the wall, batting now and again at the feathered leather hair thong that dangled from above.

The council room was one hundred feet long and thirty-five feet wide, and the vaulted hickory ceiling was hung with iron chandeliers. Tapers dripped hot wax upon us and left a trail of paraffin globs down the aisle between rows of benches. But most remarkably, from the floor to the soaring ceiling, the walls were covered over with tribal treasures that had been gifted to Uncle over the years. The air smelled of must and candle wax and slowly decaying cultural detritus. A piece of eagle down floated in the air before me. I pursed my lips and blew it onto another current.

The Sauk looked to be a narrow-shouldered people given to rounded bellies and bandy legs. None of them had eyebrows. It seemed the Sauk were averse to body hair. One boy's head was covered over with scabs. I later learned this was because his hair had been pulled out in clumps about as thick as the small finger, though the other men had apparently bought straight razors and let their wives shave their heads. Whenever any of them made the smallest movement, there was an evocative jingling from shards of decorative legging copper that sent me reeling back to the shopkeeper's store.

Bright Sun stood calmly before the assembly of men, holding in her hands a document that would bind two nations. She held the paper out at arm's length. "Two matters that confuse me. Seven is a problem. Seven says we must never again make war on the Sioux."

"So?" Uncle lifted his hands.

"They are our enemies. If they strike at us, we will strike at them."

"Bright Sun, when the Sauk make war on their neighbors, the hunting is bad. If the hunting is bad, there are no furs. If there are no furs, the Sauk people go hungry, then you come down here demanding trade credits the fur companies can ill-afford to provide you. The Sauk were deeply in arrears before your man killed that shopkeeper. And now . . ."

The warriors exchanged alarmed glances, waiting for Bright Sun to tell them what Uncle had said. Bright Sun gave Uncle William a blistering look and held her ground. Uncle continued, "And now, you have to cover your debts to us. This treaty is one way to accomplish that. You will pay your debts by giving up some of your land."

"We cannot give you more land! The traders take every cent of our tribal annuity. They make us pay too much for guns and traps and powder. It is cheating! It is not possible that the Sauk owe so much."

Uncle rose from his chair and put his palms flat on the table. "I didn't call this council for the aggravation of arguing with a woman. Now, read the treaty to those men, Miss Bright Sun."

And so Bright Sun read the treaty in a voice that echoed with disbelief. And as she read, she glanced up now and again at one warrior in the assembly, that being the odd Keokuk. What was odd about Keokuk was that he looked like a white man, dressed as an Indian, dressed as a white man. He had pale, milky skin, tiny hands and feet and bright blue eyes. Keokuk had a frizzled black goatee, which he stroked as he listened to Bright Sun. He fingered a necklace of claws around his throat as Bright Sun read to him.

"In payment for past debts the Sauk will confirm that they have ceded fifty-one million acres. For this transfer of fifty-one million acres, the United States shall give . . ."

I held my breath anticipating a sum so enormous it would cause my head to spin. I envisioned the whole tribe being seated upon three-hundred-dollar horses. Every other plainsman would marvel at the new millionaires—the Sauk tribe, flaunting their wealth in the cities along the rivers. Bright Sun cleared her throat and read quietly, " . . . shall give the Sauk people one thousand dollars per annum."

I shook my head in disbelief. Surely, Bright Sun had misread this figure

and overlooked a cipher or two. Or three or six. Keokuk said something that
caused Bright Sun to wince. When she would not repeat Keokuk's words,
Uncle William prompted her, "Miss Bright Sun, you are obligated to tell me
what Keokuk has said."

"He wants . . ." She stopped and pursed her lips, flapping the treaty dis-
dainfully. A crease furrowed her brow, and I watched her intently. Finally,
she lifted her head and said, "Keokuk wants the money given to him. Give it
to him and he will see it is handed out to those Sauk who most deserve it."

Uncle William nodded approvingly, impressed by Keokuk's good sense.
I guessed that Keokuk would keep every penny of the tribal annuity for
himself. "You are an eminently practical man, Keokuk," Uncle said.

A *practical* man. Uncle believed this was the highest compliment he
could pay to a savage. A practical red man did as he was told.

At the end of the long hall opposite Uncle William, the door swung open,
admitting a pale wedge of light and a cold breeze. It was the door leading
to the dog trot between the Clark home and the council house. Philip was
not guarding that door. Everyone looked in that direction. Thinking a gust
had blown the door open, I made as if to close it. With a harsh yell, Uncle
ordered me to stay put. I gathered my shawl up over my hair and shivered.
We waited, all of us, watching the light stream over the floor and listening to
the wind.

I saw a brown hand hook around the door, holding it ajar.

Twenty Sauk warriors filed silently into the room, led by a thin, muscular
man whom I guessed to be in his middle fifties. Seeing them enter, Keokuk's
band searched about frantically for their weapons.

The war leader at the head of the line was a full-blooded Sauk who stood
five feet eleven inches and cut into the room swiftly, without ceremony. He
looked like a man accustomed to hardship and deprivation. His face was
narrow, his nose was prominent, his mouth large and down turned. His
black eyes worked over objects and people as if he were anticipating an am-
bush. I guessed he weighed about one hundred and forty pounds.

To look at him was to know that if he wanted to make a straight leap up
and hang from the chandeliers, he could do it with little effort, then drop
upon you to deliver a lethal blow. Unlike Keokuk, this man was unadorned,
but for eagle feather plumage twined into his scalp lock. The blanket over
his left shoulder was red, and he wore fringed leggings which were his only
concession to the cold. His brown belly and chest muscles were tattooed
with graceful hieroglyphics. At his belt hung a black sparrow hawk. A black
hawk.

I rose from the chair and stood on my tiptoes in fearful expectation.

Uncle looked like a bear with a sore head. He came around the table and glowered at Black Hawk. "I will not have you in my council house, not with your feet still bearing the mud from British Fort Malden! And I'm guessing it was you who killed that pregnant woman and her children on the Cuivre River, then burned their bodies. So if you aren't here to surrender yourself to me, you'd best run before I call up the Sixth Infantry down at the Greentree."

Black Hawk held a new English trade musket covered with a red woolen slip. A bag of British glazed powder hung over his left hip. Bright Sun planted her feet solidly. As she translated, her voice filled the room, riding over the warrior's loud and staccato syllables as if the two of them were speaking a rondo of sorts. When Black Hawk spoke, his voice was a harsh rasp.

"I did not kill those white people on the Cuivre!"

Uncle William slammed his hand upon the table. "You lying bastard, who the hell did if not you? It had your mark all over it."

"I cannot control what young men from other bands do!"

"Then I'll hold you hostage until your men round up the murderers."

Black Hawk scoffed at him, "You can't hold me, Red Hair, you are not that strong."

Realizing the literal truth of this, Uncle backed away a bit, but not without looking wistfully at the door where Lieutenant Cooke stood guard, innocent of the proceedings within.

"Did the British put you up to it? Did they tell you to kill women and babies?"

Black Hawk's face sharpened with fury. "I did not kill those white people on the Cuivre! I came down the river, and some of my men went to the Cuivre, but I went to Cap au Gris. I went with one other brave, and there we separated. I saw two white men. I could have killed them, but I did not! I did not kill them because they had come to Saukenuk long ago, to learn us the white ways of making corn. They were good white men. But after I let the two white men pass by unharmed, I went up the road. There I saw one of them stumbling toward me, bleeding from his head. I saw the Sauk brave who had come with me. I told him, you have wounded him but not killed him. Do not let him suffer so! I walked away as it was done."

Black Hawk breathed heavily, like a man who had sprinted up a grassy slope.

"Those two white men had two little boys with them. I did not tell the brave with me, for he surely would have killed them. I did not kill those boys, because I have sons of my own. I know what it means to see my son killed before my eyes and to be helpless before such a thing."

I thought of the General, and I blanched. I pressed my back against the wall, willing myself into invisibility. Black Hawk continued his tirade. "I come to you from Yellow Banks, I ride along the river, leaving my people at the sugaring grounds because I hear Keokuk has come to sell Saukenuk to Red Hair. Now I hear you have put Ice on Wings in jail for saving his daughter. Ice on Wings did nothing you would not do if someone threatened your child. Provoke me to war again, and you will learn who Black Hawk is. Free Ice on Wings! I will take him home with me!"

Black Hawk's men bent at the waist and stomped until the floor reverberated like a giant drum. I jumped about three feet into the air on the vertical. The Indian objects all over the walls trembled sympathetically. Black Hawk nodded approvingly at this display. Uncle William folded his arms over his chest, and his face turned scarlet as a wound. Obviously he had determined that the best strategy for surviving a conflict with Black Hawk was to allow him to vent. Still, he couldn't resist a verbal jab. "Black Hawk, it was your men who committed those murders, and it is your men who shall suffer the wrath of the Great Father."

"Do not speak to me of your Great Father. My father was not a white man. My father was Pyesa, a Sauk warrior." Black Hawk grabbed the treaty on the desk and tore it in two. He broke the quills sitting in the jar, then held them up to Uncle and said to Keokuk's men. "What kind of men are you to drink whiskey with Red Hair and follow a woman like Keokuk? He has never killed the enemy and he has never gone into battle. Keokuk is a coward."

Despite the simplicity of his words, Black Hawk's message had great effect, for Keokuk's men hung their heads and refused to look him in the eye. Throughout this ordeal, Keokuk's contempt for his rival was apparent. Doubtless, Keokuk feared his thousand-dollar annuity would slip away if Black Hawk aggravated Uncle William sufficiently.

Keokuk spoke as if he were trying to coax a cougar into a willow cage. "Brother, things have changed with the Chemokemon."

"I am not your brother. My brothers are not women."

"The treaty giving away Saukenuk was signed many winters ago. We must find some way to live peaceably with the Chemokemon, even if that means giving up Saukenuk and moving to the Iowa lands."

When not speaking, Black Hawk's mouth remained open, and I could hear him breathing. "I did not sign the treaty. I do not take money from the Chemokemon. You would give them anything they asked for if they gave you money. And whiskey."

Keokuk tugged resentfully at his goatee and looked around at his men for reassurance, but they pretended to study the floor. A few of Black Hawk's men fiddled with greased patches and powder. I glanced at the door, and with profound cowardice, slowly began making my way toward it. But then Keokuk said something that made Black Hawk flinch: "The British at Fort Malden won't help you anymore, brother. I know you hope the British will help you. But the British have lost the rivers to the Chemokemon."

Black Hawk shouldered his gun and shuffled back and forth in a mute rage. He tried to speak but stuttered. He bent his head, pursed his lips, and finding a momentary calm within himself, said, "Provoke me to war, and you will learn who Black Hawk is!"

Black Hawk and his band filed out, but not before jostling Keokuk's warriors. As Black Hawk's men streamed down the aisle, he looked right into my eyes, and I looked straight back at him. There I saw his hatred showing as fiercely as if he had declared it to me. It was the first time I knew someone hated me. The only sign he gave to acknowledge me was a slight flaring of his nostrils. A shudder began at my scalp and worked its way to the soles of my feet, and I lowered my eyes as he passed by me. I was not desirous of knowing any more about Black Hawk than his singular glance had told me.

With a defiant flick of her chin at Uncle William and Keokuk, Bright Sun gathered her raccoon pelt about her shoulders and followed after Black Hawk's band. As I watched her go, I realized that Uncle William *had* succeeded in driving a wedge between the Sauk peoples, an accomplishment akin to tearing apart a large family.

Bright Sun did not look at me in passing, nor did she shut the door behind her. It stayed open, snuffing out the taper light and leaving us all to chill in a January wind that smelled of nothing but cold.

7

Jefferson Barracks, Missouri, January 1826

✸ I SAT alone in the quiet of Uncle William's great vaulted Indian museum. Philip, standing guard at the south-facing door, hadn't seen Black Hawk and his men enter, and I was glad of it. Black Hawk would have put a quick end to my pretty cousin. I pulled my watch from the pocket of my waistband and noted that it was three o'clock. I wondered if the General had forgotten all about me.

I began to write Mama a letter but got no further than the date. What could I tell her of these four days passing that would not cause her ruinous worry? Louisville and my dabbling former life of sixteen social calls a day, three dress balls and two formal dinners a week, seemed a distant memory.

A shrinking pool of late afternoon light fell upon me as I tried to write.

I attempted to sketch Black Hawk. The little portrait was actually rather good. I dipped the quill into the pot, but the cold had made the ink go thick. A blotch fell onto the desk, and I watched it dry, thinking, if there was ever a figure who could haunt a body, certainly it was Black Hawk. As Mama said, virtue is a good thing—until it becomes something else. And looking down at my sketch, it occurred to me that virtue might be Black Hawk's problem exactly. He called forth the twin possibilities of a man who is always just, but never merciful, a man who is so entranced by his virtuous perception of the world that everyone else is evil by comparison. Even then, I perceived the famine in his character. He required banquets of adulation to make him whole. Pulling back to scrutinize my drawing, I saw my error.

I had drawn his eyes too kindly.

When the General finally arrived, hours later than promised, he escorted me into the carriage. The tip of his nose and his ears were red with cold. After a contemplative pause, he leaned toward me with his elbows upon his knees, and covering my forearms with his hands, he tugged me close until only the edge of the carriage bench was under me. "That's two days running you've managed to get into trouble. From now on, I really don't want you going into St. Louis unless you're accompanied by an armed escort of at least three men."

"Oh, the Sauk were too worried over their treaty to give me any thought. And I don't regret having seen Black Hawk. Now I can form my own opinion of him."

"So what is your opinion?"

"Black Hawk is something more than people make of him."

"Meaning what, Mrs. Atkinson?"

"Meaning I respect him for protesting that hideous swindle Uncle calls a treaty. Honestly, fifty-one million acres for a one-thousand-dollar annuity? I don't care who the parties are, I have never heard of anything so shameful in my life. I'd go on the warpath, too."

"That treaty was made in '04 by William Henry Harrison. Your Uncle only sought to confirm it, and in doing so, obeyed direct orders from his government."

"You say that by way of exculpation?"

"No, I agree with you, Mary, it's a swindle."

"And as far as I can see, Black Hawk hugs his beliefs as tightly as you hug yours, General. By the bye, your little Red-She—knew Black Hawk was in town. She lied to you. To whom is she loyal, I'd like to know?"

"Bright Sun is loyal to herself. I don't delude myself about that. And like you, she holds to her reason by silk threads."

"Are you picking another fight with me?" The General scratched at his jaw as I inclined toward him. He grinned smugly at me and reached out a hand to pinch my cheek. I slapped it away impatiently, but he only laughed and said, "I've never given *her* a bath, you know."

"Are you implying she didn't need one or didn't want one?"

"For being so proud and scrupulous a woman, Mary Bullitt, you have a funny way of getting yourself compromised when you're in my company."

"That's plain goatish of you."

"I'm not the goat here, Mary Bullitt. You're the one who tried to despoil my chaste person by nearly pulling me into the bathtub with you. What's the matter with you, anyhow? Haven't you read any books about the role of the ideal wife?"

"No, I am blissfully ignorant of such things."

He moved his finger along my jaw and teased, "A good wife submits instantly to her husband's slightest wish."

"And what does a good *widow* do?" I snapped at his finger with the force of a pike after a tadpole.

"Jaysus, you little carnivore, you nearly took my finger off."

"Stop vexing me or I *will* bite it off next time."

The General ordered the driver to pass by the jail, where he would order the release of Ice on Wings, the Sauk who had killed the shopkeeper. He explained that Senator Benton agreed to release Ice on Wings on the condition that the General hold him as a bargaining chip to compel the Sauk to turn over the men who'd murdered the settlers on the Cuivre. A light snow drifted down, and nightfall was close upon us. The warehouses were dark and the streets were almost empty, but for a few souls riding or walking home, gathering their cloaks at their throats.

We waited in the carriage as Philip carried the release papers indoors. I tucked my hands under my arms to bring warmth into them. The arctic chill made it hard to draw a breath.

I straightened with a measure of alarm as I saw three shadowy figures emerge from the jail in a short-lived glow of candlelight. The front door banged shut, and I heard footfalls squeaking as they sank into the snow underfoot.

"Oh no!" I said.

"Now what?" The General's eyes shifted with mine.

"Look, Philip has given that little girl his uniform coat. We can't very well send her home half naked, with the weather being so cold. We could put her in the spare bedroom after you lock her father up. She could sleep at our house."

"We are not taking anyone home with us tonight. Am I being clear here? It is high time *my* house was *my* own. I intend to be alone in it this evening."

"Somehow when *you* say *house* I think you mean something altogether different."

The General seemed to think for a moment. Then he dug about in his coat pocket and removed a few coins. He opened the door of the carriage and called to Philip. My cousin walked forlornly in advance of the child and her father, who looked to have been subdued by his one night in jail. The Sauk stared curiously at the General.

"Mister Cooke, you will take these coins and buy for that little girl a proper . . . whatever it is little girls wear. Also find a boarding house that will take her in."

I put myself before him and said, "Philip has to guard Ice on Wings. You can't send a child out into the streets alone with only a pocketful of coins. Even if she knew where to buy clothing, none of the shops are open this late, and no boarding house is going to lodge an Indian child. Why can't we just—"

"Don't suggest it," the General said between gritted teeth. He paused for a moment, then pulled a few more coins from his coat pocket. They jingled in the cold air. I glanced up at the jail again and saw two white men in great capes emerge simultaneously from either side of the building. I began to rise off the seat.

I put my hand to the General's arm and said, *"Look there . . ."* but in that moment, with symmetry of form and brutal speed, the men elevated their rifles and shot both the Sauk child and her father in the back.

The girl tried to break her fall with the fragile barrier of her hands. Her ankles crossed one over the other. She fell as if she had been divinely captured in the air, then released to the earth by spirits who had forgotten her somehow. I had run at her, hoping to break her fall, and to keep her from dragging herself along in misery, but I was too slow, and her braids flew behind her. She wore an expression of surprise as she hit the snowy ground, causing it to powder the air around her. As her blood touched the snow, her life heat vapored upward in wreaths of steam above her head. I knelt before her as she shuddered helplessly. A dark clot appeared on her lower lip. I turned her over and then covered her with my cape to warm her. She shivered, then passed.

Philip mounted up and made as if to pursue the gunmen, but the General would not let him go, saying he had an idea who had sent them, and Philip did not know this country well enough to give them chase. Without waiting for the General's instructions, Philip left us to ride the three city squares distance to fetch the mortician. I held the girl, for I could think of no act more disrespectful than to require her to lie in the snow.

As we waited for Philip to return, snow soft as pinfeathers swirled out of the sky. I heard music resonating loudly in my head, as if I were standing in the center of the convent choir. I have always been accused of eccentricity, but looking back on that night, it was my attempt to put beauty to just proportion against all the ugliness I'd been witness to those two days passing. I tried to hum what I'd been forced to memorize so long ago, but my mouth and my throat were dry. The cold dissolved my voice.

When Philip rejoined us, the three of us huddled together in the snowfall. The mortician wrapped the Sauk dead in winding sheets. I thought they looked like chrysalides awaiting resurrection as something finer. The General and Philip lifted the bodies onto the mortician's dray where they were soon covered over by a second shrift of snow. I watched them roll away, glancing up at the last of the day's shadows angling off the old brick buildings. The General said, "Let's put for home. Mister Cooke, you ride inside here with us."

As we made our way back to camp, the wolves came out. Though the hills were hardened by frost, we heard them following us, as if to prevent a true crossing into a place we could never hope to understand. I could not see them, but I imagined how they looked. In my vision of them, there was a blue light over their haunches. I wonder if they hadn't gone in search of Ice on Wings and his daughter. They crept with a narrow-hipped gait under the cedar trees, gathering to retrieve the hopeless and lead them back to rights.

The horses were spooked. The General and Philip loaded their firelocks and lowered the window, anticipating the wolves would attack Philip's mount first. We never saw them. The General said the cold had drawn them to the middens for easy food. When finally, their howling trailed away, the General closed the windows. He told us that when forming a war party, the Maha took courage from the wolves by saying these words: "The wolves have no fear as they travel over the earth, so I, like them, will go forth fearlessly and not feel strange in any land."

I did not tell the General that fear and strangeness seemed the only constants in this borderland—and that the distance home seemed formidable.

⁂ WE arrived at our house on that cold night, both of us feeling on the edge of something unpleasant as we contemplated the fate of Ice on Wings and his daughter. I was subdued, and the General was caught in the workings of his own mind. He opened the door for us, and we were washed over with warmth and the aroma of chestnut soup bubbling over the fire in the dining room. It was my favorite dish. Dahlia had started the stock at dawn, notching fifty chestnuts, stewing them in a quart of veal broth, later adding the beef, ham, onions pierced with cloves, sweet herbs and stuffed partridges topped with crisp bread. My stomach rumbled in anticipation. I tapped my feet impatiently as the General removed his cape. He hung it upon a hook on the back of the bedroom door, then motioned for my cloak.

We paused in the hallway where the light was all in halves, guttering about us and making us appear more warmly countenanced than we were. I stared wistfully in the direction of the chestnut soup. He extended a courtly arm in the direction of the dining room.

"In the carriage, sir?"

"Yes."

"You said you had an idea as to who shot Ice on Wings and his daughter."

"Yes."

"Well, who, then?"

"None of your concern, Mrs. Atkinson."

"I think it is my concern."

"Of course you do."

"General, you are quite masterful at telling me perfectly nothing."

The General sighed and put his hand to my lower back to move me along more quickly.

"I know the shooters were probably Sheriff Hammond's deputies. Those deputies belong to the local militia. Like militiamen everywhere along the frontier, militiamen here are outspoken about the native peoples. They intend to see every last red man swept from the Missouri and Illinois and Michigan Territories, and so on. They killed Ice on Wings in my plain sight to send a message. That message being that the militia will 'clean house' if the army regulars won't. In all the time I've been out here, there has been rancor between my regulars and the militia. I have been fired upon more often by militiamen, particularly the trespassing squatters that my men must evict from the territories, than I have by native peoples, or by the British. You think about that."

"What will you do?"

"I am going to have my supper."

Our supper was served, and the General dismissed Dahlia. We found ourselves alone together in the spare little dining room. The table, built of the local yellow pine, was off plumb. When I flattened my palm to the corner, it bobbled. A fire smouldered in the rock hearth, shredding into white ash. We sat there silent and edgy, on terms of armed neutrality. The General took up his place at the head of the table. He poured from the decanter of watered Madeira.

"When you go chasing after Black Hawk . . ."

The General sighed in an exasperated way. "I don't *chase after* Black Hawk. I don't *chase after* any of the native peoples."

"But when you are called away to . . . to . . ."

"Drink your Madeira."

"No, it causes me to be reckless."

"Drink it all the same."

He tore pieces of egg bread into small pieces, reserving each bite for singular buttering attention before popping it into his mouth. Threadlike lines curved under his eyes. He seemed resigned to providing me some explanation. "When I go upriver, I must be keenly aware of the number of hostiles I am to confront. If I were to arrive with a small party, the young rogues would be tempted to attack for the hell of it. Nothing personal in it, they fight to gain status within the tribe. But I can't afford a single mishap in that respect. A successful attack on my command would be disastrous. Others would join in the fray, and once united, the native peoples could control the entire Western Frontier from Fort Snelling to St. Louis."

I spooned a chestnut into my mouth. It squeaked between my teeth. A wind rattled the windows, and the flames folded over the wicks in the wall cressets. "But if the Indians decide to put up a fight . . . you can't pursue mounted Indians with foot soldiers, can you?"

"My officers are mounted, as are a few light companies of scouts. But you're right, I do need horses. In the worst of situations, I'd have to call out the militia. Now, no more talk of this."

"It must be nice for you," I said.

"What?"

"Silencing people when it pleases you."

Snow blasted a gritting chill at the windows. The fire hissed as snow fell into the flue. He sliced the small drumstick from his partridge, then set it aside on the plate rim and lifted the breast with the tip of his knife. Though it had become the custom to hold the fork in the right hand, the General held the utensil in his left hand, after the British fashion. I scrutinized his movements, and catching me doing so, he paused in mid-chew, then narrowed his eyes at me and asked, "Why are you gaping at me?"

"You eat like an Englishman. It's peculiar to see."

He motioned at the fire with his fork. "Stare at the fire and comment on that for a change, will you? I feel like a specimen."

"Aren't you? Something of a specimen?" I put my fork to the plate edge. His mouth turned over in a lopsided grin. "Now what?"

"We should have taken our time with courting. At least a month."

"Very little can be done about that now."

"Still . . ."

The General shrugged and held his elbows out at an angle, pointing his fingertips at the ceiling. He looked like a plaster St. Francis summoning the woodland creatures when he did that. He said, "I would imagine all marriages begin so."

"Yes, but I don't even know your middle name."

"Don't worry yourself. I don't have one."

"Oh." I paused at this and offered, "Do you know, I've never met anyone who didn't have a middle name? The only people I ever knew of who didn't have middle names were—" And recognizing my error, I stopped speaking instantly. The General gave me a wicked look and finished my sentence for me, "Just us poor white trash and the Negroes?"

"I didn't mean . . ."

He enjoyed my discomfort. "Well, Mary Bullitt?"

"Well nothing, General." Under the circumstances, I thought it best to change the subject. I felt the blood rush to my face, and I began hopefully, "Nor do I know the names of your parents."

"John. Catherine."

I nodded solemnly as if this was a matter deserving lengthy deliberation and even lengthier discussion. "I don't think you've told me about your family."

"Carter. Thomas. Richard. Edward. Julia. Elizabeth."

"Such vivid descriptions. I feel as if I know them already."

A feathery bit of winter lingered at the nape of my neck. I closed my eyes and tilted my head aside. Mama had packed the gown I was wearing with a sachet of attar of roses. The scent wafted up from my bodice. I held my legs out straight before me and touched the toe tips of my slippers to the underside of the table. My skirts made a rustly noise. The room was cold about the edges, the winter outside so cruel that it caused the logs to pop, a noise as loud as the report from a pistol. I dabbed at the corner of my mouth with my napkin, put my fingertips to the plate edge and pushed it away from me. He did the same, resting his elbows on the table. He clasped his hands together, pressing his thumb knuckles to his lips.

I looked down at my hands and then up at him. "There is a frost on the walls that are far from the fire."

Snow fell down the flue and plopped into the hearth. I listened with too much interest to the hiss, I scavenged for something to say to him, but he wasn't making this easy in the least. He leaned on his elbows, a mild expression of contentment on his face, staring directly ahead as if in daydream. He peered curiously at me as I rose from my chair.

I walked around the table, all the while keeping my gaze on him. Despite my best efforts to appear calm, I shivered. He pushed his chair away from the table and wondered up at me. He almost smiled. His eyes were curious. He pulled me into his lap, then slid eighteen hairpins from my hair, dropping each on the floor with a tinging noise. I could feel a laughing rumble in his chest, and he said, "How many of these damn things do you have in here?"

Then he took my hand, led me across the hall into the bedroom and shut the door. The room was dark, and he left me for a moment, to light tapers. I sat on the bed, tapped my feet nervously and bit my lip. He sat beside me, and it appeared as though he was about to proffer some sort of an explanation. I did not wish to hear a speech. But the General kept talking. He said, "Now, Mary, you may not like—" But I stopped him with my fingertips to his lips and said, "What I like about the two of us being on this bed is that I don't know you at all." He lowered until his lips were close, and paused for an instant before I tasted him. After that, there was no thinking anymore, only the scratch of his jaw against my breast, my hands exploring him even as I tugged at his waist strap in the struggle to remove as much clothing as we could—until we finally gave that up, and I girdled my legs around his waist and strained up to press my mouth to his chest as I touched the small of his back. His shoulder against my nose was as warm as an apple come straight from the tree and held to my mouth under an afternoon sun. His hands were practiced, and I could not be silent under them. When we were both still and joined, he met my gaze in a way that was more intimate than touch, but knew he betrayed too much of himself and turned his head aside so that I could not see his face. That night he sought me out again. I was glad of it, I wanted to know him in every way we could imagine together. Being so new to one another, everything was exciting, and I thought about him when he was away from me.

Days later, when he was late coming home, I looked for him at his office in the barracks quadrangle. It was evening, after his adjutant had been dismissed, and finding him alone, I closed the door. Seeing me on the threshold, he set aside the letter he was writing and gave me a quizzical look.

I asked, "Did you send for me?"

He grinned and said he had not, but that I could stay if it pleased me.

"Can you imagine any way that my being here could please *you?*" I replied, brushing past him to close the shutters overlooking the esplanade.

"Well, hell yes," he said, jumping up to lock the door.

But the General favored being outside. Once he threw me into a snowbank, but as I was on the bottom, I sank deep and got cold as the snow melted under me. In the summer we rarely made love on a bed. Sometimes we lay in the tall grass with grasshoppers lisping about our legs, or in the springhouse with the creek gurgling and the milk cow looking stupidly at us, or if, on rare occasion we were in the house, I found myself precariously balanced in novel ways atop furniture not intended for sleeping. And I observed that we shared a similarity. Our bodies were finely scarred from our legs to our necks from having been cupped and bled so many times over the years by doctors. We had raised lines scarified over the skin like pearly horizontal seams. Delicate as spider webs. We looked as if we had been sewn into our bodies by a feverish seamstress with no idea of how to put us right. One night, as I lay upon my stomach, his finger prowled over my shoulder bones. He said something that I believed to have been a secret musing that he errantly gave voice to: "It is an impenetrable veil that you keep over your heart, Mary Bullitt."

That is when I thought he was waiting for me to love him first. But it was only a glimmer, as ephemeral as twilight colors or the innocent white scent of a pear in bloom. I knew the moment we stepped from our marriage bed, he would transform into the unapproachable version of himself. He would be sardonic and distant all at once. If I allowed myself to be tender, he teased and mocked me. He did not want to hear what was truly in my heart. When my husband took me in his arms, I felt as though I were with a ruling winter spirit that disappeared in the strong light of morning. Even in the deeps of January and February, he opened our bedroom window before he drew me close, as if to preserve an escape for himself.

❊ HE owned a black sleigh that was pulled by a team of grays. On the first Saturday of our married life, he tucked the lap robe around me and asked me if I was warm enough. Then he fussed with the sadiron at my feet. Still not satisfied, he tossed a buffalo robe around my shoulders. Then he took the reins in his hands and we went gliding over the snow-covered hills into the cantonment of the Army of the Frontier. His army. A stupefying cold pierced us to the skin.

Jefferson Barracks was situated atop a rolling line of limestone bluffs, in the midst of an elegant old forest of oak and sycamore, elm and hickory. The barracks were shaped like a horseshoe and partially faced with yellow limestone that glowed warmly under the diffused winter light. It was centered by a vast parade ground, punctured with a flagpole. He told me that horses weren't allowed there unless a review was being held.

The General had black locust trees planted in a half circle before and behind the two-story barracks. When construction was completed, Jefferson Barracks would be the largest military installation in the nation, and the country's first infantry school. The General was charged with running the school and training all Western infantry troops, commanding the Sixth Regiment, guarding the frontier from the Canadian border south to the Red River, and supervising the construction of any and all roads in the Ninth Military District. Little wonder he could be irascible.

He halted the sleigh along the half-built south wing of the barracks. Captain and Mrs. Ewing had invited about forty people, including Lieutenant Johnston, Cousin Philip and Lieutenant Robert Anderson, into their quarters to welcome us. We celebrated in a ten-by-ten room that smelled like newly split oak. There was a tiny bedroom off to the side, and one precious glass window that viewed the parade ground. Deliberately breaking a window at Jefferson Barracks was cause for court-martial.

The Ewings' quarters were centered by a modest table covered over with delicacies and sweets that had been procured by the guests. There was ginger cake, fruitcake, sponge cake, cheesecake, white cake and prairie plum pudding with brandy sauce. I had a little of each, and then I ate the filberts left over from Christmas. The General introduced me to them. We heard a lot of raucous jokes at the General's expense, about old bachelors giving up the life, about the last holdout having been brought down with a Bullitt through the heart. Sometimes we were so pressed for space that he stood behind me, and my skin pebbled with goose flesh as I listened to his North Carolina burr and felt him so close to me. I made charming conversation with a vengeance.

When finally the General and I took our leave in late afternoon, the others tumbled out onto the boardwalk, waving and shouting farewell to us as if we would never see one another again. The General went through his tucking ritual again with my feet and the sadiron and the robes, but when he had finished, he paused and smiled at me, then gave me a pecking kiss upon the lips in full view of the revelers, who had their noses pressed against the glass. I felt my cheeks color and I chided, "Why did you do that while they were looking?" And he said, "Because I felt like it. Are you up for a ride?" I said I was. He squeezed my hand and gave it an exuberant jiggle.

We coursed by pin-neat shanties and Soapsuds Row, which housed the laundresses. We passed the armorers, the warehouses (grain on the third floor), he pointed out rifle pits and root houses, the stables, the shooting range and the smithy's, where the clang of hammer on anvil sounded like a bell. The doors to the wheelwright's shed were open, and I glimpsed him sweating steel tires onto wooden wheels. The General pointed out the Mississippi, boned in ice, and sugared with a brown sand road the soldiers had fashioned so they could cross to the other side of the river for wood gathering. We passed children duckwalking through snowdrifts, squealing at one another.

Finally, we passed out of the camp onto a snow-covered road overarched with elm trees. The winter silence was thick upon the ears. I sighed and closed my eyes, tipping my head back on the seat, utterly content. I listened to the runners hiss over the snow. I turned my head aside and glanced at the back of my husband's curly head, and I slipped my gloves under the collar of his gray cape and tickled his hairline. I didn't bother to ask where we were going. I didn't care. The seedling that had germinated in my head was beginning to leaf out, now that I recognized it for what it was. It wasn't humility, and it wasn't pride. It was simple happiness of the sort I hadn't known since I was a small girl.

8

Jefferson Barracks, Missouri, April 1826

❧ I N the bricked kitchen behind our house, Dahlia turned the coffee beans over in the roasting pan. Plucking one out, she stepped away from the fireplace and crushed the hot bean under her thumb on the enormous hickory table and pronounced it done. When the beans cooled, she clarified them with either a lump of butter or a beaten raw egg, then stored them in a crock. For our morning coffee, she pounded the beans in a mortar, then scooped them into a small flannel bag drawn closed with string and dipped it into the coffee kettle. To clear the sediment out, she wetted a piece of catfish skin and tossed it atop the brew. When it had boiled, Dahlia crossed the yard gingerly, lofting covered pots and trays.

I brought a cup to my lips and squinted at the window. The air was smoky, for the yeoman planters around Vide Poche were burning the fields clean of last year's harvest. When I glanced through the glass, I was taken by the beauty of the hills. The windflower is the first to bloom on the limestone bluffs overlooking the Mississippi. It opens its blue, purple and white sepals in early March, drifting a soft curve over the contours of the land. Now and again, the General peered up at the hills over his spectacles as he read the post returns in our dining room.

We had been married for nearly three months and were settling into certain habits. I bent over the *Missouri Republican,* reading an article about a riot in Galena, Illinois. It appeared that ten thousand white men and Negro slaves under the leadership of a certain Henry Dodge had usurped Sauk and Winnebago ownership of some lead mines. I knit my brow, put my finger upon the article. "Husband, have you ever been to Galena, Illinois?"

He cleared his throat and said, "Hm."

"They mine lead up there with slaves? This fellow Henry Dodge has made Illinois a slave state?"

"The Sauk used to take the galena, a lead compound, out of the ground with an antler. They scrape it out of big open pits. Make bullets and other things. That's a trouble spot, up there."

I folded the paper and looked at him, chin in hand. He lifted his coffee cup, and as he had found an error, he folded the upper left-hand corner of the post return he was reading. Then he said, "It is time to put in our garden."

"It is?" I murmured with an eye on the *Missouri Republican*, "Who shall do the labor? Nicholas, Dahlia, or both?"

"You and I shall do the labor. I am a planter. You are a planter's wife."

I slapped the paper upon the table. "I had it on good authority that you were a military man."

"If we don't put in the garden, we won't have vegetables. You won't do well on a steady diet of salt beef, hardtack and whiskey."

"But I don't drink whiskey, Mister General."

"Live on salt beef and hardtack all summer and you'll drink turpentine, Mrs. General. We'll put in the garden. And soon we'll have trees. We'll plant black locust saplings all about the house. Where is your spirit of adventure, Mary Bullitt?"

"What has that to do with gardening?"

"Go put on your gum shoes. Braid your hair back, pin up your skirts and cover your hands with old dress gloves. I won't have a woman with callused hands. Meet me out back."

I put my coffee cup on the table. He pecked my cheek, then jaunted out of the house in an exuberant mood. I watched him stride across the back lawn, favoring his left leg, which bore the twelve-year-old scar of a duel. He nodded hello to Dahlia and Nicholas as he crossed the paddock. Standing at the window, I said to his receding form, "Who ever heard of anybody *planting* their own *food*? It's so *vulgar*."

I met the General on the south-facing plat. He was dressed in old tow-linen trousers. Though my vision was shaded by the broad brim of my old flax hat, the morning was bright enough to cause me to squint. The air smelled of broken loam. The willows were yellowed with the promise of leafing, and the sky was clearing itself of clouds under a southerly wind. The elms were hung with clusters of fleshy keys, and the maples were budding out with brown knobs that made me think of cloves.

"I can't believe you're making me do this. Me of all people. Planting *food.*"

I ignored the General's expression of enduring resignation. He hummed an old Scottish tune called "Miss Gordon" while I talked. He pressed his lips together, narrowed his eyes and thought about the plow before him. I knew he was examining the possibilities for modification and improvement. While I objected to gardening, he murmured to himself in barely audible undertones like a man accustomed to the company of a lunatic, "Too much drag, a steel plowshare with a pivoting moldboard would be ideal."

He complained about the colter being brittle, and wished aloud for a pivoting moldboard. I complained about walking in mud. He fluttered his fingers at me as if saying, *shoo!*

The Morgan stood compliantly as the General hooked the drawbar of the plow to him. He clapped his gloved hands together and squinted at me, "Mary, your task will be to guide the horse as I hold the plow. Unless you'd like to hold the plow."

He offered the strap to me, but I jumped away. The General stood behind the land side of the plow with the strap about his shoulders. I trudged in advance of the horse, and off we went.

After the first few feet, he had to stop to scrape sticky Missouri clay loam from the share. I crouched beside him. He swiped at the tin plate with the side of his hand. I liked to watch his hands as he worked; he applied a deliberate grace to every small motion. The sun felt warm between my shoulders, but there was a chilly undercurrent to the breeze that made me shiver. Even though we had just started, a flock of meadowlarks and swallows began their vigil, plucking up an easy worm meal from the single furrow.

After we had worked along in silence, he called at me, out of the blue, "Never touch my writing desk."

"Why should I care to touch your writing desk?"

He whoa'd the horse, brushed away clods of mud from the plow and grinned up at me. "You are too curious by half."

"Why don't you ever answer my questions?"

"Why don't you ever stop asking them?"

"There. Right there, do you see what I mean? Do you see how you just did that?"

The General straightened with a hand to his lower back, then wiped the perspiration from his forehead with his sleeve. The swallows fished the currents for flying insects, diving and soaring in pinwheels about one another until it made me dizzy to watch them.

I shielded my eyes from the glare, and for some reason unknown to me, I felt a sinking disappointment. I said absently, "Swallows are the heralds of war."

"What was that?"

"Will you be away come the summer?"

He unbuttoned his shirt so that it flapped like two curtains about his broad chest.

"I won't know until I receive orders. But you should plan for such a thing. Summer is the season for war. The Indian ponies are fat then, and the young men are restless."

I kicked at the dirt, then strode off to lead the horse.

We furrowed a half a dozen rows vertical, crossed with half a dozen horizontal in complete silence. Once we finished this, we dragged a harrow to break the dirt clods. The harrow looked like a double-hung window absent the glass, spiked on the ground side with blades to smooth the soil. We put four seeds into each little mound where the horizontal and vertical furrows crossed.

When the sun was centered in the sky, I rolled my shoulders. Abruptly, I trotted away from him in the direction of the well. He called after me, "We haven't finished."

My braid flopped at my lower back. I tossed my hands up and hollered, "Even the field hands take a noon rest!"

The willow whips tentacled about in the breeze as I lifted the stone from the well lid. I felt him come up behind me, watched as he lowered the bucket into the water. I turned away from him, shoved my hat from my forehead, then smacked the dirt from my gloves. He offered me the ladle. I looked at him over the rim as I drank. He bunched his gloves in one hand, and I noticed the sun tended to burn him most grievously atop his cheekbones. As none of the trees bordering the field were leafed out, there was no shade to be found. The meadowlarks settled into the furrows and pecked at the soil, which, despite the bright sunshine, was wintry cold to the touch. He fiddled with the well lid, sliding it forward and back as if it required leveling. I studied the small notch under his bottom lip, with its bit of dark beard stubble.

"I wish you would tell me about the gulf coast. About Plattsburgh. Fort Atkinson. You never say anything about those places—*Henry*." He started at the sound of his name, but I thought Mama's convention about my calling him General when we were alone was plain foolish.

He began to say something, but his eyes clouded over. He hesitated, then turned away from me. There was an awkward pause. I wondered if he was angry at me for calling him by his given name. I took a seat upon a rough tillering of needle grass. I coughed, then began, "You never tell me about yourself. About what you were like before we met. Do you have secrets you wish to keep from me?"

"Yes."

From under the shade of his hat, his eyes crinkled with good humor. I leaned near to him and scrutinized the play of light over the bones of his face. I touched a finger to the red crescents atop his cheekbones, where the sun had crosshatched lines into his skin. He removed his hat, showing his wavy hair to be flattened down. Then he tossed the hat onto the grass beside me, laced his fingers behind his head and reclined so that his body touched mine. His eyes were closed tight as he feigned sleep. I asked, "Of all of those places, where were you happiest?"

"Pass Christian, Mississippi. The gulf coast."

"Why?"

I studied him for a response. He hesitated, then opened his blue eyes. A tranquil look passed over him, and his countenance softened under the spell of memory. He looked younger in the state of remembrance. It nettled me a bit. The man reclining on the hill beside me was stepping through the years on awfully palmy ground from the look of the upcurve of his mouth. I nudged him and asked, "When were you in Pass Christian?"

"From 1808. Five years, all said."

"Why did you like it so?"

He licked his lips and said slowly, cautiously, "I had good friends there. I guess I came of age there."

His reticence was making me suspicious. I looked under my lashes at him and pulled a yellow bloom of goat chicory out of the ground, then tickled my cheek with the fine white hairs on the leaf.

"What kind of friends? Lady? Men?"

"Both."

"What kind of lady friends?"

He took the dandelion from me, snapped the stalk in two and pointed to the core. "Do you see how the white sap turns dark and thick when it is exposed to the air? The Cherokee chew it when they hike long distances to stave off thirst."

I gazed at him, feeling my muscles twitch from exertion, feeling flooded all through with a sense of well-being from the sun. The ground seemed to yield up, as if yearning itself green and blooming. I felt the back of my neck and my nose growing pink.

"Did you know the Cherokee?" I asked slyly.

The General's eyes flickered, turned rueful and dark. He covered them with the crook of his arm so that he had a view of his inner elbow. He said in evenly chopped fragments, "Yes. I knew the Cherokee. They are very handsome people, I think the handsomest of all of the red people. They had a grand village by our post. They are the traditional enemy of the Sauk. The Sauk would raid them every spring."

"Did Black Hawk raid them?"

With one swift motion, he hiked my skirt above the knee. He nuzzled me into forgetting talk of the Cherokee and Black Hawk. But I persisted, "Why don't you speak of your family?"

He slipped his arms about my waist. "I had one. What more do you need to know?" My eyes drifted over him and he met them. I never knew anyone who was so secretive about his family. "Do you remember your mother?"

"No." He indulged in a contemplative silence, then said, "There's no need for sympathy, Mary. We were the largest landowners in Caswell County, but I couldn't afford to pay the taxes on my inheritance. I was the youngest, and there wasn't any money left over for me. For one whole year, I sustained myself on ashcakes and molasses beer, saving every penny. Even so, I couldn't scrape up the cash for taxes, so I sold everything to my brother Edward. I wrote away for my captain's commission in '08. I never went back home, nor did I desire to. My home is here. I've passed the best seasons of my life on these plains. And I still can't bear the sight of molasses beer."

I looked down at his windburned cheekbones and blue eyes. There wasn't a bit of disingenuousness there . . . or irony. For once, the General looked to be perfectly forthright. He cast a one-eyed squint at me. "What was that you said?"

"I think I am growing fond of you."

"You *think?* Mary, it is plain that you are besotted with me."

"Now don't get carried away. I could change my mind in an instant."

The draft horse wandered off, despondently tugging the plow along until he reached a dense clump of new foxtail and ticklegrass. The General touched his fingertip to my cheek. But our quiet afternoon was not to be.

In the distance, Dahlia began shrieking. She howled insistently, in piercing intervals. The General grabbed my arms and pulled me to my feet. We ran over the slope where the wood betony was uncurling its odd little fronds. Lush patches of immortelle carpeted the thin rocky soil, promising small white rosettes in a fortnight. As we crested the hill, the General was far in advance of me. He sprinted down the slope and came to a sliding stop before the porch. I lifted my skirts to my knees and ran so fast I nearly tumbled over myself.

We found Dahlia standing on the front threshold, her hands clasped to her cheeks, staring down at a lumpen form at her feet.

The General pushed her aside, and I peered around him.

There, pooling fresh blood all over our porch, was a black bear shot through with arrows. Having seen a bounty of it those twelve weeks passing, I had lost my ladylike horror of blood. But I had never before seen a bear. Not even a dead one. I expected the bear to be clean and glossy, but it was not. Flies and gnats worried at its nostrils and the clots over its wounds. The dead eye reflected the clouds passing overhead. Its paws curved upward and its mouth hung open as if the beast were about to run off down the lawn and return to its den.

"What is the meaning of this?" I asked, my voice shaking with fear.

"That sonofabitch. Freshly dead too. Nicholas! Billy!"

The General began undressing on the lawn as if he were going somewhere. He leaned on the porch post and quickly removed his boots and socks. Then he circled round the yard, marching about hop-toed on the winter-cold grass, all the while glaring meanly at the dead bear. Flags of wood smoke from our chimneys licked at the sky. The General lifted his chin and hollered, "Nicholas! Billy!"

Both men came running as the General paced in the mud. When they finally arrived, he motioned at the dead bear. "Nicholas, ride for Johnston and tell him to bring a fully armed, mounted platoon with him. Go!"

And then the General jumped over the bear and raced into the bedroom leaving muddy prints to dry on the chilly floors. Dahlia clung to me, following me like a shadow from room to room. The General buttoned his shirt, looking about the room for something. Dahlia stood on the threshold, wringing her hands. I paced after him, asking, "Where are you going? Who did this?"

"I am posting sentries on the front and back doors. At the stables too; I'm surprised he didn't steal our horses. Don't you dare leave this house for any reason. You hear?"

I nodded, frightened speechless. He whipped open the doors of the gun cabinet and grabbed paper cartridges along with an assortment of firearms. He tossed a rifle at me and barked, "Mary, do you know how to shoot?"

"Yes."

"Do you know how to load this gun?"

"Yes."

"Good. You and Dahlia stay in the library. Keep the rifle across your lap."

"Why? Who am I supposed to shoot?"

"Black Hawk."

The General dashed back into the bedroom, then squatted and pulled his riding boots from the wardrobe. I followed after him, still gripping the rifle. I said, "But—"

"But what? Where are my socks? I need clean socks."

"Why would I take your socks? And why did Black Hawk leave you a dead bear?"

"It's what the red people call me. Zha'becka. White Bear. The sonofabitch. Coming to my house like that. *Sonofabitch!* Where are my goddamned socks? Now, Mary . . ."

"What?"

"If you fear you may be captured, you might consider . . ." Then the General put his forefinger to his temple and puffed out his cheeks.

I gasped, "I don't think so. I can't think of anything more stupid than blowing my own brains out!"

The soldiers all came in at once, shouting excitedly, and sentries were posted on each side of the house. The General dressed haphazardly; his shirt was only partially buttoned, and his trousers bagged at his knees. Billy brought the General's bay around, and I stood on the porch between the sentries, who had their bayonets affixed and looked straight ahead as if I weren't there at all. Eight mounted officers, in every variation of dress imaginable, clamored in a whirl before our door, all of them hollering. I recognized Johnston, and Cousin Philip was there too, looking grim. After a momentary lull, wherein they waited for the General's orders as he put his foot in the stirrup, the lot of them dashed off in half a dozen directions. It struck me as faintly comical.

The two sentries at the front door were Irish veterans in their late forties named Russell and Mahaffey. Russell was nearly bald and had huge bulging blue eyes. They watered constantly, as if he were ill. Russell, I noticed, had a small black gentleman's book in his hand, one of the ones designed to look like Bibles. *Silas Shovewell's Adventures with the Nuns.* He tried, too late, to conceal the title from me by covering the bridge with his hand. As it was none of my concern what a grown man chose to read, I pretended not to notice.

I motioned about with the rifle, pointing after my husband and his men. "Do either of you know where they are going?"

"All due respect, Madam General, be careful with that thing. Rifles fire bullets, don't you know?" Russell said. Mahaffey peered off at the horizon and nodded knowingly. "That would be a hawk-hunting expedition. Sport and glory. That would take the General the rest of the daylight to my way of thinking. I wouldn't put the beans to boil just yet, Madam General."

I sighed, and following Mahaffey's gaze, asked, "I should go after them, shouldn't I?"

Russell scrounged around in his pocket for something, and propping his musket between his knees, opened a small leather envelope. He stuffed a quid of tobacco into his cheek. "Madam General, I assume you are asking a question of a rhetorical nature? Because riding after the General would be an act so brashly ridiculous, that the mere formation of such a vulgar thought is beneath a fine-born lady like yourself. Wouldn't you agree, Mister Mahaffey."

"Aye. Indecorous. And foolhardy besides. High comedy."

"Or low comedy. Depending on the execution, eh, Mister Mahaffey?"

"Eh, Mister Russell."

"So, Madam General, what my colleague and I here are suggesting, with your interests exclusively at heart, is that you sit by the fire and do your tatting. Let us look after you. Our pleasure."

The two of them smiled, displaying a sad lack of teeth. Mahaffey had a beautiful head of dark blond curly hair and was about three inches shorter than Russell, which is to say, they were both a bit deprived in the legs. What the sentries lacked in height, they made up in girth, with barrel-chested physiques and enormous forearms. Despite Mahaffey's entreaties, I did not go into the house and mind my tatting. I sat upon the porch with my elbows on my knees and my chin in my hands and I said, "Mister Mahaffey, how long have you known the General?"

"That would be since '08. He recruited me and Russell at Norfolk, Virginia. We followed him to Pass Christian, then up to Plattsburgh, where the British shoved their boots up our . . . ah well, then up that great and bloody river, the Missouri, then—"

"So you've known him as long as he's been in the army."

Mahaffey got suspicious and glanced sidelong at Russell, who seemed to issue a silent caution to his friend. *Watch your words, Mahaffey, the General's wife could get you into trouble.*

"Yes, me and Russell have known the old man for a long time. We were with him when he forced the Spanish to surrender at Mobile, and when we commandeered a Spanish transport."

"You must be very proud, gentlemen."

Russell and Mahaffey cautiously accepted my compliment. Russell said, "We're not called the Fighting Sixth for nothing. We've seen our share of the worst." Mahaffey ventured, "And we got to kick it to the British, which in itself has made the whole grand adventure worthwhile."

"So you must know nearly everyone connected with the various campaigns and expeditions that the General has . . ."

Mahaffey said, "Better than anyone else, that I'll promise you. Why we know all the scrubs and each of the laundresses and most of the Indians besides."

"Then you must know that excellent translator for the Sauk tribe . . . oh, what is her name?"

"Bright Sun?" Mahaffey offered helpfully, provoking a grimace from Russell. I snapped my fingers at Mahaffey's acuity. "That's her name, Bright Sun! She is certainly a very pretty girl. And the General admires her so. He says she is a very talented translator. Why, you gentlemen must see her rather frequently, given her important role."

"Ah . . . yes . . ." Mahaffey said.

"So you two, more than anyone else, would be able to tell me more about that fascinating young woman."

The two men exchanged a worried look. Russell said slowly, "Such as . . . ?"

"Oh, whether she's married or not?"

"Ah, no. I don't think Bright Sun is married." Mahaffey seemed relieved by my question.

"I could certainly understand how the General would admire Bright Sun."

"As she is a fine translator," Russell interjected, signaling Mahaffey to shut his gob.

I said, "And she recently shared with us the best possible news, that she will soon have a child. You know, she is exotic, what with those green eyes. It's obvious to me that she is not full-blooded Sauk. Indeed, she did not resemble, in any way, the Sauk I saw at my Uncle William's."

Mahaffey interrupted me. "All we know of Bright Sun is that she is a translator for the Sauk. May I suggest that you might be more comfortable inside the house? We are not supposed to talk when we are on sentry-go. Allow me to open the door for you, Madam General."

It was apparent that neither of these men was willing to confide in me, and why should they? So I retreated into the house, intending to wash the gardening dirt off myself. I found Dahlia still in a terrible fright. I urged her into the library, but despite the General's admonishments, I did not keep the rifle across my lap. Instead, I set it atop his writing desk. A day of honest labor took its toll on me. While reading, I dozed off, and so did Dahlia. Now and again, the sentries would shout a greeting at someone passing by, which jolted us out of our torpor, but the day passed without incident.

When we awoke, it was dark, and the General had come back in a wayward mood, for though the men had scoured the prairie, Black Hawk could not be found.

9

⁂ ABOUT eighteen months after we had been married, in early July of 1827 the prominent Creole families of St. Louis hosted a dinner and ball in the General's honor. We arrived at the Chouteau mansion at three o'clock in the afternoon, then the fashionable hour for a late supper, and found the drive crowded with carriages.

The Chouteau house looked to have been shipped joist and beam on a frigate direct from Flanders. It was a massive three-story structure, with a red pitched roof punctuated by gables. The first two stories boasted pillared balconies, and the estate was closed off from the street by a limestone wall. A clutch of elaborately coiffed women in plain muslin gowns gabbled on the wide front steps. Purple clematis tangled down the pillars, and the fruit trees were laden and bending. I nudged the General's attention to the barefoot matrons and the Negro servants standing behind them, loaded down like pack mules with ball gowns.

"Why are the ladies in plain dress? And where are their shoes?"

"The St. Louis Creoles don't wear their ball gowns in their carriages. They dress upon arriving to protect themselves from mud. Careful not to touch the hood blacking. I'd hate to see your gown ruined . . . particularly since I have to pay for them now."

The carriage circled round and stopped before the portico. Billy, dressed in a ludicrous red livery, held the door open for us. Our host was Pierre Auguste Chouteau, the managing partner of a successful fur trade and general merchandising business. He comported himself after the manner of a successful businessman, laughing a false club laugh, *Haw haw,* appearing to instantly like anyone who could possibly *do* something for him. Chouteau was dark complected, shorter than the average height, and wore a heavy suit of body hair that sprouted from his cuffs and collar. His eyes were deep set and gullish, his cheekbones prominently Gallic. I stood adjacent to his wife, Mme. Emilie Gratiot Chouteau, a finch of a woman with a pleat of gray in the part of her hair, who smelled of overripe figs. Her nose was mapped with tiny red veins.

Mme. Chouteau was the most astute slave trader in St. Louis; when I came into town to shop, I often saw her buzzarding around the slave pens where the hapless souls were caged naked and forced to sit the night in their own feces. Mme. Chouteau attended auctions at the block on Fourth Street in front of the courthouse, and I am told she enjoyed seeing stripes put to African backs. On the evening of the dance, we entered the house through black doors bearing the carved images of recumbent Italian saints around the iron battens.

"Rectory doors from Ravenna." Our hosts gestured proudly.

Stolen, I thought. Pillaged. With Chouteau at my side, we led the party into the room and were seated at a long table anchored by a saddle of venison. Two hundred candles inhaled every remnant of fresh air out of the room. Young French women were placed at intervals to ornament the table. These demoiselles, as they were called, wore so many bibelots in their hair that their heads look like jeweled display cases; glittering, but empty.

One of these young girls was placed next to the General. She wore the newest fashion—a gown with enormous cotton sleeves stiffened with buckram. She was shaped like a decanter ready to be turned bottom up. The demoiselle took her seat next to the General, and her right sleeve trespassed over his chest from his throat to his stomach, across to his right arm. The General batted at the offending sleeve like an agitated cat. Alas, inevitably, the sleeve drifted back across the General's chest. Exasperated with it, and with her, he took the sleeve in both hands, rolled it to an unfashionably narrow width, then asked the demoiselle to lean forward as he pinioned it behind her back, where it stayed until the meal was over.

Her eyes welled, her lips trembled, she grimaced on the edge of a tear drenching, looking for all the world like a butterfly shorn of one wing. I cupped my hands around my mouth and lipped a message to him, *"Be nice,"* but he was too busy frowning at Chouteau about something and did not see me.

Uncle William sat on my right. He was always good company because he loved to gossip. He said in a confidential tone, "Mary, that woman across the table?"

"Yes, Uncle?" I glanced at a handsome matron with kohled eyes. "When we hosted the gala for General Lafayette here in '25, she said, '*C'est votre première visite en Amérique, Monsieur le Général?* She asked General Lafayette if this was his first visit to America!"

"You're one to talk. Didn't you give him a grizzly cub? What were *you* thinking?"

"Well, Mary, the cub had been bawling at my house ever since a Bannock Indian found him orphaned along the river. One afternoon, General Lafayette appeared at my house, and I hadn't thought to buy him a gift, so I looked at the cub and said to Lafayette, 'So, you want the bear?' I didn't think he'd accept it. A year later, Lafayette wrote me a desperate letter: '*Theez bear, he ees eating my cheeldren.*'"

The time came when I was required to speak to John Reynolds, who aspired to be the next governor of Illinois, the erstwhile boarder who had trespassed upon my marriage bed the day I arrived in Missouri. He looked uneasy in his frock coat. "Mrs. Atkinson, have you been to Europe?"

I concentrated on my plate. I can recall exactly the texture of the olives in the vol-au-vent and the Malaga over my tongue. I nodded my assent and tried to be pleasant. Reynolds said, "Me and Mrs. Reynolds, we just come back from Europe (he pronounced it, Yerp) where we saw amazing things. For instance, we went to Oxford . . ."

I peered dreamily at a fly hopping over the shrimp mousse.

"I said Oxford, England? Are you listening, Mrs. Atkinson?"

"Yes, Mister Reynolds."

"We went there for a cattle fair. Beautiful Guernseys they got. They make milk so rich it comes out orange."

"Yes, Mister Reynolds."

"But the most astonishing thing, do you know what else they got in Oxford? A big school! Oxford University. It's true. I can tell by your expression that you think I'm foolin' but I'm not foolin'!"

"No foolin'."

A servant lowered a cover of artichokes with marrow. I shivered and looked down at my bare forearms. I turned to the French doors open to the balcony and felt a cooling breeze on my nose and cheeks. I had not told the General my news, but these days passing, I had come to be sure of it. I lifted my gaze to find him regarding me across the table's distance.

"Then we go to Paris, me and Mrs. Reynolds. Now what most interested me about Paris was the gross acreage of the city, and I passed my time there trying to calculate it . . ."

The General watched me over the rim of his glass. I returned his gaze through half-opened eyes. In the carriage, on the way over, as we crossed the empty landscape, he had whispered to me, *"Where are you going?"* He had watched tensely as my cheek brushed against his knee. *"I wish to try you,"* I said. And to hear him break his silence . . . it was the first time that I had conquered him. For dessert, there was raspberry sauce over the custard. I held the fruit against the roof of my mouth.

Reynolds's face washed over with a nostalgic glow as he continued to reminisce. "When I was a boy, my favorite pastime was throwin' rocks at the darkies. You ever tried that? No? Then you missed some fun, Mrs. Atkinson. Did you hear the latest news from Galena?"

"Galena? No."

"A Winnebago war leader named RedBird has attacked at McNair's Coulee. Killed the whole Methode family. Then he continued the festivities at Prairie du Chien. Killed all the Gagniers except Mrs. Gagnier, who escaped with her three-year-old son. RedBird got the baby girl, Louisa, sleeping in the cradle though. Got her good. Scalped her so artfully, he left her alive. Stuck a knife in her throat, but still she lives and breathes."

I glared at the General, who shrugged as if he didn't know a thing about it. Reynolds balled his fists like a melodrama actor and hissed, "Black Hawk thinks the British have declared war on the Americans. Black Hawk and his British Sauk will join with the Winnebago to make war on the lead miners. To make war on ever'body. They're both British bands. All those people fought for the British in the last war."

"Lead mines are the source of this grief?" I asked.

"My dear, you are green cotton in need of drying."

"Mister Reynolds. *Please.*"

"Oh, sorry. That weren't very polite of me. Calling you green cotton."

"It's you calling me 'my dear' that I object to."

Conversation swirled around us, rose up, then fell off like the sparkling eddies in the Mississippi that trapped boatmen in dizzying circles for hours. Reynolds was eager for the éclat of being my tutor: "Mrs. Atkinson, the Northwest is rich in furs and lead. The Winnebagos and the Sauk mine the lead on their lands, then sell the surplus. And they sell furs to the traders every spring. I'm talkin' here about sixty thousand dollars in furs that the Sauk bring in every year."

Uncle William wiped the corners of his mouth, then declared loudly enough to stop all conversation at the table, "Reynolds and Chouteau want to take advantage of a small insurrection to demand that the Winnebago sacrifice those lucrative lead mines and that rich farmland up north as penance. RedBird's uprising couldn't have come at a more fortuitous time for these land-grabbers."

I widened my eyes and looked to the General, who poked his tongue into his cheek. Chouteau and Reynolds weighed Uncle's heresy.

Uncle looked at them both and scowled. "What?"

Chouteau fiddled with the buttons on his waistcoat. "*What*. What do you mean, *what?* You are a goddamned Indian lover, Clark. That's why you're not now the governor of this fine state of Missouri. And how about your pal over there? Eh? Which way is your stick floating these days, General?"

"General, Black Hawk has put you to your trumps, you have no choice but to declare war on him. You're in for a long tramp upriver," Reynolds said, licking his lips. Uncle William sipped at his chicken bouillon and looked bored. He was accustomed to provoking these men, then enduring their ranting fits. Chouteau bunched up like a badger come fresh out of the dirt and pointed at my husband. Everyone at the table tensed, even the vacuous demoiselles. The General filled his fork and then his mouth with pullet fillet larded with truffles. His eyes glittered, his entire countenance flushed and brightened.

He chewed and said none too politely from the corner of his mouth, "Good pullet."

He lifted his glass, "Excellent Malaga."

Well, it was satisfying to see that he didn't answer other people's questions either. He was consistent, I had to give him that. The de-winged little demoiselle beside him winced and leaned away from him. Chouteau drummed his fingers on the tabletop.

"General, I suffered a terrible setback this year. I'd like to see those mines taken from the Winnebago. The Winnebago have discovered they can make more money mining lead than hunting and selling furs to me. When they mine lead, they don't hunt. When they don't hunt, they don't sell furs to me . . . well, it stings to be thrown over by those who used to love me."

Reynolds commiserated with Chouteau. "Disloyal savages. After all we've done for them. They'll destroy the national fur economy with this lead mining. And the Winnebago are as snug with the British as are the Sauk. Every battlefield you come across is littered with British guns. It's true isn't it, General?"

The General laughed derisively. "If you're so concerned over the national security, Reynolds, help me request funding for dragoons for the army. I need troop-trained horses. And men who can shoot from them."

Chouteau squinted at the General, "What the hell do you need horses for?"

The General made chopping motions with the side of one hand into the palm of the other as if he were speaking to a half-wit, "Because a man on horseback goes faster than a man on foot."

"I think it's a grand idea. If I get elected, I'll back you, General. That is, if you name them Reynolds's Rangers . . . no no, Reynolds's Dragoons . . . or mebbe, Reynolds's Mounties." Fired with grandiose dreams, Reynolds smeared an imaginary horizon, thereby ending the scrapping, at least temporarily. The de-winged demoiselle pouted because the General had completely neglected to converse with her. Her spirits recovered when she was asked to break the nougat pyramid jeweled with cherries in the center of the table. She was given a hammer, and full up with maidenly venom, she shattered it maliciously, spraying candy in every direction.

And after, we adjourned to the ballroom, where the orchestra clipped into a schottische, but we were too full to dance. The musicians declared a rest to allow the nursing mothers to look after their infants. The first row of chairs around the ballroom was occupied by demoiselles, keen on stalking marital prey. Behind them, in the second row, plump matrons scrutinized the demoiselles. A disgruntled woman hissed, *"The little white dragonflies."*

Uncle William shoved us toward the dance floor, "Children, escape while you can."

But Reynolds hollered after us, "Hell, General, you ain't got time to dance, we've got to plan this war. A really big war that'll clean every Indian off those lands from the Wisconsin to the Illinois River. General?" I looked back at Reynolds as the General took my hand. The orchestra played a quadrille. The General looked doubtfully at me, "Now, Mrs. Atkinson, this isn't your best dance, try to keep your focus, will you? Try not to collide with other guests."

In the late twenties, fashionable women cultivated an ethereal look by drinking vinegar and powdering their faces with ghastly white pearl dust. Many in the room appeared quite avant in this respect, with their blue cheeks and dark half moons under their eyes. Young children scampered into the room. A couple dancing beside us broke step when the children bumped into them, and the woman's blond wig fell askew, but her partner adjusted it discreetly for her.

"Mary, will you stop treading on my left foot? It's swelling up like a rotten quince, for the love of Christ."

"How am I supposed to concentrate on some stupid dance when I've just learned you're going off to the Indian country? That is why Mister Reynolds came here tonight, isn't it? To ask for your help up north. You are going upriver after this . . . this RedBird, aren't you? And just when were you going to tell me about it?"

"Now see here, you're supposed to let me lead. And stop throttling my forearm. If you're going to be fussy about it . . . yes, it's true, I'm going upriver. Within the week."

I stopped in midstep and looked aghast at him, "This week! But that's so soon . . ."

"How did you imagine I earned my daily bread? By escorting you to cotillions?"

I blinked rapidly and turned away from him. The General turned my face with a finger to my chin.

"What's troubling you?"

"Henry, you can be so obtuse sometimes."

"What is this, Mary Bullitt? Are you worried over me? Go on. Don't be bashful. Declare your full-out love for me."

He was as sincere as a carnival barker, so I answered in kind, "The only reason I can think of to fall in love with you is that it might make me thin."

"Oh, I don't want you thin. I like you plump as a quail. I've noticed your flat belly is gone. Doubtless I've made you so happy you're filling out like a proper female."

"These Indians will put you to bed with a shovel! Black Hawk's going to join with these Winnebago!"

"Well, Mary, it is my fondest hope that the Sauk will listen to reason and not fall in with the Winnebago. My first stop upcountry will be at Saukenuk."

"Oh, you're going to Black Hawk's village! To beg for his help?"

"Not Black Hawk. Keokuk. The other Sauk. The one with the blue eyes . . ."

"Black Hawk will be there. And so will his warriors, the ones who don't like you. The ones with the black eyes and big British guns, the ones who left you a dead bear."

Mayor Lane danced by with an infant daughter on his shoulder and a girl toddler by the hand, all three of them pealing giggles. I glimpsed the orchestra behind a screen of topiaries and bouquets of oleander that gave off a sharply sweet odor.

"They'll kill you. I just know they will."

The General seemed to think this was a great lark. He said indulgently, "Are you just being hopeful?"

"Don't mock me. Sometimes you ought not to tease me so much." My stomach was cold as if I had filled it up with egg pudding. I didn't feel like bantering with him.

He caught my hand and said, "Why, Miss Bullitt, I do believe you are concerned over my person."

"What if I am?"

"What if you are?"

I leaned forward a little, then flicked an errant hair from his immaculate blue jacket. It felt good to make that proprietary little motion. His epaulet brushed at my mouth and made a small cut in the center of my bottom lip. I winced and brought my glove to it, staring at the flecks of blood on the white cotton of my thumb. I firmed my voice. "What will you do? When you go up there, I mean?"

"The Indians will surrender the murderers to me, and the whole matter will end without us firing a shot. I've done this often enough before, Mary; there's no danger in it a'tall." He tried to grin at me, but failed and, instead, looked off—over my head.

"Liar," I whispered. His words hit me like fists, because there was a heaviness in my belly now that I had hesitated mentioning to him. I felt the roots of my hair grow damp with perspiration. The candlelight streaked into ivory ribbons as the General and I moved through the crowd. Dancers clouded around us in an oriental swirl of color, wafting toilet-water scents of clove and geranium.

He led me off the floor and directed me to the balcony, saying, "You look pale, Mary. Your lips are nearly white."

A humid wind blew off the river. Yellow taper lights flickered in the windows of the buildings opposite us. In a distant allée, a dulcimer twanged.

I studied the General's profile as he leaned over the balustrade. I had thought to explain my condition to him, but no lady would ever say the word "pregnant" to her own husband. Unrealistically, I hoped that my news would cause him to reconsider leaving me. I searched for a euphemism, then said, "I am flourishing."

"Yes, you are. Missouri certainly seems to agree with you."

"No, I mean I am really *flourishing.*"

"Now you just sound vain, Mary."

"You are being dull as ditch water, sir."

He lifted his brows. "Oh, Lord, I think I understand what you mean." The General seemed a little dazed as he considered what it could mean to add even more chaos to his orderly life. He pinched his nose as if he were warding off a sick headache.

As his response was less than enthusiastic, I muttered, "I didn't want you to return and find me grown into a spacious woman."

A rare expression softened the contours of his face, as if his everyday mask had been whittled away, leaving the true core of him before me. He touched his fingertips under my chin, and his face came close to mine. His lips parted, and I thought he looked about to say what I wanted to hear more than anything. But we were interrupted by a violent braying from the dirt streets below that startled us apart from one another. We leaned over the balustrade to see a mob brawling out of the gambling shop, the GAMBLING & RYE. The rowdy gamblers shouted obscenities and cut into one another with blows that could be heard above the orchestra.

I hoped to see my husband as he was a moment ago, but when he turned to me, his expression had hardened again, and his eyes were sardonic. I felt my voice break, "A thin layer of civility afloat on a sea of blood. That's what this place feels like to me."

UNTIL the night of the Chouteau fete, our first year-and-a-half together had been a strange luxury. They brought to mind the suspended hours between darkness and light when we do nothing more than wait. But after we returned home on that particular July evening in 1827, his eyes shone at me like a nocturnal hunter's before a candle. We walked where the trees clouded like an ashy smudge on the landscape. I smelled the water upon the stones. He led me to the pond, then pulled me into the water. The summer air carried the sounds. I floated on my back and looked up at the hunter's moon, but knew it could not possibly be . . . a hunter's moon in the summer.

A war moon.

He brought me under him. I felt the sand scrape against my cheek and my breasts and knees. My fingernails scrimmed in the limestone. I dug my hands into the soil to steady myself against the force of him. He buried his face in my hair, and I felt his lips on the back of my neck. There was a jewel at my lip. I felt its delicate petal there, a jeweled shooting star near the end of its bloom, a rose crimson flower at my lip, while I strained to look up at the war moon.

I closed my eyes and saw the lake near my childhood home, where, on summer evenings, I peered at the surface waters, watching the caddis flies hatch. I tensed to watch them struggle and come to life as something dark moved through the waters, searching for them. They would drift up to the surface and float there. I held my breath in the frail instant the wind blew them to the shore, and the predator followed after. Still they lingered dangerously as they waited for their wings to dry under the changing light. There was an exquisite moment of separation as they tore free of the water and took to the twilit currents of air.

When I was young, the Ursulines would say to me, *You love yourself more than you love God.* But what did they know of such things, those bitter old women?

Because it was no longer true what they once said of me.

I loved someone more than I loved myself.

I arched my back and threaded my fingers through his hair in defiance of the war moon. Like the ancients on some sacred night, I relinquished all bonds to the earth. In the tranquil waters amidst the tall grass, I fashioned my own baptism.

10

✾ THE General sat on the edge of our bed with the knuckles of his fore-fingers pressed to his eyes. I knew he was thinking about his war. We dressed for bed in silence. Outside, the night creatures roamed freely, and every dog in camp chorused up a bark at them. A breeze off the river blew flying insects through the window, and they clicked on the floor where the wind dropped them. I imagined all of them to be winged spiders—messengers sent with dire warnings by the men who wanted to kill my husband.

I washed my face at the basin. A few droplets of water fell onto the wood surface, and I quickly dabbed them up with the hand towel. The General was particular about such things. The mirror was lit by a taper, and when I glanced into it, I could see a heaviness about his shoulders, as if a shadow spirit had settled there to weigh him down. He removed his boots and his socks, but that night he did not tend to his fastidious rituals of placement. I gathered up what he had dropped on the floor, folded his trousers and laid them atop the chair at the foot of the bed. When I sat beside him, the ropes that held the mattress to the frame creaked. I touched the dark curls at the base of his skull and twirled one of them around my forefinger.

"Would you like me to cut your hair before you go?" He didn't answer me, and I saw the crease between his brows deepen. "By the time you come home, I will have felt the baby quicken. Now and again, I think I feel him moving around, but it is too soon to know. Here . . ." I brought his hand to my waist and then held it over my belly. "My waist is nearly gone. I'm straight up and down, like a boy."

He smirked at me, then looked down at his hand over my nightdress.

"You look nothing like a boy, Mary Bullitt. I've been thinking . . . do you wish to go home to Louisville while I am away? I can buy the ticket for you and send you off . . ."

"No."

"Mary, I worry over who will look after you."

"I'll look after me. But I will not leave you. Not now, not when you're going up there. You might return while I'm away. I want to be here when you come home."

I looked up at him and was startled by what I saw. His countenance was pained and drawn. He refused to meet my eyes, as if he did not want to hear my words. He withdrew his hand from my belly and bent over with his elbows on his knees. He rubbed at the calf of his left leg and winced. "Weather in the bones. It will likely rain as we sleep."

He looked over his shoulder, as if the weather required studying, but I knew it was his way of distracting himself from what really bothered him.

I said, "You always sleep well when it rains."

I bent over and peered at the old scar. It was a long, flat ripple over his shinbone and brought to mind a dry streambed. I could see dark pieces of lead and powder trapped under the skin. I touched it gingerly, as if he had not healed. Now and again, if I watched him closely, I could discern a slight unevenness in his gait, as he favored that leg when it ached. He had been wounded over a perceived slight when he initiated a duel that nearly killed him, long ago. The General guarded his honor jealously.

"I could put a poultice upon this if you'd like."

"No. Now listen to me. Tomorrow, I begin loading the steamers. I leave the day after with three hundred men."

I feigned confidence, but my voice rang hollow and I failed to convince even myself. "Three hundred foot soldiers? That sounds like quite a sizable force!"

"The Sauk and Winnebago have four thousand mounted warriors."

Oh, Lord, I wished he hadn't said that. I could see him upon a rivery field, surrounded by hostile warriors. An idea came to me, and I gripped his hand, "Why can't you send men after Black Hawk?"

He glinted at me in a fiercely inquisitive way, as if he believed I had challenged him.

"To kill him, Mary? Is that what you want?"

"I was thinking of putting him in the guardhouse. You're the one who brought up murder."

"When you brought up the subject of Black Hawk, you suggested murder too."

"I did not. And even if I did, no one would blame you for getting rid of him. You'd be acting officially, the army wouldn't mind, St. Louis wouldn't mind, goodness, everyone on the frontier would be relieved. I'd be relieved too. There, I'm being honest. And if you ever did kill him, you would be forgiven by everyone. Even God understands a man has a right to defend himself and his home and his family. You'd be forgiven, all right." I poked the nail of my small finger into my mouth and nibbled on it as I frowned at him.

I speculated at the paradox of him. While the General had rushed to duel when insulted by a fellow officer, he appeared to indulge Black Hawk's virulent hatred. Or did he? I looked down at his scar once again. Though he willingly endangered his body, he would not risk his heart. The General was certainly masterful at obscuring his emotions. I had seen his temper only once in eighteen months of marriage. He kept his soul a cool and prudent distance from mine. I wondered if the General didn't nurture Black Hawk's enmity in a similar manner. As he did not profess love or hatred of anyone on this earth, I suspected he relished scrupling over the people who loved and hated him. He flourished upon a self-made field: The landscape of his heart was a cautious place where a judicious man could avoid entanglements. With lynx-eyed scrutiny, the General both stalked and eluded us all at once. He did not engage his enemies or his lovers.

Up until now, I had reconciled myself to his scrutiny and elusion. I drew my hands over my belly where his child grew. I wanted to say, *You've marked me, you've won, now let us be kind to one another. The time has come for the test to end.* But instead, I said, "Why are you so protective of a man who wants nothing more than to kill you?"

He took a deep breath, then spoke as if his own words were prying him apart, "It's not Black Hawk I'm protecting, Mary."

"Who then?"

"My children." He paused and looked at me as I absorbed the measure of his words. He tented his fingers, then moved his hands in decisive arcs from the wrists as he spoke. "If I were to go after Black Hawk now, without straight evidence of what he's done, if I were to send troops after him to do a cold-blooded killing or do it myself . . ."

The General spoke so tentatively that it was like watching a fox stepping into the sunlight from the skirt of a wood. I felt that if I made the smallest errant sound he would step back into the shadows again. I rested my cheek against his shoulder.

He spoke about his past with percussive force. "When I was a young officer, during the last war, I saw what the British did to people when they passed through a town. And I made a pact with myself . . . if I am given any discretion, my army won't be an agent of death. I try to keep a larger view of this frontier and everyone who lives upon it. I think of my army as being as an ice lake. And when the native people and the white settlers try to cross that lake, the ice forces them to approach one another slowly and respectfully, cautious of the ground they tread upon. I won't kill Black Hawk because I don't like what it bodes for my sons."

My army. *My* sons. "Henry, what are you saying?"

"I won't kill Black Hawk out of malice. I don't want my sons to suffer the penance for my actions or carry that kind of legacy around with them; the kind of blood corruption that springs from murder."

I shook my head in mute rejection of his dark ideal. How could he declare that our children would suffer for his sins in some Old Testament blood attainder?

"I won't kill Black Hawk, even though it would be convenient to do so. I won't do it."

He held his hands out before him, scrutinizing them for traces of something I could not imagine. I, too, found myself looking at his knuckles and his long fingers. He spoke like a man guilty of having done a crime that no one knew about. He did not fear what might transpire in the future, rather, he spoke to me in vague terms about what had come to pass.

But I refused to indulge him or his memories of distant winters. I rose from the bed. The floorboards creaked underfoot as he came up behind me and gripped my shoulders.

"Mary, you don't understand . . . what I'm trying to tell you is . . ."

I pulled away from him, he confused me with this talk. I muttered, "How can you speak of curses on our children?"

"I'm not trying to scare you. You're always asking me to tell you about—"

"Then tell me about you, not curses on our children. I don't understand why you wish for bad luck and misfortune. I don't understand you, Henry."

He lifted his hands from me, then brusquely left our bedroom.

I wish I had listened more carefully when he spoke about what frightened him. I wish I had not interrupted him, for he might have told me something that could have closed the distance between us. But I believed all of forever waited for us. I had all the time in the world.

I heard him crossing into the library. I padded in after him, tying my wrap about me. He lit the candles in the wall cressets and those upon the reading table nearest his favorite chair. The room smelled of coffee and tobacco, of charred wicks and book dust. He poured himself two fingers of bourbon, opened a newspaper and shielded himself with it. The General read the newspaper with his spectacles low on his nose. He rested his left elbow upon the chair arm, and held the long slope of his forefinger to thumb at his brow, sheltering his vision from any unpleasant distraction that might enter the room. At the moment, I was his unpleasant distraction.

I leaned against the wall opposite him with my hands under my spine. He pretended not to notice me. I studied the creases around his eyes and memorized the sunspots on his temples and the backs of his hands. This could be the last time I see you, I thought, and here we are, arguing.

I removed the paper from his hands. He did not push me away when I laid my cheek against his chest. I listened to his breathing. I snaked my arms about his waist. The skin of his back felt smooth and warm where the muscles fanned out above his waist. I traced the tip of my small finger to the knobs of his spine, and a tremor of fear went through me.

I said, "I'm sorry. I don't want you to go away angry. I don't want you to go away at all."

He said nothing, but he embraced me.

I ventured, "Promise you'll write to me. Tell me the truth. If you don't, I'll be forced to subsist on the lies others tell me. Promise me?"

He put his fingers in my hair. I felt them glide up the back of my head and come to rest upon my temple. I felt his lips above my brow. "Which version of the truth do want me to share with you, Mary?"

"Your version. Your version is all I care to hear."

I should have known better than to ask for the one thing he could never give me.

MY knees hurt from kneeling on the plank floor, and my lower back ached persistently. I did not want this task of packing my husband's things away for his campaign. There was such finality about it, as if I were folding and tucking away the short days we'd passed together.

Despite the pin neatness of our home, we were not spared cotton time and awoke to silky drifts of cottonwood achenes that lofted like powder snow, sticking to damp skin and wafting up the nostrils into the throat. I breathed in the heated July afternoon and coughed in anticipation of the languid float of seed coming toward me. But I had too much work before me to fret over untidiness. I could hear Dahlia scrubbing linens on the lawn, singing plaintively to herself, just a few rods away from my window.

> O let my children fight right on
> Upon the mountain, down in the valley
> You goin to reap just what you sow.

I leaned over the sill and cast a withering look in her direction. The sun-filled heat of the morning reflecting off the yellowing grass felt like a hostile, solid force. I could hear the noises coming from the landing where the troops were loading provender and munitions onto the steamer packets. Dahlia did not care to notice me. I coughed in protest, causing her to sing even louder. Having no effect on her, I resigned myself to packing the General's trunk.

The General's mahogany mess chest, a gift from President Monroe, was squared away at the bottom of the trunk. The flocked velvet lining in the compartments had preserved fragile Sèvres china cups, candlesticks and a coffeepot in perfect condition. But the General preferred his tin coffeepot and banged-up pewter bowls. There was a brass plate on the inside of the lid engraved:

TO BRIG. GEN. HENRY ATKINSON, FOR VALOROUS SERVICES RENDERED THE NATION, 1819.

I wrapped his favorite books in stationery paper, securing them with ribbon, to protect the pages from damp. He would not read them, but I believed the more I crowded his trunk with talismans from home, the greater protection would be afforded him. I removed the dark hair from his brush, cradling a soft nest of it in my palm, and I put it into my hair receiver. I would plait a bracelet of his hair entwined with mine and wear it for luck until he returned safely home to me. I placed his hairbrush into the small daub kit along with his razor and strop, cakes of soap, a bone-handled toothbrush and salt. I enclosed a few shoe nails in the event the heel plates of his boots came loose. Then I put the Sully oil miniature of myself atop his shirts.

I lifted the corner of the blanket on our bed. It held the scent of the two of us together. With careful precision, I clipped a corner and placed the small swatch atop his spare uniform coat. I touched the fabric of his shirt one last time before I shut the lid.

I rose from the floor and patted the front of my skirt free of dust and cottonwood seed, then looked around the room, wondering if there was anything I had forgotten. I wanted to show him that I too could be fastidious and conscientious. I opened the wardrobe doors and searched the bottom boards for small objects. I tugged open the drawers of the chiffonier, but all the necessaries had been packed. I nodded my satisfaction with my efforts and, wiping my hands on my apron, strode into the library, thinking to check his writing desk.

His words came back to me: *You are not to touch my writing desk.*

Seating myself, I opened the middle drawer. I shifted its contents to have a better look. Sticks of red sealing wax rolled into a corner of the drawer. I lifted his stamp, engraved HA, in Spencerian script, and there saw a notched lever.

Mary Bullitt, you are too curious by half.

Isn't that what he said of me on the day we planted our garden?

I touched the lever gingerly and heard a spring releasing from somewhere around my knees. Pushing the chair back, I tilted my head and frowned at the underside of the desk.

A small secret drawer protruded by my left knee.

I stared at it, wondering if I should push it back into its place without looking. Obviously a secret drawer was meant to hold secrets. I had begun to believe the General might trust me a little, and to look into this drawer would imply a distinct lack of trust and a boatload of snoopiness on my part. Wouldn't it? I touched the edge of the drawer.

I wouldn't look.

I squeezed my eyes shut tightly.

If I just felt about . . . what harm was there in feeling about inside the drawer without looking? I was doing just that when my fingertips came upon something supple and small, with a leather cord—a pouch that fit into the palm of my hand.

I opened my eyes.

It was a small deerskin bag, worked with blue beads and porcupine quill in a fanciful design, heavy with small objects. I loosened the drawstring and emptied the bag's contents on the desk. There was a bear tooth. A bit of bird feather. A lump of lead. One mountain lion claw. A nondescript clump of fur. One dried scrap of flower. And a tiny note, replete with misspellings, written on parchment in a wavering hand:

> bare for pwer, feather egle for brav,
> tree cat klaw to kil yur emmy, fox klever
> and (indecipherable).
> thees mak u live fur evvr.

I held my hand to my bodice to calm the gimlet pierce in my vitals.

These make you live forever.

Though I shook with fury, I knew a cold resolve. With the side of my palm, I scraped the objects, note and bag into my left hand and crossed the room. The day was hot, but I built a fire. When the flames flicked steady

over the logs, I threw the pouch and its contents into the hearth. I watched
the childish note catch the sparks.

Make you live forever.

I lifted the shovel and forced the bag deeper between the logs to speed
its destruction, then held my knuckles to my mouth. I took a deep breath.
Why would a man keep such a thing if it didn't come from a woman he
loved? I wavered and considered trying to dig the little bag out. I should not
have burned something that belonged to the General. I paused. No. No, I
had a right to be indignant, didn't I? Let it burn. I'd meet his betrayal with
one of my own. I returned to the desk, rearranged the contents, then closed
the secret drawer.

I sensed a presence on the threshold and spun around guiltily. I hadn't
felt so acutely bad since I was thirteen and my Calvinist governess found me
standing with a pair of pinking shears over her two sliced up dresses. Her
dresses looked as if they'd been chewed by some saw-toothed beast. I took
a deep breath, clasped both hands tightly before my waist to keep them
from trembling. But I felt the color creeping over my face from my neck to
my eyebrows.

"Philip! You startled me."

"Oh, sorry about that, Mary. I hope you don't mind me stopping by unannounced."

"Don't be silly, I'm always eager to see you. Come in."

My cousin was dressed in gray work fatigues and a forage cap crowned
with regulation yellow lace. It was a hideous uniform, but practical for the
labor of rolling barrels up the steamer planks. In the space of one year,
Philip seemed to have grown from a boy into a man. He was no longer frail
and slender, but had become muscular. His pale complexion was now
weather stained, and he comported himself with a new confidence.

He lifted his nose in the air and sniffed. "Mary, what are you cooking?"

My hands fluttered to my face and the back of my neck. I smiled weakly.
"Nothing, I was just burning . . . ah, paper."

Philip tugged at his collar, and his auburn hair fell over his forehead. He
nodded absently, and surveyed the room. "I wanted to see you before I had
to go. I don't know what to expect tomorrow. The boys tell me boarding for
a campaign is a frenzy. So this might be my last opportunity to visit."

"Then please sit. Would you like something to drink?"

"No. You sit too. And stop rubbing your hands on your apron, you'll wear
the skin away from your finger bones."

"Philip, you must promise me you will be cautious."

He shifted in the chair and squared his shoulders, but then said rather bashfully, "No chance of me getting hurt. I'm going to be the General's tent mate. How about that?"

"That's the best possible news." I looked away from him, at a squad of mounted officers riding past our window. "The whole camp seems bursting with excitement. Are you packed?"

"I am, Mary. I'm eager to see what the Indian country is about, having heard so many stories, and none of them true. I've written a letter to my mother, would you mind posting it for me?"

"Of course I'll post it for you." I took the letter from him and studied the address. "How is your mother getting along?"

Philip colored dark red. "You know that when my father passed, so did the money?"

"Yes, I know."

"Mother pretends not to mind, but I know she minds well enough. She's sixty-one this year. Some days, I begin to fold money into the letters I write her, but then I can't bring myself to do it. I can't send the governor's daughter five dollars. She's an awfully proud woman."

I gazed out the window, thinking of Catherine Esten Cooke sitting alone in that big house in Loudon County, Virginia. In 1776, the British navy captured an American warship off the coast of Bermuda, and a thirty-year-old naval surgeon named Stephen Cooke was delivered to Governor John Esten as a prisoner of war. It was a most delightful incarceration wherein Dr. Cooke roamed the island at will, attending cotillions, concerts and dinner parties. Though soon exchanged, Cooke often returned to Bermuda, and in 1782, he married Catherine Esten, the British governor's sixteen-year-old daughter. The couple lived in St. George, where the lilies bloomed in profusion. Philip was named for that place.

I came out of my reverie, murmuring, "I remember you telling me about the lilies."

"Mother talked about lilies before she gave me bad news. She told me about the blood cup lilies when Father died, she told me about the orange-freckled lilies before I was forced to go to West Point at fourteen. I don't think I much care for lilies."

"Will you write to me, Philip? You can include your letters with the General's. I'm sure he won't object in the least."

"I most certainly will write to you."

I nodded, but then we both fell silent. A squad of bandsmen shuffled by, carrying serpentines and drums. We listened to them chattering about the departure. Philip took a deep breath and said in an embarrassed way, "Yes, well, here's the other thing I came to tell you. I know what I am going to make of myself, Mary."

"Oh?"

"I have purchased for myself a journal and a mahogany traveling writing kit. There are plenty of fellows back East earning a fine fee for writing western military adventures, and most of them don't know what they're writing about. Me? I can write from experience on the frontier."

I admit I wasn't paying attention to Philip. I glanced guiltily at the fireplace once again, speculating on what the General would do when he discovered my little crime.

"Philip, if you have a spare moment, write to me and tell me what the General is about, even the little things."

My cousin stiffened. "You mean *spy* on the General, don't you? I won't spy for you, Mary, not on my commanding officer."

It was my turn to blush, for Philip's bad opinion of me. "Philip, how could you think such a thing? While you are having your grand adventure with the Lake Nations, I'm left behind to conjure all manner of horror tales about the both of you lying injured on some field. That is why you must write to me. To reassure me. I'm bound to hear all sorts of rumors that aren't true. After all, the General is going up to the country where Black Hawk— and that awful Bright Sun—malinger. I don't trust her. Do you?"

Philip squinted at me and asked, "Trust who? Who are you talking about, Mary?"

"Never mind."

"Be careful, cousin. And . . ."

"What, Mary?"

"Look after the General for me, will you?"

BEFORE sunrise, on the landing at the base of the bluff, the air smelled of smoke off the steamer boilers and the dense marshy odor of a thirsty river. Servants lofted burning oil rags atop stobs along the rickety wooden stair. The river made soft lapping sounds against the strand on that torch-painted night. I stood by the willows so near the General that the line of our bodies touched from shoulder to knee as we observed the commotion of the boarding. The soldiers' families lined the shore, the women's pastel gowns billowed in the darkness like the sails of ghostly clippers. A few infants wailed, but most of the children were so sleepy they made no sound. Some curled up in the grass and slumbered in their nightclothes.

Three stern-wheel steamers, the *Essex,* the *General Hamilton* and the *In-*

diana chuffed at anchor. The iron-plated pilothouses were pocked with bullet dents. The General told me that Indians shot at the pilothouses purely for sport. The packets gave off flags of smoke that hung in the still air. Now and again, I covered my nose with a handkerchief, for it was like breathing burnt oil into the lungs. I saw Surgeon Gale, looking ghoulish in his black uniform, directing the loading of crates of medical supplies onto the *Essex*. The engines of the steamer packets groaned as the rousters fed them corder. A faint glow of candlelight could be seen from the pilothouse and the navigator's cabin, and candles hung in small lamps from the deck ceilings.

The General held his bay and watched the regiments assemble.

A bead of perspiration lingered on his temple. The strand was crowded with light artillery drays and troops in various attire. It was eerie, the way the regiments emerged from the darkness and came into sharp relief as they neared the candlelight reflecting off the water. The infantrymen in blue uniform coats and white trousers looked miserable under their tall plumed leather shako hats, designed to impress the enemy with the soldier's height. There were even a spattering of bandsmen unaccountably dressed for a concert performance in red-and-gold coats. The troops filed on to the packets silently, except for the sound of their boots on the boarding planks and the soft clanking of their belongings jumbling about in their haversacks.

The horses whickered in the darkness and stomped impatiently.

I turned my attention to a fine-looking squad of young riflemen standing at ease along the hills. They wore gray uniforms with a high choker collar and carried pear-shaped brass powder flasks, leather-strapped black bags and haversacks. *A soldier's uniform must fit him tightly so that he never forgets the authority of the state,* I mused, wondering where I had heard that said before. Probably the General quoting someone else. A few burly sergeants hauled a caisson loaded with kegs of whiskey for the daily ration of one-half gill.

I scrutinized the passing columns of blue and gray and red uniforms, searching for Cousin Philip, but I could not pick him out. A few riflemen had been assigned to shoot stray dogs that pestered the processional and the horses. Now and then, I heard the sharp crack of a rifle report.

I gathered my paisley shawl about my shoulders against the damp chill. An order was given for a cadence, and the band played the "British Grenadiers," a curious selection, to my mind.

Billy led the General's horse up the plank. I put my hand to the General's arm. Though I knew protocol would never allow such a thing, I wanted him to embrace me. I needed to feel his arms about me. He paused and contemplated me, as if there were something he had forgotten to say. I gave him a pleading look, then just as quickly, glanced down at my feet. But ever proper in the presence of his men, the General granted me nothing more than the slightest bow.

He said, "I shall see you before Christmas, Mrs. Atkinson." And he turned on his heel, then walked away and up the plank.

In that moment I experienced a sharply limned premonition. It coursed through my veins, merciless and incandescent. All of the gentle months that had been allotted to us had come to a close. And I felt as if I had wasted them. I envisioned the years before us lined up like peddlers at the back door, waiting patiently to deliver things we didn't want to own.

I could not see him through the gloom as he took up his place on the officers' deck. I stood on my tiptoes, pulling the shawl tighter still and strained at the *Essex*. The packet whistles blew, signaling the time for departure. A triumphant cry went up from hundreds of men as the paddle wheels battered the water. They made a thrumming vibration that I could feel into the center of my being. The water was low, ribbed out with gravel shoals and sandbars that threatened a slow journey upriver.

I stood on the shore until I could no longer hear nor see the steamships, when the strand was again given over to darkness and the promise of another morning. Behind me, a thicket of indigo bush spread its heavy panicles, dark as wine, in a fragrant curtain. The leaves made a silky noise as they trembled in the dark breeze. The night insects whirred about my ears in blind search for me.

The other wives trailed away, but I stayed in place, staring at the fleshy waves, dreading the days to come. A haze formed over the river. It concealed the water from me and spiraled white the length of the strand. When it drifted over me, I breathed in the cold mist, and I steeled myself to the inevitable. I would have to wait and nurture hope as my husband hastened to the stronghold of his mortal enemy, Black Hawk—and to the village where a beautiful young Sauk woman who loved him, waited for him.

II

Jefferson Barracks, Missouri, June 16, 1842

❧ If I want to know what happened during the seasons of war that Bright Sun spoke of over my husband's grave, I must commit a trespass. And now that Philip and the General are gone, I have the freedom to do as I wish. It is time I pieced the years together. So I rise wearily from the leather chair and step into the bedroom where my little son sleeps. I find the old trunk in the corner, covered by an embroidered linen sheet. I remove the sheet and read the dull brass plate over the trunk latch, engraved *Philip Saint George Cooke.*

I lift the lid noiselessly. Philip's civilian shirts, frock coats and trousers are tightly folded in layers. I lift each layer gingerly, searching for the journal. I see a bundle of ribbon-tied letters addressed to Philip in a scrawly feminine hand, letters from his mother, his sisters and schoolgirls in Virginia who once admired him. There are vests, kidskin boots and a bottle of clove cologne; vestiges of Philip's former life as a Virginia gentleman.

I find the calfskin-bound journal under Philip's white cambric nightshirts. After closing the bedroom door, I clutch the stolen treasure against my ribs and take up my place in the General's chair. My heart is pounding as I look at Philip's journal. It is locked with a leather thong that attaches the back cover to the front. I hesitate as I touch the binding. This book holds the secrets Philip recorded when he accompanied the General to the Indian country. I am sure it contains glimpses into my husband's life that I was never afforded while he was alive.

If I wish to understand those lost years, I must violate Philip's privacy, breach his confidence and destroy his property. I take a deep breath.

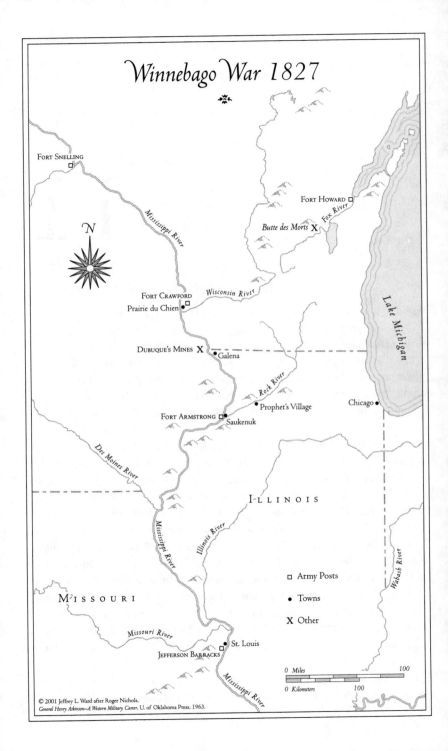

Winnebago War 1827

Fort Snelling □

N

Mississippi River

Fort Howard □

Butte des Morts X

Fox River

Fort Crawford □
Prairie du Chien •

Wisconsin River

Lake Michigan

Dubuque's Mines X
• Galena

Rock River

Fort Armstrong □ • Prophet's Village
Saukenuk

Chicago •

Des Moines River

I L L I N O I S

Mississippi River

Illinois River

Wabash River

□ Army Posts
• Towns
X Other

M I S S O U R I

Missouri River

□ St. Louis
Jefferson Barracks

Mississippi River

0 Miles   100

0 Kilometers   100

© 2001 Jeffrey L. Ward after Roger Nichols,
General Henry Atkinson—A Western Military Career, U. of Oklahoma Press, 1963.

Then I cut the leather thong and open Philip's journal. The General often teased Philip, calling him the most prolific diarist in the Army of the Frontier. Philip is reported to have left three trunks full of diaries, journals and manuscripts addressed to his brothers (who are published authors), at Fort Leavenworth. These pages are cross written. Being short of paper, Philip turned the pages on their side and wrote from bottom to top.

He recorded whole conversations. There are long musings on philosophical questions and love poems of the alabaster-breast variety to Rachel Hertzog, a judge's daughter in Philadelphia. I set those aside as they are none of my concern. I flip over the first third of the book, detailing his days as a cadet at West Point and his first year at Jefferson Barracks, though my eye is keen to any sentence bearing my name. He notes passages he intends to publish by marking them with a star; he has tucked a letter from Lindsay & Blakiston, Publishers of Philadelphia, into the end paper. I sink deeper into the old leather chair and introduce myself to the General's world.

Journal of Lt. Philip St. George Cooke
23 July 1827

I write this over a crate marked ONE HUNDRED U.S. ARMY TROUSERS that now serves as the casket of a Dutch stoker. He was scorched to death when he overloaded the steamer's boiler. I do not know his name. Johnston said the stoker smelled sweet when he was cooked alive. Given he was cooked, he will keep nicely until we can bury him on Rock Island. By that time, I might be dead too. If the Indians kill me out here, I want Brother John to dig me up and rebury me on the green lawn of my mother's house in Loudon County, near Leesburg. Because they are going to kill me. I am sure of it. My only hope is that this journal will somehow get to John. I want him to know how it was for me.

John, if you are reading this, I am probably dead. And this is how it was.

We began our hunt for the Winnebago RedBird after passing over the Des Moines Rapids. The day I was almost killed began hissing hot. The gallinippers were bent on making a living from me, so I slapped them from my face in an unfriendly way. Our boats formed up a line one hundred yards distant from one another as we moved upriver. There being no wind, the boiler smoke fell on us like a fog. A steamer paddle makes a lot of noise. If I were to stand on the shore, I could feel the steamers passing by through the rumblings in my leg bones.

I was ordered to the Texas deck to join the General. He put a field glass to his eye, looking off to the east. Ignoring me, he cursed for a few minutes straight without once repeating himself. He sure swears fluently.

Soon the rest of us glimpsed the cause of the General's worry. There, on the east shore of the Mississippi, were two thousand mounted Saukies. Their faces were painted half white, quarter green, quarter red. They looked like raptors about to rip us to ribbons. Those Saukies sent up their roar like screeching demons so that my ears throbbed at the pain of their yelling.

The drummers sounded the long roll. The General gave the order to position the swivel gun and four-pound guns over the east shore. I ran down the stairs to the boiler deck, tore the paper tip off a cartridge for my musket and spilled gunpowder all down my lower lip. I got the unpleasant taste of linseed oil and turpentine on my tongue, and it stayed there too long a while. My hands shook as I tried to affix my flint. Then I prayed, Priming, please be dry. I said to myself, "We got us one shot, sir. That is all."

I felt a severe stomach wracking when I looked up from my musket. The General gave the order for the *Essex* to hove to and drop plank. He couldn't mean that, I thought. No man in his right mind would bring us in close to those Saukies. Feeling my guts boil near to exploding, I searched the deck for a slosh pot to ease myself. Anyhow, there I was, tending to my business, when the General gave the order for his bay to be brought up from the stern for him. Seeing this, about a half dozen others volunteered to join him and had their mounts brought round too. I couldn't be the only one of the staff left huddling on the boat, so I did the same.

But not in the same spirit of self-sacrifice.

The General lashed a brace of pistols along his saddle, but held his Hawken out in his right hand, parallel to the ground, as if it were a rudder of sorts. The Saukies made insulting noises as we came down the plank, whistling and sniggering. I looked back in mournful longing at the three boats behind me. The decks were full of soldiers at arms. There I was, under a hot sun, nose to nose with the Saukies. Behind me, 310 not very accurate gunmen had orders to shoot into the crowd if the General were taken. I gritted my teeth and girded my belly for gunfire taking off the back of my skull.

If Black Hawk wants to shoot the General through the heart, now would be a good time for it, I thought. I looked at nature's children. The faces of the Saukies bulged as if they had a generous plug of chew in both cheeks. But then I saw the reason for it. The Saukies held bullets in their mouths, spit them into the muzzle so as not to require a greased patch, because a wet ball sticks to the powder. They hooted for a while. But seeing they had no effect on the General, they all sort of fell silent and just stared at us. I guess they were as muddled as we were about what to do next.

The General looked up and down the line as if these were his troops and he was having a review that displeased him. When he saw the Saukies wearing blue U.S. Army uniforms from the last war, some of them shot raggedy with bullet holes, the General moved his tongue over his back teeth as if they were sticking with popped corn.

Keokuk greeted the General, but in a manner not too friendly. Bright Sun behaved as if the General were an unpleasant acquaintance. On her back, she had a papoose board, and a little infant slept there. Keokuk wore bits of lead on tin strands pierced through his ears and a bunch of sumac tied to his hair roach. He came forward and asked, "Zha'becka?"

I guess that's what these Indians call the General—Zha'becka.

Another shout went up from the Saukies, and more shots were fired in the air. All their guns and a few of their swords were British made. Keokuk yelled something that was echoed down the line. Those Saukies looked huge sitting their horses, painted fierce and smelling all musky like the hides they wore. Their eyes told us they wouldn't quarter doubt over killing us.

The General gave the command for a few companies to disembark and form up with the riflemen in advance of the infantry. I heard a lot of thundering as the men came down the plank behind me and formed up lines. I tried to keep my expression firm, but my left eyelid twitched, and my shako slid down my forehead on account of the sweat springing out of my head.

Keokuk motioned the General to follow him. Then he and Bright Sun turned their horses in the direction of the village. I thought, "That's it? They're letting us through?"

So in our group there was me, Lieutenant Albert Sidney Johnston, a big gap-toothed bastard who pesters and bedevils me to no end; Major Kearny, who almost never says nothing at all; and the General, of course, along with some others who I won't mention here.

The Saukies began breaking up into curious but menacing groups that followed us as we rode away from the safety of the boats. Saukenuk put the white frontier towns to shame. I guessed there were about ninety fine, large bark-slab houses, or wickiups, facing east. The streets were broad and straight, and young braves sat before these wickiups smoking in neat ells. Upon seeing us, some shouted insults we could not interpret and for that I am grateful.

As we rode up the broad village main, the General paid particular attention to the British flag drooping off an effigy pole in the middle of the road. "Your friends have been here," he said, grinning at Kearny, who was once a British prisoner of war. We rode past three huge piles of lead, at least forty-thousand dollars worth—just sitting there for the taking—that the Sauk had mined during the summer.

Keokuk led us into his wickiup. Once inside, I realized that this house was nearly sixty feet long, constructed of bark slabs with a pitching roof. I was careful not to walk upon the rush mats underfoot as my boots were muddy. Two long platforms stretched the length of the wickiup. A couple hundred dollars' worth of trade goods were piled high on those platforms. I wondered if Keokuk was planning to open a general store.

Bright Sun, our translator, sat on the General's right side. Apparently, she had gotten over her bad mood. When she sat by the General, she moved her shoulders so as to cause her hair to swish like a horse tail. The General stretched his arms over his head as if he were thinking of a nap and Saukenuk was the most comfortable place in the world. Since he had confronted those Saukies on the shore, his eyes were brighter and his face was all lit up with excitement. His expression was one I have seen on men who win at gambling.

Looking into the back shadows of the wickiup, I spied six womanly figures, seated along the wall. Johnston nudged me with a wink. "Keokuk has got himself six wives. I'd either be busy splicing with them, or I'd be gone deranged because of them. Don't know which."

"What is it you want from me, Zha'becka?" Keokuk asked.

The General said, "If the Sauk go to war with the Winnebago people, I will have no choice but to bring down the whole force of my army on Saukenuk."

Keokuk's mouth turned down and puffed out. He rubbed his eyebrow with one finger and thought about it. The General leaned forward like a man on the edge of a gorge and asked, "Am I mistaken in thinking you can control your Peace Band?" Keokuk scratched his arm in a lazy, amiable way. "I can control them if it is worthwhile for me to do so, but Black Hawk's British men do as they please. And you must understand that I feed six wives."

The General's eyes looked like slits. He said, "Johnston, bring your saddle here."

"Is he going to feed my saddle to Keokuk's wives?" Johnston asked.

The General said the Great Father cared for his Sauk children, but then he threatened the Sauk with ruin if they made war on the white people. The General gave Johnston's saddle to Keokuk. "I want a box of money too,"

Keokuk said. The General gave him twenty dollars in specie out of his own pocket. Then we left Keokuk's wickiup. And I sighed in relief, believing all of our worries about the Sauk were at an end.

Which only goes to show how green I am.

The General paused, looking up and down the wide streets of Saukenuk. "I would like to pay a visit to Singing Bird." Seeing everyone else around me tighten up, I asked who Singing Bird was.

"Black Hawk's wife," the General said, pinching the bridge of his nose. Bright Sun motioned in the direction of Black Hawk's lodgings, but Major Kearny looked flummoxed.

Kearny said, "Sir? Are you sure you want to go to Black Hawk's *house?*"

"He came to *my* house uninvited, didn't he?"

Behind us, Keokuk shouted a proclamation of peace to the Peace Band, who were huddled round him. Our parade rounded a broad corner. Bright Sun told us to halt before a fine-looking wickiup with a bough arbor and green-and-yellow rush mats at the entry. The wickiup was surrounded by a thick fringe of young tobacco plants.

We found a Sauk woman sitting under the bough arbor before a cook fire adjacent to a wickiup. I could not guess her age. Upon seeing the General, the woman looked away shyly, then wagged her finger at us in friendly remonstrance. Singing Bird—*Asshewqua*—wasn't Sauk. She looked so different from the rest of them. Kearny told me she was a Cherokee, and that Black Hawk had captured her when she was a girl, during a raid down south. I thought her a figure of beauty. She motioned us to sit, but I felt skittish, waiting for Black Hawk to jump out of the shadows at every turn.

Mats made of cattail flags hung above my head. I sat near a few poles covered with ropes of dried pumpkin, I looked at my mat. Four surly red panthers returned my stare. As the General settled in, a huge medicine bag, a buffalo-skin monstrosity, hanging from the rafters in the northwest corner caught my attention. I got to my feet, crossed the room and reached my hand to touch its crackling black surface, but Singing Bird, Bright Sun and the General all hollered at me in unison. I jerked my hand away quickly.

The General grumbled, "You idiot, they think a white man touching that bag would mean the end of the world. Sit down. Keep your mouth shut." I stared at the Trojan buffalo and fully expected Black Hawk to jump out of it and kill us all.

Singing Bird sat on a mat with her legs curled under her to her left, a bowl of blackberries at her side. When she spoke, Bright Sun translated her words. "You are getting fat, Zha'becka. Men do not get fat unless their women make them happy."

The General patted his belly and grinned, "My woman does not cook."

"Do you make this woman sit up late by the fire, worrying where you have gone?"

The General shook his head in mock sorrow and pointed to his head. "Now that I am a gray-hair I do not wander around so much during the night."

Singing Bird looked sadly over her shoulder, under the eaves of her wickiup and off in the direction of the horse pasture. She wiped her eyes with the back of her hand. They looked solemnly at one another.

"I remember the day I last saw you. Every moment of it. I keep count of the winters," the General said, and his face was drawn down like that of a man about to be shot.

"Black Hawk remembers the day too. The two of you are much alike. Perhaps that is the reason for the trouble."

"Perhaps," the General said. "Then again, the reason for the trouble could be you."

Singing Bird smiled almost flirtatiously. The General seemed pleased and continued, "I come to you, Singing Bird, because I know that you, more than any other, can help Black Hawk to know what is right."

Singing Bird put the bowl off to the side and looked past the General. "Zha'becka, why do you come to my house? Heh. You must wish for death to do this!"

I got nervous and looked over my shoulder. Johnston did too. The General lifted his hands as if to placate her. He said, "Singing Bird, I do not believe anything frightens you, least of all Black Hawk's anger. But I fear for you and your children. You must tell Black Hawk that joining the fight with the Winnebago RedBird will be dangerous."

Singing Bird looked sharply at him. "How much money did Keokuk take from you?" When he didn't answer, Singing Bird seemed to read the General's mind, and she scoffed, "Keokuk is rotten as the inside of a fallen tree. And living peacefully with the Chemokemon is more dangerous than fighting them. Heh. My husband was attacked by the Chemokemon when he hunted his own lands. He was beaten by three white men who stole his gun and his horse. My husband is a proud man, Zha'becka. First you ask him not to fight with RedBird. Then you tell him to give you Saukenuk. He cannot give him the land where his dead lie buried. You will pull your plows over our bones. You would not give him the land where your father lies buried."

The General and Singing Bird stared at one another, but it was the General who looked away first.

Singing Bird said, "And the British have never lied to him. He will never forsake his British fathers just as he would never forsake me. My husband will never surrender to you. He will die to protect Saukenuk. You and I have no quarrel, Zha'becka. But your Chemokemon have put a gun to the hearts of my people. What choice do we have . . . do *I* have?"

"Singing Bird, I would never put a gun to your heart. You must trust me when I pledge that I would never harm the children of your body."

"I fear the day will come when you will do just that, Zha'becka." Singing Bird stared pointedly at Bright Sun. "And there is something you should know. It is the *women* who urge their men to follow my husband. It is our *women* who plant the corn. The Chemokemon want to take our corn lands. Heh. Even now, they tear up our fences, they claim our corn fields for their own. They do not let our women harvest the corn they have planted. So you see, it is the *women* who stand behind my husband and urge their men to fight with him. You know, Zha'becka, women can have very strong ideas. Stronger than the men most times."

The General looked in surprise at Bright Sun, who cast a complacent sideward glance at her infant. Singing Bird said quietly, "If you fight us, you will find me standing beside my husband. And though I cannot speak for her, I think Bright Sun, too, will fight with us."

The General put both hands to his temples and winced at the floor. But after a long silent while, he took Singing Bird's hands in his. The General bowed good-bye to her, and Singing Bird's mouth quavered as if she were about to cry. She followed us out and watched us leave.

I was curious about the history of that friendship and what gave rise to it. Later that night, over two fingers of bourbon, I tried to ask the General about both Singing Bird and Bright Sun, but he changed the subject and would not speak of it.

The General was grim as we rode out of Saukenuk. Doubtless he had greater hopes for his meeting with Singing Bird. Our parade passed along the fine streets, by the large, neat wickiups. I could see women bent over the knee-high corn growing on the bluffs behind the village, and I thought upon Singing Bird's message: *It is the women who stand behind Black Hawk . . . because of the corn.* At the base of the corn-tilled bluffs, I saw a cemetery. A few young men were tending graves and painting the posts that marked each burial plot.

I began to ask the General about that cemetery, when he ordered the scouts to scour the countryside for Black Hawk and RedBird. I was told to join the scouting party again. The same Saukies who met us at the landing watched us sullenly as we proceeded north along the river.

The weather was heavy, and I guessed we would have nighttime thunderstorms. The General rode with our party, directly ahead of me in the line. The cut banks of the river were lined with blooming mulberry trees. After a time, the landscape turned rough. We were surrounded by a heavy forest and by beetling crags of rock that came out of the river. Sometimes we sank in marshy holes that we couldn't see until we fell into them, because of the weeds.

As the afternoon wore on, our squad broke off from the rest of the company. We wound through the dense brush and wood. We scoured nettle patches for Black Hawk and the Winnebago RedBird until sundown, but we found nothing. I figured Black Hawk was smarter than to squat in poison ivy.

Then the skies opened; it rained pitchforks, and the lightning hit so close we could hear the crack! of wood splitting, and we could smell the burn. I touched the top of my head. Finding my hair still there, I gave my scalp a congratulatory pat. We rode back to the boats in the downpour. Off on a distant scarp, a blade of lightning stabbed a cluster of pine trees. That was something. When hit, the trees exploded, and sparks flew everywhere.

The General looked over at me, rain dripping from his chin and his hair going curly. He grinned as if he were having the time of his life. As I speculated what was going through his fertile brain, he shouted over the weather, "Just think, your West Point classmates are keeping books at the War Department about now. But this life . . . *this life has got flavor,* hasn't it, Mister Cooke!"

After last roll was called and the signal gun on the *Essex* sounded tattoo, we returned to our cabin. The General and I instantly took to our cots, being needful of sleep. But it was not to be.

Just as I was falling in, our cabin door burst open, and there stood Bright Sun, sobbing her heart out. As she had gone swimming to reach us, she dripped water all over the floor, but when I peeked into the papoose board on her back, I saw it was empty. I wondered where her little baby had gone to. As if to answer me, she pulled it out from under her sodden blanket and held it out at arm's length toward the General, before returning it to her back. He made a sympathetic tsking noise, and she ran to him, clinging to him. The General hushed her up and shoved her briskly from the cabin.

I sat up in my bed, listening to her weep. The General put his arms about her. That took me aback. He saw my shocked expression and shut the door. I heard him ordering the sergeant to find food and quarters for Miss Bright Sun and her child.

He came back to the cabin a few minutes after having left it and went to sleep. I have learned that Bright Sun is to join our expedition into the Winnebago country. The General says her services will be invaluable there. We shall see.

The General doesn't like being in the cabin except for sleeping. Most nights, he is on the pilot deck alone. I can see him because of his pipe. One night, I invite myself up there, and he offers me a smile of whiskey. Death has a way of making me want to be full sewn up—drunk, that is.

The General smoked on the pilot deck and looked off at the dark hills passing away from us. The stars were low and bright as New York nickels and seemed to swing over us. I could hear bats whirring over the flyway. Out of respect for him, I waited for the General to speak first.

Finally he said, "April."

"Sir?"

"April."

"Oh?"

"When my war comes with Black Hawk, it will be in April. Of some year. Not far off."

"Is that so?"

"The Sauk live in Saukenuk from April to October. One April, they'll come back from winter camp to find Saukenuk full of white squatters. *Pioneers.*" The General said those words fiercely as he sipped his whiskey. He drew a breath and continued, "*Brave pioneers.* They like to paste together legends about themselves being courageous before the *savages.*"

I had never heard the General hurl inflammatory talk like that before. I mumbled, "But, sir, their lives are tough."

The General's countenance was partially obscured by shadows, but his eyes looked wily.

"Calling themselves *pioneers* is a neat way to excuse themselves from the obligations of their faith. Unless the Commandments have been amended to allow murdering, stealing, cheating and lying. Has that happened lately, Mister Cooke?"

"I don't know, sir. I haven't been back East in a while."

"Mister Cooke, do you think there can be such a thing as a *Christian* soldier?"

I think I must have looked panicked by his question, because the General laughed at me. Mercifully, Kearny and Johnston came up to the pilot deck to let us know we would have roasted venison for our late supper. We had eaten earlier but were still hungry. It was a stringy buck brought down by a rifleman. This time of year, even the buffalo cows are thin and poor as they have just come round from calving. Johnston brought his damnable flute. He serenades us with songs about maidens floating facedown in Scottish lochs. Besides, he looks ridiculous playing it, being big as an elephant.

An express just arrived from Fort Snelling. Me and the General both got letters from Cousin Mary, neither of us had time to read them; a body can write a letter without it having to be long and longer. I adore that girl, but she does tend to go on. The important thing is the General received orders urging the Sixth Infantry to Fort Crawford. It was abandoned by the army, giving the Winnebago the idea that the army had run away from them in fear. We hear reports the Winnebago have closed the Mississippi at the mouth of the Wisconsin. We will travel north on the Mississippi, then make us a right turn on the Wisconsin River.

On to Winnebago country.

12

Jefferson Barracks, Missouri, Summer of 1827

⁂ I PAGE back through Philip's journal, rereading the lines wherein he speaks of Bright Sun's baby, of Bright Sun sitting beside the General at Saukenuk, of the General's apparent affection for Black Hawk's wife, Singing Bird—and I am at a loss. Philip writes just enough to raise even more questions and prompt more suspicions from my suspicious mind. This is precisely the sort of vexing that isn't good for a lonely widow left alone with her ruinous doubts and her vigorous imagination. These shadings of past events do not illuminate my understanding of my marriage to the General, but only nurture my speculations about him.

And despite Philip's comments, I was not and have never been one to "go on" in my letters. I simply believe a civilized letter should be possessed of a beginning, a middle and an end—as opposed to Philip's letters, which tended to be little more than a pitiful list of requests for ointments and salves, interspersed with complaints about his aching feet. Even so, I have to smile in remembrance of Philip, for I reciprocated his affection, I adored him in turn. Besides, I worried for him—and for my husband. The General's letters from the Indian country were suspiciously banal, filled with observations about the scenery, amusing anecdotes about the men and questions about my health. They were the sort of letters you'd write to a child, an elderly aunt—or a pregnant woman like me.

When he returned home from the Winnebago War, I peppered the General with questions until he held up his hand and laughingly said, "There was a little arguing and some distant gunplay, Mary; rest assured I was not involved. Look at me. Do I look like a man who has been shot at?" I scrutinized him; he cast a cautionary glance at my enormous belly, commented upon my delicate state before changing the subject and diverting my attention. Though I missed my husband terribly that summer, I enjoyed the company of Mama and Eloise, who came to look after me. Fearing for my well-being in his absence, the General had purchased steamer tickets for them to come on from Louisville.

On the day Mama arrived, the steamer *Josephine* was the thirtieth packet to berth at St. Louis, and the stage of the water was so excessive that the towpath at the base of the bluff was hidden. The *Josephine* idled in the channel and waited for a landing to clear along the levee. I could barely contain my excitement. I jumped from the carriage and ran through the mud, past the rousters dumping wooden crates and stacks of pelts onto the levee. I avoided the cranky mud clerks, who studied bills of lading and declared sugar missing and whiskey in short supply. The white plaster buildings on Rue de la Tour reflected the sunlight, the apple trees flowered along the shore and the fetid silt along the banks swarmed with flies.

The engines of the *Josephine* wheezed to a halt, and the plank slammed into the mud. The levee was chaotic with shouting laborers, horse traffic, frustrated passengers hollering at their servants to look after their baggage and frantic *chausseurs des bois* scrambling back and forth. A few genteel Frenchmen in surtouts were discharged from their carriages by wives who feared guests would be lost forever on the levee.

Mama took my face in her gloved hands. They bladed straight out from my cheeks and she exclaimed, "Why, Mary, you look fine as a carrot fresh scraped."

Eloise slid her hands around my enlarging waist. "Fine as all the root vegetables put together, then mashed with butter!"

A pilot aboard the Josephine screamed at some Indians floating by in bull boats with birch bags full of honey they'd come to sell in the city. "Move the fug out of the way, or be ground to mince, y'red bastards!"

Mama adjusted her bonnet and pretended not to hear this. She said brightly, "Where is your house, Mary? Can we see it from here?"

"No, but I can point out Uncle William's house to you. Shall we call upon them?"

"I think not," Mama said, tugging upon her waist, then peering off in the distance. "Perhaps tomorrow."

"Mama, who is bringing your valise and hampers?" I asked, standing on tiptoe to see around her. She waved blithely at her servants. "I have brought you a box of medicines; the Bateman's Pectoral drops, jalap, tartar emetic,

Essence of Peppermint by the King's Patent, calomel, a jar of leeches and a ball of hat lint to plug wounds."

Eloise clasped her hands behind her back and tapped a dainty toe at a snail in the mud. "And I've brought you ague, dysentery and dropsy so Mama can make herself feel useful while we're here."

Mama was brightly observant of St. Louis, remarking on how quaint and French it was, and as we passed out of the city, then through the gates of Jefferson Barracks, I sensed she was impressed by the grandeur of the place, the elegant old forest, the formal limestone buildings, the gardens at every turn. The carriage wheeled up before our house. I took Billy's hand and stepped down the pedal, then turned happily to Mama. She halted in mid-step, her face puckered with despair before she covered her nose and mouth with her handkerchief. Then she snapped away from me, and I saw her shoulders trembling.

"Mama!" I asked, "Do you wish to lie down?"

Mama heaved a sob into her handkerchief. "Oh, Mary, I never imagined what you meant by a 'modest' home. It is a hovel, isn't it?"

I shuffled uncertainly, looked up at my house, then back at Mama, who shuddered. She dabbed her red nose and squared her shoulders. "A life poorly furnished is miserably lived, and if you must live in a hovel, I shall see to it that my daughter has the most opulently decorated hovel in all of Missouri."

"But, Mama, I like my house. What's wrong with my house?"

"It's just so . . . so aggressively . . . *humble*, Mary."

"You've thrown Mama upon her beam ends once again," Eloise whispered admiringly.

The next day, there were mists over the river and over the streams we crossed. The few buckeye trees held back by the barrier of the tallgrass savanna looked in a fragile state, greening out timidly, with buds so small they looked like petit point. In a few weeks they would boast creamy yellow flowers. I crushed artemisia underfoot, and the woody stalks sent up a scent of evergreen and sage. I rolled my shoulders and lifted my face to the sun.

Eloise's thin voice trilled, "Where are you? Sister! Come out of hiding."

I was hiding from them because I had grown tired of their fussing and constant attention. I needed respite from their chattering and womanly hovering. I had drifted off to a place where they could not find me, even if they began their search at dawn and looked for me until sunset. The savanna of big bluestem leafed around me in mottled purple and red. The tall grass geysered upward, each stalk splitting into three fingers that seemed to beckon and tempt the scissor-tailed flycatchers into spying upon me. I watched them dive, flickering a snow-white underbelly, disappearing in a black flash of tail feathers. The sky over my head shone like a mirror, but I could see very little of it. I lay in the understory where the compass plants point their leaves due north and summon the lightning. The orange lilies powdered my dress when I rolled near to them, and the earth under my knuckles exhaled a moist and powdery odor.

I reclined in the tall grass, felt the roots of the giant plants embracing under me in intimate union, and I knew a reflective calm that sang through my blood. I turned aside, under the sun's heat, but was sheltered from its light as the forest of grass closed eight feet above my head. I felt the damp under my elbows, I breathed through my mouth and tasted the flavor of the air. I hollowed my tongue to drink in the fragrances around me.

I felt his presence in shadowy relief before I saw him.

I dared not breathe with him so close. I heard the trade bells jingling on Black Hawk's snakeskin armbands as his eyes bored at me through the branches, each leaf wavering before his countenance like a timorous spirit. He had followed me here. He had searched me out, and now I was alone, far from the rest of them, lying in the tallgrass like a sacrifice. Even if I could rise up fast enough, I could not outdistance him. He came near me steadily, his dark eyes inquisitive; with one hand he parted the grasses, waiting for me to run. That I did not attempt escape baffled him. I propped myself up on my elbows and watched him stepping toward me.

In a moment, Black Hawk crouched before me.

I was paralyzed with mute fear. I tried to set up a shout, but my voice did not issue. He crept closer and clasped one hand over my stockinged ankle, and with the other, pushed my skirt to my knee, then higher, where the stocking ended and the flesh of my leg was exposed. He paused, breathing through his mouth. I stared at his hand over my leg, the beauty of his fine bones against the green silk fabric.

He bent near enough that I could see the yellow flecks in his eyes, and I realized my need to share in his secret. I gave my consent by saying nothing. My eyes riveted upon his hands, pushing the silk up and up. He looked down at me, and then at himself, unfastened his breechclout and knelt over me. He took my face in his hands and forced me to look into his eyes as he thrust himself into me. I linked my feet around his slim waist, my hands slipped over the cool skin of his buttocks, I put my mouth to his neck and licked the salt from him.

The tall grass bristled against my bare skin, my skin was damp where he rubbed against me; bits of leaves and damp root flecked in my hair and over my skin, while the sun angled in the western corner of the sky.

These dreams of Black Hawk began the night the General left home for the Winnebago War. And each dream was more vivid than the last, leading me to believe I had admitted a storm-blooded apparition in my sleep. Each time, he slid his hands over my throat, then down my belly, and his original intent was lost in seduction. Yet I feared for him whenever he sought me out. I knew he required sustenance from me. I understood that he could not survive without joining to me. Outside the tallgrass there was nothing but danger waiting for him—perhaps oblivion. I watched him go, then tried to gather up the shredded remnants of my gown about me, covering myself in silk as green as corn leaves, my hair the color of the soil, my skin smelling of him.

All flesh is grass, says Isaiah somewhere in the Bible.

"Mary!" They edged through the savanna, looking alarmed, and Mama's heliotrope cologne drifted over me like a benediction. I lifted my gaze to her, and she knelt, then began plucking grass from my hair. "Are you faint?"

Eloise floated down beside Mama and tilted her narrow face at me. One of her hair combs had slipped out, and she looked as wild as if she had just stepped from the ark. She scrutinized the ground around me and narrowed her eyes.

"What were you doing here, Mary?"

"I must have fallen asleep."

Mama dropped a little and studied my eyes to diagnose my mood. I felt heavy and otherworldly all at once. Eloise reached out her bird-boned hand and touched the stalks where they had bent. Her eyes roamed suspiciously over me, then over the clearing I'd made for myself.

"Sister has wrigglers in the blood. The General's been away, and when he gets home she'll have grown so large it'll be the gandering months for him, and he won't have anything to do with her. How awful, as Sister's become accustomed to regular—" Eloise drew her lips over the slight protuberance of front teeth and gave the wind a pecking kiss.

"Eloise, we've got to find you a man, you're turning strange." Mama sighed, giving me a hand up. "Mary, put your arm about my waist: there you go, dear. Eloise, what are you looking at?"

"What is this thing?" Eloise bent from the waist and plucked up a copper legging jingler. "It looks like some kind of Indian ornament. Mary, does this look like an Indian object to you?"

"Put that down!" Mama said sharply.

Eloise slipped the legging jingler into my hand. It felt cool and sharp.

I tucked it into my pocket and allowed myself a secretive smile. As usual, nothing escaped her. She glanced pointedly over her shoulder at my sanctuary in the tall grass, then whispered, "Sister, who are you becoming?"

In late July, the cicadas took up that odd paper-over-a-comb thrumming that rises and falls over the twilight, I picked up a small gray pebble and tossed it. The sunset was green; they often are over the river country, when the tall grass and the giant old trees send up the breath of living, coloring everything with a shimmering light, like standing water. The bridal veil was in full bloom, long white whips curved sorrowfully over the grass. The steamers coming up from St. Charles whistled now and again, and the air was tainted with smoke. Eloise and I had been out for a constitutional, walking in the humid twilight, when she slipped her arm through mine and asked, "Do you miss the General when he is away?"

"The summer is passing off so fast."

"That's no answer."

"Sometimes I turn about to tell him something, and finding myself alone is the grayest feeling I have ever known." I handed my parasol to Eloise, then bent over a fiery patch of butterfly weed and waved the monarchs away with my hand. A few of them alighted on my gloved knuckles. I allowed them their rest, but snapped a few gummy stalks and held the hot-colored blooms a safe distance from my skirt. Eloise tucked them into her gathering basket.

"This is a day for trumpets. My sister has fallen in love."

"I said I missed his presence." The sun was at a cruel slant, I tipped my reclaimed parasol against it.

"It's the same thing, Mary. Is he in love with you?"

"He is cautious, prudent, judicious in all things."

Eloise had a slippy little-girl voice, and she asked mischievously, "Even in your *relations?*"

"He has a very cautious heart, Mama said—"

"You took marriage advice from the unhappiest woman in Kentucky?"

I let my chin drop at the tense and unpleasant memory of my parents together. "Pa had other women, Lu."

At this Eloise leaned forward. "And some of them lived under our roof." Looking away from me, she asked, "Does the General have other women, Mary?"

"These smell cloying, don't you think?" I asked, lifting a snippet of bridal veil to her nose. Eloise lifted a brow at my evasion, but she let me slip. We left off the conversation of our parents, seeing no point in revisiting what we knew to be true. It would have required us to condemn them or understand them, and neither of us was in the mood to do either. They had their own losses, and we saw no point in acquiring them for ourselves.

"You ought to keep a madstone to put upon any bites your children might suffer. Madstone draws out poison. Madstone can do other things besides." Eloise stood and made a little stamping motion with her feet, so that I could see her soft brown boots, laced up the instep. After setting the gathering basket beneath an elm tree, she whirled, with her arms outstretched. Her skirts mushroomed out, her hair combs flew off and were lost in the grass.

We shared the one bed, Eloise and I, as we had when I lived in Louisville. She slept with her face smashed into the pillow, her mouth open a bit, and I slept curled on my left side. Mama slept on the trundle below us, complaining of my house even in her dreams.

One morning, Eloise rode beside me as we descended the sunflower road into a country gold as a hawk's eye. The sunflower trace was no more than two dusty wheel ruts trimmed in cottonweed. The leaves of the plants were silvery green and shaped like sickles. I could smell the dusty fragrance of the yellow strikes, and I reached out to touch the heads bristling with tiny hairs. Bees droned in the lazy air.

I dashed after Eloise and rounded down the knoll, across a broad, grasshopper-filled meadow. They clicked and whirred before me, alighting now and again with a dry clutch upon my skirts. I flicked them off, but in crossing the meadow I accumulated bits of purple floret from button snakeroot and gray-green horsemint about the hem of my gown. We trundled down the sunflower road into a country rippling with heat. I glanced over the tidal pool of yellow strikes and green stalks. That is when I spied the woman eight rods distant, barely visible in her dun-colored clothing against the bald spot on the hill.

"Eloise, look! Don't you see her? That woman." I sheltered my eyes and pointed across the swale. Eloise rubbed the dust from her nose, glanced in that direction, then said in an offhand way, "She looks like she needs help."

"I don't think she needs help. She's in mourning."

"How do you know, Mary?"

The sun was oppressive. I grumbled, "A woman doesn't have to wear black bombazine to be in mourning. She doesn't have to be standing over a grave."

We silently considered this as we gazed in that direction. Eloise observed me shifting uncomfortably on the sidesaddle. "You had better start switching off, Sister, or your right cheek is going to be much bigger than your left. Let's go see her."

"I don't want to, Lu. It doesn't feel right. We should just let her be."

"Fine. If you're afraid, I'll go alone."

"Eloise, it's an intrusion. Eloise! Come back here!" But Eloise was fired with zeal and eager to reform. She cantered like a crusader up the trace. I coughed at the glinting ball of dust she sent up.

Seeing Eloise approach, the Osage woman scooped a handful of cold ashes from the fire ring and blackened her face. She looked dully at my sister as she smeared them over her forearms. There was a weariness in her shoulders, the bones of her face were sharp and her bare limbs were all at angles. Eloise dismounted and approached the Indian woman on her toes, crouching, touching her fingertips to a patch of cottonweed.

She tilted her head, then asked, "Do you need help?"

The woman sat motionless with a fixed downward gaze.

I dismounted, picketed my mare with the coiled rope alongside my saddle. The mare jerked her head in a swoop away from me, then foraged at the grama grass with dull tearing sounds. There was a clump of pickleweed behind me, flowering in a ball-shaped cluster of mimosalike leaves. When I touched them, they curled shut in protest.

"She looks to be starving," Eloise declared.

I yanked her away from the Osage woman. "Eloise, let's say that Mama had gone to Cave Hill to visit Pa's grave, and let's say that a swaggle of Osage women came racing after her with a basket of blue buffalo tongues whilst Mama was saying her prayers, urging Mama to eat! eat!"

"That would be gross impudence."

"Precisely."

"As Mama would never tolerate such a thing from red people."

The Osage woman lifted a white blanket from the ground, then drew it over her head. She tucked up her knees, causing dust to swing in the air around her. I stared at the fine ridges of bone on the tops of her feet and the dirt between her toes. The woman shifted her weight and put her forehead to her knees.

Eloise notched her face up awkwardly until she was darkly flushed. "Where is your family? Where . . . is . . . your . . . family?"

I lost my patience and my temper. I clutched my sister by the throttling collar of her riding habit, slipping my fingers under her neckcloth and hoisting her so that she flailed, her face red from choking. The forty-eight buttons upon Eloise's bodice jiggled in the sunlight, her skirt—thirteen yards of polished Carolina cotton—flopped, her tricot drawers with the little straps over her boots flashed under the prairie sun, and she waved her brown leather gloves, scattering the dragonflies and gnats.

"Sister! Put . . . me . . . down. Damn you!"

"Not until you promise to leave this woman in peace."

"Ack!" she said. Eloise was a little slip of a thing, not more than ninety pounds. I dropped her, and she scowled up at me.

"You are the worst human being that ever lived or walked on the earth or—"

"Yes, I'm terrible. Now you apologize to this woman."

"I will not," she said, tossing her chin up and pursing her lips.

I made another threatening jab at her collar, and Eloise curtsied peremptorily, then mumbled, "Sorry." I tugged Eloise to her feet and dragged her toward her horse. All the while, she stared back regretfully over her shoulder.

Eloise said, "You act like you know everything, Mary. Like I'm bad for wanting to help."

"Eloise, it's just that I have grown tired of seeing everything native to this place killed off, penned up or somehow altered to suit the newly arrived."

I did not look at the Osage woman again. I was embarrassed for the both of us, and angry at myself for not following my better judgment. A straight wind came off the horizon, causing the dirt to waver up in a dense brown curtain. August was nearly upon us, and I had not received a letter from the General in a fortnight. The newspaper accounts were scanty, but I heard through the military grapevine that my husband and his men were about four hundred miles north of St. Louis on the Mississippi River, at Fort Crawford. There were lots of rumors floating around, including one that Black Hawk and his band of British sympathizers had split from the Sauk Nation and joined forces with RedBird and his renegade band of young Winnebago warriors.

Every night, when I lay beside my snoring little sister, I clasped my hands together and stared at the ceiling, pleading, sometimes even bargaining with heaven to keep my husband safe. "If you bring the General back alive," I would say, "I will never lose my temper again"; or "I will be the most courteous woman you ever saw"; or "I will knit stockings for all the poor people at the barracks."

One night, Mama heard my prayers, and she whispered, "Mary, the General is a battle-hardened veteran, and shrewd besides. I doubt that any man could get the better of him. If you want to pray for someone, ask God to find a husband for Eloise. She's becoming jittery in that spinsterly way. Now go to sleep."

By August, I couldn't remember a single promise I'd made to heaven, which is just as well, because I broke them all.

13

Journal of Lt. Philip St. George Cooke
3 August 1827

What we are doing now is waiting, and I am very good at that. Each day, at dawn and three hours before sunset, I ride with a scouting party between the Wisconsin and the Mississippi Rivers. My circuit goes eighteen miles each route into a scrub-oak and pine-tree country. We look for RedBird and Black Hawk. I am always happy when we do not find them.

I am turning into bacon. I smoke under the engine boiler and fry under the sun and eat nothing but salt pork in putrefaction. The company cook wears a kerchief tied over his nose when he hacks the pork out of the barrel from whole gray hogs packed ass end up in salt. We boil it with churts of blackened cottonwood. This, according to regulations, will dissolve the rot and make it fit for eating. The flour barrels are so thick with fat black bugs that I could fish for weeks with the bait that collects in there. The company cook calls them thickener, and when he fixes the flour up into flapjacks by adding buffalo tallow and river water, the bugs pop in the grease.

The General has picked me several times for officer of the guard—except that we have no guardhouse, so I look after the sentries. My first duty was on a night when the monsoons came. I put on my india-rubber cape, then slogged in the rainstorm from one end of the boat to the other, up and down the decks, dumping water out of my boots.

I found the sentries, Russell and Mahaffey, smoking whilst sitting atop the gunpowder barrels in a lightning storm. I motioned at their pipes and said to them, "You boys will soon go to your kingdom."

The sentries looked up at the lightning tearing sheets across the night sky.

Russell said, "No harm. Mahaffey's ass will mute the explosion."

Still and all, I made them stop smoking. Russell and Mahaffey have been with the General since '08 and have followed him all over this country, from Plattsburgh in New York, to Fort Atkinson on the Great Plains and now here. They told me stories I preferred not to hear, about the dead rotting in coffins above the ground on the gulf coast. They were with the General at Pass Christian when Russell formed an unnatural attachment to a deceased consumptive girl named Janie. Russell boasted about how he visited her nightly. About how the grinding noise of the granite lid being shoved aside from the sarcophagus aroused him, and how Janie was still fresh, although declining in the humid climate.

"And it was on just such a night as this, when Russell was standing over Janie"—Mahaffey waved at the sky—"and the lightning struck the ground a piece not too far away."

"I almost rode that lightning bolt to Jaysus," said Russell. "My shoes smoked."

"But Russell ain't touched himself since," Mahaffey said with fatherly pride.

"Ain't," Russell held up his hands as if that proved something.

"You two ain't right," I said.

"No, we ain't," they agreed, but contritely.

4 August 1827

☙ I NEED catarrh ointment as my nose is so swollen I cannot breathe for trying. I cannot deceive myself. I think I contracted a violent cold in Galena, which is unpainted shanties on a mud cliff overlooking a sluggish yellow river. After the Winnebago RedBird had his spree, white squatters and their families came fleeing here in a panic. They crowd twenty and more to a shanty. Men and women alike have shaved their heads, so they all look like trolls. The General met with the local citizenry. They demanded the General inspect the abatises they had thrown up around their taverns, gambling dens and whorehouses. Then there was the prickly incident with Mr. John Reynolds, a local magistrate who aspires to be the governor of Illinois.

We found him holding court in a windy shanty. I stepped after the General onto a sloping floor. Hizzoner Reynolds stirred his breakfast brandy with a hair comb as he presided over squabbling Galenians. The lawyers had to step around mounds of dog shit on the floor. Hizzoner cleaned his fingernails with a fork as he listened to arguments. Afterward, Reynolds invited all of us into his chambers. This was a cubbyhole furnished with a necessary chair and a writing table. Reynolds sat upon the necessary chair whilst he and the General spoke. I didn't pay their conversation much mind until Reynolds raised his voice to the General.

"Sirrah, while you're here, sweep the red people from this state."

"By what account?"

"The Potawatami steal chickens and hogs from God-fearing white people, the Winnebago men can't resist ravishing our women—"

Johnston whispered to me, "Those must be some desperate Indians."

"And no man gets elected in Illinois unless he kills Indians," the General said dryly.

"Am I going to be forced to call out the militia?" Reynolds asked, pouring himself another brandy.

"You don't have the authority to call out the militia, *Mister* Reynolds. And even a governor lacks authority to remove native people from federal lands."

"But come harvesttime, I will be the governor, and I have a right to repel an invasion of the State of Illinois, General. I was just trying to do you a favor, let you have a little glory . . . let you add to your military reputation on my home ground. So as you would remember—"

"You best go back to your mama and your buttermilk before I find a hole and stick you in it," the General said. He is not so popular in this region as one might think.

The General gave us an afternoon's leave, but he pulled me aside and cautioned, "Mister Cooke, when you are with these daughters of joy, I suggest you keep your gun and your money close at hand. Do you understand me?" I said I did.

Me and Johnston found ourselves wandering in a marketplace of feminine wonders. The whorehouses had poetical names, given they were mostly shacks. Johnston took me to a place called the Bake Oven. Three girls offered their bottoms for five dollars a throw, and three girls went for two dollars. A blue curtain printed with lilies hung right down the center of the parlor, the idea being to keep enlisted men separate from officers. The place was crowded with bluecoats from all over the Northwest Territories.

Me and Johnston patiently waited our turn, having a look at the girls as they came out. My hopes were quickly dashed. We sat on these rickety old ladder-backs lined against the walls and tapped our toes and stared at the raggedy blue curtain. I wished for a drink, but it is against the law in Galena to serve liquor in a whorehouse. I twiddled my thumbs, kept my chin down and asked Johnston, "What name are you going to give her?"

Johnston sneered at me. "What do you mean? She don't care about your name." I looked up at the ceiling, then down at my thumbs and asked, "But what if I make a mistake?" Johnston said, "You can't make a mistake, you're in a whorehouse. Look here, this ain't like your wedding night; all these girls been bit by the trouser serpent. What's going to happen is this: she'll ask what you want—"

My voice squeaked in an embarrassing way, "What I want? I'm here, ain't I? Ain't it obvious what I want?"

"See here, Cooke, you like pie, don't you?"

"Sure I like pie."

Johnston counted on his fingers, "You got your lemon pie, your pecan pie, your apple pie and your peach pie. Let's not even get into cake. You ain't ready for cake."

"I don't follow. Here she comes—quick, tell me what to do."

"Just ask her if she's got a special of the day and then let her do it to you. And don't give her your goddamned name." Anyhow, I picked a dark-eyed girl with dark hair and hoped for the best. I followed her down a narrow hall into her crib, and the door didn't quite shut. The room was so small, we couldn't stand side by side for falling over her little bed. She put the money I gave her in a lockbox.

I introduced myself as John Quincy Adams.

She greeted me by opening her dress, "Charmed to make your acquaintance, Mr. Adams." At least she was friendly. She reclined and held out her plump arms, the tops of which had fine, dark hair. She asked if I wanted something *special*. Not having a clear idea of what that could be, I got into her and said, "Just the straight up, thank you."

About midway, I found her so much to my liking, I asked her if she would charge me double if I rode her twice. She said she wouldn't as I was the prettiest man she'd had all day. Somehow, I think the compliment meant more to her than it did to me.

The third time she charged me for.

Anyhow, I was eager to be out of Galena, as it is a dangerous place. After we left, I could scarcely stay awake for all my exercise. Johnston came down the steps buttoning his jacket and wearing a gap-tooth grin. He said he had two girls at once, and they both fell in love with him. Johnston said that once he's had a woman, she follows him around like a dog. I told him I've seen plenty of dogs following him, but no women.

We got back to the boat in time for lights-out. I passed by the big mess room, and through the door, saw the General hunched over a table that was stacked with maps and reports. He had several dozen tapers burning. I thought to go in and say good night, but fearing there might be rouge and cheap eau de toilette all over me, decided against it. The men are playing dice and losing money back and forth. Dice are against regulations, but the General has allowed it else there would be nothing to do but scratch at ourselves.

5 August 1827

✦ WE have made camp on land around abandoned Fort Crawford. The Winnebago summer camp is about twenty miles north, on the Wisconsin River. In a day or so, we are going northeast up the Wisconsin to meet those Winnebago, which may be my final day of reckoning on this earth. Red-Bird's attacks on those families at McNair's Coulee coincided with the army abandoning Fort Crawford under orders from Washington. So RedBird thinks the army is afraid of him.

I am writing this by light of a candle stub. I have finished a letter to Cousin Mary. I hope she sends me all the medicines I asked for. The General sat there awhile with her last letter, reading it over and again as if he were real worried about something—but of course he never says what that might be. He is old-fashioned and believes a gentleman should not speak to others about his wife. Anyhow, the General is in a terrible foul mood. Tonight, he met with Kearny and Colonel Zachary Taylor, the commander at Fort Armstrong, who has come up here to join us. The General has black shadows under his eyes from lack of sleep; he pinches the bridge of his nose and scowls at me through his spectacles as if I am the cause of his troubles.

Also I have learned to shut up, for he dislikes much talk.

Bright Sun entered the tent and sat cross-legged right in front of my cot, saucy as you please. The General had just come back from a review and told her he was expecting a Winnebago chief, then he asked Bright Sun to stay close to translate. The General left again. Bright Sun slid the papoose board off her back and put the baby to rest on the General's bed. I told her she ought not to do that. She said the General wouldn't mind. She opened my writing kit, held the bottle of ink to her ear and shook it like a rattle. I don't know what the hell she expected to hear from my ink bottle, but I snatched it from her.

One of the officers' servants, a Negro boy, walked by with a tray. Bright Sun watched him pass, then asked, "You own slaves too?"

I said that I was opposed to owning human beings.

Bright Sun looked at me contemptuously, then announced, "That is because you are too poor to own slaves. Or you cannot capture them. You should raid another camp and take some. People would think better of you. I know I would. We had two slaves. Then Tree Striker married one of them." Bright Sun looked deeply disappointed by Tree Striker. She said, "I have been to Dodge's mines and I have seen the Black Frenchmen. (She meant Negroes.) I have heard their songs. One of the songs, I liked. Here, I will sing it for you."

I tried to edge out of the tent to get away from her.

But Bright Sun followed after me singing "Keep Me from Sinking Down" with a Sauk cadence and in a nasal tone so that it sounded nothing like the Negro spiritual. When she had finished, she glanced smartly at me and demanded, "What does the song mean? Are they afraid to fall into the lead-mine pits? Are they afraid that they will be covered up by the water in the pits?"

I admonished her to return to the tent where she had left her baby alone. She wouldn't go until she had her answer. The girl has a head that's hard as quartz. I said, "Bright Sun, that old spiritual is from Psalms. It's about a captive people who fear there is no hope of rescue."

Bright Sun said, "Those Black Frenchmen must be poor warriors to let the Chemokemon work them like animals. And you must not be a very good warrior if you can't steal some slaves of your own. I would like to have my own slaves. And twenty horses. Cooke, I am thinking you are poor. Or you are afraid or you are weak."

"And I am thinking you are the rudest little cider-squeezer I have ever met."

She wrinkled up her nose and pushed her face up to mine, "What does this mean, 'cider-squeezer'?"

6 August 1827

T H E R E is a strange Indian village due north of our encampment ruled by a man called White Cloud the Prophet. The Prophet's village (also called Prophetstown) is a jumble of mud huts, torn wigwams and primitive lean-tos. It is a settlement of Indians who have been thrown away by their own

tribes on account of moral decay. What this means in Indian terms I am not
sure. But I did see a lot of crippled people and about a dozen dwarves.
Which struck me odd. One thing is sure, this place is nothing like Saukenuk.
Packs of big-ribbed mongrels nipped at us, and the few ponies we saw were
swaybacked and covered with sores. No children could be found in all of
the place. The absence of children in Prophetstown made all of us nervous.
Johnston peered into the Indians' cook kettles. "No infants stewing here, sir."

Our council tent was put up quick as a blink on the outskirts of Prophetstown, and the troops formed up to let the Indians know we had not come
to eat and drink only. Bright Sun stood off to the General's left side with her
hands clasped before her. She swayed on her feet with her eyes closed, as if
she were sleeping upright.

Surrounded by troops, our confidence bolstered by two four-pounders,
we settled in to wait for the Winnebago Prophet to come visit. But One-Eye
Decorah, a Winnebago chief, was our first visitor. He had bushy white hair
and a cataract thick as a plate over his left eye. His right eye was gone, there
being only a fleshy socket. One-Eye Decorah wore a rabbit-fur sporran over
his breechclout, and a woman's tartan sash over his shoulder.

"Who does he think he is? Robert the fuggin' Bruce?" Johnston said.

I could tell the General liked One-Eye right off, because he ran his thick
hand over his eyes and cupped it over his mouth to cover his smiling. He
cleared his throat, trying not to grin as he greeted the old Sauk. Anyhow, as
One-Eye Decorah rummaged in the possibles sack hanging by a leather
thong around his neck, he cradled an open umbrella over one arm, hunch-
ing up a bit on that side. Steel needles clinked against flint and some tin
items. Clink, clink and so on as we all sat there, admiring the Highland Winnebago. Finally, with a look of mingled relief and pride, One-Eye Decorah
pulled a crumpled ball of paper from the sack and offered it to the General.

The General carefully flattened the paper out with his hands. Leaning
over the table, he handed the note to me. Johnston and I read it in unison.

> This Indian who calls himself One-Eye Decorah
> cannot be trusted as he murders on a whim.
> Lewis Cass,
> Governor of the Michigan Territories.

Bright Sun crossed the room, looked over my shoulder and read the
note. She made a face at the General, then at One-Eye Decorah. If she'd
had a gun with her, she would have settled everything right then by exe-

cuting the poor old bastard. She hunkered down between me and John-ston.

"Any man who would offer that note so pridefully can't be all bad," I said.

Johnston snarled at me, "It says as plain as can be that One-Eye is a crook, and Cass would know well enough."

Bright Sun interrupted. "I think the General should kill him right now."

"Why?" I asked. "Because One-Eye trusted what some white man wrote down about him? Wouldn't be the first time."

Bright Sun sneered at me. "I have lived here a little while longer than you, Mister Cooke. I would think you could listen to what I say. Heh?"

"Cass knows enough of One-Eye to send him out into the world with a written warning. It don't get much clearer than that, you rube." We all paused at the wisdom of Johnston's words.

Bright Sun muttered, "Cooke, you are such a green-foot."

Johnston whispered to her, "Ah, Bright Sun, I think you mean greenhorn, don't you?"

Bright Sun shook her head, "I saw Cooke's feet, they are green like a dead man's, covered with death mold. Green-foot. He stinks like a swamp."

"What the hell were you doing smelling my feet, Bright Sun?"

"I came into the tent, I could not help but smell them."

"Cooke! Say One-Eye were a white man? And say this white man was il-literate and gave you the same note, what would you do then?" Johnston asked.

"I'd hear him out."

"Oh, bullshit. Stop reading that garbage that Mister James Cooper writes. It's ruining your common sense. You seen any red-skinned nobility the whole time we been out here? Hell, the whole time we were in Galena with those chawbacons, did you see any white-skinned nobility? I didn't think so. And why is that, Mister Cooke? Because there ain't no such thing as a noble anybody."

"Mister John-stones, what is a cider-squeezer?" Bright Sun asked, making a face at me.

"Shh," I said.

One-Eye glanced opaquely in our direction, then hoisted the Scotch um-brella up and down in small rhythmic movements as he spoke. As he had tied old snake rattles and trade bells to the underbracing, the umbrella served as musical accompaniment. One-Eye talked on, but none of us understood what he was saying. Least of all the General. He tossed his hands up.

"Bright Sun! Are you working, or is this one of your high holy days?"

She jumped to her feet and began translating in a low voice.

"Great War Chief of the Blue Coats, I come to warn you about the one who is known as the Winnebago Prophet. He is an evil man, but the people in Prophetstown are even more evil. You can see this by looking at them. The Prophet leads them in warfare against anyone for anyone who will pay him. The Prophet lies to Black Hawk, and Black Hawk listens."

One-Eye paused and gazed raptly at the bottle of rum on the General's table. The General motioned for One-Eye to help himself. One-Eye gulped loudly, wiped his mouth and continued, "I have admired Black Hawk these many winters. He is a good and honorable man. Black Hawk can hunt like a long-tail tree cat, and he is a fearless warrior. But in these, his last years, Black Hawk listens only to the Prophet's words. Why? I do not know, but it makes my heart heavy to see him misled by an evil man. Do a good thing for your bluecoats and for Black Hawk and his British Band. Burn Prophetstown. Send the Winnebago Prophet away to the northern lands of the British fathers. Burn Prophetstown."

One-Eye finished his speech. He stood quietly, waiting to hear what the General had to say. "Mister Decorah, let me make sure I understand what you are saying. You have come here today to ask me to burn the Prophet's village because it will be in my best interests to do so?"

"Yes."

"And by burning the Prophet's village, and exiling the Prophet, Black Hawk will lose both his spiritual advisor and access to the Prophet's mercenary forces?"

"Yes."

"Mister Decorah, have we ever met before?"

"No."

"Then why have you formed a sudden affection and concern for my person?"

One-Eye paused a long while, looking at the General in a confused way. The General motioned at One-Eye's tartan with his forefinger and asked, "Did the British officers at Fort Malden give you those things, Mister Decorah?"

One-Eye looked down at his sporran, patted it fondly. "Yes. The Long Knives."

"And did the Long Knives give you guns? Glazed powder? Did they promise to send Long Knives into the Winnebago land?"

"No, no. No guns. No powder."

I tried to discern what motivated One-Eye. Had he heard that Keokuk's band of Sauk would not aid the Winnebago in their fight against the Americans? The Winnebago must be awfully angry about that betrayal. It made sense that the Winnebago would want to stick it to the Sauk warriors. Was One-Eye trying to exact some sort of revenge, or was he acting in the General's interests? I couldn't tell, but it didn't make sense to me that he would be here warning us when, within a week, we'd be surrounding his village, threatening his people and demanding the surrender of RedBird and a passel of his best warriors.

Johnston whispered, "He's a spy is what he is. Taking British coin."

I said, "He's starving. All the people are starving. If you were hungry, you'd take money from the British too."

"Like hell I would. He came down here to size up our troops, meet the General face to face and assess the odds. He's going to run back to Saukenuk and then to Fort Malden and report to the English. I'll lay odds we have to go up against a British regiment at One-Eye's Winnebago camp."

The General leaned back in his chair and took the measure of One-Eye. He dragged imaginary circles on the tabletop with the tip of his forefinger. "What I don't understand is why you have come alone, Mister Decorah? Where are the other chiefs?"

One-Eye began repeating his whole message, but the General stopped him with an uplifted hand. "Yes, I took it all in the first time, Mister Decorah. Why don't you see the orderly sergeant on your way out and get yourself a twist of tobacco and some coffee?"

Bright Sun escorted him through the tent flaps, rolling her eyes in a saucy way at me and Johnston. I was beginning to like the little cider-squeezer's spirit.

A quarter of an hour later, when she returned, Bright Sun escorted White Cloud the Prophet through the flaps. The Prophet was taller than the General, about six foot and rich in flesh but little else. I guessed him to be in his early forties. He had a long black mustache and matted black hair. "My men say they saw One-Eye Decorah riding away from your camp," the Prophet began. The General ignored this, but the Prophet continued, "You can't trust One-Eye. Everyone knows that."

He rubbed a hand over his belly rolls, pinching one of them fondly, then said in near-perfect English, "I tell Black Hawk my dreams. He follows my dreams. He does as I say."

We all perked up at this. The General's eyes went small, and he lifted a quill and scratched something out. "I hear you poisoned your first wife, Mister Cloud," the General said.

"Away she go. Ffft." The Prophet wiggled his hand in a downward motion like a falling bird. He wiped at a bead of sweat falling between his breasts. He had breasts like a woman's. Those were confusing to see.

"Have you met recently with Black Hawk, Mister Cloud?" the General asked. "Do you know where I might find him?"

In response, the Prophet looked at Bright Sun, but she looked away from him quickly, as if repulsed by his appearance.

The Prophet spoke in a singsong voice that was as flat and bored as a man who is reading aloud a bedtime story for the hundredth time. "If you make war on Black Hawk, the thunder gods will strike you down, Zha'becka. They will strike down all the white people with a sickness, and you will disappear from these lands. *Yo ko ho the he he.* And all the rest, and so on."

The General yawned. "Any more hocus-pocus before you take your leave, Mister Cloud?"

The Prophet made a delicate fanning motion over his nipples and said in the same bored voice, "The winter is close for your last war, General. My dreams will decide what happens in this country. You will not long be the great war chief of the bluecoats. *Yo ko ho the he he.* The rest you can guess about. You will not be war chief of the bluecoats for much longer."

Chin in hand, the General regarded the Prophet. "That is wishful thinking, sir . . . by the both of us."

After the Prophet left, the General turned to us and said, "Gentlemen, I want a scouting party to monitor the Prophet's movements. I wouldn't be surprised to find Mister One-Eye Decorah and the Prophet are acting in concert to stir up the entire region. If I moved against either party, it would be to the advantage of both. It would give them the excuse they need to form a confederation of the Lake Nations."

"Like Tecumseh did in the last war?"

"Yes, like Tecumseh."

The General is in better spirits as he is soon to meet with Governor Cass with news from the Winnebago council at Butte des Morts. We press on to the portage between the Fox and Wisconsin Rivers, where we are told thousands of Winnebago have assembled.

I would be lying if I didn't admit that my heart jumps at the idea of so many hostiles.

10 August 1827

✢ I HAVE never been fond of drink, but these days passing, I am beginning to see the reason men take it up. Truth is, I'm having a jigger as I write
this. It is out of medical necessity as I could not hold the turkey quill for
shaking. Two days ago, we were forced to abandon the steamboats to move
northeast up the twisting Wisconsin on our way to meet the hostile Winnebago tribe.

We boarded keelboats and gaff-rigged mackinaws and struggled up the
river. We were facing a strong head wind, so we had no choice but to pole
and tow. I volunteered to assist with the towing. It made me uncomfortable
to sit like a nabob on the deck and watch the enlisted men, roped like animals, pulling us thigh-deep in river silt.

My towing inspired Johnston to join the men at the poles. Which meant
he walked the cleated deck, shoving off with a pole to the bottom of the
river. He saluted me every time he ran to the back of the line to shove us off
again. He was getting on my nerves. So there I was, towing the keelboat upriver and falling over and dangling upside down by my ankles until Johnston
hollered, "Look at Cooke there, dangling from that rope as if it were his
mama's titty! Look at Cooke all wet! What flat rock were you on when the
cow took a piss?"

That did it. I released the rope and waded the river. Then I swam it until
I reached the keel. I flung one leg over the side, then jumped on Johnston
and began pummeling him with all my might. Which wasn't much com-
pared to Johnston's might. He threw me off. I lay on my back like a helpless
beetle with Johnston's fist coming straight into my face. But the General
pulled Johnston off me.

The General said, "Johnston, I'm considering the choke box for that."
Which caused Johnston to shudder. In the choke box, you have to squat or
be strangled with a red welt about the craw. Now, I was not eager to know
what the General had in mind for me, but he only said, "Mister Cooke, get
back to your post!" That is how my clothes got washed without me having
to remove them. The hours wore on, and I kept to my towing until somebody hollered, "Hostiles!"

Bugles sounded the alarm. The drums played the long roll. Gunfire broke
all around me. We ropers squatted down in the tall weeds, letting go the
ropes in our fear. I fell belly-down into the shallow water with rush grass all
over my nose and hoped I was invisible. The boys from behind us fired over
our heads onto the prairie. A few ramrods whizzed above my head like pro-

jectiles, and seeing them fly, the soldier next to me gaped in a big-eyed way and said, "I guess the General knows who needs to spend more time on drill."

Then we heard the General holler, "Remove those goddamned ramrods before firing!"

The artillerymen lit the six-pounders. Canister shot hit the prairie and sent up fountains of dirt. I looked back over my shoulder. I said to the fellow next to me, "We ought to swim or we are sure to be butchered." Like turtles, we backed into the water, keeping our noses out of it. We slid back until we were in deep enough to turn. Which was when the hostiles spied us. My friend shrieked when the balls fell all around us in the water. We could hear the Indians whooping for the sport of firing at us. I put my head down and paddled for my life. I squiggled so as not to be such an easy target. I lifted up to take a breath, and there went a ball right before my nose.

I heard the General direct the riflemen to fire at the Indians who could be seen in the narrow clearing and the infantry muskets into the piney woods, which were blazing with musket fire. I was swimming in that water forever. I approached the hull and tried to clamber up, but Johnston hollered at us to climb up the port side as we would be too easy to hit coming up the starboard. Lucky for me, our keel drew only nineteen inches with the boat fully loaded.

Then, as quickly as it had started, the Indians stopped firing on us, turned tail and fled

I had just come up on the deck when it stopped and somebody hollered, "Let's go after them! They're riding away!"

Our mounts were brought out of the hold, and our keelboat dropped plank. We walked the horses down onto the marshy shore, nervously looking about for Indians. At the command, we mounted up and were told to search for the warriors who had fired on the boat. The General said that, if possible, we were to bring the hostiles in alive. He wanted to question them to learn the whereabouts of RedBird, and maybe even Black Hawk.

The big bluestem was high and thick, a grand cover for hostiles. As we rode into it, I struggled to keep hold of my blowy breechloader in a wet hand. Coming over a hillock, I saw what the General was after. Three horsemen on skinny brindle Indian ponies sped away down the hill in three directions, and the General motioned us after them. Me and Johnston went center, but the General and Kearny and some others took left, so I did not see their pursuit.

Johnston called at me, "What kind of Indians are these? Sauk? Winnebago? What?"

I didn't know. None of us did, including the General. The Indian we were chasing made as if to hide in a dense pine stand. I was trying something new, that is bringing up the reins to my teeth like a circus rider whilst filling my breechloader. It struck me as a dashing thing to do at the time. But maybe not, as I accidentally dropped my cartridge. Then my jaw was nearly torn off when my damn horse shied around the coming trees.

So I hollered at Johnston, "Are you loaded?"

He shouted, "Hell no."

I said, "Well, for shit."

"He's getting away," Johnston said, "I'm going around him. Up around and then back. I'll pincer him."

It sounded complicated. It sounded like running away. I was about to tell Johnston not to leave me alone, but Johnston disappeared into the tall grass and beyond into a wall of dense pine. The Indian descended a ravine, and when I followed, I found myself alone in a bug-clouded ditch. When Johnston finally appeared, I said, "That was some pincering action, you jackass."

"How'd he get away? We could have popped him to sky-blue fits! Where did he get to?"

"We wouldn't have lost him if you hadn't gone off in the opposite direction."

We bickered like two quilting ladies until Major Kearny rode up on us, out of breath.

He said, "The General got Black Hawk. Come on, then."

14

We got back to the keel, and the troops were crazy with excitement over the General's capture of Black Hawk. But while the others were milling and staring at the old Sauk, I was distracted by a strange sight. Bright Sun stood away from Black Hawk with a blanket over her head. Given the heat of the day, I thought it odd for her to be covering her head with a three-point blanket. Seeing me, she wiped her cheeks with the back of her hand and strode off to the stern of the keel. I watched her go and wondered why she was behaving so. Then it occurred to me that Bright Sun might have told Black Hawk how to find us. That she might be a spy for the Sauk. She lived with them, after all—lived in Black Hawk's wickiup.

I pushed past the others to get a look at him. Black Hawk knelt on the deck, under a mean sun, with his wrists tied at the small of his back. His head was bald except for a scalp lock, from which fine graying hair hung fanlike over the back of his head. He had a prominent, hooked nose and large high cheekbones. His eyes were smart and wild, as if he were in charge of all of us and just playing along to humor the group. Nobody touched him or taunted him. We just stared at him. He was a man of about five feet eleven inches, and every stitch of him tensed with muscle. His hands were lean and fine and could make quick work of a body.

If I took the measure of the man by his enemies, the General was surely a lord for Black Hawk's hatred.

Johnston said, "I'm of a mind to give him my saber and let him and the General go at it. That would be a fight to see. Cooke, wouldn't you like to see those two old fellers pounding on each other?"

"You would have to watch from on high as an angel," Kearny said, shoving Johnston back for his foolish ideas.

The General came out of the hold with a bunch of keys and ordered us to follow after. The General's coat looked to have been rent by a knife. The arms were soiled black. We waited patiently as he removed it and folded it over a barrel as if it were in fine condition. His shirt was soaked clean through with sweat, and the legs of his trousers were sorry with grass oil and mud. I heard him make a snorting noise and saw there was blood coming out of his nose. There was also a deep gash over his left eye. The General pulled Black Hawk to his feet by his manacles, then dragged the old Saukie so that he had to walk backward. That's when I noticed the knuckles of the General's left hand were cut up. One side of Black Hawk's face looked to be swelling, and his nose traveled in several directions at once.

We descended three creaking steps, then stopped on the straw-covered floor. In the hold, there was one compartment with a heavy oak door in which a square of iron lattice covered a tiny window. The dark was suffocating hot. The General slid a key into the lock, then opened the door and made as if to throw Black Hawk into the cell. But Black Hawk squatted with his legs wide apart and resisted being thrown.

The General and Black Hawk stared at one another like dogs before a skirmish.

Two dark-red angry streaks came into the General's cheeks under his gray beard. His eyes got mean as a badger's. I saw his elbow cant back as he pulled a dirk from his waist strap. He put the tip of the blade to Black Hawk's throat. He pushed hard enough to pop a red line right below the Sauk's jaw. Then that red line began leaking blood steadily. Black Hawk didn't flinch, except for his nostrils flaring out and the corners of his mouth trembling a bit. He looked down his nose at the General . . . daring him to cut his throat. Black Hawk's ribs flared out as he was breathing in short bursts.

Black Hawk said something so low that only the General could hear it. He repeated the same words over and over in a mocking way. The General was wound tight, angrier than I've ever seen him. He yanked Black Hawk's head backward by his scalp lock and said, "Don't you say it." The General seemed to forget we were in the room, and Kearny looked worried.

But seeing the General lose his temper, Black Hawk knew he had the better of him. He almost smiled, and he repeated those same words. It was having a lethal effect on the General. He began to slice the soft skin under Black Hawk's chin. He was a moment away from severing the old Sauk's soul from his body when Black Hawk tensed and dipped his knees. The

General shoved Black Hawk into the cell so that the Saukie fell on his ass. Just that quick, Black Hawk was up on his feet again with his hands still tied behind him. Black Hawk charged at the General. The General popped Black Hawk with his hand as if it were a good-sized cudgel, sending him reeling back into the cell.

Slamming the door shut, the General then put his face against the iron-lattice window and began talking to Black Hawk in a voice that sounded dry and harsh.

"It was no accident I found you up in the north woods those many long winters ago. I hunted you down. I searched for you when you joined the British. And so you know . . . what I did to your boy? I'm glad you saw it all. Because when you killed her, I was close enough to see you doing it, but too far to be of any help to her. You and I have struck a bargain in this life, friend. I have to live with your sins. You have to live with mine."

The General walked away glazey eyed as Black Hawk pitched curses at him.

We were all agitated that night. The General didn't sleep at all but paced the deck until reveille. I couldn't sleep either, thinking of Black Hawk separated from us only by a wall. I jumped up with every creak of the keel. There were false alarms every few hours. I rose about two o'clock in the morning and pulled my trousers on under my nightshirt. Then I went belowdecks, into the hold, to Black Hawk's cell.

I found Mahaffey and Russell playing cards, having set two candles atop their black leather cartridge boxes. They greeted me in a friendly way but were reluctant to look away from their cards. The lard candles flared atop the cartridge boxes, about to melt and send flame scooting directly into the balls and gunpowder.

I said, "You boys are intent upon blowing yourselves up, aren't you?"

"If I die I get to see Janie, and she's got tits that weigh five pound each, I swear to you. First thing after dying, I'm goin' to swive Janie, right in front of St. Peter's gates. No kissing, no groping, just swiving. Lift her dress and swive her," Russell mumbled.

I looked at Mahaffey. "Is he talking about the dead girl again?"

"The course of true love is mysterious," Mahaffey muttered, studying his cards.

I looked in on Black Hawk. He was awake. He stared at the door with his mink-bright eyes as if entranced by the view. One side of his face was purple and green and swollen.

"Mahaffey," I said, "could I have a word with you?"

"Sure," Mahaffey said. "Russell plays cards like a fockin' Mormon."

The keel scraped a gravel shoal with an agonizing drag. The two of them turned their ears to the floor in an analytical way. But then Mahaffey brightened and asked, "What can I do for you, Mister Cooke?"

I pulled him out of earshot and whispered, "Mahaffey, you've been with the General since the beginning?"

"That's right."

"You were with him when he killed Black Hawk's adopted son?"

"I were."

"What did the General mean when he talked about seeing Black Hawk kill 'her'?"

"Who?"

"The General said he saw Black Hawk kill some woman."

Mahaffey looked up at the ceiling and appeared to contemplate my question, but I could see he was thinking about which lie he'd tell me. He breathed through hair-clogged nostrils, then shook his head. "I wouldn't know the first fockin' thing about it."

"Ah, Mahaffey, I'm not trying to get anyone in trouble. I'm just trying—"

"I wouldn't know a fockin' thing," Mahaffey's voice shot up loudly as if he were picking a fight with me. For a moment, I thought he was going to send his keg-sized fist into my listeners. Mahaffey's florid cheeks flopped a bit as he dropped his jaw. His few remaining lower teeth were surrounded by small pockets of blood. I gathered the impression that Mahaffey had served me some truths and some lies, but if put to the test, I could not tell which was which. As I walked off, I heard Mahaffey insulting me.

"Fockin' hothouse lettuce. Asking questions he ain't got no right to . . ."

I could have had both Mahaffey and Russell brought up on a whole menu of charges, but the effort would have brought as much hardship upon me, besides which, Mahaffey could tell the General I had been spying into his past. I knew it was dumb of me to ask those questions as well as to let their insubordination slip.

12 August 1827

THE next day, we turned Black Hawk over to Major Riley without a whit of ceremony. The General wasn't even on the boat when Riley and a company of men transported Black Hawk back to regarrisoned Fort Crawford to be held on charges. He was off riding with the scouting party. Still, seeing Black Hawk go put us at our ease, and the mood of the command improved considerably. But the General is solemn and concentrates all of his energies on the coming battle. I believe he dreads our meeting with the Winnebago. I know I do. The General has gone very thin. And he still does not sleep. I don't know how a body can get along without food and sleep.

That night, after we made camp, I determined to take a short walk between the camp and the keels in the river. But as I set off, I came upon a curious sight. On the shore, screened by a cluster of willow trees, I saw the General standing near to Bright Sun, with his hands upon her shoulders. She bowed her head. He appeared to be the one doing the talking. Bright Sun looked angry. She kept trying to turn away from him, and he kept trying to spin her back around by putting his hands to her shoulders. I saw him give her money, which she accepted.

Then about eight friendly Sauk with that familiar bald look to them came riding up the shore. The General greeted them, then said good-bye to Bright Sun. She got up on a piebald pony and rode south with them, presumably to Saukenuk. Bright Sun did not look back. But if she had, she would have seen the General staring after her.

Not long after that, a few of us officers were sitting on the deck playing brag, which the General taught me for the exclusive purpose of having someone lose to him. Gradually, everyone else headed off to bed, leaving me and the General. We were playing cards over a flour barrel, before a hurricane lamp.

The General said, "The thing is, once we have our war, it will mean the end of them and the beginning of more of us. It will mean the end of something more than I care to lose. And there won't be any territories and one day there won't be any West to be had."

And I said, "Who are you talking about?"

"The red people. They're being ruined."

And being a little sotted, I interrupted him saying, "Sir, the Winnebago look to kill us."

"It could come to that," the General agreed, studying his cards.

"I find that an awfully heavy hog to hold, sir."

"That's because you're young and stupid, Mister Cooke. My cards say you owe me two bits, which doubtless you do not have." Which ended talk right there as I am gone broke over playing cards with the old man. In lieu of two bits, I offered him cinnamon candy. He called me green and would not take it.

So I went to bed. I had been dreaming of the General holding Black

Hawk under his knife. In my sleep, I saw the knife pop the skin of Black Hawk's throat and linger there. I watched the General take Black Hawk's taunts and respond with his own. I awoke and sat up. Seeing the General's bed had not been slept in, I lit a candle. A thought had come to me. The General could have killed Black Hawk with a flick of his wrist. One tiny motion. A clean slice and all of his troubles would have gone away. But he hadn't killed Black Hawk, had he? I put the General's words together, and suddenly, I began to understand.

Once we have our war, it will mean the end of them. . . . It will mean the end of something more than I care to lose. . . . You and I have struck a bargain in this life, friend. I have to live with your sins. You have to live with mine. . . . This life . . . this life has got flavor, hasn't it, Mister Cooke!

That's when I understood the General would never kill Black Hawk. If the old Sauk died, it would be under someone else's hand. Because without Black Hawk, the General's life would make no sense at all.

15 August 1827

So now there is something wrong with my feet. In between my toes has gone all sore and itchy, and they smell worse than ever. The General barks that my feet make the tent smell like bad cheese. He is one to talk, as he looks like hell, all skinny and burned and his whole face covered in beard. His hair is so long, it hangs down over his collar, Jesus-style. I sleep with mosquito netting over my bed, which is an effective way to trap mosquitoes close to my skin.

The General won't use netting. He said he had yellow fever in Louisiana, and what else could these mosquitoes do to him? He gets up before dawn and swims in the river and scrubs himself with a green weed called artemesia. This he learned to do from the Indians. One thing is sure, he smells sweet—like sagebrush. Last night around midnight, I roused enough to observe him as he paced in front of the tent wearing nothing but his trousers and his spectacles on his nose. He was smoking a mixture he made up himself, of willow bark and kinnikinnick-weed and only a sprinkling of tobacco. I was sleeping when he came back into the tent and lit all the candles, which woke me up.

He offered me his cigar pinched between his thumb and forefinger. I declined. He went back to smoking, but opened some of the books Cousin Mary had packed for him. Inspired by something, the General spread out foolscap on his writing table, and began sketching out flywheels and pinions and gear-driven paddles, muttering *hypotenuse* and other mystical phrases favored by engineers. He squinted through the smoke. He noted measurements in tiny script at key points over rays and right angles. He cocked his head aside this way and that, like a pointer I once owned, as he examined his creation.

He's got rats in the upper story, I thought, watching him talk to himself.

He glanced down at himself in surprise when he dropped an ash on his pant leg, leaving a scorched hole there. He clenched that damned cigar between his teeth. Then he raised his nose to an alert trajectory and frowned at me and said, "Mister Cooke, why don't you step into the drink? Maybe a big wind will come along and blow the stink off you." I groaned and covered my face with the pillow, then fell back to sleep with the sound of his quill nib scratching at the paper.

18 August 1827

✥ WE have forged forty miles northeast on the Wisconsin in two days to reach the portage between the Fox and Wisconsin Rivers. At this point, the Fox River is shaped like a fishhook and the Wisconsin is shaped like the inside of somebody's elbow. The portage is the skinny stretch of land between the two rivers that Indians and fur traders use as a land bridge to cross from the Fox River to the Wisconsin River. They climb out of their canoes in one river, hoist . . . or portage . . . their canoes over their heads, walk across the land bridge, then drop their canoes into the other river.

One-Eye's Winnebago village was hundreds upon hundreds of tipis set upon this portage. The village stretched away in a morning fog as far as the eye could see. Indian ponies moved through the mist like ghosts. I had never seen a village so big. I am told this is the largest settlement of Winnebago in the territory, and I believe it. RedBird came out of this particular village. We came here to demand the elders surrender the murdering bird to us.

The General called for the troops to disembark, and we established our camp on the west bank of the Wisconsin, in the inner elbow of the river, directly across the water from this enormous Winnebago village, and prepared to host a parade and review the next day. The idea being that we would overwhelm the Winnebago with the appearance of a superior force, and they would catapult the murderers of the white families in our direction. Our keels were cordoned up the Wisconsin River, around the portage on the west side, and the sentries on the decks paced with their arms at the ready. The troops were on tenterhooks.

As dawn broke, the Winnebago woke up. There looked to be about ten-thousand sleepy people, mamas, old ladies, a million dogs, little boys and warriors gathering on the riverbank and pointing at us. They looked friendly. We relaxed a bit. A few of the children waved shyly, and I waved back.

Johnston said, "Look at those pretty girls over there. Invite 'em over for coffee."

"Johnston, this ain't some goddamned sociable," I said.

"Not yet, it ain't. That's because those girls haven't met Mister Johnston."

My men formed up in a corridor that led from the river to the General's tent. We were joined by 140 armed Menominee allies, the Rice People as they like to be called. The Menominees are enemies of the Winnebago and the Sauk. I don't think it's a good idea, them being here, but they have *horses.* And the General said he'd sooner trust the Menominee at his back than the Illinois militia. That was a striker. So there I was with my men, and behind us, the Menominees chattering in their language. We had Indians before us and Indians behind, and if put to the test, I could not discern my allies from my enemies. What is more, I feared the Menominee would decide to have at the Winnebago on a frolic. And there would be me and my men stuck in between. Meantime, me and Johnston flirted over a river's distance with those pretty girls.

Governor Lewis Cass had been in the Winnebago village hosting peace councils when we arrived. He was close to being the ugliest man I had ever seen in my life. His whole pocky face threatened to slide off his skull under a cap of slick, black hair. He had broad bony shoulders, but no muscle, just this hollow chest above a sagging belly.

In fact, the Winnebagos' name for Cass is Big Belly—a good name for him.

Cass crossed the river in a bull boat atop a stack of wolf pelts, looking like a man of Gotham gone to sea in a bowl. A Menominee warrior, a leather thong clamped in his teeth, swam Cass across the water. Upon stepping ashore, Cass asked me to lead him to the General's tent. I obliged him. But when we got to the tent, the General wasn't there. Which didn't bother Cass, who sat at the General's desk, then began rifling through his orders, reports and correspondence. There being only the two of us in the tent, I said sternly, "Mr. Cass, you had better step away from that desk or . . ."

Cass raised his brows at one of the General's documents. "Or what, Lieutenant? What are you going to do to me?"

It made me furious that I couldn't think how to answer him. I wasn't sure I could do anything to a governor. But my temper came up, and I raised my weapon just a little and said firmly, "Governor, you ought not to read the General's papers. Now you put that down and step away from the desk, or I'll take you to the guardhouse."

"Don't be foolish, Lieutenant. You're not going to put the governor in the guardhouse." Cass then read aloud a private communiqué from General Gaines to General Atkinson. "'Inflict on the Winnebagos exemplary punishment. Demand a cession of the entire lead-mining region as a price for their bad conduct . . .' Well, good afternoon, General Atkinson."

I quickly stepped aside and avoided looking at the General.

"You shaved lately, General?" Cass smiled, still holding the order from General Gaines.

I watched the two of them. The General didn't say anything. Cass smiled even broader, but it changed from an expression of insolence to one of submission. The General walked around the table, dragged the chair away from it, then, with one hand, shoved Cass to the floor. Cass reached up for the General's forearms in a clumsy manner. The General caught Cass's wrist in a way that crippled Cass's whole person, until Cass was begging for mercy and sinking on his knees. I thought, Now, I would like to know how to do that trick, and I crossed over, hoping the General would order me to shoot the governor. The General released Cass.

Cass made ready for fisticuffs, a ludicrous picture, given his scrawny arms and big belly. He circled round with his fists raised like a ninny and bellowed that the General had better enforce the order to burn the Winnebago village. The General ignored Cass. Cass churned his fists in the air. The General moved a few reports around, then said, "Now, Mister Cass, do you wish to return to your family with your knowledge box broken?"

Mr. Cass dropped his fists. "No, that sounds less than ideal."

"Then stand down."

Cass licked his lips and glanced around the room nervously. He put his hands to his hips and shifted his weight, then motioned at the General's table. "You got orders there. You can't just ignore orders to destroy them Winnebagos. I want to see you do it."

"I will not slaughter noncombatants to provide you and Reynolds with entertainment."

"But the order from Gaines says—"

"Mister Cass, I long ago learned to distinguish between the stated policies of my government and the growlings of testy men."

"You could go into that camp right now. You could make short work of them and remove a difficulty . . ."

"I get nervous when politicians refer to human beings as *difficulties*."

"What I meant was—"

"You aren't thinking clearly about the repercussions. Always think in advance about the repercussions. That way, you won't have to suffer them yourself."

"I don't follow, General."

"I came here with clean hands, seeking the murderers of two white families. If I burn that camp and shoot noncombatants, the acts of those murderers will be forgotten. We would have ourselves a little war. And a war would abrogate the responsibility of the entire tribe to deliver the killers to me. I do not want any act of mine to cause the original crime to be forgotten."

This apparently made sense to Mr. Cass, who teetered away spouting that he had complete faith in the General. When Cass left, the General exhaled loudly and put the heels of his hands to his eyes. He lifted his spectacles from the desk and placed them over his nose. Seeing me shuffle foot to foot, he motioned at the chair across from him. I sat warily and watched him.

"I need horses. Lewis Cass and John Reynolds are the devils with whom I may one day have to make a dangerous bargain. That is why I went mild on Cass. He can get me horses. The War Department can't and won't finance troop-trained horses or men who can shoot from them."

I thought of the disaster awaiting us across the river should the Winnebago decide to attack our forces. He handed me some paperwork. As I left, he said, "Thank you for looking after my interests, Mister Cooke. And feel free to throw Governor Cass in the guardhouse when it suits you."

20 August 1827

A FEW days later, we crossed the river with the intent of showing our force to the Winnebago, the idea being they wouldn't attack if they believed us to be mighty. I tried to look mighty and hoped for the best. The General took a command of 310 foot troops, plus 200 men from Major Ketchum's command. Doubting their impartiality and self-control, the General left the Menominee in camp. The sun was hot upon us, and there was little wind. My brains felt to boil under my shako, and the men were awfully sore footed. It was frightening to walk into a place where we were outnumbered three to one by Winnebago warriors, ten to one if I counted babies and old ladies.

You could look down a line and see all the troops sweating from fear and from standing still in that heat. Then the General held a parade and reviewed the troops. He kept a sly sideward glance on the Winnebago chiefs as he went down the line of the regulars. The Winnebago looked vaguely offended when the artillerymen blew a stand of cottonwood to smithereens. However, it being done, the Winnebago women gathered up their wood baskets, slipped the leather thongs over their foreheads and set off to harvest firewood. The band played, the riflemen fired volleys into the clouds and blew up a lot of smoke. Winnebago men, women and children gathered curiously about us, pounding their own drums at the spectacle of the men marching in formation. I kept a wary eye upon the crowds, but their faces seemed friendly.

Then the General rode over to where the chiefs sat their mounts. With the aid of a three-hundred-pound translator named Antoine Le Clair, the General asked for the surrender of the Winnebago RedBird. The dust tossed up by people and horses turned the air around us brown. There was disgruntled murmuring from the red people who surrounded us.

One-Eye Decorah looked worried. He came forward and lifted his right arm to the sky. "Do not strike. When the sun is there tomorrow, we will come to council."

The General was satisfied by their offer and thought it fair to wait, but insisted that each of the chiefs give him one son to accompany him back to camp as a hostage to show their good faith. Eight young Winnebago men were brought forward and put under guard. The crowd didn't like that. They began whistling and jeering as the boys were led away over the river into our camp. We retired across the river, posting sentries and troops all along the shore. Bonfires burned at fifty-foot intervals. The fire reflected against the water like a great orange shield between the camps.

But the deadline came and went with no sign of One-Eye Decorah.

I was beginning to wonder if we had been duped into delay while the Winnebago prepared their offensive. The General was meeting with his field and staff officers, preparing for the worst.

We had not slept for waiting. Even as I write this, I can hear the sounds of the Winnebago camp across the river. At night, the tipis look like great orange cones illuminated by the fires. I could see families moving around inside them, going about their daily business. It seemed peculiar that we would have to move against them. I hoped not. I could not move against women and little babies.

The Winnebago keep fierce-looking effigies on high poles. They were ghastly heads of beasts or people made up of animal skins. The effigies flopped in the wind. As the General had just come in, I joked, "At least you can take comfort you don't see yourself depicted on those effigy poles."

He grinned in response. "Or perhaps, Mister Cooke, I simply do not recognize my own image."

23 August 1827

↠ THE mounted Winnebago chiefs descended into the Wisconsin, a wide river with a pebbled bed. The inlets swirled gray with the horses crossing; the river boiled under them. There we were, across the river from them on a sort of peninsula, surrounded on three sides by the Wisconsin River. We all looked to our commanders, waiting for word to fire, because the young Winnebago men slammed canoes into the water. They howled and sang and shot the sun, paddling with feverish energy around the keels in the river in a threatening way.

All of them were painted up for war.

Why isn't the General giving the order to fire? I wondered, chewing my bottom lip as I aimed my musket across the river. I watched the General for the word. I could see his jaw working in tiny movements, he squinted through his field glass, he talked the whole time to the officers nearest him; the calming talk one uses around a nervous horse.

Johnston said, "They look hostile, they're acting hostile, I think we should take the upper hand here. Why ain't he ordering it?"

"Johnston, maybe you were right about One-Eye Decorah."

"Of course I was right. He's a goddamned crook."

"Oh shit, how many do you suppose there are, Cooke?"

"In the canoes or on horses?"

"Shit."

Another wave of Winnebago warriors on horseback suddenly appeared in the distance, behind us. They must have crossed the Wisconsin where it bends back on itself, northwest of us, then ridden around our flanks. I heard the troops calling out to their commanders, asking them to give the fire order. I began composing my last will and testament in my head.

"Johnston, if they kill me—hey, Johnston, listen. If they kill me, I want you to give my journal to my Cousin Mary. The General's wife? Tell her to publish it posthumously . . . except the part about us going to the Bake Oven . . . and tell her to send the money to my mother."

"Cooke, I ain't got time to worry about that. Jesus, look at that group coming up behind us. Goddamnit, there's got to be three thousand behind us and half as many up front of us. Don't you let them cut off my balls. Or dig out my eyes. I hear they like to do that. You promise me, Cooke."

"Why the hell should I promise *you* when—"

"I ain't got time to argue with you, Cooke. Why ain't the General giving the order?"

There was an insane uproar of noise all around me. The horsemen coming from the east were nearly upon us. The warriors in the canoes shouted encouragement at the horsemen. Their women crowded the opposite shore, drummed an uncertain cadence, danced a simple step forward and back and blew a shrill flute that sounded like a pennywhistle. And coming up over the hill behind us were more Indians, all of them painted up and carrying weapons.

"Uh-oh," I said, poking Johnston in the bicep. "Look behind us. We're all surrounded."

Johnston turned about fast with his eyes bugging.

I looked a last time at the General, and his nostrils were flaring out as if he were trying to smell his way to a decision. He raised his left hand in the air, and there was a harsh sibilance up and down the line as we elevated our weapons. Still they came at us. I guessed in the first wave there were nearly five hundred Winnebago horsemen in the advance.

Then I saw why the General had hesitated.

Centered amidst the painted horsemen were nearly a dozen men carrying small scraps of white fabric. He had seen what I had not . . . that the Winnebago carried with them barely discernible flags of surrender.

"Why are their surrender flags so small, Cooke? What kind of idiots are they?"

"Well. Maybe they don't have a lot of experience at surrendering."

Seeing our men at arms, the Winnebago halted in the center of the river. They looked confused and frightened. I saw One-Eye Decorah look around in a panic. He hollered something at the men in the water. The Winnebago around him took up the call, and the men in the canoes fell silent. So did the women on the shore. The General, trusting in One-Eye Decorah, gave the at ease command, which we obeyed, reluctantly.

One-Eye and his men still paused in the river.

We looked at them and they looked at us and nobody trusted nobody. Seeing we were in a dangerous spot, the General ordered the eight Winnebago hostages brought forward in a hurry.

Meanwhile, I waited. And I sweated like a fount on a holy day of obligation.

The Winnebago hostages were brought around, and the General made it plain they were no longer hostages. Seeing their release, One-Eye relaxed and motioned his men forward. They came slowly, some with their hands far out from their weapons, to reassure us.

I said to Johnston, "Phew. It looks as if we are not going to hit the silks today."

I was eager to see RedBird, to look at the face of a man who was known to be an efficient killer of babies and women. RedBird directed his pony with his legs, for his left hand was filled with an ornamental pipe, and he held a white flag of surrender in his right. As he entered the camp, he was followed by one hundred of his warrior kin, some of them bearing American flags. He was dressed head to toe in white deerskin hunting shirt, leggings and moccasins, and on his head a bouquet of scarlet bird feathers. As he passed by me, I put my hand to the hat plate on my shako. It rattled with his booming voice as RedBird sang his death song.

But when the General motioned for RedBird to be put under guard, RedBird asked permission to make a speech. The General consented reluctantly, which did not please any of us. RedBird turned to his people and began to speak. We exchanged nervous looks.

RedBird bent to the ground.

We elevated our weapons, expecting him to draw a knife from his leggings.

But instead, RedBird pinched up some dust between his thumb and forefinger and shouted, "My life has left me like this." And he let the dust fly. Then he said, "I have done wrong and do not wish my people to be punished for my bad acts. So do not put me in irons, for I will not fight you. My life is gone behind me."

Then RedBird snapped his hands behind him to let us know that all was in the past.

The entire Winnebago Nation accepted this as RedBird's moment of death. The screech they set up caused all of us to jump. We aimed at the crowd, expecting them to rush us. But Kearny and the General, nearly in unison, shouted at us to stand down. They knew what the Winnebago were about, even if we didn't. The General quickly declared a peace, and the eight hostage warriors were returned to their fathers. He said that the Winnebago chiefs should follow him to his tent to celebrate their new friendship.

The General held the tent flaps for the chiefs in a gentlemanly style. He offered each chief a small bag of North Carolina tobacco, explaining that it was grown on his native land, which delighted the chiefs who took to smoking it instantly. The chiefs said they refused to speak further with Mr. Cass, whom they accused of forking. The tent grew so foggy with pipe smoke, I waved a clear space in the air now and again. Kearny and the General sat on one side of the table. Antoine Le Clair, or Fat Ass Le Clair as we call him, spread his bounty over three shuck-bottom chairs, heaving out each sentence with great effort. He lacked both Bright Sun's talent and her good looks. Seeing him in her stead made me realize I missed her the smallest bit.

Everything was going smoothly until Kearny's Negro boy rose up and walked circles inside the tent, spraying eau de toilette on the floor. This was the servant's own idea. He was relegated behind the Winnebago and was unaccustomed to the musk smell of their tanned deerskin clothing. I jumped up and put a stop to his perfuming, as I did not wish the Winnebago to take offense.

That was pretty much the whole dance. Major Whistler took RedBird and Wekau under guard to Fort Crawford, which the General has regarrisoned. They are to be kept there, pending trial.

At twilight, the General stood up before a line of campfires. He shouted the proclamation of peace to the Winnebago people, which Fat Ass Le Clair translated for him. The Winnebago women and children stared at the serpentines and drums. They nudged one another and laughed, thinking our music ridiculous, particularly "Parade." I have never liked it, thinking it long and dull. Anyhow, that night, bonfires burned brightly in the Winnebago settlement, and the warriors danced about with buffalo effigies, howling to a drum cadence that came over the water to us. We had been invited to join the dance, but the General politely declined. There was a festive mood going all around. Johnston approached the General with a bold request.

"Sir? Me and Cooke here, well, we have met some real nice Winnebago girls who have invited us to their tipis for coffee and—"

I glared at him for including me in this. The General interrupted him, "No."

"Ah . . . sir? What if the girls come over here?" Johnston made swimming motions with his hands as if the General couldn't grasp a river crossing.

"No."

"Aw sir, those girls look real nice. . . ."

"I said no. Johnston, didn't you ever hear about William Ashley and the Arikara in 1823? He and his fur-company employees went up the Missouri, counciled with the Arikara, arranged for a friendly horse trade, then that night, twenty of his men slept in the Arikara lodges. At dawn, they were all slaughtered, along with nineteen horses on the strand. The beach was greasy with human and horse blood."

"That's what I like about you, sir. You're well-scienced in the ways of these Indians. Ah, now, I ain't serenading you, sir, how did you see those little bitty white flags the Winnebago were carrying? I didn't see 'em. And Cooke sure as hell didn't see 'em?"

"I didn't see the surrender flags either," the General said.

Johnston momentarily lost the power of speech.

So I said, "Then why didn't you give the order to fire?"

"The women played flutes and drums on the shore in plain view. They had their babies with them, there were old ladies and old men there too. If the Winnebago intended to make war upon us, they would have sent the noncombatants away to a safe place. They didn't do that."

Johnston, whom I have decided to name Lieutenant Lickspittle, popped his fist into his palm and said to the General, "Young men may have the advantage of keen eyesight, but old men have something better . . . insight. General, I would follow you off a cliff."

I squirmed in embarrassment for Johnston. It's ugly to see a man slobbering like that. As for the General, he looked as if Johnston had just offered him a glass of pond water with green scum over it. "You'd follow me off a cliff, Johnston?"

"Yessir."

"But if you followed me off a cliff, it means you'd land right on top of me, and if the fall didn't kill me, you sure as hell would."

"Oh no, sir. I'd jump wide, like this, real wide, like on the other side of the cliff." Johnston slid one palm past the other off in a trajectory to show the General just what he meant.

"But if you jumped off the other side of the cliff, you wouldn't be following me. You'd be insubordinate, wouldn't you?"

Seeing Johnston scramble was torture enough for anybody, so the General sent him off fetching a bone, just to get rid of him. Looking sour, the General said, "He called me *old*."

So that was the whole of the Winnebago War, which to my thinking, wasn't a war at all. But the white people in the region called it a war, so as to feel there was justification for making trouble in the future with the red people. Besides, you can tell stories about yourself and bravery if you call it a war, can't you? Nothing has been settled about the lead mines, which is the real cause of trouble in the Lake Region. Dodge's slaves are still in shackles, while his white miners continue their thieving. More squatters are moving into the Sauk and Winnebago lands. Black Hawk and RedBird are in custody, and that ought to put us at our ease.

But I have my doubts.

I feel as if we have marched away from an arsenal, and though we have taken with us all the cordite and fuses, still we have left behind kegs of powder heating under an Indian sun. I don't know that we have truly solved the problem, but I am still in my skin, which is saying something.

15

Jefferson Barracks, Missouri, July 1830

ON the Fourth of July, people came to Jefferson Barracks to picnic and to watch the fireworks. The General hosted a parade and review. The offices' wives draped bunting and regimental flags over the hot yellow stone of the barracks. The colors flew from the flagpole, and the quadrangle was filled with a burgeoning crowd dressed in summer whites; ribbons fluttered from straw hats in pale colors that mocked the heat. Senator Thomas Benton was there in his shirtsleeves, milling through the masses, shaking hands with voters as his lovely daughters followed behind under green parasols. Children scurried and hollered, weaving through the throng, snapping willow whips.

Soldiers in gray fatigues sat alongside the stone walk upon the esplanade in the afternoon sun. Some boys were playing hustle cap with the tin lid. A pouf of dust flew up as they fidgeted their boot toes in the dirt. One small boy murmured, "Call it," and the other would say heads or tails, and then the boy holding the lid would flip it. A pile of stone marbles, brown and calcareous, lay before the cup of his hand. Families had claimed every pool of dappled shade from the black locust trees, and they sprawled under the elms and the oaks and listened to the band play marches.

Eloise cocked her head like an inquisitive bird, then rushed at me, saying, "Sister, you look spectral. I want you to rest right this minute. Sit down."

I lowered myself at the base of an elm tree. The roots pained out of the limestone like rheumatic knees. I picked up an elm key, and its beige wing crumbled between my fingers. Eloise fluffed down beside me with crisp little movements. She was light boned as a kestrel, and just as keen at per-

ceiving truth swimming under opaque surfaces. The skirt of her gown
bulged with the rolled newspaper she had thrust into one pocket. From her
other skirt pocket, she removed a copy of *A Vindication* and caressed the
spine, looking through the trees to where the bluffs fell off in scarps.

"You look tired. So does the General."

"He doesn't sleep."

"And you?"

"I don't sleep when he doesn't." Groups of women floated by, arm in
arm, chattering. They greeted us with nods and smiles. The steamers coming up from St. Charles whistled now and again, and the air was tainted with
smoke. Eloise fluttered her hand at Mrs. Kennerly. She said cautiously, "Well,
Sister, I may as well read this to you." She tugged at her waist pocket, un-
rolled the newspaper so I could see the masthead—the *Miners' Journal of
Galena*—and read aloud this flagged announcement,

> In the case of <u>United States v. Wekau,</u> for the murder of Methode and
> family, a *nolle prosequi* was entered and the prisoner discharged, Red-
> Bird having died of dysentery in prison. There being no bills found
> against a Sauk chief named The Black Hawk for attacking and firing
> upon keelboats, he was also discharged.

"Black Hawk has been released? They let him go?"

"Sister, it looks that way."

I snatched the paper from her and read frantically. "Why would they let
him go?"

"It's Independence Day for everybody, I suppose."

I kept my moody silence. An image came to me of Black Hawk running
through a cool forest, over a fern-covered ground that slowly filled with
shadows. Off in the distance, buttes curled like lion paws, and atop each of
them, his warriors awaited his homecoming.

Uncle William crossed the lawn with a stiff gait. He held my two-year-old
daughter, Elizabeth, and my three-year-old son, Walker, by the hand. "Like
herding cats," Uncle wheezed, eagerly handing the children over to me.

Our blanket was next to the Johnstons'. Mrs. Albert Sidney Johnston had
gone so thin since having a child in April that she looked a mere shadow of
her former self. Her cheeks were white and hollow. When we embraced
one another in greeting, I could feel her ribs through her dress. Her hair
smelled like a pelt. I knew Doctor Harding had prescribed a strict diet of Ice-
land moss and goat's milk to cure her of summer troubles. He bled Mrs.

Johnston three times a day to clear her lungs of fluid. She pressed her small finger to her pale lips and glanced around the parade grounds for sight of her husband.

Uncle opened our picnic basket too roughly, and the contents clinked. I paused to feel through the brown paper for breakage. I had hastily packed four glasses: gooseberry jam sealed with a white circle of writing paper dipped in egg; precious pie plant; piccalilli, a relish of onions and peppers; and lastly, one glass of Dahlia's coveted walnut catsup. Thinking I was distracted, Uncle stole into the picnic basket with a guilty look.

"Uncle, you put that apricot tart back in the basket! We're not eating until the General and Cousin Philip join us," I said.

"But I'm hungry," he whined, peering into the basket.

"Me too!" my son, Henry Walker, said.

"What are we having for lunch, Mary?"

"Fried patties of grouse with piccalilli or walnut catsup, peas cooked in butter with onions, apricot tarts, biscuits with gooseberry jam or pie plant relish—and all of this from my garden, can you believe it?"

"Oom-pah-pah," Eloise said, bouncing Elizabeth up and down on her lap in time with the band music. "What I can't believe, Mary, is that you eat radishes for breakfast."

"What's wrong with radishes for breakfast?" Uncle asked, breaking a piece of crust off the tart and popping it into his mouth. "All of the St. Louis Creoles eat radishes for breakfast. And green tomatoes for lunch. Now, there's a food I do not understand, thick rinded, hollow centered and lumpy-bumpy. Ah, Hermitage Moussec! Yes, m'dear, fill my glass." I did so, then Eloise held her goblet under the bottle with one hand and squeezed my daughter, Elizabeth, with the other.

"And what do you have in your basket, Mrs. Johnston?" Uncle asked, and Eloise nudged me and whispered, "He sounds like the wolf in 'Little Red Riding Hood,' doesn't he? Say, Mrs. Johnston, don't feed him anything or Uncle will follow you home, devour your grandmother, then he'll turn three circles and nap before your fireplace."

Mrs. Johnston's dark eyes flashed at Uncle. She pinched his cheek playfully. "William Clark, you can nap before my fire whenever it pleases you."

Uncle blushed scarlet and lofted his brows roguishly at her.

The pale blue ribbons Eloise wore about the crown of her hat tempted little Elizabeth. She grabbed at them with her fat fists and tried to put them in her mouth. Then Elizabeth's eyes brightened, her mouth opened in an expression of silent delight, as she strained to be free of Eloise.

"What are you going after there, baby? Oh no you don't, you don't want that old cricket."

"Tandy. Tandy," Elizabeth wailed. Once a day, at least, I hooked my finger into her mouth and liberated ladybugs, water bugs and grasshoppers from under her tongue.

The boardwalk filled up with spectators. They applauded the troops and waved small flags as the band struck up "Yankee Doodle." As the General passed by with his regiment—the Sixth Infantry—he glanced over and gave Walker a little salute. Walker raised both arms and said, "Up, Pa, Up!" I took Walker's small arm by the wrist and wagged it in the General's direction, then turned over my shoulder and gushed to Eloise, "Oh, isn't the General handsome!"

"No, he looks like a monument to himself. All that's missing are the pigeons."

"I'm hungry," Uncle William said. "At the very least you ladies could start bringing out the plates and flatware, couldn't you? I'm getting whittled on this wine."

Mrs. Johnston extended a cold plate of something brown and gelatinous to Uncle William. "Try these jellied calves ears flavored with sweet woodruff."

"Mrs. Johnston, there is nothing I like better than meat strongly flavored."

"Spoiled. He means spoiled. Uncle William likes his oysters, his rabbit and his beef spoiled and rank. But at least he doesn't eat radishes for breakfast like Sister Mary," Eloise said, laughing.

"Oh, leave off on me, Eloise. By the bye, Uncle, did you hear the authorities at Fort Crawford set Black Hawk free? Do you have any news of that?"

Uncle frowned into his glass, dipped his forefinger and smeared a winged creature out of his wine. He glanced up at me and mumbled, "Black Hawk's probably gone running to his British allies at Fort Malden for aid and succor. Besides, Mary, there's bigger news afoot than Black Hawk."

"What could be bigger than Black Hawk getting loose?"

Uncle dabbed a blotch of brown jelly from the corner of his mouth. "The Indian Removal Act has been passed into law." Eloise and I looked to Uncle, waiting for his explanation. He sipped his wine and said, "President Jackson is trumpeting the Indian Removal Act, and it's going to change the General's life in a big way. No more summers at home, m'dear Mary. Pack his bags for him."

Mrs. Johnston peeled a napkin from a plate of crayfish and handed it over the basket to Uncle. He squinted at their antennae, then said, "President

Jackson is going to force the General to remove every red soul from their homes on the east side of the Mississippi to the west side of the Mississippi. Beginning with the Sauk. Your husband is going to be one busy man."

"But the treaties . . ." I began, and Uncle shook his head solemnly,

"They'll force them to sign treaties all right, Mary. And then, every red man, woman and child will be forced out of their homes into a new land, a land foreign to them in every respect, because President Jackson wants to secure the country for white settlement. Tens of thousands of red people will be forced to wander homeless and defenseless. This crayfish is marinated, isn't it, Mrs. Johnston? In what?"

"Slippery elm bark."

Eloise smoothed a hand over Elizabeth's curls, and I took her into my lap. "Uncle, when will the act take effect?"

"I'm meeting with leaders from the various tribes—Mary hand me that napkin will you—in September. Jackson told Congress, 'The red man must submit to civilization, and if he doesn't he will 'erelong disappear.' Or something to that effect. The poor souls. Damn it all. I'll admit to you, Mary, I hold no great fondness for Black Hawk and his band. But . . . I feel I've abrogated my responsibility to them in some respect. We're going to move the Sauk into the heart of Sioux territory. Human sacrifices. I tell you, I'm dreading this council in September. The General will be there as will Bright Sun and Keokuk."

Uncle said this last part casually, but I caught him peeping at me, his eyes bright but cautious. Tens of thousands of people would be forced out of their homes. The idea of it sickened me. Worse yet, the General would be required to enforce this law. I knew what this "Removal Act" meant—it meant a war. The native people would never allow the government to shove them out of their homes and off their lands without a fight. I know I wouldn't.

My daughter, Elizabeth, scrunched up her mouth, brushed at her face with her fingers and whined, "Itches. Itches. See? See?" She lifted her little pink face to me, distressed by the mosquito bites on her delicate jaw. There were pink bumps up and down her forearms, she had scratched tiny blood spots atop some of them.

"Don't scratch, Elizabeth. No scratching."

I kissed each cheek and pronounced her better.

Eloise raised herself up to kneeling and waved at Cousin Philip, Lieutenant Johnston and the General, who were laughing about the bets they'd placed on the horses during the afternoon races.

Seeing his father, Walker ran across the lawn in his body-forward, awkward baby way, his little fat legs seeming to lag and his arms flailing. The General bent and clapped his hands, encouraging him to come on, then hoisted Walker upon his shoulders and gripped a pudgy knee in each hand. Walker clasped his hands over the General's face and beamed proudly. The General named Walker for a sixteen-year-old boy who had been the hero of Lake Champlain. Walker was plump as a dumpling.

"Are you hungry, Walker? I'll wager you are," the General said, lowering the boy to the blanket. The General motioned to Cousin Philip. "Cooke, sit down next to your Cousin Eloise and tell her why she ought not to allow Swedes to come calling on her."

Philip gawked at Eloise and asked, "Why are you letting a foreigner call on you, Lu?"

Eloise wiggled her shoulders coyly and popped part of a biscuit in her mouth, "He's not a 'foreigner.' He's a baron. Baron Frederick de Kantzow."

"That's worse, Lu. You could have your pick of boys here, gosh knows they're lonely enough."

"Oh, now there's motivation for you, Eloise," I said, laughing. "Desperately lonely men."

The General and Uncle exchanged a skeptical look, and Uncle asked, "Eloise, how much money does this 'baron' have?"

Eloise stiffened. "Why? Do you doubt he's really a baron?"

Uncle shrugged, but the General quaffed his wine, and after a pause said quietly, "I do. And even if he is a baron, he may not have a red nickel to his name."

Eloise fluffed about, a hen in a snit. The four of us fell silent. Walker fisted a hunk of patty into his mouth so that most of it hung over his bottom lip. His eyes watered with the exertion of chewing. I cupped my hand under his chin and said, "Spit it out, Walker. That's too much." I wrapped it in a napkin and pulled Elizabeth against me as I tried to balance a plate on my thigh.

Elizabeth sat drowsy eyed, with her forefinger in her mouth. She startled, gave a fearful jolt and her eyes flew open. She pointed above the General's head and she cried out, "Scratch!"

A boy with a shock of brushy brown hair, a broad face and green eyes, stood over us. He was dressed in a brown linsey-woolsey shirt and pants that shredded about the ankles. He touched his muddy work boot to the edge of our picnic blanket where the General sat. The General had his back to the boy and did not acknowledge him.

I smiled a chilly smile of the sort I reserve for people I dislike and asked, "What is it?"

"You ain't rememberin', is you."

Eloise looked him up and down and said contemptuously, "Why would we?"

"I ain't talking to you, skinny missy."

My eyebrows flew up, and I was about to hold forth with the boy on the decline of civility when the General exhaled in disgust, set his jaw and began to stand, but Cousin Philip said, "Allow me." Philip put his plate on the blanket, wiped his mouth with his napkin, then rose stiffly, saying, "Boy, it's not polite to intrude on people you don't know a' tall."

The boy, I guessed him to be about sixteen, perhaps seventeen, shuffled in place, and his flat green eyes turned cold. I scrutinized him, feeling the color rise in my cheeks at his rudeness. He had the most lifeless eyes I had ever seen. The boy pursed his lips and narrowed his eyes and blurted, "I s'pose it was fine enough for you to come into my house, and for my ma to feed you, but now I ain't good enough for you to say hello to?"

My skin prickled, and I put a protective arm about Elizabeth. "I remember now. You're the boy who was torturing that gander behind the house."

Uncle William begged Mrs. Johnston to fill his plate with cock's comb sauced in mushrooms. He ate steadily and voraciously as if this were a competitive event, seemingly oblivious to everything.

The General sighed and got to his feet, his knees made their familiar noises of protest and agony, popping and creaking. He began to hold forth, but Cousin Philip was having none of the boy's nonsense. With a swift motion, he twisted the boy's wrist so as to cause him to wince. I frowned at the ingenuous way Philip had put the lock on the boy and wondered where he had learned such a thing.

Philip said, "You're going to come with me peaceable-like."

But the General said, "What is your name?"

"Reason, Reason Stillman. You folks came to my ma's house a time ago and you ate at our supper table. My ma? She talked about that supper like she had been receiving royalty, she talked about it to all the neighbors until the day she died, like it was the best thing ever happened to her, to wait on you. 'William Clark of the Corps of Discovery ate my owl soup, so did his niece, the belle from Louisville, the rich girl what they call the Bullitt Beauty, and her new husband, the Great Western General.' Well, I knowed better then and I knowed better now. Ma's passed over, but I knowed better than to think you folks was anything special. You're just uppity. Now I try to be friendly and I see I ain't good enough for you."

"What are you doing here?" the General asked.

"I'm on my way up north. I hear tell the Saukies are goin' to be sent packin' and I intend to git some of that land for m'self. I heard the big Saukie village is free for the taking October through April. They leave big wood houses without no locks, and nobody watching, either. If I have to, I'll shoot a few Saukies, then I'll take m'land."

"All right, I've heard enough out of you," Cousin Philip said, easily looping both of the boy's wrists in his hand and dragging him along the lawn.

"Hey! Hey! You take your hands off a me, you yaller-legged chicken. You let me go." Reason Stillman struggled in Philip's grip, but Philip talked to him calmly, as if the boy were a riled barnyard animal. Reason wheeled along on bowed pins at the predictable angle of a body being dragged. He harangued Philip relentlessly. We heard Philip say, "Why I think the best thing for you might be an upside-down bath in the hogshead. What is that I smell on your breath? You been drinking, haven't you?"

I peered at the General, and I saw something there that looked like shock. Elizabeth and Walker looked to their father for reassurance. Elizabeth rubbed her hands over her cheeks and wrinkled her nose again and yawned. "Itches. Scratch."

The General took his seat, but he looked past me at the river, in a pensive mood. I passed an apricot tart to him. He poked the tart with his fork then set the plate aside. "Let's take a walk with the children before the fireworks start," he said.

Uncle was asleep by then, and Cousin Philip sprawled facedown on the blanket, moaning about having overeaten. Eloise lay on her back with her head upon Philip's shoulders. Her eyes were heavy lidded. She held a book of Keats and read aloud in a drowsing mumble, "'When I have fears that I may cease to be . . .'"

"My poetry's better," Philip said into the blanket. "Nobody dies in my poems."

The General put Walker back on the throne of his shoulders, and I held Elizabeth's hand as we slowly made our way past one family after another, pausing before each of them to say hello and ask after their health, and were they enjoying the festivities, and wasn't the weather more temperate than it had been of late? Then we left the crowd and brought the children around to the open ground in the west where the fireworks were set up.

Russell and Mahaffey stood before a prodigious quantity of gunpowder, swinging oiled torches perilously close to the combustibles. They had volunteered to light the rockets. Upon seeing us approach, they saluted the General. Russell's watery blue eyes bugged with excitement, and words came tumbling out of him.

"General sir, this night, Mahaffey and me are sending these rockets into the kingdom of the unknown. I could end this night perforated like a sieve. The fire will be enormous, a Genesis sort of fire, and I don't doubt that I will know an ecstasy of the like not experienced since Emperor Tiberius was at Capri."

I had no idea what this man was talking about.

Mahaffey thrust himself before Russell, backhanded his colleague, then bowed to me with a flourish and said most humbly, "Madam General. Please forgive the ramblings of this walleyed savage standing behind me. On Independence Day, Russell is overcome with gratitude to be here rather than in England, where none but noodles have the world in charge. General sir, your children are beautiful miniatures. Would the boy like the honor of putting fire to the fuse of the first rocket?"

"*No!*" The General and I cried in unison, pulling Walker back.

As we departed, the General mockingly made the sign of the cross over them and asked if they had made a last confession and did they wish to unburden themselves to him? No thank you, they said politely, as the General was a member of a church founded on the balls of Henry the Eighth.

"Good-bye Mr. Russell and Mr. Mahaffey," I said.

"Good evening, Madam General."

We watched the fireworks from the lawn before our house.

Fiery chrysanthemums bloomed out of the black sky in red and green and silver so that Elizabeth, standing with one arm about my knees and the side of her face in my skirt, looked up in awe, and I saw those flowers reflected in her dark blue eyes. She gasped, she pointed and said, "Frowwersh. Shtarsh."

The air was scented with gunpowder and trees releasing their summer oils into the night. Someone threw blank cartridges onto a distant bonfire. I lifted Elizabeth, and she splayed her hands, trying to touch the magic in the night air.

"Ffwt!" Walker said. "Bbbbshshquap! Zzzftbrr." Walker could make the oddest sounds. His cheeks vibrated, his tongue hummed so that he sounded like some small manufacture of wheels and cogs and pistons. He made exploding noises that began deep at the back of his throat before wiggling out of the General's arms. Nicholas, Dahlia and Billy stood on the lawn too. And when the last spray of light vanished, Dahlia gathered up the children to put them to bed for me.

The General and I lingered on the lawn, listening to the crowds retreating in the distance and the steamer bells calling the St. Louis visitors to board. An easy wind blew over the grass scattering the mosquitoes, the leaves rustled and it grew cool. We stepped onto the porch, I reclined upon one of the long chairs the General had built.

He said, "Stay right there, Mary, don't go anywhere."

"Where would I go?" I yawned, crossing my ankles and lifting my face to the breeze.

"I'll be back shortly."

"Mm." I said, closing my eyes and smiling to myself. It was quiet but for the crickets, the night birds and the river sounds. My gown ruffled a bit in the breeze, my petticoats seemed to glow in the darkness. The stone foundation of our house wheezed the musty odor of sunless soil. I heard his steps recede into the house, a drawer sliding open, the children muttering protests as Dahlia urged them to bed, his footsteps coming nearer down the hall, then onto the porch.

He tossed a package into my lap and said, "Open it."

Then he sat in the chair beside mine. He glanced aside at me as I untied the string and opened the large brown paper envelope. I gave him a quizzical look. "Harp strings? But these cost fifteen dollars. You must have sent to New York or Charleston for these. And my harp is in Louisville."

The fan of lines about his eyes deepened as he smiled at me. "No it isn't. It's on a steamer, under the watchful eye of Captain Keyes, and it will arrive here tomorrow. Will you play something for me when it arrives? Like the time I heard you playing at your mama's in Louisville?"

"You remember that day?"

"Of course I do."

"Still, to have spent so much on new strings and having it shipped . . ."

The General moved his shoulders back the smallest bit, and he set his jaw as he always did when he was in a mood against arguing. My voice faded away to nothing as I waited for him to remonstrate, but instead he spoke in a restrained and thoughtful way: "I like the idea of having that harp here, is all. It makes me think of your old life in Louisville when you wanted for nothing, when your life was one of grace and ease. My children should have music in their house, and their mother ought to have . . . anyway you'll need these new strings as the harp looks to have been hung on the willow, by your mother's account."

When I said nothing in response, only touched the paper over the strings, the General asked, "How can you ask if I remember that day? Of course I remember that day."

During my confinements we returned to Mama's house in Louisville, where she cared for me, helped my babies come into this world, then insisted that I rest for three weeks after the births. The General passed his days at the War Department and his evenings relaxing with me and the children in the luxury of Mama's hospitality. Elizabeth had been a particularly difficult labor, as she weighed a shocking ten pounds at birth. Walker weighed nine pounds. There had been some measure of damage that required monotonous bed rest, and late one December afternoon, as Walker and newly arrived Elizabeth napped, I slipped unnoticed from my bed. I donned a wrap and descended the stairs slowly, with great pain and discomfort to myself. I held tight to the handrail, and my legs felt wobbly.

I opened the door to the chilly music room, where, years before, Eloise had pleaded with me not to marry. The walls were pale, the air so cold I could see my breath. The room smelled of beeswax polish and wintry abandonment. The settees and *bergère* chairs were upholstered in pale yellows and dove grays, and the wood was painted white with faded gilt. The large windows brought the snowscape into the room. I crossed the floor to my harp, which stood covered with dust before the cold fireplace. I wiped the dust from it with the sleeve of my wrap and ran my fingers across the strings.

Feeling worn in spirit, my body tattered and exhausted, I wanted the solitary pleasure of creating music for myself. So, in a manner uncharacteristically hesitant, I took my seat in the chilly room. I wanted the strings to sound correctly, to prove to myself there was something of the old me still left. Please let me remember, I thought, as I pressed my cheek to the cold rosewood and touched my hands to the strings. Something simple, perhaps, "Star of the County Down." That's easy enough. I could play that from memory. I closed my eyes, because I did not want to see my fingers fumble. My shoulders hunched a bit in anticipation of error.

I smiled to myself when the first notes sounded in the lonely room. I played the "May Song" from memory too, my eyes closed, my senses filled up with music. When I had finished the piece and stilled the strings, I glanced up to find the General sitting across from me on the yellow *bergère* chair. I remember that I turned scarlet, fumbled my words, looked away. I suppose I resented his intrusion a little. No. No, I resented him being there more than I would admit to myself

"Play something else," he said.

And I did, but then the music was for him, not for me.

I played a song I first heard when I was sixteen years old, in the spring of 1820, while I was living with the Ursulines. I was drawn to the balcony overlooking the fountain where a young Irish woman was washing altar linens. She wasn't much older than me, and the *place* was covered over with apricots blooming decay. The woman's hair was auburn, and her fair arms disappeared into the water of the fountain. Each Wednesday, she sang to herself, and to anyone else who would listen to her. What could a man do to make a woman so mournful? I had wondered, leaning over the balustrade, watching the sun glint off her copper hair. The laundress turned and looked over her shoulder toward me, sheltering her eyes with a wet hand. She couldn't see me though, as I was behind the sun. In August, when the courtyard was heavy with the fragrance of catalpa blooms, I noticed that her belly was rounded. The verses seemed to change, *"Where are you going, across the water? Take me with you, to be your partner."* In October, the grounds smelled of smashed persimmons and damp brown leaves, and I could see that the heavy work taxed her. She stopped often as she scrubbed, she lifted the white linens with clumsy effort, *"Sun, moon, and stars from my sky you've taken. And God as well, if I'm not mistaken."*

In December, the laundress did not come. I asked one of the nuns where she had gone, but she made a clicking noise and said the woman had died of something I didn't need to know about.

When I finished playing the song, the General lowered himself next to me. He asked what the music meant, and whether there were words to go along with it, but I could not translate those emotions for him. It would have been as if I were betraying that girl's secret. I dropped my chin and would not meet his gaze.

He said, "Mary, that was beautiful. Very beautiful."

It was a rare compliment—one of the few he gave me in sixteen years of marriage. I kept it safe within me, and opened it up on the worst of days, remembering how he knelt beside me, and that he had said something I had done could be beautiful in his eyes.

16

St. Louis, Missouri, September 1830

🌬️ IMAGINE for a moment that into the same house, with bedrooms separated by three narrow feet of hallway, you place one fervently passionate young man of seventeen and one lissome, dark-eyed girl of fifteen. The boy and girl took every meal together. They passed fevered glances at one another in the library of the house, touched hands in passing. They spied upon one another, they shared secrets and took long walks, and the heat transferred from one to the other was so intense that neither of them slept at all.

He whispered through the keyhole of her door, "Come walk with me." And she rose from the bed in her white nightdress, whispering back, "Wait for me on the back piazza." He did. She appeared, hugging herself, with her black hair shining loose. The boy licked his lips and brushed the lock of hair from her shoulder, but his knuckle passed over the round swell of her cotton-covered breast. He withdrew his hand as if it had been burned. They could not speak of their desire as they lacked the vocabulary of experience, which was for the best as they were, in the eyes of the world, brother and sister.

Yes, well, it sounds worse than it was, for the girl was Mary Radford, daughter of Harriet Radford, Uncle William's second wife, and the boy was Meriwether Lewis Clark, or Lutie as he was known to us, Uncle's firstborn son by his wife Juliet. Lutie and Mary Radford were second cousins, so there wasn't any *dangerous* degree of consanguinity—but the situation was unsettling all the same. When Uncle married Harriet, she moved into the house on Vine Street with her fifteen-year-old daughter, prompting poor Lutie to spiral into a tizzy of lust.

Lutie's manly resolve to restrain himself was dashed to ecstatic bits that night on the back piazza when Mary Radford threw her arms about his shoulders and kissed him with her mouth open. He feared all the arteries in his body had exploded. The two of them began slowly, tentatively, but they kept up these exploratory trysts every night, and sometimes during the day, removing sheaves of modest clothing. They met secretly in the root cellar, gnawed at one another until their lips were swollen and perspired until their undergarments stuck to them.

They romped in the carriage house too, until one fateful day, Uncle William decided to have a look at some old tack to determine whether additional purchases were really necessary. In his customarily obtuse fashion, he walked about humming, muttering to himself, his white hair like a halo around his head. He tinkered with a tenuous-looking throat latch, he winced at frayed harnesses, he shook his head at the sad state of things generally, then hoping for the best, he yanked open the warped door to the storage closet and there, amidst the spare bridles, he found his stepdaughter in her natural state with her stepbrother, both of them straining toward earthly bliss.

I am told Uncle shrieked and ran from the building with his hands cupped over his eyes.

I know about all of this because Mary Radford told me herself, intermittently weeping, and detailing one lubricious session after another though I tried (really, I tried) to silence her with assurances that after the first anecdote I had grasped the general state of things. And I mention this little love saga, because in September of 1830, the lives of those two young lovers became inextricably bound up with an Indian scare, an almost-duel and the General's infamous blue curses that shocked the delicate ears of the society ladies of St. Louis scarlet.

But I am getting ahead of myself.

Uncle William arrived at our home two hours after the incident in the carriage house. He leapt onto our porch, dabbing his forehead with a kerchief. I feared he would have an apoplectic fit. He accepted the General's offer of a potation, downed it in one swallow, then gasped, "Write a recommendation for Lutie to West Point, General. Write it now. I've got mine here." He waved a missive about, then refilled his glass. "I'm outfitting the boy with a five-year-old gelding and three hundred dollars and shipping him out."

"Why?" the General asked.

"He's playing Romeo to Mary's Juliet."

And so Lutie was sent East on a steamer headed for New York. Mary Radford disobeyed Uncle William and saw Lutie off at the levee. Two years passed, and during that time, Uncle—who was obtuse to the point of sadism at times—wrote letters to Lutie, most of them filled up with talk of Miss Radford's debut, her beauty, and how she was being feted by everyone from the Prince de Joinville and Prince Frederick William of Wied to officers from Jefferson Barracks. But Lutie learned that no one was more assiduous in his courting of Miss Radford than Major Kearny.

Major Stephen Watts Kearny was the most eligible bachelor in all of St. Louis, which was saying something, given that men outnumbered women two to one. In his early thirties, Kearny was a tough veteran of the frontier, perceived by many as a harsh disciplinarian. He was very serious about most everything. So both the General and I were baffled when Kearny began courting Mary Radford, who was by then a seventeen-year-old slip, with little troubling her aside from the color of her gown and who was named on her dance card. Major Kearny approached Mary Radford with a vehement sincerity that made me cringe in fear for him. He declared that he would obliterate his opponents by sheer will, he would make Mary Radford see she required his guiding hand, his protective arm, his earnest heart.

In bed one night, the General said to me, "Kearny is quenchless over that girl."

Kearny proposed marriage. Mary vacillated. Kearny proposed again. And again. He argued his case, Mary demurred, thinking of Lutie and the love letters he wrote to her every day. But Uncle said that if Lutie ever tried to touch Mary Radford again, Uncle would exile him to Algeria to live with the Arabs. Foreseeing a Lutie-less future, Mary Radford agreed to wed Kearny on the last day of September in 1830.

The wedding was to be held upon a perfect autumn day, the sort of day when the air sparkled with a seasonal chill but the sun was warm and the grass had gone red and yellow on the hills. Eloise, Dahlia, the children, the General and myself crammed into the carriage. But when we turned onto Vine Street, there was a jam of conveyances, and Indians on piebald ponies and their women with dog-pulled travois mingled amongst a clotted river of expensively dressed Creole families.

About a hundred Plains Indians had assembled for the council on Indian Removal that was scheduled to take place the following week. The Clark lawn was submerged under geodesic willow lodges and cattail flag–covered *pukwe'gans*. The lawn was pocked with fire rings, the air was redolent with boiling meat and roasting meat and frying meat.

Wedding guests in stovepipe beaver hats and gowns as soft as London smoke walked stiffly and rapidly up the brick pathway. They looked neither left nor right, clearly frightened out of their wits by the Indians. The guests scurried to the entrance where the Negro butler whooshed them inside with a worried look about, then stood guard at the door.

Eloise darted up the walk, holding Elizabeth and Walker by the hand. I adjusted my bonnet, looped my arm through the General's and straightened the kinks out of my spine. A low wrought-iron fence separated each side of the yard from the walk. Upon seeing the General arrive, his old friends and acquaintances came up to the fence to greet him. Bright Sun was there. I smiled my special chilly smile at her, I asked after her young daughter, I inquired after her health. I was proud of myself for carrying off a civil conversation without demonstrating any jealousy whatsoever. The General was more enthusiastically inclined to her than I would have liked, but all the same, I was painfully gracious.

The Clark house was crowded to suffocation. We could not move without everyone in the room having to adjust their stance. Glasses clinked with precious chips of ice salvaged from last winter's river and sawdusted to perfection in the icehouse. Guests discreetly hooked fingers into their drinks to fish out small bits of wood dust. The late afternoon light ochred and sifted through the brown oak leaves framing the windows. The Indians pressed their faces against the glass, cupping their hands about their brows to see inside the Clark house. They rapped on the glass, talked through it, signaled to us and made faces.

Down the hall, in the ballroom, the orchestra tuned up before the open windows, and the caterer and his staff bumped and nudged their way through the crowd, lofting trays. The florist walked about with shears and twine, tweaking arrangements of stephanotis, forced jonquils and hothouse roses. The baker fussed over an uneven spot of icing upon the wedding cakes.

We found Major Kearny, Cousin Philip and Lieutenant Johnston milling with a dozen other officers in a mahogany-choked anteroom off the center stairway. They smoked pipes and nipped from pocket flasks. Major Kearny looked hollowed out and sickly nervous. His eyes worked up and down the staircase, and beads of perspiration dewed on his forehead. He paced across the room with his arms folded across his chest. I thought he was going to be sick.

The orchestra struck up incidental music, which gave me pause. It was familiar, and though I could not place it, I knew the simple melodies were inappropriate for a wedding. I frowned and listened more closely. No, it couldn't be. Just then, the officers stepped from the anteroom, squinting and listening to the music too.

I nudged the General, "Is that chow call? And stable call? For wedding music?"

Cousin Philip and Lieutenant Johnston burst out laughing. Kearny skated into the hallway over wax-slick walnut floors. The General tried to be help-ful, but he wasn't. "Good idea on the music, Kearny. I like it. Is lights-out next? Or maybe roll call?"

"Nothing is going right today. Nothing." Major Kearny's face was a knot of frustration and worry. He slapped his gloves in his palm and looked about helplessly. He tugged me away from the General's side. "Mrs. Atkin-son, would you check on Miss Radford for me? I have a bad feeling."

"Major, you're just nervous. Everyone is nervous on their wedding day."

"No. This is different; she may have doubts."

He gripped my forearm tightly, squeezing a yes out of me. I slipped from the anteroom, passed up the stairs, being careful not to step upon the girls huddling in the corners telling secrets. I peered down the stairwell as the Reverend Mister Thomas Horrell—the skittish rector from Christ Church— was urging the guests to take their seats in the library for the ceremony. Then I knocked on the door. It whipped open, and there stood Mary Rad-ford, dressed in a rose-pink gown, darkly violet blue lobelia sprouting all over her head, and her eyes small from weeping. Upon seeing me, she dragged me inside, then sank to the floor, a despondent pink bubble.

"Why, oh why, is this happening to me?"

"Where is your mama, Miss Radford? I'll go get your mama. Or Uncle William."

"No, no, no, please no. Uncle William is so peculiar. And Mama wouldn't understand; they blame Lutie for everything. But you'll understand. Please help me. Please, Mrs. Atkinson. Everybody's scared of you. They'll do what you say."

I frowned at her, deciding whether I was flattered or insulted. Then I thought of poor Major Kearny and put myself back on the road. Miss Rad-ford made skupping noises as she choked back her tears. I patted the top of her little eggshell skull.

I said, "I really think you ought to talk to your mama about this. I'll fetch her up for you."

"*No!* I can't talk to her! She doesn't know anything about being in love— look at who she married the second time around. She *sleeps* with Uncle William."

Eloise knocked on the door and I admitted her. She sat on the floor with her legs straight out before her, her jaw hanging slack, her eyes wild with envy. She stared inelegantly as Miss Radford recounted a litany of petting and panting, without omitting a single lubricious detail.

Eloise asked, "So what did *it* look like?"

Miss Radford sniffled, and shot a swollen look at Eloise. *"It?"*

Eloise kicked her heels against the floor in exasperation. "The central matter of curiosity. Mister Clark's birkie."

I scowled at my sister. "Really, Eloise. His *birkie?*"

"His fugleman. His wire-puller, his whipper-in, his factotum."

Miss Radford wintled across the floor on her bottom until she slumped beside Eloise, who rolled her eyes and bared her lower teeth. "I'm asking you to describe it exactly. When you touched it, what did it feel like? A bird? A serpent? A desert lizard?"

A dozen tiny furrows appeared on Miss Radford's blank brow. She attempted to answer Eloise's question with an artistic loose grip of her little hands, one stacked upon the other, but this was lost upon Eloise. "I am sick and tired of nobody ever giving me an answer," she fumed.

"Eloise," I said helpfully. "A tulip."

"A tulip?"

"A stalk, a bloom."

Eloise squinted up at the ceiling, silently repeating, A tulip, a tulip.

Miss Radford threw herself against the lavender silk of my shoulder and left a wet stain of misery there. I mopped at her nose with a handkerchief and began, "Miss Radford . . ." But my little speech was stillborn, because the entire house rumbled with booted footfalls thundering hollowly up the staircase.

"Mary Radford, don't you do it! I'm coming for you," a voice shouted.

And then followed a chorus of male voices shouting, "Get him! Somebody stop him! I'll mow him down, I'll shoot him dead on the landing! Check your priming!"

Lutie whirled into the room and brushed his long hair out of his eyes. He shoved a highboy before the door, a chiffonier before the highboy then fell to the floor like a postulant before Miss Radford, who scrambled to him on her hands and knees. The lovers percolated longing and woe. For a few minutes, I allowed them their effusions, considering that they were much like retrievers being returned to a bird-rich field; you had to let them shake off the hunt lust before they could reason with a task.

"Mister Clark! Miss Radford! Get up off the floor. Compose yourselves."

I was surprised when they obeyed me. Clinging to one another, they cast a wounded look at me. I clasped my hands before me and began firmly, "Should you decide, Miss Radford, not to go through with this wedding, at the very least you owe Major Kearny a discreet explanation. Oh, stop it, both of you. Lutie, put your hands in your pockets. Miss Radford, splash your face and stop whining. You must stop behaving like rutting goats if you expect to be treated like adults."

"Mrs. Atkinson, how did you know to marry the General? What was it about him?"

"He came along in the off-season when I was bored. He promised he wouldn't go feeble."

In the hallway, a blue wedge of angry officers pounded upon the door and crushed against one another while the General shouted above the din, "Mary! Are you in there?"

"Yes!" Miss Radford and I responded in unison.

"Is Tomfoolery in there with you?" the General asked.

"Henry, that is not his name."

"Why, it ought to be. Goddamned Tomfoolery!"

"Lutie!" Major Kearny growled. "Lutie, you come out here and face me like a man. You stay away from that little girl! Lutie, you coward, come out of there now!"

"I am not a coward!" Lutie retorted.

"I contradict you, sir!" Kearny shouted back.

A red-faced Lutie stood on tiptoes, balled his fists and shouted at the door, "I contradict you twice. Maybe three times! And a hundred times after that. Forever!"

There was a disgruntled silence, then Kearny spoke. "Lutie, I challenge you. Meet me on Bloody Island, tomorrow at dawn."

I interrupted that nonsense. "Major, don't be ridiculous. You're not going to shoot a boy. Not this boy at least."

To the General's thinking, an insult to his closest friend and favorite officer was the same as an insult to his own honor. He was working himself into a rage. The General rapped on the door as if his knuckles bore the authority of the state. He drew a breath to stoke his fulmination. "Mrs. Atkinson, I demand that you come out of that room. You will bring Miss Radford with you. Miss Radford, you will marry Major Kearny, do you understand me? I order you to marry him. Come out here before I knock this door down."

Eloise laughed. "The General huffed and he puffed and he blew the door down."

I said, "You can't order Miss Radford to marry Major Kearny."

"Like hell I can't. This is a travesty, it's a heap of horseshit that a seventeen-year-old bit of fluff . . . is affronting one of my officers."

"General Atkinson, I am not fluff. Don't you call me fluff. I'll tell Uncle William, I will."

"Lutie! Come out here, I am going to horsewhip you, you horny little bastard. Goddamn it, I am sick and tired of this shit. I hate weddings as it is, and you're dragging this one out, which is cutting into my card-playing time. Little sonofabitch."

From the room below us, I heard women gasping with predictable shock. The officers in the hallway fell silent. It occurred to me that a chorus of guests might be observing all of this from the foot of the stair, so I asked quietly, "General, is Reverend Horrell standing out there?"

"Yes," he admitted, his tone surly.

"Are there ladies and small children out there too?"

"Yes," he growled

"Henry, come to the door." I moved the furniture, my husband poked his face into the interstice. Our lips almost touched. I pecked him on the mouth, which unsettled him in the manner intended. He blinked and mumbled something. I patted his cheek with my fingertips, and in a whispering voice, I said, "You ought not to curse before the minister, ladies and children."

"Mrs. Atkinson, you are being insubordinate . . ."

"Yes, yes, this blustering is very impressive, but you can't order Miss Radford to marry Major Kearny. As embarrassing as this is, we aren't going to resolve this by allowing either Kearny or Lutie to kill the other, are we? Well, are we?"

Another hard silence from him, some conspiratorial murmuring in the hallway until I said, "Henry, send the hanging posse back downstairs. When Miss Radford is calm, I'll ask for Major Kearny. Doesn't that sound like a good idea? Of course it does. Go on, now. If it makes you feel better, you can threaten Lutie one last time."

"Come out here, you little pisser!" The young officers joined in, "Yeah, come out here, you pisser!" A moment of expectant silence followed. And then, "All right, Kearny, join me for a jigger in the study, the rest of you too. What are you waiting for?"

"But General!"

"I said we're moving out!"

"Yes, sir." The stomping and grumbling receded in the distance. Lutie swallowed hard and wore a panicked look. He paced about, searching the floor for bits of wisdom that may have fallen out of his pockets. Then he turned to Miss Radford.

"I am poor. At least I will be until Pa dies, and he ain't showing any signs of faltering. And even if we married, he'd cut me out of the money, wouldn't he?" Miss Radford didn't say much. I sensed Lutie was a bit relieved by her hesitancy. Doubtless he conceived the romantic notion of rescuing her, but having made his appearance, Lutie realized he wasn't prepared to keep a wife. Particularly not one as expensive as Miss Radford.

I put my hands on Lutie's bony shoulders, his dark head drooped. I lifted his chin with my hand and said, "Lutie, no decisions need be made today. Sleep in the carriage house until you can talk this over with Miss Radford and your pa."

He gulped, then looked over his shoulder at Miss Radford, whose mouth was trembling.

"Now, Lutie, say good-bye to Miss Radford."

"Good-bye, Mary. I'll come for you tomorrow morning. I will. You'll see."

"Good-bye, Lutie."

I shoved him out the door. I watched him walk somberly down the steps and past the study where the officers were cloistered, drinking of course—fueled with whiskey, bourbon and hurt pride.

That was when I recognized my mistake. I should have sent Lutie out the back door.

Upon seeing him pass by, the officers roiled out of the room after him. Lutie kicked up a sprint, so did the blue wave. I scrambled down the stairs with Eloise in tow. Lutie dashed out the front door onto the brick walk, then ran past the native peoples convening on Uncle's lawn. The officers ran after him, Cousin Philip in the lead, as he was the slightest and swiftest and eager to win points with his comrades. About a half dozen Indians, young turks of an impulsive age who considered William Clark their friend, thought Lutie to be in danger. Out of bold loyalty to Uncle, the Indian warriors chased after the officers.

Seeing himself the reluctant head of a parade, Lutie scurried around to the back of the Clark house, entered the back door, ran through the ballroom and into the grand library where hundreds of wedding guests were seated. Upon seeing the terror on Lutie's face, the guests rose to their feet. When they saw the Indian warriors—who believed themselves to be coming to Lutie's aid—they knew there must be an Indian massacre in the making.

"The Indians have come to kill us!" a woman screeched; worse—everyone believed her.

Some tried to jump out the huge windows, others knocked over chairs. Dowagers and elderly men in colonial smallclothes escaped down the hall and out the front door. I flattened myself against a wall and stood on tiptoe so as not to be trampled. I glared at the General over a thundering herd of Creoles.

"This is your fault," I said.

The General cupped his hand to an ear and pretended he couldn't hear me.

The Indian warriors went bug eyed at the sight of the stampeding white people. They turned tail and scurried out the front door. The peaceable red peoples camping on the lawn jumped to arms at the sight of what they believed to be an imminent massacre by bloodthirsty white people, but quickly discerned that the wedding guests were panicking for some reason unconnected to them. They were baffled by the matrons and demoiselles collapsing in the street because they could not exert themselves and simultaneously breathe in their tightly laced corsets.

One week later, Miss Radford married Major Kearny at Maracastor, Uncle William's country house. Mrs. Kearny presented Major Kearny with eleven children, proof positive he met some of her expectations. But on that last day of September 1830, all we knew was that I had failed to patch together Major Kearny's wedding ceremony. The wedding guests went home. We stood in the viburnum thicket, watching people crowd out of the house and onto Vine Street.

Bright Sun turned to Uncle William and asked, "Mister Clark, will you talk to the people today? Call them to council now. They want to hear, then they want to return to their homes. The Sauk most of all. The Sauk have something to tell you."

AUNT Harriet, dressed in midnight-blue silks, wearing an exotic blue rebozo over her graying curls, tried to block the door with her considerable person, but the native peoples entered her house anyway. They didn't speak English, so they couldn't be faulted. A company of officers performed guard duty, Johnston patted the chiefs down for weapons, Cousin Philip collected knives and flintlock pistols in a heap by the viburnum bushes. The rest of the soldiers took up guard points about the house and down the hallway. As they had been imbibing before the wedding ceremony, some of these sentries looked unsteady on their feet.

As the Indians marched through the door, Aunt Harriet signaled them to stop, but with her arms raised above her head, it looked as if she were surrendering. The Indian chiefs held their arms up too, reflecting Mrs. Clark's surrender posture, thinking this must be the greeting she preferred. She pointed and poked in the general direction of the council wing.

"Go around to the council house. The council house!" They ignored her. Aunt Harriet finally slumped on the staircase, rubbing her eyes, trying not to cry. Uncle wearily directed the delegation into the ballroom, but Aunt Harriet said, "Oh, Willie, we may as well feed them. All this food going to waste."

And so about seventy Indian chiefs were led into the dining room, where the table had been laid out with covered dishes and silver serving utensils. They plucked slabs of ham and medallions of veal out of sauce with thumb and forefinger. The chiefs assumed the serving utensils placed beside the dishes were gifts intended for them and pocketed them accordingly.

The General and I came up on the line and found no ladle beside the mashed turnips. He pushed up his sleeve, dunked his hand into the turnips and slopped them onto my plate. He grinned at me as he wiped his fingers on the tablecloth.

"You're enjoying this, aren't you?" I said.

"Yes. You never let me eat with my fingers at home."

I moved on down the line, dipped my chin and asked in a low tone, "How do you think they will take the news?"

"Badly. To use your words, Mrs. Atkinson, the Removal Act is a swindle."

"What will you do if—"

"Agh, there won't be an 'if.' The Removal Act will be read aloud in several languages after which the men will retire to council together over the implications. They'll gather with your uncle again tomorrow. Pig's feet souse? No? How about fried apples?" He lifted a silver lid and squinted at a white soup, shook his head and replaced the lid.

"Aren't you worried? After all, aren't you the one who's going to do the 'settling'?"

"Yes, but peaceably. Oh, look, salami of duck."

"You hope, sir."

"No, it's duck salami, I'm sure of it."

"Henry. Are you going to disobey a direct order?" I whispered.

"No."

"Then what?"

"There are ways to accomplish this without hurting people. Tea rusk?"

"Uncle said that the hunting was poor west of the Mississippi, and that the red people who lived there now were fighting with one another over hunt lands. He said most of the plains people were going hungry. Why would President Jackson send more people into an area that was depleted of game?"

The corners of his mouth turned down; his eyes had that familiar dark look. I looked down at my full plate and then up at the General. "President Jackson intends to starve them into submission, doesn't he?"

"He hopes that intertribal warfare will finish the rest as they fight to control hunt lands. How do you suppose the Sioux will react when they hear the Sauk are being moved onto their hunt lands, keeping in mind the Sioux and Sauk have been at war for about two hundred years?"

We stood by the windows, face to face, intimate as new lovers, leaning into the curtains with plates in our hands. "What will you do?" I asked. The General glanced out the window and feigned a light tone, but his voice was bitter, "Tell me, Mary. Do you think there can be such a thing as a Christian soldier?"

IN 1830, there were six thousand soldiers in the entire United States Army spread over six thousand miles of inhabited ground. Most frontiersmen had never seen a United States soldier and they preferred it that way. Large standing armies brought to mind the brutal excesses of Europe and the oppression Americans had sought to escape. Every frontier cabin boasted one gun posted above the door, for a man could not rely upon the government to defend him. He had to rely upon himself to protect his family. I shared the General's hope for a peaceful future. I doubted peace was a possibility. The General had made peace in difficult times many times before, but this time would be different.

The orchestra had been dismissed. The assembly of chiefs sat upon the ballroom floor with clean plates before them. Cousin Philip Cooke, looking frazzled with his hair mussed, rubbed at his eyes and penned notes, pausing now and again to massage a cramp out of his hand. Near his feet sat a minor Sauk chief adorned with an otter-fur hat, a pair of exquisitely worked moccasins with broad, generous flaps, an ornately embroidered breechclout and little else. He had twined a magnificent piece of horsehair plume and turkey bristle into his hair roach. From the corner of my eye, I glanced sidelong at the hollowed flank of his buttocks, then at his profile.

Every Sauk in the room looked gaunt and hungry.

Uncle shifted about before the orchestra screen of red roses and yellow jonquils, green vines and white stephanotis. He held an official-looking paper at arm's length. He struggled with the size of the print as he read aloud the full text of the Removal Act.

I observed Bright Sun with a sharp eye. Now and again, she looked pointedly at the General. Occasionally, he regarded her too.

When Uncle finished reading the Removal Act, the chiefs looked about to one another, whispered about this new law, then fell silent—from disbelief or confusion, I know not which. They seemed to pass the idea around amongst themselves for consideration.

Then Bright Sun requested permission to address the assembly not as a translator, but as a representative of the Sauk people. Uncle refused. I thought he looked frail, with his shoulder-length white hair hanging loose and brushed off his high forehead. There was a curve to his shoulders I had not noticed before.

"Clark, there isn't any harm in Bright Sun having her say. I'd like to hear her out," the General said.

Bright Sun took a deep breath and held her hands flat against her ribs to keep them from shaking. She kept her chin high, but kept her eyes downcast as she spoke in a strong voice that carried throughout the ballroom.

"When the Sauk left Saukenuk to hunt last winter, the Americans stole into our wickiups. A Chemokemon family—I mean to say—some Americans, took Black Hawk's wickiup. This is my home too. Our family returned home in the spring to find strangers living in our home! But we did not harm them, we left them in peace. We built a new wickiup and we did not raise our voices to them. We thought we could live in peace.

"I tried to make corn for my daughter. But the Chemokemon say I cannot make corn. When I plant the seeds, they come the next day and stand over my garden with their guns and tell me they will shoot me if I return. Then they fenced my corn lands.

"The Americans brought barrels of whiskey into Saukenuk to sell to the Sauk men and boys. Black Hawk will not drink the whiskey and he will not let his men drink the whiskey. So Black Hawk put his axe into the barrels, and the whiskey poured into the dirt. The Chemokemon said Black Hawk must pay them for the spilled whiskey. Last winter, we received an annuity of one thousand dollars. The traders took nine hundred dollars. They gave one hundred dollars to the squatters who complained about the whiskey.

"This winter, the Sauk people will be hungry. The Great Father tells us we must go to the Iowa lands with Keokuk, to our new home. Keokuk and some others have gone to the Iowa lands. They tell us the ground in Iowa cannot be broken for corn with hand tools. They say the grass is so dense it cannot be broken. When the Chemokemon plant the corn in the Iowa lands, they have oxen and plows. Yet we are expected to do this with hand tools? What will our people do if they cannot hunt and they cannot make corn?

"I say to you, Red Hair, your treaties with the Sauk are no good. Why? The cornfields around Saukenuk do not belong to the men. The cornfields belong to the Sauk women. The women break the ground, plant the seeds and make the corn. Not the men. The Sauk men could not sell the cornfields to you, because the Sauk men do not *own* the cornfields. The cornfields belong to the Sauk women. Look at your treaties, Red Hair, do you see the names of any Sauk women there? No. The Sauk women will not leave Saukenuk. We will not move."

Despite my jealousy of Bright Sun, I was moved by her courage. And I thought her argument a good one, but I wondered where the Sauk would remove to, if they believed the Iowa lands were unsatisfactory? Her speech garnered no response from the chiefs, as she had delivered it in English. Clearly Uncle and the General were her intended audience. Uncle folded his arms across his chest and did not respond to her, recognizing there was no need to respond, for the other native peoples had no idea what she had said. He turned his face away from her and said, "You receive a fee to translate. I don't give a damn about your opinions."

Bright Sun lifted her chin so that her face was parallel with the ceiling. It was an awkward stance, but then, as I scrutinized her, I saw why she was doing it. Her eyes were swimming with tears. She began to retort, but the General tipped his head near to hers and said, "Miss Bright Sun, why don't you and I have a talk in the hallway so you can tell me more about Saukenuk in private?"

He waited as she looked about the room. Upon seeing the General motion in the direction of the door, I rose and followed after them. I was not about to leave them alone.

Uncle William declared the council adjourned. It certainly hadn't seemed like much of a council to me. I had expected to see Keokuk, perhaps even Black Hawk. The red men about me began to drift out of the room.

Cousin Philip rose stiffly from his chair, blowing on the ink-wet sheets of paper.

Bright Sun looked over my head at the door and scraped her nails along her temples. The General stared at her hands and face in a covetous way that caused a pang of jealousy to shoot through me. He said in warm tones, "If the worst is to happen, for your safety, for the safety of your child . . ."

Her tongue darted over her lips, and she shook her head and looked away. She folded her arms over her chest. "You have not cared before this moment about my daughter. She is four winters, but she would not know you. Why would she?"

They shared a look that made me shiver. He looked at her in a way that he had never looked at me. He stepped forward and lifted his hands as would a supplicant.

Bright Sun said, "Do not begin to care, not now when I must choose for her. You must know something. You must know that when I see old women in my village beaten by white boys just because they try to harvest what they have planted, my heart is with Black Hawk. And when I wake in the mornings and wonder if tomorrow my child will be shot down by the lead miners who come through our village, my heart is with Black Hawk."

Bright Sun pointed a finger at the General and said, "It no longer matters that I have known you . . ." She paused and cast a baleful look at me, "Zha'becka, if I must choose between your rules and my people, I will follow my people."

Bright Sun pulled an embroidered broadcloth shawl about her shoulders and fled noiselessly. The General's face was clouded with sorrow, and I knew at that moment, if I had not been in the room, he would have run after her. He would have pleaded with her and consoled her. I knew this because his face told me it was so. The look in his dark blue eyes was one of the purest torment and longing.

I remember that my throat ached. I was ashamed of my self-deceit, of having fooled myself into believing that his affections had ever belonged to me. In four years of marriage he had never said that he loved me. He never said it, because he did not love me. He kept his heart locked away and held me at arm's length, and now I knew why. I turned crisply away from him, my heels made a clicking noise on the floor as I brushed past him with my head down.

He did not call after me. I glanced over the balustrade at him. He walked out the door and onto the brick walk, searching the makeshift shelters all over Uncle's lawn for Bright Sun.

I lifted my skirts and I dashed up the broad stairway to the nursery and found our children napping on blankets upon the floor. I told Dahlia to leave us alone. When the door clicked shut behind her, I covered them protectively with the wool blankets. My heart raced, my stomach heaved with fear for us and what my children might suffer as they came of age in a house where their parents did not love one another. One day, some cruel gossip would tell them that their father kept another woman, that he had children by her; one day someone would torment them heartlessly over his indiscretions. I opened the window and stood before it, watching the sun descend behind the hills. The ropes of a stained baby jumper dangled limply from the corner like a noose that jangled with the late evening breeze.

What could a man do to make a woman so mournful? A small bitter catch lodged in my throat as I remembered the laundress. The baby turned about inside me, wedged itself on my left side. I looked over my shoulder at Walker, who had his face smashed into a pillow, his mouth open slightly, one arm trapped under his tummy.

Someone had left a knitting basket by the fire with the work of half a stocking. This was how women endured their marriages, my mama included. Mama busied her hands with petit point, with knitting and sewing so that her head could pretend that her husband wasn't dining with his mistress, or lying with one of the offering girls at the dozens of bagnios in the city, or slipping into the maid's bed after dark. And when he was with Mama, she allowed him to know, by her dignified comportment, by her brittle silences and by her wounded looks that she knew all about him.

The General would shred my heart before this was over, but I vowed to keep something of my dignity despite him. During that long afternoon, the General did not look in on me or our children. That was when I knew my guesses were not guesses at all.

17

⁂ I KNEW something was wrong because they were gathered about the bed, clutching Bibles and psalmbooks. I saw my cousins Louisiana, Octavia, Celeste, some friends of Mama and Eloise, all of them dressed in black bombazine. It was daylight, noon perhaps, but the curtains were drawn and the candles were lit, dozens of them on the tables about me. The air was stale and smelled of blood. A basin by my head held a styptic solution and rolled lengths of muslin. I thought I saw the shadowy form of Doctor Harding off in the corner, but I could not be sure.

Reverend Shaw, who had officiated at my wedding, stood solemnly at the foot of the bed.

I wondered if he had come to yell at me for not attending service the past four years.

The General sat on the bed beside me, hugging my arm to his chest, clasping my hand to the side of his face. Mama sat on my left, her eyes rimmed red, and Eloise had her hand on my feet. Sister was stroking the bones of my ankles through the blankets. It was so peculiar, and my mouth was dry, so dry I couldn't lick my lips for trying. My feet were cold. I didn't understand why, because I was covered in many blankets and the fire was stoked to blazing.

I looked up at the General and asked, "Where are the children?"

"Dahlia is looking after them."

"I want to see them."

Mama dropped her head then, and so did Eloise, and a few of the ladies in the room began sobbing. I made a face at them, the most sour face I could muster under the circumstances. I said, "What is wrong with you people? Mama, why are all these ladies here?"

"They're here to visit you, Mary."

"But I don't even like them."

I felt the General's chest rumble under my arm, and he was smiling, but his eyes were moist. I lifted my lids—they felt so heavy—and he squeezed my hand. I whispered for him to come nearer, and he did. He bent over me and asked, "What can I do for you, Mary?"

"Tell me the truth."

"Yes."

"Why are they here?"

His eyes glistened as he whispered to me, "They're here to vex you, Mary. They heard you required vexing." I sensed the falsity in his bright tone. He paused. "We had ourselves another boy. He's a big, fine boy with lots of dark hair."

I tried to manage a smile at the idea of another baby. "Another baby that looks like you. He must have come out nine years old with his own pony. It felt that way." I closed my eyes and struggled to breathe. I was glad to feel my husband's face so close to mine, the almond smell of his breath comforted me. I said, "Henry, send them away. I don't like them being here."

The darkness was so pleasant and difficult to resist. I felt as though I were sinking into myself, like the first rain of spring sinks into the thirsty soil of the savanna. I knew what was happening. I felt myself draining away, becoming weaker with each breath I took, but I suffered no pain, just a drifting into the quiet.

I remember Mama saying long ago that we begin to die from the feet up. My limbs felt like cold iron, too heavy to lift. It wasn't so bad. It wasn't bad at all. It meant I wouldn't have to fear for myself or him or the children any longer. It was so easy that I felt pity for all the people I was leaving behind, living their lives of struggle and woe.

When I awoke hours later, the General was in the same place, lying beside me, stroking my forehead, cupping my face in his hand. I turned my face to meet his and found him riveted upon me, his eyes heavy with pain and mourning.

"What's wrong with your eyes? They've gone all red."

He didn't answer me. He was wearing a mood I'd never seen before and did not recognize. He looked afraid, and something more than afraid—hopeless. I said, "I dreamt of our garden. I was in our garden with Walker and Elizabeth, picking lilacs. It's odd, that day you took me to the south plat and we plowed up the ground together?" I paused to draw my breath, tried to wet my lips. "I never thought I wanted a garden. But when you're away, upriver . . . the children and I pass the whole day there. I'd like a garden for butterflies, with bee balm perhaps, Elizabeth loves butterflies, they're the only insect she doesn't try to eat."

One of Mama's servants came into the room and carried away a bundle of sheets, then shut the door behind her. In the hallway, Mama spoke softly to Doctor Harding and the reverend, my cousins conversed with Eloise in solemn church voices. It was a background noise like an autumn creek, dry and low, the voices of women murmuring regret and concern. I heard a servant bringing them coffee; I could smell it, I could hear the ceremonial clink of silver and china.

"They're drinking coffee in the hallway? I must be in a bad way if Mama is serving coffee in the hallway."

An unfamiliar noise issued from the General's throat. He tried to conceal it. He turned his face away from me then, and I heard him scold himself, "I told myself I wouldn't do this."

"Do what?"

He stared down at the pillow and would not answer me.

"Henry, is it snowing?"

"Yes."

"What kind of snow?"

"Small icy pellets, the kind that tumbles down like rocks."

"I like to sleep when it snows."

"Mary, you don't want to sleep in this snow. Stay awake for me. Awhile longer."

I felt so sorry for him that I decided I could no longer hide from him or myself. My pride wasn't of much use to me anymore. Though it had once fortified me, my obstinance now felt like hard-edged scree burdening my spirit, sloped over me in a confining way. I was tired, and he looked so miserable. I wanted to reassure him, I wanted to give him something, a small gift that he could choose to open or keep in its wrappings.

I lifted my right hand to his cheek, caressed the beard stubble with the back of my fingers. I looked him in the eye and said to him, "I have decided not to care about her, Henry. I don't care anymore. I want you to know that I love you all the same. I always did. I think I loved you from the moment I lay down on the floor of that horrid inn beside you. All I know is the moment I met you, you changed me. There. I said it. I'm free now."

He slid his hand gently over my ribs as if I would break. He shook his head, began to say something and then stopped. He lifted his eyes to mine. He said, "Stay here with me. Please."

Once again, he had not responded to the question implicit in my confession. It didn't vex me, it merely made me sad for the two of us. I stared up at the ceiling and tried to see into its vaulted depths. "You never did say please before."

He brought my hand to his lips, he put his lips to my brow. He said, "You see, Mary Bullitt, you have to stay with me. You have to teach me good manners."

I wanted to close my eyes and rest again, but he wouldn't let me. His body seemed to radiate a halo of heat. His lineaments were sharply drawn. He was so ferociously *alive* . . . I remember thinking, Why, he'll never die. He'll just go on and on like one of those ancient shires that plods the barley fields season after season. He curled himself around me then, his body heat radiating right through the blankets, willing health into me. "Open your eyes, Mary."

"No, I'm tired."

"Wait. Don't go. Listen to what I have to say . . ."

He whispered his plan as I began drifting away again, he told me he was going to transfuse me with his strength, that my whole being would filtrate with life, his life. After all, he said, he could accomplish anything. If he could bring whole nations of people to order, if he could command so many men and so much wilderness land, why couldn't he have what he wished?

He told me he would require God and the angels and all of the saints to pay him heed. He shifted his weight so that one of his legs pressed over my knees, his body was half across mine as if he hoped to trap me under him to prevent my ascending. I imagined that the sound of him being alive came to me, a humming noise of unfathomable strength, a beating of wings, the sound of hooves galloping over soft earth.

I drifted off and had a dream that I was afloat upon a tranquil river. The shores were lined with violet-colored houses, each of them bursting with a divine light.

My feet began to warm.

❧ O N the first spring day of 1831, I sat against the stone wall of the foundation of our house, sans bonnet or hat, raising my face to the warmth of the new sun. Our third child, Edward, nursed at my breast, his soft birdlike head seemed fragile on the stalk of the neck. And the sun on my skin, how good that felt, as if it were drawing growth out of me, just as it drew frail white shoots out of the earth itself. Walker and Elizabeth played a few yards away under a makeshift tent they'd made of a blanket I'd tossed over dogwood bushes.

The General held a black locust sapling in his hands, he turned about, surveying the sloping hill around our house with a critical eye. The saplings stood at attention in an arc about the house where he planned to sink them.

I followed his gaze and said, "Don't plant them too deeply, now."

He straightened as if I had insulted him, then peered at me from under the rim of his hat and said, "What makes you think I don't know how to plant a tree?"

"All I'm saying is, don't dig the hole too deep. You'll want to leave room for the root ball to breathe up top."

"Are you giving me gardening advice, Mary Bullitt? This is the woman who thinks planting *food* is *vulgar*?"

"Fine. Don't listen to me. But I'd hate to see those little trees die after you've taken such care bringing them from Virginia, and you having paid so much for them. Go ahead, drown them in dirt. Good-bye, little trees. I'm glad to have made your acquaintance."

The General cleared his throat and set the tree on the ground. He raised his chin and squinted down the slope at Walker and Elizabeth. He came to sit beside me, drew up his knees, removed his hat, rested his head against the wall and sighed. His hand stole up to the blanket, and he peeked at Edward's mouth bubbling over my breast.

The General made a face, then looked at me and said, "Does it hurt when he does that?"

I yanked the blanket back over myself and slapped his hand away. "Why? Are you hungry too?"

He touched his hand to Edward's fuzzy head and said, "You know we can't have any more. The doctor says we can't."

I glanced away from him, but not before he saw the disappointment all over my face.

"Mary. Don't be blue. I have . . . ideas."

He leaned forward, smiling as if he knew a secret.

I narrowed my eyes at him, "What *ideas*?"

He ignored the question, and waved a hand over the half circle of trees. "Now what do you think of this plan? Do you like them there, or should we spread them a bit farther back from the house?"

That afternoon, as Edward slept in his basket and the children played in their tent, we quibbled and jibed ceaselessly over those trees. That hole's too deep, this one is too close to that one. I dug holes, I carried pails of water with bails so rusted they left orange crescents on the palms of my gloves, I held the trees while he filled in around them with soil. He kissed me once for each tree we planted, which was a bad idea, given our constraints. Constraints made temptation so much sweeter. It got us all riled up.

Elizabeth and Walker ran breathlessly up the slope, calling after us, "Come see the baby mice we found. Mama, come see!"

"Don't you touch them. Mice are filthy creatures."

"Mama, they're just babies. They can't be dirty. No dirtier than Baby Edward, and you let him in the house."

"Elizabeth, what is that in your hand, Open your hand, dear." She did, and I winced at the small pink round worm there. "Put that mouse back in its nest."

"Mama, I can't, it will die. Come see." Walker waved us over somberly, put his hands on his hips and turned a professional countenance to his father. His posture said, this is a manly matter that needs to be settled amongst men. "So what do *you* think, Pa?"

"I think they're mice."

"Tell Mama we have to keep them in the house else they'll die."

"No."

Elizabeth stamped her feet, shook her head hopelessly and wiggled her shoulders to let me know just how exasperated she was. Then she clasped her hands together and lifted her face to her father. "Oh, I'll feed them and I'll clean their box and I'll be really, really good if you let me keep them."

The General's eyes twinkled at me. I hated it when he tried to charm me into surrendering a righteous point; I hated it more when I gave in to him. Elizabeth was resorting to desperate measures; she began to weep, pausing now and again to peer up at me to see if she was having an effect. The General said, "Well, Mrs. Atkinson?"

"You can keep them on the porch in a butter box with cotton batting. But the porch is as close as I'll let them come to being in the house. Do you hear?" Elizabeth and Walker accepted these terms, albeit unhappily. They scurried off to the house, shoulder to shoulder, looking back as they whispered plots to one another.

The General grinned at me and asked, "Are you going soft in your old age, Mary Bullitt?"

"No. The cats are sure to get them on the porch."

🪶 BEFORE bed each night, the General read the children a story. Their favorite was "A Week-end at Grandmama's," the tale of a wicked Yankee child who is spanked into an epiphany by his firm Southern grandmama. When the General finished his story, I gave the children a song on the harp. I would take my seat upon the little stool, press my cheek against the smooth rosewood and close my eyes as I placed my fingers upon the strings. Elizabeth liked "Turkey in the Straw" and "Nine Miles from Louisville," old-time dancing tunes.

Lying on his tummy, Edward balanced on his hands with his legs straight out behind him, his head bobbled as he tried to see his brother and sister dancing awkward circles, stopping to clap or stomp the floor. They couldn't manage to do all three at once. And each evening, after they had their song, Dahlia gave them warm milk and put them to bed.

After a full day of tree planting, my shoulders were sore, but I felt the sun's heat still inside me as I bowed to kiss the children good night. I straightened with a hand to my lower back and closed their door. I tossed the General a questioning look, because his face shone with mischief. He took my hand and hauled me into the bedroom. He crouched, reached under the bed and removed a small mahogany box.

I kept a suspicious distance, staying safely near the door. "What is that?"

"Come over here and see for yourself."

"No. Tell me what it is." The General would not be swayed. He sat on the side of the bed, put the box next to him and removed his boots, then his socks, and then he began unbuttoning his shirt. He smirked a little to see me squinting at the box.

"You are too curious by half. This is killing you, isn't it?"

I huffed across the room, sat next to him with the box between us and began unbuttoning the waist and then the cuffs of my work dress. I ignored him when he grinned and tapped the box's lid, I unlaced my boots, and seeing his settled so neatly, tossed mine carelessly on the floor, then I threw my stockings in a heap, along with my blouse and skirts. I sat in my chemise on the side of the bed and said, "What's in there?"

"I told you I had ideas, Mary."

"What sort of ideas?"

"To begin with, I am not going to have a chaste marriage. I'm not that honorable."

I felt a sudden surge of panic as I thought of my last ordeal. He was in an amorous mood, and I missed him terribly. But I would not martyr myself in childbed . . . I was singularly unfit for martyrdom. I felt slightly queasy when he put his hand to my arm, and I looked away from him.

He said, "Tea."

"What?"

"After the doctor talked to me, it occurred to me that here was something I could do for you. For us. Tea." He opened the box. It was brimming with shiny white and pale yellow plant seeds. He held one between his thumb and forefinger and said, "We're going to make a cold-water infusion with these seeds for you, and you're going to drink it every day for six months. No more babies. Ever. The Osage woman I spoke to said the Osage ladies made a tea of these seeds and they had no more children."

"Are those Osage ladies still alive?"

"Of course they're still alive."

"How do I know it won't make me sick? What plant did these come from?"

"It is called yellow puccoon, or Indian paintbrush. It blooms in big yellow mounds all over these prairies. You'd recognize it if you saw it."

"And it won't make me sick?"

"She promised me it wouldn't make you sick. She said she drank a tea made from the puccoon and never had more children. She pointed out other examples. Do you want me to drink it too? Because I will."

"Yes, that's a grand idea, and leave our children orphans."

I tried to imagine the General approaching an old woman and asking her for advice on how to prevent babies coming to be. I told him this, and he said he wasn't the least bit shy about it.

His eyes shone at me. He moved the box aside and brought me to him, saying, "I am a man who has been too long in the desert."

"HURRY, hurry, hurry it along." He motioned circles with his hand, as I scrambled for my riding habit, my boots, my hat and my gloves. I grumbled and circled about, it wasn't even dawn, the light in the room was chilly, thin and gray, but I could hear larks singing. Dahlia had packed a breakfast for us. The General and I planned to ride out alone for the first time since Edward had been born. The horses were brought round out front. I scrambled into my heavy old Directoire riding habit.

"This skirt and jacket weigh thirty-seven pounds. Did you know that?"

"Well, Christ, Mary, take the lead out of the hem, I don't care if your skirts fly up. Why make yourself miserable?"

"Where are those gloves, I always keep them . . . oh, here they are."

"Will you hurry? I want to get into the woods before the sun is up too high."

I thrust my hand into the glove at a high velocity and felt my fingers puncture something soft and wiggling.

I turned to my husband. A look of pure horror went across my face as I dropped the glove. I tried not to scream. "My glove! There's something *living* in my glove!"

The General snatched it up and peered one-eyed into the lining. "Not anymore. Elizabeth hid those damned baby mice in here. You exterminated them nicely."

"Ugh. My fingers! My fingers!" I sank my hands into the basin, squirming with revulsion at what I had done. "What do we tell Elizabeth and Walker?"

The General set his jaw and said sternly, "I will speak to them when we return. When Elizabeth goes snooping into your drawer for the glove, we'll let her find this empty one and panic for a half day over her deception."

I heard him exit the house with the glove. He returned with it, having emptied it of mouse babies, and placed it in the drawer.

When the General and I arrived home, Elizabeth was predictably inconsolable over the mice; Walker was morose and silent. He glared accusingly at me until I confessed all, which only caused Elizabeth more anguish.

I made a big fuss over the funeral. We would dig a grave under the dogwood bushes, we would put flowers atop the dirt, I would even stick a little soapstone carved with each baby mouse's name there.

But it wasn't enough.

"Will you make the grave under my window so I can see it?" Walker sobbed until his nose was swollen.

Yes, I said, of course I would.

"And Daddy will stand over the grave and he will shoot his rifle twenty times, just like when they bury the soldiers?" Walker asked.

"The band will play "Roslin Castle," and we'll put the casket on a caisson?" Elizabeth sniffed.

I quirked an eyebrow at the General.

He said, "Now look here, military funerals are for soldiers. Not rodents."

Elizabeth threw herself to the floor, and Walker declared us the meanest parents that ever lived. But the General stood firm and refused to give the mice a twenty-gun salute.

18

✳ THE apricot trees were in bloom at Maracastor, Uncle William's country estate outside of St. Louis. The General and I had come with the children for the Easter holiday. Maracastor was originally called *maraiscastor*, which meant beaver marsh. It was twilight. I reclined in a hammock, in an iris-colored gown, and listened to Aunt Harriet, Mary Radford Kearny and Sister Eloise laughing and chattering in the house with Walker, Elizabeth and little Edward, whom we called Ned. They were coloring Easter eggs. I had retired from a two-hour frenzy of egg coloring after my children had dunked nearly three-dozen eggs. They were enraptured by the miracle of egg dye. I looked at my hands. My cuticles were blue, green and yellow.

The General sprawled beside me under the generous canopy of an elm tree before the green pond. He watched the trout jump for midges. A plate of preserved plum heath peach, picked from trees in Uncle's orchard that grew as tall and narrow as Lombardy poplar, sat at the General's elbow, while he contemplated the size of the fish breaking the surface of the water. He flicked an ant off a peach slice and savored the juice on the tip of his tongue. The lazy sound of his voice told me that the General was enjoying an abiding contentment.

"Ever tried those white plums, large as an egg, that I grow? No? I'll bring you a dozen stones to start you. I'll pack them in sand and send them over," the General said.

The cicadas serenaded us as the sun dropped. Eloise's thin laugh trilled out of the windows. "Sounds like Eloise has poured herself a toddy," Uncle William drawled.

A servant crossed the lawn with a tray, refilled our glasses, then wiped down the old wooden table and chairs in the apricot grove where we had taken our supper. The General and Uncle spoke about politics and shared news from the War Department.

Aunt Harriet held the back door open. Walker, now five, Elizabeth, four, and Ned, aged two, came running toward us, each bearing a willow basket. I smiled at the sight of their bright heads. Their pale frocks seemed as summer clouds to me, drifting and benign. Eloise and Aunt Harriet floated out onto the cool green lawn in their embroidered muslin gowns and country bonnets of woven flax and straw. The children giggled and knelt by my hammock to display their craft.

"Now, why have you dyed all of the Easter eggs blood red?" I asked.

Walker held one aloft and admired it, then passed it into the General's outstretched hand.

"Red rolls faster. I want to win the egg roll this year."

"They look like big, fat rubies. I think they're lovely," Eloise said, laughing.

"I think they're perfectly sinister."

"Mary," the General said, "I am in a heap of trouble if you think the color of an egg is going to decide my fortune this summer."

I straightened and peered suspiciously at him. Where was the General planning to be this summer?

Eloise proposed a hiding game, then chased after the children. They went running wild through the yellow forsythia, over the grass jeweled with anemone and jonquils. Now and again, they ran over to me to report on their screeching pursuit of insects. Walker was in the thick of the mischief. Elizabeth kept apace, hollering after little Ned, "Lazy boots!"

These inscrutable epithets of hers, I had yet to understand. Then Elizabeth coaxed Ned into acquiring her bug-eating habit. Ned snapped up a lightning bug, then wobbled around in his pale-yellow leggings, scrunching up his face and smearing his tongue against the roof of his mouth.

Eloise called from the edge of the lawn, "Sister! I'm not putting my fingers in his mouth."

The General finished his drink, slapped the arms of his chair and crossed the grass to join us. Upon seeing him, the children screeched and darted off, hoping he would pursue them. Ned tried to scamper away while my forefinger was still hooked in his mouth. The General was dressed in country clothes with his sleeves rolled up. I glinted up at him, and he extended his hand. The lines about his eyes had deepened, aided by years of sunlight reflecting up from hard, baked dirt and the glare from the western rivers.

"Take a walk with me."

I nodded in the direction of the children, but he cut me short: "Eloise! Mind the children."

"Fine, Brother Henry, but I'm not sticking my finger in their mouths."

The sun had dropped low in the sky. The grass underfoot was soft and broke to an elm wood on the western slope. We walked along silently, hand in hand, and I knew where he was leading me—to the small river that cut through the center of the trees and fed the marshes. The grass spoiled the blue silk of my slippers, so I paused and leaned against him as I unlaced them. He took them from me and folded them into his pockets. The grass felt delicious, I curled my toes, grasping at it. But when I looked up at him, his expression frightened me.

"Oh, no."

"Now, Mary, it's not as bad as you might think. Up north, near Saukenuk, some Menominee Indians hid themselves in the tallgrass and waited for a small group of Sauk to come near them. You know how easy it is to hide in a stand of bluestem. Sauk women and children got away by crossing the Mississippi River, but a lot of Sauk men were killed. Naturally, the Sauk avenged their dead by attacking the Menominee, and now, we expect the Menominee to retaliate. The initial killings happened when the Sauk were on their way to council with Major Bliss from Fort Crawford. So the Sauk hold us to blame for putting their people at risk. But I am concerned the white folks in the Lake Region, who are frightened out of their wits by the threat of an Indian war, are going to jump in and start shooting Indians at random, because they don't know an ally from an enemy."

"Is Black Hawk involved?"

"I have reports that he is preoccupied with removing his band to the Iowa lands. I do not expect to encounter him. My mission is to apprehend the Sauk and Menominee who started this mess, calm the remnant group of Sauk left in the Lake Region and present a reassuring presence for the whites in the area. I'm taking two hundred men with me—"

"Two hundred! What can you do with two hundred men?"

"Enough. And I intend to pack the summer uniforms, but, Mary, I can almost guarantee that I will be home by the end of May. I will make arrangements to see that funds are available at your disposal, and I have written a will—"

"Don't say it."

"Naming you my sole beneficiary and executor of my estate. It is in my center desk drawer."

"I hate this. I hate that you've written a will."

There was an awkward silence wherein he pulled my slippers out of his pockets and tapped them together in an absent way, looking off to the north as if he were trying to guess what it held for him.

⚜ I PACKED his trunk for him. But this time I included snippets from each of the children's blankets too. And I asked each child to give their father one small token that he could look at each night when he thought of them. I advised them to select something that was very dear to them. This prompted a scurry of intense child-talk in the nursery, as each of them decided among their most cherished possessions. Walker somberly presented me with "A Week-end at Grandmama's," saying he wouldn't want anybody else to read it to him anyway. In truth, I think he was happy to be rid of the book. Elizabeth parted with a porcelain-headed doll that was so beloved that the paint had been worn from her face. Ned decided the best gift was one of self, and he tried to squeeze his chubby little body into the trunk. I praised them for their selflessness.

They didn't care. A new moment had arrived with a new distraction: they heard Billy bringing the little dapple gray pony around from the stable for their riding lessons. Billy dropped the mounting block on the lawn, and they ran out the front door, arguing over who got to sit little Cherokee first.

I got to my feet, crossed the hallway and saw the General standing beside my harp in the library. I gave him a questioning look. It was midday, a busy time when he was ordinarily inspecting troops, meeting with his officers, local politicians or War Department officials. He had his hand atop the dark, glossy wood of the frame. When he would not look up at me, I stood opposite him, with the harp between us. I could sense, as surely as if he had said it aloud, that he had a foreboding and had come home to look in on us.

I urged him to rest. He sat in his chair, and I put my fingers to the harp's strings. As I played, I saw him relax, and he closed his eyes. I could not speak of my concern for him. But in that moment, I wondered if, when he lay atop me in my childbed as I was so near to dying, he hadn't given away too much of himself, particularly now that he was going to a place where neither life nor death mattered a great deal.

I drew a breath and tipped my ear. The music was an intimate link that joined me to him. I could feel it coursing between us, binding us against the currents of wind and water and the destructive will of others.

***

✳ I SHIVERED and awoke, having dreamed of apocalypse, I dreamt of flames that rushed before me, devouring all living things. I ran from it as fast as I was able. I gathered the children into my arms, but I could not carry all of them by myself. Walker kept falling behind, and I couldn't find the General. I awoke with my heart racing, my throat hurt from crying in my sleep. My skin was damp and chilled. I raised myself up on my elbow and looked down upon him as he slept beside me.

His hands were folded upon his chest, his face was silvered by the moon haze, his wavy hair now threaded with gray. I touched his brow.

The slant of the shadows over the floor told me it was after midnight.

I sat up. I would keep watch over him these next few hours. I would keep a vigil for him in this gloom, even though I could see only the shade of him beside me.

We watched him go before the sun came up. The air was the color of frog skin, snags and sawyers shone out of the water like black molars. I stood on the shore with the children huddled about me, asleep on their feet and clinging to my skirts. I held Ned in my arms.

Two hundred men boarded the *Chieftain*. The horses exhaled wreaths of vapor, and Walker complained of the cold, damp air.

He threw his plump arms around the General's neck and kissed him on both cheeks. The General lifted Elizabeth and hugged her until she protested that he was squeezing the grape juice out of her. He kissed Ned too, then took him from my arms and settled him upon the ground.

The General embraced me, and with a dramatic downward swoop that he meant to be funny, kissed me long and soulfully, until the men on the boats stomped and hurrahed the silent levee.

Then he left us.

From his place upon the texas deck, the General raised his hand, sending a wordless farewell to me. I watched him being taken by the shadows, into the sputtering gray mists upon a river of cloud.

The night after the General departed for Saukenuk, I sat with the children on the porch. I wrapped them in blankets, and they hugged their knees and lifted their faces at the sky. We had come out to watch the star fall with Nicholas and Dahlia. The star showers had caused a panic amongst the drunkards at the GAMBLING & RYE in St. Louis, who drank themselves into a stupor in anticipation of the apocalypse. The four of us ate popped corn, shivered in the damp chill and praised the sky. When a bright streak coursed the horizon, Dahlia said, "Looks to me like the Star of Bethlehem."

And Nicholas said, "It gave up being to shine. Old star couldn't bear to watch what's coming for them poor red folks up north."

Walker turned a confused face to him. "What red folks?"

"Them Sacks, what they call them. Poor old star couldn't bear to witness what's coming. So he gave up and fell."

Dahlia rubbed her hands over Walker's narrow back and said in a scolding tone directed at Nicholas, "Walker, there is some folks like Nicholas here who thinks you can tell what is coming from the direction of the wind. Or mebbe how a rooster picks up grain, or how wax turns once it's dropped in water. This fool would live by the way his name was wrote in ashes."

Walker returned his attention to the sky, and I chided Nicholas. "As for me, I prefer to gauge my days by the way a hatchet balances upon a stile."

"Huh. And that stile be cancered through with rot, about to fall on your head. You all jest better remember it was pride what ruined them angels."

"Nicholas Brooks! Git. Now, I said!" I was glad Dahlia had come to our defense, as I was not in a mood to argue with him. We watched Nicholas lumber away, and Dahlia wondered aloud, "He sure is cranky tonight, ain't he?"

But Nicholas lifted his face to the dark sky and began to sing, delivering to me a message he dared not speak in plain words, "You'll hear the sinners moan, to wake the nations underground, lookin' to my God's right hand when the stars begin to fall."

19

The Black Hawk War, Spring & Summer of 1832

I COLLECT to myself the bits of the Black Hawk War, hoping to lay one fact beside another and find a contiguous truth. For ten years I have kept to my journey of looking and listening, but time has taught me that perhaps I shall never truly know all. I hold Philip's manuscript in my lap, and though I have not yet read his musings upon the war, I trust in his compassionate heart and his innocent eye. I hold Bright Sun's hesitant and despairing voice in my memory, and I know she had nothing to gain by concealing or obscuring what happened to her.

Perhaps now I shall give to myself the gift of my own history. I hold that summer of 1832 unto myself, finding it difficult to resist fashioning a cool and pale surface over those events, and thus console myself that the General could not have . . . surely he would not have allowed . . . But I am my history. And the Black Hawk War is part of me. It was a dark fabric, loomed upon a frame of deadly ambition, laced together at angles by Me'um'bane the Bright Sun.

At my request, Bright Sun met me upon the strand along the river on a warm day in October of 1832—in the autumn immediately following the summer of the war. By that time, she had been at Jefferson Barracks for over two months, inhabiting vacant enlisted quarters with another Sauk family until the Indian agent could arrange to transport her to Keokuk's village. Bright Sun wasn't a prisoner of war, nor was her presence unusual in the larger context of things, as there were many native peoples—including nearly a hundred refugee Sauk—camped in and around Jefferson Barracks.

She greeted me, wearing a simple deerskin tunic, no shoes. Her glossy black hair fell loosely to her waist. I had never seen Bright Sun in such plain clothing before. She sat rather immodestly with her long slender legs stretched straight before her as she traced the river with her gaze. The beach was dry, only mildly troubled by sand flies. The steamers could not run, for the water was in a low state.

"Where is Zha'becka?" Bright Sun asked, sifting sand through her fingers. "He has not come back to you?"

"The General is still in the Indian Territory. He should return within a fortnight," I answered evenly. "I expect he shall wish to speak with you when he arrives, Bright Sun." I said this last bit cautiously, scrutinizing her face, but she did not react at all.

"I will leave here before he comes back," she said simply. When she would not meet my eyes, I spoke to the river.

"Bright Sun, will you tell me about Bad Axe?"

At the sound of the words "Bad Axe," Bright Sun drew in her breath sharply.

"There were atrocities," I added firmly.

Bright Sun lifted her right hand before her face and blinked at the hazy sunlight like someone waking from a pained dream, then plucked softly at the air before her. "It is a cheery word—atrocities. It sounds like spoons and ladles clanking in an iron pot."

I studied her, but the dreamy look vanished, and her face hardened.

I said, "I am told that if Black Hawk had seen the cities of the East with his own eyes, there would not have been a war. Keokuk had been to Washington City. He could guess what was possible, how powerful the Americans could be. But Black Hawk could not."

Bright Sun's eyes locked upon mine as if she were wavering between presenting a challenge or concurring with me.

I continued, "Black Hawk could not think upon the larger world because he did not know of it. He believed the entire army consisted of the few troops with my husband, and the one company of infantry at Fort Armstrong. Black Hawk thought that all of the white people in America were those living in the Lake Region. He could not guess how many we were."

Bright Sun squared her shoulders and tipped her chin away, but did I glimpse a hint of agreement in her countenance? I think I did. Emboldened, I ventured, "Please. I wish to know what happened to your people at Bad Axe. I don't understand why it happened. And the only stories I hear are those that the militia politicians have published, and they are so ribboned through with lies that I cannot believe the first word that is said."

She did not respond, and so I offered, "I shall return the favor in any respect you like."

"Anything I want? You will give it to me?"

"Yes, Bright Sun."

She hummed tunelessly—it was more rhythm than melody—and I could tell she was trying to decide whether she wanted to speak to me or not. She hummed, paused, hummed and raked her fingers over the sand. When Bright Sun gave no sign of speaking, I thought to prompt her.

I said quietly, "In the spring of this year, the stars fell like water from the sky. After the General's boats departed Jefferson Barracks, I looked up at the star shower carving brilliant washes into the night."

Bright Sun tilted her face in my direction but would not meet my gaze. She spoke to her feet, resting her chin upon her knees.

Bright Sun's Story

BLACK Hawk said the stars were the Old Ones who fell to earth to lead us to a new place where the Chemokemon—the Americans—could not harm us. After wintering at the sugaring grounds, we returned home to Saukenuk in the little frog moon to open the caches we had carefully filled with corn and pelts. But the Chemokemon had opened our caches and stolen all of our food and furs, worse, they had stolen our seeds so that we could not plant the corn! We knew we must send them away. We did not wish to harm the Chemokemon, or to say bad words to them, because we knew they would send the bluecoats after us, or worse, the militia.

It was decided we would have a Night Feast. This is a powerful ceremony for sending away bad spirits, and we could think of no spirit worse than a Chemokemon.

The young men prepared a feast of dog and venison. All of Black Hawk's band came into our wickiup. Black Hawk sat behind the fire, facing the east door, and he smiled to see his friends. The young men gave each guest a stick representing a piece of meat in each of the kettles. The young women looked about at one another with shining eyes as Black Hawk stood and welcomed his brothers and sisters. He made a speech of hope.

"My brothers and sisters, we offer this kettle of food to the Great Spirit, *Getci Munito,* we offer this corn and set it aside for the Thunderers, we offer the quail to the Water Spirits, we offer the pumpkin and the fruit of the land to the blackhorns that run over the tall grass. We offer these things in the hope that once again Saukenuk will be ours and we will be allowed to remain in the home of our fathers."

Then Black Hawk threw tobacco on the fire.

Singing Bird cooked eight pieces of boiling meat, then ladled them into one bowl. Then the young men had a contest to see who could eat the fastest. Their eyes watered. They yelled to feel the boiling meat going down their throats, and the women laughed and clapped.

The first young man to swallow all of the boiling food was Whirling Thunder, Black Hawk's oldest son. Whirling Thunder jumped to his feet and ran to touch the lance at the end of the lodge. He was supposed to make a speech about how brave he would be in war, but his throat had been burned. His eyes watered as he tried to cough out his words. He bent over the lance, trying to brag. Even the women guarding the east and west doors against evil spirits pulled their short pipes from their mouths, then laughed at Whirling Thunder.

I sat upon the platform on the north side of the wickiup. The drummers took their places beside Black Hawk. Then I stood opposite Singing Bird, and we faced one another and danced to Fire-Keeper, then we danced to Night Sun. Another woman raised a blanket over our heads with the Night Sun woven into the fabric, and we danced to send the Chemokemon away.

My daughter, Kamia, had known six winters. She clapped her hands, and her blue eyes sparkled to see the women sending away all bad things. My infant son watched me dance as he lay upon a deerskin robe stuffed with cornhusks. He was born in the moon when the geese return in the blizzard cloud, and I named him *Naso'nomuk,* but we called him Little Brother. When Little Brother was born, Black Hawk made a cradle board from a living burr oak tree, for it is bad luck to put an infant into a cradle board made of fallen wood. The living spirit of the tree makes the infant grow strong. Little Brother liked to kick at the moving foot board.

The fireflies swarmed over the dirt paths outside the wickiup. Some of them floated inside, and that was how I knew it would rain that night. Singing Bird and I danced until our skin shone, and though our faces were calm, our hearts were not, for we could hear the Chemokemon, outside, taunting us. They wanted our men to come out of the wickiup and fight them, they wanted this because they were drunk on the *tu'xe*—bad water. Our men ignored the Chemokemon voices until they went away. I believed our Night Feast had been successful.

But one sleep later, the Indian agent came into our wickiup. He said, "Black Hawk, you must take your people to the other side of the river and never return to Saukenuk. Keokuk has left with his people. They will make a new life in the Iowa lands. You must go to the Iowa lands also."

I knew the Iowa lands were not a good place for corn; the earth was so thick it could not be cut with our tools. None of the women wanted to leave Saukenuk, so we spoke our hearts to Black Hawk and asked him to find a way for us to remain in the Lake Country, our country.

Black Hawk asked the Prophet and One-Eye Decorah to smoke with him and to share their wisdom. I did not like this idea, for I have never trusted either man. One-Eye Decorah and the Winnebago—they call themselves the Fish People—have never been friends to us. I did not trust them because the Fish People seemed willing to do anything to make the Chemokemon happy.

The Prophet said to Black Hawk, "Friend, you cannot let the bluecoats move your people across the Great River Mashisi'pu to the land where the sun disappears. The Asha—the Sioux—live there. The bluecoats will move your people onto the Asha hunting lands. The Asha will surely kill all of your women and children."

Black Hawk nodded to hear this. "We have been at war with the Asha for two hundred winters, and now that the blackhorns are scarce, the fighting for hunt lands will be worse than ever. Keokuk tells us to go to the Iowa lands. But the women of my lodge and many others do not wish to go where they cannot plant corn. And the young men are ready for war, the ponies are fat and lazy and the warriors have been quiet too long in their lodges."

One-Eye said, "If you travel up the Rock River, you will meet your good friends the Fish People, the Winnebago. The Straight-Cut Hair People, the Kickapoo. The Burnt Legs, the Potawatami. And most powerful of all, the Long Knives, our English fathers."

Black Hawk thought upon this a long while.

"How can I know you are my friend, One-Eye? I have heard you are angry with us for not helping the Fish People fight Zha'becka and his bluecoats five winters ago?"

One-Eye said, "Friend, you fought with us against Zha'becka, the bluecoat war chief. You attacked their boats on the Ouisconson. Then you sat in a Chemokemon jail for your Winnebago brothers. Your people fought beside us. Now, I offer my hand and my war club."

And the Prophet waved his long feathered pipe over the fire and said, "I am half Winnebago, half Sauk. So you are my brother, Black Hawk. Bring your people north to Prophetstown to live in my village. Your women can make corn at Prophetstown, you will find a new and happy life amongst my people, and we will stand beside our Yellow Earth brothers under Zha'becka's guns."

But still Black Hawk hesitated. I wanted to tell him to speak to Zha'becka before doing this, but I knew that Black Hawk was too proud. He hated Zha'becka. And Black Hawk liked the new way in which my people—the Yellow Earth People—admired him and spoke proudly of his war victories. The bold young men wanted to make war, and they asked Black Hawk to lead them. Though Black Hawk had never been one of our tribal chiefs, he was our best war chief, and he was proud that some called him "Brain-Splasher," that is, War Club.

One-Eye leaned forward and pointed at the rocks around the fire ring. "Zha'becka trusts me. When I am on Zha'becka's boat, I will count his men, I will see for myself the size of his force, and I will come back and tell you what I have learned. Once you strike upon Zha'becka and his bluecoats, and take meat from them, we will join you, and so will the Burnt Legs."

That is how Black Hawk came to believe the Fish People would help us to find a new place. Now the Yellow Earth people had split into two bands, those who followed Keokuk to the Iowa lands and those who followed Black Hawk. The young men crowded around Black Hawk, they called him "Honored Uncle." They listened to his war stories and made Black Hawk feel proud once again. And the women followed Black Hawk too, because of the corn.

Black Hawk is my near-father and I love him, but he can be too proud. He is like the mouse that sees and tries to hold close all the small things nearest to him. But a mouse cannot see the distance, and he is unable to guess at the places beyond him. Such was Black Hawk's weakness—to see only what was before him. One day, before Fire-Keeper showed his face over the edge of the land, Black Hawk woke me.

"Daughter," he said, "the Prophet will let our women make corn at Prophetstown. Help Singing Bird bundle the *pukwe'gan* and bring only what is necessary. I will give you one horse for your children." As we bundled our things and tethered the travois poles to the horses, my near-mother Singing Bird would not speak. I knew our journey would not be good by the look on her face. There were tears in her eyes as we rolled the cattail flags. I tied the strap for Little Brother's cradle board, I lifted Kamia onto the horse and put my arms around her. Her body felt rigid in my arms, and so I knew she was frightened, and I drew her closer to me.

We looked around at our people—the Yellow Earth People. We gathered up everything we had to march to a place where we hoped we would be left in peace. After the sun dropped, we began our long walk toward the Cold Sky. Sometimes Kamia rode before me on the horse that Black Hawk gave to us. Sometimes she rode behind me and sang a song to Little Brother.

Black Hawk told our warriors to beat their drums, to sing the Wolf Song to let the Chemokemon know we were fearless. Hearing our music, Kamia tried to sing along, but her little body was stiff with fear. We could hear Zha'becka's boats. Kamia watched the river behind us for signs of Zha'becka coming near. Her little face was shaped like an acorn—pointed at the chin, wide cheekbones—and her eyes were blue as the sky. Her cheeks grew pink when she was flustered.

When Black Hawk saw how frightened she was, he touched Kamia's chin and said, "Do not be afraid, Daughter. One day, you will tell your grandchildren about how you came to live in the safe place. You will tell them about our great happiness."

Journal of Lt. Philip St. George Cooke, 12 April 1832

★ I F my troops are in a sharp mood, they can load and fire their muskets four, maybe five rounds in two minutes. If they aren't aiming at all, just pointing in the direction of a thicket? They can load and shoot three times in one minute. But the hostile target must oblige us by being ideally about 130 yards near. If the hostile is beyond 450 yards, we may as well sing him a welcome song as we wait for him to ride upon us. And he will come riding a well-trained horse that he guides by a buffalo-skin slipknot around its lower jaw. But if it's raining, all bets are off, because a baptized flint won't fire and wet priming won't fire. You may as well barber your own scalp from your head and hand it over to the Saukie, and thereby save yourself some pain.

I drill my men on loading protocol, and when we have finished, we drill again. I tell them it must be as instinctive to them as taking a piss. Indians hate the army. White people hate the army. When you live in a place where everybody hates you, it is a wise thing to be able to load your weapon quick and correct.

14 April 1832

★ A R R I V E D at Fort Armstrong at the mouth of the Rock River. Around two in the morning, we saw runners along the shore, in the forest, carrying torches. The sentries called alarm, the long roll was sounded. The General jumped out of bed, grabbed his spectacles and his rifle and kicked me, "Cooke, get up!" So out we go into the pitch blackness, and there are about fifty Sauk Indians standing on the shore, signaling us to let them board. They're half hidden by the trees and weeds. The General put a field glass to his eye and tried to see what was before him.

He handed the field glass to me and said, "Who the hell is that, can you see?"

"Sir, I think it's . . . that's Keokuk, sir. And some of the Peace Band."

The plank was lowered, and the troops stood at arms as the Sauk friend-lies thundered up the deck to greet the General. Keokuk brushed a hand over his long hair. He was winded and panicked. The General directed us into the big room on the main deck that the troops use for mess. I had eaten quail for breakfast that was raw in the center. There is nothing worse than raw bird. It came back to visit my tonsils every few minutes.

Anyhow, me and Johnston were sitting side by each at this long table, and the General was standing before us. Keokuk leaned against the wall of the cabin, and about a dozen of his men lounged about on the deck in the dark, under the torches. Our translator, Fat Ass Le Clair, sat with his hands on his knees, heaving in every little breath. He was still in his nightshirt. It was an ugly sight, his round white calves all covered with black hair. When Fat Ass spoke, his jowls jiggled.

Keokuk swallowed his drink, then said, "It is Black Hawk and the British Band."

"What about them?"

Keokuk pointed at the black land behind him. "They move up the Rock River. For the swamps. Black Hawk says you have taken Saukenuk from him, but he will not let you remove the Sauk people to the west side of the Mississippi. He knows the Sioux will kill every Sauk that crosses the river to the west side. And Black Hawk has come under the spell of the Prophet. The Prophet told Black Hawk to go up the Rock River even as we speak. Black Hawk will hide his women in the swamps, then he will come for you. He will strike at you once the women and children are safe."

The General turned away from Keokuk, put his hands on his hips and kicked at the wood planking. "How many mounted warriors does Black Hawk have with him?"

Keokuk looked around at the Peace Band. They talked for a moment in Sauk. Then they fell silent, and Keokuk said, "Five hundred Sauk warriors, one hundred Kickapoo warriors, one hundred Winnebago, one hundred Potawatami. He is taking the British Band to Prophetstown. The Prophet promised him that *all* of the Winnebago, Potawatami, Kickapoo and British will join the Sauk. Then there will be too many warriors to count. The Prophet has convinced Black Hawk that he will be like Tecumseh, a leader of all the red nations."

Johnston looked sickly white. I felt the quail coming back to visit. I took a few deep breaths and reached for my penknife to cut the turkey quill to a sharper point, then examined the ink stains on my cuticles. Johnston whispered, "Well, Cooke, I guess we are in for some warm action."

The next morning, after reveille, Black Hawk serenaded us from his camp about eight miles to the north. As I jumped into my trousers, I could hear, but faintly, his drums and his pipes and his women squawking. His drums sounded like the inside of somebody's chest, the heartbeat of a runner; boom-Boom, boom-Boom. Johnston faked a shudder and drew his finger across his throat. The troops heard the drums too. As most of them were with us on the Winnebago campaign, they were reluctant to go slogging up the Rock River once again after Black Hawk.

The General stomped back and forth on the deck, looking at the direction of Black Hawk's Sauk musicale.

I said, "Sounds like they're daring you to come on, sir. What do you think?"

"Sounds like somebody whistling past a boneyard to me, Cooke. The louder they are, the more scared they be."

Me and Johnston sat in the big main-deck parlor, watching the rain clouds roll up the Mississippi, listening to the men grouse of boredom. This has been a cold spring and it has rained every day. The troops are grateful for their winter capes. I rubbed the cold out of my hands as I copied the General's orders and heard a light rain falling upon the decks. A damp gust blew across the room, from one open side of the big cabin across to the other.

Johnston scribed a letter from the General to Governor John Reynolds of Illinois. In this letter, the General didn't exactly ask for the militia to turn out, but to my mind, he hinted things were worse than they really were to get Reynolds to send out mounted militia troops.

I thought, Well now this is a slippery trick.

Because if the General describes an alarming situation on the frontier, but doesn't formally request the militia callup, Governor Reynolds was bound to send them anyway. When the General was out of the room, I whispered to Johnston, "I don't think we need all those militia, do you?"

But the General returned and took a stick of wax out of the writing kit on the desk. I watched it drip thick and red onto the paper overlap. The General let it set a minute, then pressed his seal into it.

He handed the letter to me. "Take this to Black Hawk. Bring Bright Sun and her two children back with you. Tell her that, for her own safety, she must come to me, and I shall see that she is looked after."

The General turned lazily, but his eyes were shrewd as he looked at the weather.

27 April 1832

~※~ As we came into the camp, Black Hawk's warriors were itching to fight us, but we carried white flags big as bedsheets. One knocked the white flag out of Le Clair's hand and threw a British Union Jack atop him so as he looked like a fat red, white and blue ghost.

Black Hawk stepped out of a tipi with a British flag wrapped like a robe about his shoulders. Bright Sun followed behind him. She looked at both me and Johnston, and I could see the poor girl was scared, pleading with her eyes. It nearly cut right into me to see her strapped like that. I wanted to fetch her up and take her back with us, but what could we do? There were twelve of us. We had walked bold as you please right into a camp of nearly three thousand Indians, if you counted women and children along with the warriors.

Fat Ass Le Clair cleared his throat and his wattles jiggled. He read a letter from General Atkinson that said, "Black Hawk, come back to Fort Armstrong and you will not be harmed. Tell these men whether your heart is good or bad. If it is good, we can make peace. Your women and children will be cared for. No one will be harmed."

Black Hawk seemed to think about this. Two of his sentries motioned for us to follow him into the tipi. They stood over us with guns pointed to our heads. We weren't allowed near the fire, which I rightly perceived was an insult from the Sauk. I was surprised to see both the Prophet and One-Eye Decorah there. One-Eye had given up his colorful tartan sash and was dressed in regulation white wool army trousers and the sort of red broadcloth shirt that a whiskey trader might fancy. The Prophet and One-Eye pretended they did not see us. They looked right past me and Johnston, as if we weren't there at all.

Bright Sun huddled off with Singing Bird, opposite us, with the two little children. Outside, the young men started a fire, shot their guns, pounded the drums and danced around in what I presumed was a war dance. They burned Le Clair's big white flag. Whirling Thunder stepped outside and told them to be quiet, as the elders couldn't hear themselves speak.

Le Clair, sitting between me and Johnston, whispered a translation of

Black Hawk's conversation with the other two Indians. The Prophet urged Black Hawk to turn us over to the warriors outside the tipi. He said, "I would like to see their throats ripped out, I have a good lance tipped with two *cathu*—rattlesnake fangs filled with poison. Let your young men use the lance against these bluecoats. It will prepare them to fight and make them strong for the coming battles with the Chemokemon."

Me and Johnston exchanged a look.

One-Eye said to Black Hawk, "No, no. Do not listen to this old fool, the Prophet. Instead, accept this gift of tobacco as their ransom. One day, friend, you can kill all the bluecoats you please. But not today. Zha'becka is too close."

Black Hawk took the tobacco and made an unhappy sound, then he, the Prophet and One-Eye stepped out of the tipi without looking at us. Johnston said, "Bright Sun! Is Black Hawk going to bar-bee-kue us, or what the hell?"

"Bright Sun, the General wants us to bring you and your children back to the boat. Come with us, for your own safety as well as your children's. C'mon old girl."

Singing Bird grabbed Bright Sun by the arms, and I thought she was going to shake the younger woman. Le Clair translated as she said, "Daughter, if you choose to go to Zha'becka, I will not think badly of you. Black Hawk will be angry, but one day he will forget his anger. Go. Take the children and go!"

But Black Hawk came back into the tent, alone this time. Bright Sun looked pale, drawn and trapped. Black Hawk said to Antoine Le Clair, who translated his words, "This is my message to Zha'becka. Tell him I do not understand why he asks whether my heart is bad. My heart is not bad. I think upon my children, of taking them to a place where they can make corn and be safe and live without fear. We will go up the Rock River."

I stood there looking at Black Hawk, and I wanted to hit him upside the head. It was all about his pride and vanity, about looking mighty before those eight hundred warriors outside the tipi. Black Hawk turned from us and said to Antoine Le Clair, "One-Eye Decorah will go with you to see Zha'becka. He will speak for me."

Bright Sun began to say something, but her voice caught in her throat.

I was disgusted with the stupidity of the whole thing. I said, "Bright Sun, we'll help you pack up your things. Come with us. General Atkinson sent us here for the purpose of bringing you and your children to safety." But Bright Sun looked in a panic, and I could tell she felt she was betraying Black Hawk and her people. She turned her back to us, crouched over her two children and would not speak to us again.

I left feeling an injustice had been done, but by whom, I could not say.

The General watched us cross the river from the promontory at Fort Armstrong. Me, Johnston and Fat Ass, along with the other men in our escort, stepped into these fragile shallops. Me and Johnston, being the two tallest and heaviest men in the command, were jittery about letting Fat Ass join us in the boat.

I could see the light reflect off the General's field glass as he watched us cross the river, and I knew he was looking for Bright Sun in one of the shallops. He stood before the stone powder magazine, and when he realized we had come on without Bright Sun, he threw both his cigar and the map he was holding to the ground in disgust. He walked in circles, threatening me, threatening Johnston, cussing buck and kicking up dust.

I gave my full report, but the General paced back and forth with his arms folded over his chest and his head down. Johnston said, "Sir, there weren't a whole lot we could do . . ."

The General looked ready to shoot both of us. "You have failed this mission in every respect," he said. Johnston protested, but I dragged him off before the General pummeled us with blows and curses.

I remember thinking, Why didn't you go after her yourself, then?

One-Eye interrupted the beginnings of the General's fitful tirade upon my incompetence. He sipped from a jigger, then looked at the General through his silver-blue cataract and said, "Zha'becka, do you know I have told Black Hawk to come back? Go down the Rock River, I said to him, come to council with Zha'becka and stop this foolishness. I said to Black Hawk, old friend, Zha'becka will not harm your women and children, if only you come to meet with him. But what does Black Hawk say? *My heart is bad.*' He says he hopes to fight you one day and settle all. 'My heart is bad,' he says. What is bad, I tell him, is that he listens to the Prophet."

I couldn't believe my ears.

Johnston and I scrambled to tell the General that One-Eye was making up lies, that this was not what happened at the Sauk camp. At great bodily risk to myself, I put my hand on the General's uniform sleeve and forcibly turned him away from the Winnebago chief. I said, "Sir, you have got to believe us. We were there. We heard Black Hawk say that all he intends to do is to find a nice safe place for his women and children—"

The General cut me off. "So that he can organize his forces, hide his families in the swamp, then strike at us without having to worry about his non-combatants."

Johnston frowned at the General, looked at him as if he thought he was crazy, "Sir, that ain't it . . . that ain't what we're saying . . ."

But the General didn't want to hear it.

He came into the sleeping cabin on the *Chieftain* around one o'clock in the morning. I was sitting up on my bed in full uniform, waiting for him. I stood when he entered the cabin, looking slope shouldered, red eyed and weary.

I said, "Sir, I was there with Black Hawk. His real worry is protecting those women and children. He didn't say his heart was bad. The other two, Prophet and One-Eye, egged him on, but all Black Hawk said is that he is going up the river to find a safe place. Those don't sound like the words of a hostile to me, sir.

The General sighed and loosened his cravat and scratched at his jaw. He rubbed his eyes with his thumb and forefinger, then yawned. "Isn't this a circus of demons?"

"You said yourself that Black Hawk's band was scared."

"Cooke, you were his *hostage*. If One-Eye hadn't ransomed you for a carrot and twist of tobacco, you'd be baking with butter sauce over Black Hawk's fire."

We sat there a longish time. Then the General said, "Mister Cooke, I need my sleep. So do you." He licked his fingers and snuffed the candle, and a few moments later, I heard him snoring.

9 May 1832

WHENEVER Colonel Zachary Taylor—the commanding officer of the Fourth Infantry out of Fort Crawford—wanted to mount his horse, he'd bellow, "Johnston!" And Johnston would roll his eyes, but then he'd crouch before the old man with his hands linked like a small step. Then Taylor would use Johnston for his mounting block. The Colonel's legs are so short he has a hard time getting atop his horse. Our company of spies proceeded in an easterly direction and wound along a game trail through a pine forest, as we were now hunting Black Hawk, hoping to detain him and his band before they committed a murder that would throw us reluctants into a real war. The trail was musky with feral scent marking and oily weeds, and our horses tossed up icy mud behind them. Our party split into three lines, and I found myself at the head of our unit.

When I rounded the bend, I was the first to discover the Indian boy.

His body had been staked spread-eagle fashion to four stakes so tautly it was suspended inches above the ground. I dismounted, my men circled the perimeter and presented arms. I crouched to examine the Indian boy, who was perhaps twelve years old. He had been skinned with a flaying knife, a work so finely done that there appeared to be no injury to his muscles, which were raw and shiny. Gnats and ants crawled all over him. But there was an even more devilish aspect to his suffering as every skinned inch of him had been pierced with pine needles. Finding this entertainment insufficient, his torturer had set fire to the pine needles.

The boy was still breathing. He lifted his lids and looked dumbly at me. I turned away from him. He made a grunting noise after me, begging me to do what I had resolved to do. With my back to him, I loaded my flintlock pistol, concealed it behind me, then returned to his side. I put my hand over his eyes, and he obliged me by closing them.

Quickly, as mercifully as I knew how, I emptied my pistol into his head.

My troops leapt at the sound of the shot. I stood there stupidly, feeling sick, wondering how me and some unknown had unwittingly conspired to kill a mere boy who is now stained into my memory. Johnston said, "I'll wager whoever did this is still close by."

Upon hearing the gunfire, Colonel Taylor and his men hurried to join us. Johnston helped me untie the boy, we set a detail to digging a grave for him, but Colonel Taylor stopped us and told us to move on.

I said, "Sir, don't you think we ought to say . . . words?"

Colonel Taylor drew himself up, looking baffled. "Words? What words?"

"I was thinking a few words of the 'funeral nature,' Colonel?"

"You want to say Episcopalian prayers over a dead Indian? I thought the ceremony was meant to honor the dead, not comfort the first lug what happened upon the body, eh?"

But that didn't calm the dark feeling inside me, not exactly premonition, but something more dense, like a squally certainty.

"There is a brigade of Illinois militia making camp about two miles distant. I want to have a look-see at them. Johnston!" Colonel Taylor roared, waiting for his mounting block.

About one mile later, we passed a white boy, about nineteen years old, walking along with a musket over his shoulder, carrying a stringy blue heron. The heron flopped over his back, limp and dull eyed. The boy wore a bright mustard-yellow shirt and gray cassinette pants. At first I didn't think anything of it, but as I rode by, our eyes met. I called back along the line to halt, because I recognized him. It was the boy I had had to drag away from haranguing the General and Cousin Mary at the Fourth of July party two years ago.

"Reason Stillman. What the hell are you doing out here?"

He lifted the heron, then looked up and down the line at us. I dismounted and said, "Put your musket down." He did. Then I said, "Show me your hands."

"Why do you want to see my hands, you stuck-up?"

"Show 'em to me."

Reason Stillman's palms were black with pine resin. He grinned and snaked a look down the line, "Ain't you scrumptious in your blue coats with the shiny buttons."

I jerked him around, and Johnston tied him up with a hemp rope, binding him by his elbows. "Why did you do it?" I said, yanking the rope tight and hoping his hands would gangrene.

"I didn't do nobody."

"The Indian boy."

"Oh, him. I saw him when I was bagging this bird. But he was dying of his own self. Dying of the summer troubles. You goin' to make me ride with you? So as you can try to bugger me?"

"I am of a mind to drag you along like the livestock you are."

"Suit yourself," Reason said, "but my pa ain't goin' to stand for this. I'll remember your name, I will. *Cooke*."

"That ought to fill a whole day for you, Reason."

"My pa won't take kindly to this. He says wax figgers would be better Indian fighters than you tea-sippers. He's a militia major. Major Isaiah Stillman. You hurrah-boys," Reason scoffed.

"He's a major because he couldn't raise the battalion to make himself a colonel?" I laughed.

Johnston snorted. "Any farmer who's fifty miles from home is a colonel, if he's a hundred miles from home, he's a general, meaning your pa is still disgracefully close to home."

The militia camp was a sight unlike anything I had ever seen in my life. Fifteen hundred sloppy-drunk country rubes in baggy trousers and straw hats squabbled behind two stumps. Upon those stumps stood two potbellied men with their hands atop whiskey bungs who were begging the men to choose them as their officers. As this was the election season in Illinois, every aspiring politician in the state had volunteered for duty. A man of about forty with dull yellow hair wheeled on bowed pins through the crowd. Upon seeing us, his eyes lit up.

"That's my pa," Reason said, puffing out his bony chest. Major Stillman brushed past Colonel Taylor, took my hand in his in the preacher handshake and said warmly to me, "General, sir, I am so honored . . ."

THE BOOKWORM

08/15/03 13:54   K   0   10576
1@ 14.00 0743223772 20%$ 11.20
        GOOD JOURNEY

SUBTOTAL $ 11.20
SALES TAX @ 7.000% $ 0.78
TOTAL $ 11.98
TENDER Cash $ 20.00
CHANGE $ 8.02

Your Savings! $ 2.80

RETURNS WITHIN 21 DAYS WITH RECEIPT
        SALE PURCHASES ARE FINAL

"I'm not the General," I said, "and I believe this boy of yours has committed the murder of an Indian child . . ."

"Hah! You done bagged yourself a savage and we been here but one day, son!"

Colonel Taylor interrupted this prideful speech. His white eyebrows were thick as autumn caterpillars. "You will report to Fort Armstrong with your men to be mustered into federal service," he said.

But Major Stillman balked at this. "I cain't. We are the Wolf-Lick Rifles, you see. Our commander is Governor John Reynolds; we answer to him and him only. Reynolds tells us where to go, and we range river to river."

Colonel Taylor shoved his nose against Stillman's. "You deaf?"

"No."

"Then report with your troops to the commander in chief, immediately."

"Ugh, that would be up to Governor Reynolds, as he is—"

But Colonel Taylor turned on his heel and gave the order for us to return to camp.

"What about the prisoner, sir?" I asked.

The colonel looked scornfully at Reason Stillman. "Release the little and degenerate piece of shit to his old man." Colonel Taylor lowered those white eyebrows at me, and I did as I was told, but with a warning look to Reason Stillman that he was now in my sights.

20

Indian Territory, Spring of 1832
Bright Sun's Story

I T had been thirty-nine sleeps since we were forced to leave Saukenuk. The creeks and rivers ran cold under our feet, spreading over ground where river had never gone before. We hid in a thicket along the creek from the Chemokemon soldiers passing by us. Governor Reynolds was with them. We knew these were militia soldiers—they were not wearing the blue coats. They were drunk and had trouble staying on their horses.

"They are hunting us," Singing Bird said after they had passed by without seeing us.

We made a camp upon the banks of the Kishwaukee River. Black Hawk told the young warriors to tie the British flag to a high pole. I spread our deerskin and buffalo robes over the mud. Singing Bird and I fought the stinging wind as we struggled to put up our *pukwe'gan* and tie the cattail flags around it to protect the children from the rain. When Kamia was afraid of the storm, Singing Bird told her the booming noise was the Thunderbirds, the giant eagle warriors of the North, throwing bolts of lightning at the ground to free their brothers held captive under the earth by the Serpent Gods of the dead. She told Kamia the Thunderbirds had come to protect and watch over the Yellow Earth People.

We shared food, but there was so little. I removed the last of the parched corn from my pouch, I turned the pouch upside down, shaking every bit of corn dust into the buffalo bladder. I added some water and made for us a corn soup, flavored with slippery-elm bark. Singing Bird held Little Brother close, rocking him with his little head under her chin.

I said to her, "My milk will not come."

She said, "It is because you are too thin. Here, take my soup, I am not feeding an infant." But I knew it wouldn't matter, so I gave Singing Bird's food to Kamia, and she swallowed it greedily. There were shadows under her eyes.

She said, "Mother, what is this moon?"

"This is moon in which the Yellow Earth People plant the corn," I said, hiding my sadness because I feared I would never again feel the warm earth under my hands as I planted seeds.

While we ate the corn soup I had made, a horse stopped before our *puk-we'gan*. Whirling Thunder pushed aside the elk-skin flap and ducked inside. His tunic and leggings were shiny with rain. Singing Bird cried out happily to see her son return safely from the hunting party. Whirling Thunder bashfully offered his mother three rabbits, but we were not bashful about accepting them and quickly skinned them for our pot.

Whirling Thunder hunched down beside Black Hawk. He looked around nervously, then said, "Father. We have been lied to by the Prophet and One-Eye. They are liars like the Chemokemon."

When Black Hawk said nothing, Whirling Thunder almost shouted, "No one will help us. I met with the Prophet. He said, 'Tell Black Hawk to turn back, he will not make corn at Prophetstown.' Then I went to One-Eye's village. I smoked with One-Eye Decorah. He said, 'The Fish People will not help the Yellow Earth People.' And Father, the Long Knives never said they would fight with us. Father, our enemies have said these things to us because they want the bluecoats to destroy us!"

As Black Hawk smoked, his face was sharp.

"Do they say why their hearts have changed?"

"They are afraid of these Chemokemon soldiers, they call them 'militia.' They say there are two armies coming for us now, the bluecoats—Zha'becka's bluecoats—and these militia."

Black Hawk's body tensed as he sat before the warming place. The light faded and the sun disappeared behind the trees, and still Black Hawk thought upon what he must do. At last, he said, "These children are thin and we have no more corn. We will surrender to Zha'becka."

Kamia climbed into my lap and hid her face between my breasts. I felt relief when I heard Black Hawk's decision, because I knew we could not walk so long without food. I whispered to Kamia that perhaps soon we could return to Saukenuk, and we might not have to walk so long anymore. I wanted to give her something so she would stop worrying about Whirling Thunder's news.

So I scraped my hand into the dirt around our robe. There I found a few wet and blackened cottonwood leaves from last fall. I put my lips to Kamia's dark hair and said to her, "Look, Kamia, I will make a village for you."

I made seven tipis of the cottonwood leaves. Kamia lay next to Little Brother and told him a story. The north half of the circle were the Sky People and the south half were the Earth People, and everyone was happy because the hunting was good. But we made the mistake of taking Little Brother from his board and laying him too near the cottonwood village. His hand smashed the tipis to bits that disappeared into the dark air around us.

Black Hawk knocked the ashes from his pipe and said to Whirling Thunder, "Son, tomorrow, you will take three messengers to the Chemokemon camp. Our scouts say this camp lies a very short ride in the direction of the coming sun. Very close. Tell the Chemokemon I wish to speak to Zha'becka, that I will come to him in peace. I will bring forty warriors with me. We will watch you from the hills. When you raise your hand to let me know they have accepted our peace offer, we will join you. Only after Zha'becka promises not to harm the women and children will we bring them out of hiding."

Whirling Thunder's face was angry. "You trust this Zha'becka? I thought you hated him!"

"I do hate him."

"Father, I do not wish to surrender."

Black Hawk looked at Kamia and Little Brother. "Nor do I. But now a great army comes after us. And I must protect these children."

I went to sleep hungry and dreamed of food. The next morning, Kamia awoke, weeping from a bad dream. She pressed herself up against me, and I stroked her hair. "What is it that frightens you, Daughter?" I asked as I wiped her wet cheeks, but she refused to tell me.

Singing Bird clapped her hands together, bent down low and said to Kamia, "Look, Granddaughter! The sky is blue. Go out into the sun and run four circles, then run seven more."

A cool wind blew away the clouds, but the air shimmered like water. Kamia ran to where the tall grass came to her waist, and she danced in the light. Her blanket fluttered in circles around her. Black Hawk, Whirling Thunder and the other warriors rode to the Chemokemon camp, hoping to council with Zha'becka and his bluecoats.

Kamia happily waved good-bye to them and danced seven circles.

In Black Hawk's absence, our warriors spread out over the country, searching for food. They hunted for blackhorns, but found only small animals. Some hunted through the day but found no game. Singing Bird showed me how a bladder filled with boiled corn gruel, thin as water and sweetened with chokecherries, could be tied to a turkey bone to feed Little Brother. He did not like this, but what could I do? We were all hungry.

The Kishwaukee River is surrounded by marsh. There are few fish there. But Singing Bird and I knew this was a good place to look for water-lily root, as we could eat the long, narrow tubers. The air was cold, but we were grateful for the warmth of the sun.

Journal of Lt. Philip St. George Cooke, 11 May 1832

ACCORDING to army regulations, we have an obligation to journal the day's events on campaign. This is called sedentary duty. As we are force-marched such long distances, if I write, I must do so at the expense of eating, and I have grown so skinny, Johnston has nicknamed me "Sliver." So, with our wall tent pinned open in such a way that the tent is an awning, me and Johnston and the General tried to get a few things done.

As we did this, a crowd of militia boys gathered in a half circle before our tent. They sat attentively and observed us as if we were putting on a puppet show for them. I glanced up, and there must have been thirty of them just sitting there, watching us. They had no clue as to military protocol.

Anyhow, when I finished scribing a letter from the General to Governor Reynolds, I said, "Major Stillman's Wolf-Lick Rifles have still not come in for the muster?"

"Like a pack of dogs running the deer," the General said absently. "My spies tell me that a militia regiment under Stillman is camped at Old Man's Creek. That's our next stop."

I said, "I don't understand by what authority Stillman's volunteers are—"

The General tossed a portfolio onto the table. "Governor Reynolds has fashioned his own army, one that will do his bidding. Reynolds is using Stillman to make his political reputation with his Illinois constituents." His voice dropped away to an interior sort of musing, "Reynolds's Rangers, Reynolds's Dragoons, Reynolds's Mounties."

The General has us march eighteen miles a day over a fine prairie and forest country, hauling wagons of provisions and leading strings of mules with backs and bellies gone raw from the surcingle. His spies tell us Black Hawk and his followers are three miles distant from Old Man's Creek. We are hurrying to greet them, but all armies are obliged to feed themselves, and we are no different. The oxen-pulled wagons sink in the boggy soil, and we are slowed because it rains every day.

It rains. Then it rains some more.

We are further hampered by the mounted volunteers, who are as much good to us as a weeping canker on the ass. The militia breakfast each day on crackers and whiskey. This morning, after fortifying themselves, they commenced an irregular firing at the head of the line. Our men instantly formed up, preparing to meet the enemy, but we learned the militiamen could not resist firing at a hapless deer that crossed their path. The volunteers finished the day by crying out an Indian alarm that threw us once again into formation.

We have since learned they did this as a ruse to dump their provisions, for they do not believe they should be troubled with carrying their own food.

I share a small tent with the General. While on march, we sleep on our blankets, but last night, around midnight, the General sat with his feet in a bucket of rare water . . . that is, it was warm. His trousers were rolled over his knees, his spectacles low over his nose. He held a taper aloft so as to read a communiqué from Secretary of War Lewis Cass. His expression told me it was yet another carping missive. President Jackson issued an order to the General directing him to "attack and disperse" Black Hawk's band. This gives the General no discretion in his dealings with Black Hawk. Jackson wants a body count, but the General still believes peace is possible.

Bright Sun's Story

BLACK Hawk and Whirling Thunder looked grim as they ducked into our *pukwe'gan*. Singing Bird cried out to see them, and threw her arms around Black Hawk's neck, kissing his face, but he smiled shyly and held her at arm's length. We scurried after the men, eager for news. We built a fire to boil water-lily roots, but Black Hawk told Singing Bird to kill one of the dogs. We would have a dog feast to celebrate his victory.

Singing Bird turned a sharp glance on Black Hawk: "Victory? Was there a fight?"

"Yes!" Whirling Thunder shouted. "We have defeated the Chemokemon's millisha. We went into their camp looking for Zha'becka and his bluecoats, but they were not there! Instead we found these Chemokemon fools. They are the greatest cowards that ever walked the earth. Kamia could frighten them away, that is how afraid they are of us. But Black Hawk will share our war honors, he will tell you!"

Black Hawk began his story.

"As the sun fell behind the hills, I watched the Chemokemon camp from a ridge covered with short trees. That hill overlooks a wide swamp, covered with many-whips-bending trees. There was some dry ground, and then beyond that, a creek. The creek was flooded, but the Chemokemon made their camp along it.

"Whirling Thunder and two others rode slowly down the hill, carrying white flags before them, planning to surrender and ask the Chemokemon war chief for peace."

Whirling Thunder said, "They swayed before their fires."

Black Hawk continued, "As Whirling Thunder came near, the Chemokemon fired their guns at him! Tree Striker was killed. Whirling Thunder dropped the white flag, turned his horse and sped away from the militia camp. The militia pursued Whirling Thunder and Dark Antler, shooting at them.

"We were few, and they were many—about four hundred, but I told my men to have courage. Four hundred militia against forty Yellow Earth warriors . . . The forty of us charged down the hill, into the Chemokemon camp.

"But seeing us ride upon them, the militia screamed like women, then turned and fled before us. I tell you, I was so surprised that I laughed out loud. So did Whirling Thunder.

"As we charged across the wooded land after the retreating militia, we slapped our axes against the wood. It sounded to the militia as if we were splitting skulls with our axes. Then, we made loud cries of dying and agony to fool the militia into believing many of their number perished in the swamps. And this worked!

"It was now growing very dark. The militia horses panicked at the sound of our approach. The Chemokemon were confused by the darkness and our noises. Our few men surrounded the camp, forcing them to run for the swamps. Most militia carried their guns with them, but they stumbled and fell into the water, and their guns would not fire. Those white men who had working guns shot and killed their own men. The militia war chiefs cried out to their men, 'Do not run,' but the militia were such great cowards, they did not listen to their leaders.

"I found one large white man sitting a horse that was tied to a tree; he begged the tree to release him, as he was so frightened he could not do this himself! Another Chemokemon stole a horse that he could not control. At first the horse ran to safety, but then the horse turned around and carried the militia soldier into our midst! We took eleven scalps."

Black Hawk fell silent.

A gray foam boiled atop the kettle of dog. I looked at its brown eyes and its open mouth, and my stomach felt sick. We spoke no more of this battle. It meant nothing to me, and I did not wish to celebrate. Singing Bird and I were sullen and watchful. We did not now have more food because these militia were dead or fleeing from us in fear. We could not return to Saukenuk because Black Hawk had shown his bravery. It meant only bad things for us. Until that fight, I had hoped that Zha'becka and Black Hawk could find peace. Now, Black Hawk had humiliated the militia and had taken scalps.

Now I knew peace was impossible.

The news of Black Hawk's victory over the Chemokemon passed over the Lake Region like a rainy wind. Within six sleeps, all of the tribes that had once refused us help, now came to join with us. It was time, the Burnt Legs—the Potawatami—said, to take meat from the white people.

Journal of Lt. Philip St. George Cooke, 16 May 1832

OUR tent is black with mold, as we must fold it in the rain and unfold it in the rain. I sneezed and shivered and watched the mud trickle along the bottom of my blue wool blanket. I could feel the cold seeping into my clothes. I reached for my haversack, removed a handkerchief of cinnamon candies and popped one in my mouth. I offered one to the General, but he grabbed a handful, packing them into his cheek until it bulged. "Get enough, did you?" I asked.

Private Russell poked his melon-sized head through the tent flap. He wiped the rain from his face. "Sir? Something happened at Old Man's Creek you ought to know about."

There being no standing room in the tent, the General dragged a gray blanket around his shoulders, pulled on his boots, then walked out into the mud. I followed him. We try to maintain bonfires at forty-yard intervals around the camp, and at any given time, there are 120 men on sentinel duty. The fires reflected off the heavy cloud cover, burnishing the air over us, protesting the drizzle with fat columns of smoke.

Major Isaiah Stillman and his rat-goggled spawn Reason shivered, hugging to themselves, under the canvas awning I'd strung under a buckeye tree for the sake of counciling. They looked to have gone for a mud-swim. Their mules stood dismally in the storm. I glanced up at Major Stillman, his mouth was open and he was breathing hard. I noticed his teeth were onyx black from taking too much calomel over the years.

Following the General, we grouped under the awning, which swooped threateningly overhead, pregnant with three hours' downpour. I stood between Russell and Mahaffey, who held a running commentary—they being married mind and soul to one another.

"Mister Russell, the waters are out once again this evening."

"Aye, it's a most vigorous defluxion we're enjoying, Mister Mahaffey."

"General!" Stillman cried, clutching at the General's arms. The General pried Stillman's hands from his biceps and shoved them in the direction of their owner. "General, there has been a great battle, a terrible battle at Old Man's Creek! We have just come from there."

"But your camp is twenty-five miles distant . . ."

"The way I run was not a little, General, it was stir or git beat . . ."

"Beat by whom?" the General asked coolly, lighting his pipe.

The exasperated Stillman fairly shouted, "Black Hawk! He come down from the hills with a thousand men in columns, with such discipline, like Roman centurions . . ."

Russell turned thoughtfully to Mahaffey, "He means legionnaires. Here is a man who don't know his Latinity."

"Black Hawk and his troops come down howling at us with the precision of Wailington's men in Spine," Stillman gasped, wiping the mud from his face.

Mahaffey cocked a brow, but I said, "Shut up," before he said anything.

Stillman continued: "Me and Reason here, we stood our ground, we drew our weapons, we fired at those Indian ghouls coming at us out of the darkness, but we was overrun! There was so many of them, they was bloodthirsty—as usual—they was surrounding us, but me and Reason, seeing there was only three hundred of us and *four thousand* of them—oh, sir, the results was tragical. I don't know how many of my men got killed."

The General eyed him suspiciously through his pipe smoke. "Why did you engage Black Hawk in the first place?"

"They just come at us is all. For no reason. That and Governor Reynolds, he ordered me to go after Black Hawk. He did. But I didn't. But he did order me. I got the order right here." Stillman stuck a muddy hand into his pocket and withdrew a crumpled paper, extended it to the General, who would not take it. The General held the stem of his pipe between his teeth and stared coldly at Major Stillman, and I began to realize, as if it were day-dawn, just what Governor Reynolds and Isaiah Stillman had done.

Before this fiasco, we were chasing Black Hawk in the hopes he'd turn around, peaceable-like, and go to his new home in Iowa. Now, the militia had started a war that neither the Sauk nor us army regulars wanted. And having started that war, the militia ran from their enemies and left us regulars to clean up after them.

"Where are your men now?" the General asked in an abrading tone.

"Don't know. Ever'body scattered, it was ever'man for hisself. Governor Reynolds included; he ran too. Me and Reason stayed together, but aside from that I don't know where my men might be."

"You lost three hundred men in the swamps!"

Stillman shuffled, his eyes darted over the line of fires about the camp, then returned to the General's face. He tried to argue on his own behalf, but failing this, let his shoulders drop and stared at his feet. Reason Stillman, a flatulent little fart if I ever saw one, boasted, "I kilt eight . . . no, I kilt ten savages with my own hands!"

Reason glared. "You shoulda seen what they done to Harkin on account of him bein' bald. As they couldn't scalp him, they cut off his head. I tell you, I am goin' to kill every one of them, nit and lice. I have a right after what I seen done at the Battle of Old Man's Creek."

"*Stillman's Run* is more like it." The General's eyes were malevolent.

"It has a cachet." Russell nodded approvingly at Mahaffey, *"Stillman's Run."*

I could see the General was sickened by this senseless and stupid act by Stillman. If we only had been a decent-sized corps of dragoons, we could have advanced quickly after Black Hawk and his people, we could have been in a position to accept Black Hawk's peace offer.

The General told Russell to summon Colonel Taylor and the officers for a council of war. At the General's council that night, after advising the officers about Stillman's Run, it was agreed that a peaceful resolution might yet be found. But we have to get a messenger to Black Hawk, requesting that negotiations be opened before other tribes take advantage of the Sauk victory and spill more blood along the frontier.

Once that happens, all hope for peace will disappear.

23 May 1832

❧ O N a sunny day, at the Davis farm on Indian Creek, Governor Reynolds barely contained his enthusiasm: "This is exactly what I feared might happen," he said. But I wasn't fooled. He thought this catastrophe justified Stillman's Run in a retrospective way. This confirmed his every political ambition and purpose.

Mrs. Pettigrew said, "Mr. Davis had a longtime running disagreement with the Potawatami over the fishing of this stream you see here. When the Potawatami came to him and asked him to stop damning the stream so as to allow the fish to get down to their village . . ." Mrs. Pettigrew removed a small Bible from her pocket and held it to her flushed cheek as if it were cooling ice. Then she continued, "Davis beat their leader with the butt end of his gun. That was a mistake. Should have shot them clean out."

I removed a cinnamon candy from my pocket, and when nobody was looking, stuffed it into my mouth so as to settle my stomach. We had, all of us except the General and Colonel Taylor, doused our neck cloths in rum, then tied them over our faces. Sixty troops stepped gingerly before the barn at the Davis farm. The flies formed a black aerial wave over the lawn. I tried not to look at the barn, tried not to look at the yard, which left the sky above and the faces of the people standing around me.

"Bellflowers." Mrs. Pettigrew sighed, looking at the eight settler women off in the distance. She was right. They did look as bellflowers. The Potawatami had tied eight settler women by their ankles from the hog hooks in the barn. I saw their legs white as stalks holding the bloom of their skirts.

The white children had been brained by the Potawatami, then hacked in pieces at the same time the war party killed the livestock, and the troops were picking over the bloody ground, trying to figure out what was what. The bodies of the settler men were strewn over the yard, and ravens hopped impatiently over the roof of the house and the outbuildings, protesting the troops messing with their supper.

The General brought in his lips, sucked them in so as they disappeared. I could see the outlines of his teeth against his skin as he tried to keep his stomach down. Colonel Taylor turned his lantern-jawed, scruffy old face to the General and began, "Who?"

"Potawatami. They're taking advantage of the momentum from—"

"The Battle at Old Man's Creek," Colonel Taylor finished the sentence for him.

"From *Stillman's Run*," the General said.

Governor Reynolds, sensing a thrashing coming on as the General's anger grew, slipped away. The General's eyes watered and followed Reynolds toward the creek, like the rest of us, he just didn't want to look at this mess anymore. "Black Hawk will begin a series of raids for supplies and horses, that is, now that his women and children are secure in the swamps," the General said.

"He's making war on you?" Taylor asked.

"Not exactly. He's meeting his logistical needs. I don't think he had any part in this. I think if we see him it will be around Ottawa, Kellogg's Grove, Apple River . . . wherever he can get fresh horses, food for his women and children. The Winnebago will join him next, if they haven't all ready. It is critical that we keep the road from Galena to Dixon's Ferry open. If we don't do that, my lines of supply and communication will be cut. We need to send out patrols of two companies . . ." The General pinched the bridge of his nose and squinted at the slaughter.

"Jaysus, but that's—" Colonel Taylor began. But the General went on, "What he'll do is keep the main body hunting around the swamps, preparing for any major offensive I may throw at him, but he will, in combination with the other tribes, send out small parties to harass all the settlements along the line. Diversionary feints." The General winced at the flies swarming over the dead. "Sergeant, get those men busy digging a trench to bury the livestock!"

Mahaffey and Russell lumbered across the yard, neck cloths tied over their faces. They waved two red-calico sunbonnets at us. "The two lasses belonging to these hats have been taken, sir. You think they're still alive?"

Mrs. Pettigrew choked back a sob, snatched the bonnets away from the men. Probably she intends to sell them in Galena as souvenirs, I thought uncharitably.

"Rachel and Sylvia Hall. Poor girls. Poor, poor girls."

"Mrs. Pettigrew, they're alive and well. If you don't recognize them amongst the dead, then they're hostages. And if they're hostages, it means we have a good chance of ransoming them," General Atkinson said.

Mrs. Pettigrew flashed a cutting look at him. "If they're very lucky, those Indians will kill them. What decent man will have them after they've been with Indians?"

The troops milled over the scene, a detail dug oblong holes, another stood beneath the settler women, calculating how to disengage them from the shambles. Sensing the General had cooled, Governor Reynolds rejoined us, put his hands in pockets and kept his gaze upon his feet.

The General motioned us away from Mrs. Pettigrew and said, "Tomorrow, I am going to ride to Ottawa to meet with the mayor and arrange for a transfer of about one-hundred fifty stand of arms to the citizens. These people are always telling me that they can spring forth like minutemen, fight a war before noon and return to their plows after dinner. We'll give them an opportunity to prove themselves. It is a fifty-five mile distance across the Ottawa plain, but we can cover that in a day if we bring along remounts. Governor Reynolds, would you care to come along and bolster the morale of your constituents?"

"The Winnebago and Potawatami are all over that plain!" Reynolds squeaked. "And, ah, hell, this ain't my war no more, this is Michigan's war, given Black Hawk is running up that way."

The General stared at him and waited.

"Ah, no. I think I'll stay here and . . ." Governor Reynolds looked around helplessly.

"Cram pork and whiskey down your gullet? Colonel Taylor, I need you to stay with the regiments. But Johnston and Cooke, you'll come with me."

I concealed the cinnamon under my tongue with some effort.

"How many men we taking with us?"

"Six," the General said, stepping around the dead. I followed after him, my eyes watering with the effort of keeping my stomach down. All I could think of was that, if we were killed crossing the Ottawa plain, I hoped I didn't leave remains that so closely resembled red pudding.

21

As had become our custom when he was away on campaign, the General paid passage for Mama and Eloise to come on from Louisville to be with me. Our days passed after the old pattern, we rose at a languid hour, then took breakfast with Walker, Elizabeth and Ned. After eating, we changed into our walking-out gowns, and often took the carriage to St. Louis to pay calls. But on particularly hot days, we did not visit our friends in the city, instead, we donned simple cotton shifts that floated loose over the skin, we patted big-brimmed hats atop our heads, then passed the day in the cool woods playing with the children, reading and, sometimes, gardening.

On one such day in July of 1832, when summer heat seemed to both breathe up out of the soil and shimmer down at us from a cloudless sky, Mama and Eloise settled with the children in the shade, while I worked in my garden. The meadow broke to woods where Mama and Eloise were, just a few rods away from my work place. Though the post was nearly deserted of troops, the bugles still sounded calls for the regiments. Faintly, off in the distance, I could hear the few remaining men going about work details.

Elizabeth sat on Eloise's lap. She tilted her head away from Eloise, who poked around in my daughter's ear with a wadded piece of cotton. Eloise squinted and held the cotton up in the dappled sunlight.

"Mama," Eloise said, "this little girl has very dirty ears."

Elizabeth wrinkled her nose and stared at the cotton. "What is that stuff, Auntie Eloise?"

Mama patted Elizabeth consolingly. "That, my dear child, is ear wax. Eloise, save it in the ear-wax jar; come a rainy day we'll polish the floors with it." Elizabeth howled her dismay and ran off to join the boys as Mama and Eloise laughed after her.

With Eloise's help, the children had, once again, dragged bed linens over the long grass and tented sheets over the lilac bushes. For a goodly long while, Walker and Ned confined themselves to the tent, and I could see their silhouettes as they played.

Their voices carried in the humid air. Walker said to Ned, "I'm afraid I'm going to have to amputate your leg, soldier. Don't move else I might ax-ski-dentally cut the other one off too."

"Cut them both off," Elizabeth said. "We can build a fire and eat them for supper. Plenty of meat on those fat baby legs."

It was hot under the sun. We called this grasshopper weather. I snipped salsify and put it into my gathering basket. I lifted the wood mulch about the black raspberry vines and peeked at the roots. Black roly-polies tumbled out of the soil. I tugged the straw brim of my hat down over my cheeks and wiped an itch from my jaw with the back of my glove. I turned at the sound of a man running. His shadow fell over me, and I squinted up at him. I recognized a young Negro boy of about fifteen—one of Uncle William's young servants. I leaned back on my haunches, dropped my shears into the basket and sniffed.

"Mrs. General?" The boy bent over, clutching his knees, breathing heavily from the exertion of having run all the way from my house, where his horse was picketed.

"Yes?"

"Mrs. General? I gots a word for you from Marse Clark. He say you best git down to his house right now. He say there is some people you gots to talk to. He say them people you got to talk to gots a letter for you from your man . . . 'scuse me, mistus . . . from your husband, the Marse General."

With a pounding heart, I scrambled to my feet and seized the youth by his shoulders. "What is it? Has the General been injured?"

He panted and shook his head. "No, mistus, it ain't that. I'm s'posed to say, 'Now, don't you be fearful.' But it's news from the war, and General Clark—he say it's news you should hear."

"You run back to my house, you tell Nicholas to have my carriage brought round!" I snapped at him, then lifted my shift to my knees and sprinted over to tell Mama and Eloise. Alarmed, Mama jumped to her feet, declaring, "I am coming with you." She looped her arm in mine and we ran across the meadow.

Within two hours' time, Mama and I arrived at Uncle William's house. We were both flushed from the heat. Though it was noon, the streets along the river were nearly deserted as the St. Louis Creoles had taken the sensible measure of napping through the hot weather. Uncle greeted us in hushed tones and ushered us through the door. He was wearing a white shirt and had opened his collar and rolled up his sleeves.

Upon seeing Uncle, I feared the worst, despite his messenger's reassurances. I felt a sharp rise in my stomach and a renewed terror that my husband had been hurt. "What has happened?" I cried as Uncle William tried to calm me. "Has the General been hurt? Tell me the truth."

Uncle murmured that the General was alive, but struggling in the territories to bring the war to a conclusion. Gripping my arms, Uncle said, "Mary, there are two refugees here. They are called Rachel and Sylvia Hall. They have been sent downriver by your husband. He ransomed them from an Indian called One-Eye Decorah. Now, these girls witnessed a most terrible massacre at Indian Creek by the Potawatami tribe. Your husband entrusted a letter for you with Rachel Hall. The General also wrote to me, via Rachel, and asked that you and I work together to find these girls a place in St. Louis. But I am going on. Come, come, you must meet these young ladies and hear their terrible story."

We followed him down the hall to the little sitting room adjacent to the main staircase. It was dark—the heavy velvet drapes had been drawn to block the sun—and the space was still and thick with summer. I paused on the threshold. I was sun-blind and waited for the forms within the sitting room to resolve themselves into people. Aunt Harriet perched stiffly on the horsehair sofa, her back ramrod straight, tapping her fingers on her lips as she gazed worriedly at two young girls eating at a round table before the window.

I was introduced to Rachel Hall, aged seventeen, and Sylvia Hall, aged fifteen. The girls had been dressed in Aunt Harriet's old gowns, in colors from a spring twenty years previous; Empire sylph gowns baring much bosom-age. They had almond-shaped gray eyes that glittered starvation, and they looked almost beautiful, after the yearning way of victims. When I joined them at the table, they met my gaze shyly.

It was tacitly understood by all in the room that the Misses Hall would not—indeed, could not—speak until they had eaten. They were thin to the point of frailty and gripped their forks in their fists, then lowered their faces over thrice-filled plates with daunting concentration. Sylvia confused a slice of egg bread for a sea sponge and swiped her plate, gobbling the bread in such a way as to cause gravy to rain down her wrist like a topaz bracelet.

Rachel glugged her water, wiped her mouth with her palm and gasped her satisfaction.

"When we was with them savages, they tried to feed us duck embryos roasted in the shell," Rachel said.

"But we ain't eating *that,* we told 'em," Sylvia chimed in, then nodded to Rachel, who continued, "Bad enough they come on and kill ever'body."

"As if that ain't bad enough," Sylvia agreed. Without a word of prompting from Uncle or me, they began their story. The sisters linked hands over the table and stared at one another, remembering the morning of the massacre.

Rachel said, "I was sitting on the bed, plaiting Sylvia's hair, and she scolded me for pulling it so tight that her eyes tilted up all China-style. There was three families, all of us living together in one house. The Davises, the Pettigrews and us, the Halls. We come on together for protection from the Indians what were killing ever'body on the frontier."

Sylvia lifted her pale eyes to me. "I looked out the window as Rachel plaited my hair and saw—it looked like a hundred—Potawatami running across the grass right at our house. Mr. Pettigrew, he hollered for the women to hurry and latch the shutters, but it were too late."

"Too late," Rachel echoed, rolling an orphaned bit of potato around on her plate.

"The first thing the Potawatami did was to shoot the men what stayed, but you know, most of our men was out in the yard, and they runned when they saw those Indians, runned and left us all by our own selves."

Mama and Aunt Harriet exclaimed in horror, causing Sylvia to halt uncertainly. I glanced impatiently at Mama, then nodded at the Hall girls, urging them to continue.

"Two of them savages held our brother Jory by the arms—he were fourteen—the third shot him. The red men just brained the babies and little ones, held 'em by the ankles, smashed their heads against the nearest thing—the rock hearth, the logs of the house, the stumps. That left the womenfolk, there was eight womenfolk."

Sylvia nodded. "The savages laughed, they made geese noises, 'squawk, squawk,' when they chased the womenfolk, grabbing 'em by the skirts, laughing in a mean mockin' way. They tomahawked the women. Me and Rachel here, we stood on the bed, holding each other, we thought of runnin', but there wasn't no room for it. So we stood on the bed."

I cupped a hand over my mouth, then whispered, "What did you do?"

"We screamed the whole while, but we didn't really knowed it." Sylvia trembled, withdrew her hand from Rachel's and brought her feet up on the chair so that her knees were at her chest. She wrapped her arms about her legs. With a quavering voice, Rachel blurted, "They did things to the bodies. All of the bodies cut up in pieces. We was there on the bed the whole while . . . It seemed they passed off a long while just cutting into the dead."

Sylvia sighed. "The noise of their knives going into the bodies, I hear it all the day and all the night."

Mama rose then, and taking both girls by the hand, led them over to the sofa, where she and Aunt Harriet put their arms about them and murmured in maternal tones. I left the table too, and sat beside Uncle William, I leaned forward to hear more, but Sylvia had begun to cry in low, harsh sobs that shuddered through her.

Rachel, however, was dry eyed and shocky. She said, "Then the Potawatami came for us, but instead of killing us, they put us each on a horse with one of the red men before they rode off." Rachel fell silent, scratched at her temple and stared dazedly past me. She muttered, "Them savages, they talked about us, I knewed one of them wanted to force us to lay with 'em. But the One-Eye Indian, he wouldn't let that happen."

Sylvia stopped weeping for a moment and nodded, wiping her nose with Mama's handkerchief. "That One-Eye, he wouldn't let 'em do that. He put a squaw on-a both sides of me and Rachel, he told them other savages to get on and to go on."

Rachel interjected, "But that ain't to say that we think they're good. That ain't what we're saying at all. Because do you know what they did, right in front of us? Right that very night?"

Aunt Harriet, Mama and I shook our heads in unison. Uncle said, "What happened?"

Sylvia whispered, "That night the Indian men and women danced over Ma's scalp. I recognized it was hers because her hair is chestnut color." Sylvia dissolved in tears, crying into her hands, "We thought they was gonna kill us for sure. Or force us to lay with 'em. But they din't."

"They din't," Rachel said.

Sylvia put a wet hand to her chignon. "One of the young boys cut my hair and kept some of it. I din't like that. One-Eye, I could tell he was askin' me, did I want to be nice to the boy what cut my hair? Did I want to mebbe be with that boy?"

Rachel's brow furrowed. Her stoicism intrigued me, and I guessed that she felt some duty to be strong for her younger sister. She pursed her lips and studied Sylvia, then said gently, "Sylvia, we don't know anything like that for sure. All we know is what we saw. Then One-Eye took us to see General Axson."

I started and put my hand to Rachel's forearm. "You *saw* my husband?"

She looked surprised. "That your husband? I thought it were your pa." Seeing my expression, she put *her* hand atop *my* forearm. "He were alive, if that be your question, but he were real skinny; all his men were sick with flux. They are tryin' to cross a huge swamp, then woody mountains, with foot soldiers and big old wagons. Looked tough to impossible in my thinkin'. I ain't never seen no military camp a'fore and I was a little gooched by it, so many white tents all of a row, so many menfolk all busyin' about."

"Huh," Sylvia raised her eyebrows, sniffling. "Your old man, he wears the spectacles and has an all-gray beard?"

"General Axson, he was kind to us, but he din't talk a long while to us or nothin', bein' full up with troubles as he is. He brought us into his big tent; there were a lot of soldiers in there. They was all gentlemanly to us. He paid One-Eye two thousand dollars for us. At least, that's what we heard tell. General Axson told his soldiers to bring us blankets and find us food. He asked us to bring you a letter, and General Clark here a letter." Rachel looked at Uncle William, who crossed to the table where the Hall girls' plates were, then handed the letter to me.

I held it against my heart as fervently as if it were the General himself, and I was impatient to leave the room and read it. But I waited for the Hall girls to finish their tale.

"Mostly General Axson just wisht' us well, then sent us on our way," Sylvia muttered.

I asked, "Why did the Potawatami attack your family?"

Rachel shrugged, "Weren't even our family they was after. I guess we was just their sweepin's."

Sylvia's eyes suddenly flashed with anger, and she snapped, "Were the farmer Davis who beat one of 'em with his rifle when the reds came to ask him to lift the dam from his stream. Reds say they lived on the fish, but the fish don't come no more after the dam."

Rachel said, "Sylvia, ain't goin' to do no good to get riled."

"I don't care," Sylvia yelled, startling Mama and Aunt Harriet. She snarled, "That's why my ma's dead. And my pa and my brothers. They're kilt over Davis's dam and his stupid fish. Twenty white people dead over fish, all 'a'cause of them savages."

Rachel plucked at her gown, then said dully, "We ain't got no home. We ain't got no kin. I don't know what will happen to us, Sylvia. That's what we got to think upon."

Mama interrupted then. "My dear girls, you can rest assured we will take good care of you. We shall raise a subscription for you."

Mama and Aunt Harriet launched into a fervid discussion of fund-raising as I slipped out into the hallway with the General's letter. I broke the red-wax seal stamped with his initials and read eagerly. The letter was dismayingly short, but I didn't care—it was a letter from my husband, and my heart was gladdened to see his familiar script.

My dearest Mary,
I have little time to write, forgive the brevity of this note. I am a bit afflicted by ague, but otherwise I am in vigorous health. This campaign has been the most difficult imaginable, there is no fair field of honor in pursuing starving Indians, but I console myself with the promise that I shall soon come home to you and the children. Send a letter via the express man who accompanied these girls, let me know of your days.

And that was all of it.

I imagined he had had to write this in the presence of others, and in great haste. I reread it, taking comfort from the idea that a scant few days before his hand had touched this very paper, and I smiled that he had evidenced his old habits—even though he was doubtless in grave danger, he wrote only of his worry for us. How I missed him.

Rather bashfully, I held the letter to my nose, but it smelled of nothing at all. Even so, I folded it and tucked it reverently into my waist pocket. Then, reluctantly, I returned to the sitting room, where the presence of the Misses Hall served as a vivid reminder that my husband traversed a brutal and dangerous wilderness.

I was haunted with worry for him, I kept a hand over his letter as if I could protect him from harm by memory and touch.

Bright Sun's Story

⁕ IN the month when the blackhorns bellow, we entered the sacred place the Yellow Earth People call the Trembling Lands. Horses sank when they stepped upon the sod afloat on marsh waters; I had to lead our horse through the swamps, walking in water up to my waist. I took comfort in knowing my children were kept dry, and Kamia bravely took Little Brother's cradle board over her shoulders so that he would not fall.

When we had walked nearly ninety sleeps, I became sick with fever. Little Brother sucked feebly from the turkey bone, but I put him to my breast to calm him. The fever made me weak. Each day, I carried Little Brother until my back was cut, blistered and bleeding.

Sometimes, I fell far behind in the line until I was with the old and sick. Kamia would not leave my side. She held tight to my hand the whole day until we made camp. Then I knelt alongside Singing Bird and scraped at the earth with a deer jawbone to build our fire pit. But knife pains shot up and down my back. I hunched over and breathed in sharp pants. The muscles of my back cramped into hard knots from the strain of carrying Little Brother.

Singing Bird lifted the cradle board from me and gasped. She said my skin was bleeding through my tunic. Singing Bird put heavy rocks near the fire until they were hot. She found someone in camp who had buffalo tallow and rubbed grease onto my skin. Then she wrapped the stones in hides and placed them on my back so I could not move. The warmth pressed the cramps from my muscles. It had been so long since I had known comfort, that I wept into the robe. My worry came out of my eyes, I think.

Singing Bird murmured, "Calm, calm, Bright Sun." And she rubbed tallow into Kamia's feet. She covered Little Brother with tallow too, then lined his cloth with the down from cattail seeds. That was the best night of all, for Black Hawk brought down a deer. Our *pukwe'gan* was crowded as we shared the meat. Someone said, "This must be the only deer left in the Trembling Lands."

After the night of the deer feast, the Burnt Legs, Fish People and Straight-Cut Hair people who had joined us after Black Hawk fought the militia at Old Man's Creek went away and returned to their homes. It frightened me to see them go—this meant we were now alone in our journey, and alone if we had to fight the militia.

Kamia put her finger in her mouth and watched them go. She asked if we could go with them.

I wanted to say yes, but I said, "Kamia, we will stay with Black Hawk. He is the strongest warrior. He will protect us." The other tribes had heard that thousands of militia have joined Zha'becka's army and all of them want to kill us. The scouts ride behind and ahead of the lines, and they tell us the militia ranges closer to us than Zha'becka's bluecoats.

One morning, Black Hawk gathered all of the men together on the shore of Mud Lake, and he said to them, "Brothers, we have joined together to help one another, but now our numbers make us vulnerable to the Chemokemon. We must divide into groups and go different ways, for if we remain together, Zha'becka will surely find us."

Soon, there were only a few hundred of us left who hoped to cross the

Great River Mashisi'pu. We knew our enemy, the Asha, waited for us there, but at least there might be some chance the Asha might not kill us. There was nothing left for us to do but walk.

Perhaps we would walk until we crossed the medicine line where the Long Knives ruled the lands. As we moved toward the Cold Sky, the old and sick quietly left us. They stopped without a word along the trail and sat beneath a tree with their possessions gathered around them. If an old man stopped, so did his wife. This was their dying place. I nodded good-bye to them as I stumbled past, my hand upon Kamia so she would not straggle and be lost.

We were a silent march of spirits through the rain.

Journal of Lt. Philip St. George Cooke, 18 July 1832

THE General ordered a force of approximately four hundred men to patrol the Galena road and keep it open for communications. So when an express man arrived in our camp at one o'clock in the morning, the sentries called him safely in, but the militia sentries camped on the opposite shore fired at him for sport. The express man delivered a handful of missives. But seeing the top one was from Washington City, the General tore off the wax seal and read it. He looked like a man already defeated. I didn't say anything when he dropped the letter on the blanket.

The General said, "You thirsty, Cooke?"

As yes seemed the only answer, we covered ourselves with our india-rubber capes and slogged over to the council tent, which gave us some standing room. The center of the tent was a huge mud puddle. The General poured me a smile, then we took our seats on warping old chairs and listened to the rain leak through the canvas. We could see our breath.

He said, "Cooke, I have been replaced."

"What?" I started, banging my glass down on the table.

"President Jackson says that as I have not—let me quote him precisely—'attacked and dispersed' Black Hawk's band, General Winfield Scott will be replacing me."

"But—"

"Scott is rushing here from New York with a battalion of fresh recruits."

"Cass is Jackson's new Secretary of War, isn't he, General?"

The General didn't answer me, but I saw the revenge in the replacement order.

"I should have shot Cass when I had the opportunity." I spat. Then I paused and recalled a recent letter from home. "I hear the cholera is raging in New York. Have you heard that?"

"Yes. I received a letter from Mrs. Atkinson. She tells me that the Northeast is in a panic over the epidemic."

"So Scott is bringing cholera ships west? Scott can't possibly get here in time . . . why, we're almost upon Black Hawk. And I'll tell you what, I'd like to see Scott do better through this marsh and quicksand. I'd like to see if his foot soldiers are magical-faster than our troops. What the hell does Cass expect when we're chasing horsemen through swamps with infantry? And besides, he'll bring the cholera here and infect our troops. Damn, I've never had the cholera. Have you?"

I went on in this vein, knowing there was no purpose to my venting.

A ghastly irony came to me—the cholera might delay Scott long enough to allow the General to find the Sauk, engage them in battle and thereby save his military career.

The General, having made his announcement, was silent while I ranted. President Jackson is up for reelection this summer. I guessed Jackson disliked the questions he was getting from Washingtonians. And Lewis Cass was finally getting his revenge on a man who refused to kill Indians for him during the Winnebago War. The General handed me a letter from the Secretary of War. Cass's letter referenced the General's prudence and judiciousness.

The General laughed bitterly. "I've never known those words to have such pejorative color before." He refilled his glass and lofted it to me. "As I see it, Jackson has given me an ultimatum. Race Scott to the killing ground and save my military reputation, or end my career in disgrace."

I took a deep breath and said cautiously, "Cholera might slow Scott long enough . . ."

"To give me time to find Black Hawk? Now I'm pinning my hopes on the plague?"

The General's voice sounded thick, as he poured himself another. "Maybe you're right, Cooke. Cholera may save me yet," he muttered. He downed his drink quickly and took a fourth for himself. "Because I've got to land Black Hawk before Scott lands me."

I put my hand over my glass and refused his offer of a refill, as reveille was in an hour. I watched him wipe the corners of his mouth with his thumb and forefinger and prepared myself for yeasty eloquence.

"My old man used to say the greatest sacrifice was that of self." The General rubbed his eyes.

"Oh," I said, studying the expanding mud puddle.

"Never made a damn bit of sense to me. Does that make any sense to you?"

"I think you ought to try and sleep, sir. The solution will come after we've slept some."

He ran his hands over his temples and scratched his scalp. He made as if to pour himself yet another drink, but I intervened and slid the bottle away from him. He didn't seem to much notice. He drew in a breath and got up shakily with a hand to the table.

"The real reason everyone counsels against revenge . . ." the General cupped the jigger absently. "There is no such thing as revenge. Just isn't possible."

I drew my hands up under my armpits to warm them, then shuffled foot to foot as I stared at the General. I could see my breath when I spoke. "Are you the one looking for revenge, General? Or are you thinking someone is out to get it on you?"

The General lifted his chin, glared out at the rain. I thought he looked really drunk. Drunker than I'd seen him look before. He put his fingertips on the rickety table. His voice sounded gravelly. "Cooke. How old are you?"

"Twenty-four."

The General laughed harshly, "Christ. You're about as old as my career." He coughed hard, shuddering, bending over. When he righted himself, his eyes were mean and small. He muttered, "About as old as vengeance."

"What do you mean, sir?"

"Aw, what the hell. Never mind."

As I could tell he wasn't about to explain himself, I told him I was going to sleep. He didn't argue, and he didn't say anything more about revenge.

19 July 1832

❧ RELATIONS between us regulars and the new volunteers—Dodge's miners from the lead region—are so bad the General has ordered them to camp on the opposite shore. Last night, a militia sentry, overmuch nervous, shot one of his friends while he was taking a piss. Which only goes to show the militiamen are more dangerous to their friends than their enemies.

We are lost in the country the Indians call the Trembling Lands. Now and again, we see Black Hawk's spies watching us from a distant hill. We find the dead along the trail, and Dodge's men fight amongst themselves for first rights to scalp the corpses. The regulars aren't interested in that sort of trophy. We're too busy trying not to drown, starve or waste away from the dysentery.

To cross the marshes, we throw up causeways made of bushes and grass over the quicksand. The troops put a shoulder to the wagons to shove them every foot of the way, and those of us who are mounted don't have it much easier. I tried a valiant jump over a ditch, miscalculated quicksand for turf and my horse dumped me in the drink. So now, I have caught the regimental cold in addition to my bowel troubles.

After a full day of marching, it is my duty to seek and assign campgrounds to the companies, and nobody is happy with me. I am not to blame for the boggy ground or the rising creeks, yet I hear much grumbling as the men lay out their camps. Johnston and me and Lieutenant Anderson stand over the baggage wagons and supervise the unloading, or it would never get done, and without unloading, the troops can't set up camp. We assign men to cut wood for fires that do not burn under stormy skies, others fetch up water, if there is any to be had, and the rations are dwindling, which many take for a blessing.

The rain has forced those troops with less-skilled company cooks into eating nearly raw pork and raw corn dough. After my troops clean their arms, I inspect the men as they stand in the rain with sore, wet feet and bellies full of dough. But just when sleep looks possible, we must see to the horses. Johnston has offered me a dose of calomel for my dysentery. I don't want to take it, for I have a sore in my mouth from it, and it is causing me to drool like a baby. Anyhow, I don't want black teeth like Major Stillman.

20 July 1832

WE'VE been wandering through tamarisk bogs, searching for Black Hawk's trail. He could make our travails even more miserable if he sent small parties back for us, to snipe at the defile, which seems to stretch out for a hundred miles. This country is too tough for marching in squads. Every man has to pick his way through the forest and the bogs. Black Hawk could simply send a war party to steal the militia's horses and he'd win the war. I don't understand his absence on this campaign, it is eerie and makes me suspicious. I am wondering if he is holding out some deadly trick for us.

A scouting party consisting of me, Johnston and the General struck off in search of the Sauk trail. Johnston grew disgusted with our slow pace and careful looking. "I will find that trail and get back to you before this hour is up, sir!" he declared, then descended the steep hill rapidly, crossed the river bottom, forded the waters and appeared on the opposite bank of the river.

Meanwhile, me and the General followed Johnston to the river bottom. There, at the base of the bluff, broad as Rue d'Eglises in St. Louis, was Black Hawk's trail. All that was missing was the signpost. The trail was marked by cairns of kettles, pelts, utensils and cattail mats, not to mention the odd butchered horse, which was nothing more than hooves and a bit of gravy. I couldn't believe Johnston missed it. The General squinted up across the river bottom at the sound of Johnston's whistle. He put the field glass to his eye and laughed as he passed it to me.

The General waved back. "That's right, Johnston, keep on a-going. Say hello to the goddamned Hudson Bay men for me when you reach Canada."

The day after we found Black Hawk's trail, I entered the council tent to deliver the morning report to the General. I overheard Colonel Taylor say, "I know you don't want to leave your regulars behind, but you've got to go with Dodge's horses. Take those militia by the short hairs and ride on ahead of us with them. I'll stay behind and march up on you, I'll have no problems with the regulars, but General, you can *not* let the militia get ahead again."

The General folded his arms across his chest. "No, no, no. In this spongy turf, I think my troops can outmarch the militia. These miners don't know how to bring a horse through difficult country. Think of the swamps we've just crossed."

"Go with the militia," Taylor barked. "Knock Dodge on his ass and take charge of his men."

"Why? If I do just that, then we encounter the Sauk, those miners are more likely to shoot themselves than the Indians. It'll look like epic suicide. Now I am thinking that upon reaching the Wisconsin, I will turn back all but the best riders and best shots amongst the militia, give each man eight days' rations and leave the provender wagons behind. Then I'll move both the militia and regiments out at the same time."

"I don't like it," Taylor said.

I have to admit, neither do I. Once again, a militia force of poor dubs roams close on Black Hawk's heels, while we infantry regulars struggle to keep a pace. I fear for the Sauk women and children who cross Dodge's path.

I have just penned cause for my own court-martial.

Dodge, whom Johnston has nicknamed Ivan the Turrible, commands three hundred Irish and German miners on mules, each of them with a bottle of blackstrap in their pockets. They are so rough that Dodge has been known to buck the rawest of them. This means Dodge ties them up with a rope an inch thick in an uncomfortable position. But the German recruit that Dodge bucked chewed through the rope, got loose, and I am told blood flew all over the camp.

Reason Stillman, that piece of trash, has joined with Dodge and can be seen in the same bright-yellow shirt day after day, toadying after the old man. As I write this, Dodge's mule-militia ranges ahead of us by about one day, and I fear for the red people who cross his path. We marched yesterday twenty-five miles over the roughest country imaginable. It is all morasses and defiles. These briared hills are so steep, we have to go over them at a crawl. We must throw up causeways over endless muddy bogs, most days we swim after our horses.

We march through ravines, surrounded by high bluffs on all sides. Black Hawk could repulse us instantly with well-placed snipers. Why he has not attacked us is beyond me. He could make us pay dearly for every inch of ground we pass by placing snipers on the hills, he could easily bring the militia to a halt by stealing their horses. All these things he is capable of, yet he takes no action when the smallest action could ruin us. Maybe he isn't much of a war chief after all.

As we are unable to pitch tents on these slopes, we sleep under cover of blanket in mud holes. Upon deserting a camp, we leave a landscape of rain-filled depressions behind us. I am too tired to write more.

Bright Sun's Story

✣ W H E N we came to the river called the Ouisconson, my people stood on the shore, staring hopelessly at the gray and flooding river. The Yellow Earth People were still many, but we were spread out along that river in a long line. My eyes felt hot and dry, and I was confused.

Singing Bird stood beside me, alert as a deer. I could not understand why she looked around wildly. Then, seeing an untended horse, she leapt away from me and returned with the animal. Black Hawk rode up to us then. "Singing Bird, cross and meet me at Bad Axe. Go!"

I turned, confused. Suddenly, a war whoop flew over us, screaming from down the trail. There were howls of panic, and we heard a dull thumping and crushing noise. It was the sound of a melon dropping. I could not move. Neither did Kamia, who freezes like a trapped fawn when she is frightened, hoping her stillness will send the danger away.

I saw white men on horses, riding slowly through the rain with their blood-stained swords and their guns pointed at us. They stepped through the rain, they came at us through a fall of water. It was not the bluecoats, but the militia. For a quiet moment, those of us on the river shore did nothing but stare at the men coming toward us on their horses. I wondered if this was a gray-and-silver dream come to life.

Then the roar of noise around me scared me so I couldn't think. Gunpowder smoke burned in my nose. I felt as though I were swallowing the clouds and swallowing burning gunpowder.

Black Hawk shouted at me, "GO! GO!"

He shoved the four of us roughly into the water behind the horse Singing Bird had taken. He forced Singing Bird to put her arms about my waist, he told Kamia to cling to my chest the way a baby clings to its mother, and not to let go no matter how tired or afraid she might be. He shouted at me, "Bright Sun, hold to this horse's tail and swim the river!"

Then Black Hawk slapped the horse on the ass, and it bucked into the river, pulling us along. The water embraced me like the arms of many cold ghosts. Singing Bird and Kamia held to me as Little Brother cried from the shock of the cold water seeping into his cradle board. I felt myself slipping. Behind me, I heard the screams of those who hadn't escaped as the militia horses bore down upon them.

Our men stayed behind and fought Dodge and his militia and helped the women and children escape across the Ouisconson.

When we reached the shore, we scrambled, Singing Bird and I; we put Kamia on the horse's back, Singing Bird struggled up behind her, then gave me a hand up with Little Brother. We rode away, but I looked behind for Black Hawk and Whirling Thunder. I ducked from the snarl of bullets. Our horse galloped through the underbrush, as frightened as we were. After a while, we slowed the horse to save its life and ours. We came upon many like us who had escaped. Some followed after.

For two sleeps, we rode and walked northwest, through the woods, from the Ouisconson river to the place where Black Hawk said he would find us, to the mouth of the Bad Axe River. There the Bad Axe River pours into the Great River Mashisi'pu—the Mississippi.

All of our belongings, our cattail mats, travois and *pukwe'gan* poles, our blankets and our robes were left behind on the shore of the river. We scrambled down jagged-rocked cliffs growing thorn bushes and pine trees. The cliffs dropped off in sluices to a marshy river bottom that was hard to cross because it was full of fallen timber covered by stinging sloughs grass. The marsh opened to a sandy beach that stretched along the Bad Axe River. And in the Bad Axe River, there were many islands grown over with willow trees.

Singing Bird kept a steel and flint attached to her waist, and seeing it still there, the two of us were relieved. She built a small, smoky fire, and my children huddled upon her lap, shivering, with frightened eyes. As it began to rain, and as we waited for Black Hawk, I searched about the marshes of Bad Axe for something to keep my children warm and dry. I left the children with Singing Bird and walked along the river bottom, gathering sedges and rushes to weave a roof for my children. I would not let them sleep in the rain. I searched for food too.

The land was so strange. The current of the Bad Axe was swift as it flowed into the Great River Mashisi'pu. A heavy gray fog descended upon us as Fire-Keeper sank behind the hills. I looked at the willow islands and the river, and I thought, I should cross with my children right now. I must not wait for Black Hawk and the others. This feeling was very strong inside me, as when you come upon something that startles you in a wood and you wish to run. I wished to run. But crossing the Bad Axe was a frightening idea, for we would have to hold tight to one another, and the Bad Axe could pour us into the Mashisi'pu, where we could easily drown.

I should try to make a raft for myself and my children, I thought, looking about for large pieces of wood. I told myself to do as Black Hawk had asked, to be grateful we had made it this far, alive and together, and to trust in his wisdom as a great war leader.

Whenever the geese wished to return home to Saukenuk after a long winter, they flew inside a storm, protected by the four winds and the clouds. Perhaps the Yellow Earth People are like the geese, protected by the rain and the storms that have covered us for so many moons as we walked in search of the safe place.

I collected the rushes and sedges, but they cut my hands, small, sharp cuts that left green streaks on my skin. I looked across the Bad Axe River one last time. I put my hand over my heart to make it beat more calmly. I reminded myself that Black Hawk was so powerful a warrior that all of the Chemokemon in the West feared him, even Zha'becka.

22

✤ W E have come upon another militia rout, another abysmal militia fail-ure. With a tactical brilliance most major generals would envy, Black Hawk held off Dodge's militia with fifty men, while managing the most difficult of maneuvers, a river crossing with women and children while under fire. Black Hawk managed to transport most of his noncombatants safely across the Wisconsin.

If Black Hawk's spies are keeping their eyes upon us, they must return to camp and report to the old Sauk that we bluecoats pass our days paying re-spects to the militia dead. It sure seems that way to me.

We came upon the battlegrounds of the Wisconsin in a red sunset, top-ping the high grassy plain in time to see twilight shining off the red tonsures of Dodge's scalped militiamen. We found no Sauk dead because Black Hawk requires his warriors to carry their dead off the field for a burial with honors. The five militia dead, as usual, had been mutilated. It isn't a good thing that I am no longer shocked by what I see.

Dodge met us, looking obstinate but dejected. The prodigious braggart said to the General, "We held our ground, Black Hawk pushed at us, but we held firm."

The General bellowed, "You jackass, then you did exactly what he wanted, stayed put so he could get his women and children across the water."

We are camped on the Wisconsin heights, overlooking the river. Another storm is coming up from the northwest. Upon arriving at this section of the river, I found the General stepping over Indian bodies, turning over those of the young women.

"She's at their mercy," the General said, his voice sounding cracked, and I knew he meant Bright Sun. Some days I find him in advance of the columns, scouring the underbrush as if he expects to find her hiding there. I do not know what pull Bright Sun has over the General, but there is some ferocious bond between them. The strain of this life and its secrets has sliced into the old man's body and spirit.

The General is back to his old habit of pacing the campgrounds all night like an unplanted ghost. He stops at each company cook fire, chats with each goblin group, then moves on. He despises giving up control of anything, a proclivity that is near to finishing him off, and, I think, distracts him from our larger mission. I have seen him checking on the horses, reviewing rations for the regiments, riding along on scouting sorties and coming back to oversee the guard mount post. It's lunacy. Also, he takes stiff doses of whiskey every evening with his supper. And he has come down with a wet-lung cough, in addition to the old yellow fever coming back to haunt him. Between the two of us hacking, drinking carminatives and chewing magnesium tablets, our tent resembles an infirmary.

An express man came with a letter from General Scott declaring that he has been detained in Chicago as his troops have been decimated by the cholera. Thanks to General Scott, every river city in the West is now suffering the epidemic. We have not heard from Cousin Mary recently, and I worry that the cholera may be in St. Louis.

Still, Scott intends to leave his troops behind and race up here, hoping to add to his military reputation by assuming command of this campaign, So the General, true to his word about not being in mood to sacrifice his military career, is merciless in forcing the men forward.

Here the General's prediction to Colonel Taylor has proved correct: Since the fiasco at the Wisconsin, we have outmarched Dodge's men, and each day we arrive at our camp hours before them. We marched two days without fresh water, my wood canteen has gone moldy, but I fare better than Johnston, who drinks out of one made of india rubber. The water tastes fetid. As it rains most nights, we eat cornmeal dough and raw pork, and most of the men have the dysentery.

But last night, with rifle as sole commissary, I shot a doe. I had followed the spoor a long way, careless of Indians or other danger as I was so hungry. The General, me and Johnston roasted collops of venison atop sticks, we made a paste of cornmeal and braided it round twigs and baked them over the fire. I was a gustatory hero for thirty minutes. The General made me tell the story of how I tracked the deer.

"The tracks being the least edible part of the beast," the General said, laughing. It was good to see everyone's spirits raised a mite.

1 August 1832

❧ I was standing for a moment before our company cook fire, trying to dry my clothes after a rain had soaked them, when the scouts came riding into camp. Everybody got excited, and the call was sounded for the field officers to come to war council. As tired and wet and sick as we've all been, we are glad to have this news.

Our scouts found Black Hawk's camp at the Bad Axe River, which is only a four-and-a-half-hour march from this place. The General issued the order that the troops strike camp at midnight tonight and march as soon as possible thereafter. Before sunset, we heard a plaintive cry from the hills. It sounded like the banshee-women Russell and Mahaffey talk of. Upon hearing it, the General quickly finished the evening inspection, then rode to the edge of our campsite and strained to hear better. His eyes moved over the heavy pine forest and steep hills before him. He motioned a Menominee over, then pointed in the direction of the pleading voice.

The Menominee shrugged to let us know he couldn't translate the words. Nobody in the camp could translate, it sounded like Winnebago, but the Winnebago scouts have left us and returned to their village. I stood there too, listening to the voice rising and falling, repeating the same words over and again.

Dodge joined us and said, "I think he is challenging us to a fight."

The General didn't answer.

"Should I send some of my men up there?" Dodge asked. "Bring that Indian down."

"What if he's suing for peace?" the General said. Dodge gave him a disdainful look as if the General had just confirmed all of the criticism of him with that statement.

The General rode back to camp, told Colonel Taylor he had something to look after, then indicated the direction of his search. He advised Taylor that if he didn't return by midnight, to assume he had been killed and move out with the troops anyhow. He ordered me to accompany him, and we set off over the grassy plain, in the direction of the steep, pine-covered scarp as the sun disappeared behind the horizon.

We climbed into the forest, but the horses balked and nearly lost their footing. I heard owls, lots of owls that I knew weren't owls but Indians talking about us, and the night air seemed green blue. No moon, just a sluggish low cloud cover and mosquitoes big as birds. We dismounted and led the horses over a muddy incline. A drizzle fell, causing me to feel even more miserable than the hopelessness of the General's search.

We could hear the banshee voice, but there was no trail to speak of, just pine trees growing dense as the hair in Colonel Taylor's ears. What the hell am I doing here? I thought. Then, as the rain dropped in sheets, the General hollered into it, "Come down here!"

The banshee call stopped then, so did the owl noises, and we did not hear them again.

For a time, I waited, but the rain came heavier, and lightning jagged across the sky, then hit something on the promontory above us. I swear I heard a rock split. I said, "Uh, I am thinking of going back now."

The General led his horse over the slick ground without saying a word to me. A wild storm broke at midnight. The lightning hit pines all over the hills, and as we were on an elevated plain, we were at great danger of being struck. When we got back to the camp, I noted that I had one hour in which to sleep.

But the winds came up so strongly that our tent shook, then surrendered to the force and turned itself inside out. I jumped into my boots and hollered above the wind, "What is that shaking?"

I thought it was an earthquake.

Mahaffey and Russell ran up to us, "Sir, the Indians have stampeded the horses!"

The General and I loaded our pistols and ran to join the line around the tents. There, coming toward us, was a bulging-eyed, arch-necked plague of horses, careening through the camp. Johnston threw himself up a tree, hugging bark as sorrels and roans brushed against his legs in their sprint for freedom. Upon hearing the alarm, our regulars formed up their lines before the tents, bearing arms that shone in the firelight, and their presence confused the horses into thinking they were something large and solid. Luckily, nobody was killed.

After all this, we had to try to get some rest if we were to meet Black Hawk within a few hours.

My horse, being a somewhat indifferent twelve-year-old, loped in my direction, hoping for an oats bag. I picketed her adjacent to my tent, dropped upon my blanket and slept for thirty minutes.

The Bad Axe River, Indian Territory, August 1832
Bright Sun's Story

⚜ W H E N I was a girl, Singing Bird told me tales of the ghost villages in the tallgrass lands that were crowded with spirits of the Old Ones who had not followed the stars. These phantom villages must not be disturbed or desecrated. When the Yellow Earth People came upon a ghost village, they made offerings to the spirits of fatted buffalo, of corn and pumpkin. I wondered as I walked through the mists, if the Yellow Earth people had become a village of ghosts, only we did not know ourselves to be so. I thought this place called Bad Axe would be a good settling ground for ghosts. When I walked, I had to stop and lean against trees; I used a tall stick to push myself along as I searched for something to feed my children.

I found three marsh tubers that were beginning to rot from all the rain. After I scraped them free, I stared at the wound I left in the earth. We never dig roots from the soil without returning something to our mother. We put a twist of tobacco into the ground to thank her. But I had nothing to give her.

The fog was dense over us. I returned to our smoky fire, where Singing Bird praised what I had found, but the marsh tubers were bitter and very hard. Kamia rested her head in my lap, and I stroked her hair. Whirling Thunder was one of the last warriors to arrive after the fight on the Ouisconson. I looked up at him and thought of how strong and bold he was. He never showed fear or looked hungry, though I knew he had been fasting nearly three days now.

He took my hands in his and said, "Little Sister, I have gone to Zha'becka's camp!"

Singing Bird's eyes grew big. She wiped her hands upon her tunic and frowned at him, "Son, do not frighten your mother this way. What are you speaking of?"

"I went to the hill overlooking Zha'becka's camp as Fire-Keeper was slipping down the sky, and I told him the Yellow Earth People want only peace, that we will surrender if only he will look after the women and children. I told him this in Sauk, and I told him this in Winnebago."

I felt my heart leap with hope at this news.

Singing Bird asked, "What does your father say about this?"

"It was Father that sent me to ask Zha'becka for peace."

Singing Bird said, *"Henekohe,"* which meant all right.

Kamia sat cross-legged beside me, frowning downstream, and Whirling Thunder poked her playfully. "Why do you wrinkle your face, Little Kamia?"

Kamia turned to him and said, "I feel the ground shivering under my legs. The river is making a noise and sending it to Grandmother Earth and she is speaking it through the bones of my legs."

We all turned and stared at the water. There, coming toward us, out of the mists was a huge steamboat, thumping the water, making it angry with noise and waves. Some of the women cried out in fear, but Whirling Thunder lifted his brows, and his eyes grew wide. "Mother," he said, "I believe Zha'becka has sent a boat for us!"

But I was doubtful, for I have been on those boats, and I have seen how Zha'becka makes the bluecoats stand proudly on the decks. I strained but I did not see Zha'becka on the highest deck with the glass to his eye, and I did not see the horses at the back of the boat. And there were only a few bluecoats standing on the front of the boat.

I grabbed Whirling Thunder by the arm and said sharply, "I know Zha'becka better than anyone. This is not him. This is a trap, tell the people to hide!"

Whirling Thunder was confused for a moment. He looked again at the boat, and I pointed to the Chemokemons loading a cannon and pointing it at the shore. But Black Hawk disagreed with me. He said, "I know the man who owns that boat. He is a good man."

I said, "Father, I do not think this is wise. Look, those men are loading their guns. They do not wish to make peace."

One of the bluecoats shouted, "Black Hawk, you and two men come aboard to surrender. Come out from those trees."

Black Hawk squinted at the boat and looked to be thinking about this. He could not see the young warriors crouched in the tall grass behind him, who were loading their guns. Black Hawk nodded, then he said, "I will go on that boat. I will bring these children to a safe place. Help me to find a white flag. Bright Sun? You say the words for me. Say the Chemokemon word for 'surrender.'"

But I did not believe the bluecoats. Whirling Thunder said to me in a low voice, "Tell the boat to pull to shore. Tell them to come to us."

I began to shout surrender. I began to tell the bluecoats Black Hawk would come aboard with two warriors, until I saw the bluecoats on the deck pouring powder into their guns. I backed away from Black Hawk. I put my hand around Kamia's wrist and stepped backward, into the woods.

The bluecoats on the boat yelled, "You are trying to trick us, and we won't be tricked, Black Hawk!"

"Run!" I shouted, grabbing my children just as the first ball fired into the grass and landed, sending up a shower of dirt. The Yellow Earth People dashed toward the base of the great rocky crags and hid themselves.

I found Singing Bird, and we carried the children through the grass, jumping over fallen trees. We splashed into the sloughs—deep ditches of water to our waist—to reach the base of the high rocky bluffs behind us. From there we watched the fight. Our men concealed themselves behind rocks and logs to shoot at the boat. I counted only six bluecoats on this boat, I did not see Zha'becka or any of the soldiers I knew. They filled the big cannon on the front of the boat and aimed it into the grass. Kamia screamed when the shot hit the ground, we closed our eyes and turned away as the smoke twirled up from the grass.

I was grateful that the stormy weather brought darkness early. As I hid with Kamia and Little Brother, I heard the bluecoats shouting that the boat was out of wood and had to return downriver. Twenty-three Sauk warriors were shot and killed. Singing Bird shook her head, her eyes filled with tears when she heard the terrible sound of women and children wailing when they found their men dead.

I was frightened by this. But I began to realize how bad things were after the boat left. Those bluecoats and their guns delayed our crossing of the Bad Axe and the Great River Mashisi'pu. They trapped us in the river bottoms for another sleep. And I knew an army was coming for us from the Ouisconson River. I huddled with my children beneath a dogwood thicket and kept them close to my body for warmth as the rain fell.

That night, in the rain, Black Hawk helped me tie logs together in a raft. He said to me, "Daughter, when the sun comes tomorrow, cross the Great River Mashisi'pu. Once you cross the river, you will be in the safe place." Singing Bird frowned at him, but Black Hawk said, "Take the horse, cross the river. Promise you will go at once when Fire-Keeper comes up."

"But why don't we cross together?" I asked.

"Whirling Thunder will help you and the children. You are young and strong, it is important you go upon waking. I must stay behind and look after the sick and the weak."

I promised him I would cross the river, but I begged Whirling Thunder for help. So much deep, swift water frightened me. I tried to think how it would be to swim with my babies across deep gray water, without being able to touch the river bottom. The river dreams troubled my sleep, I felt the cold currents swirling around me, curling under my chin as I tried to breathe. I slept badly that night; the fever seemed to hold onto my bones. I kept Little Brother under me, but he did not like my heat and wiggled about. Kamia was silent. She did not sleep, but lay with her whole body pressed against mine, from her head to her toes. Whenever I looked at her, she gazed into my face, awake and alert. She lay clinging to me all night.

The next morning, Fire-Keeper climbed into the heavens, above a white cloud over the Bad Axe and the Great River Mashisi'pu. To see the mist lying like a soft spirit over the water, to see Fire-Keeper raised my spirits.

Black Hawk was nowhere to be found, nor was Singing Bird. I guessed they had gone to find food, so I rested a moment, alone with my children, I put my finger into the corners of their eyes and removed the sleep sand. Then I stood stiffly and ran my hands over my back. There were water-filled bumps on the skin over my bones where the cradle board rubbed against me.

I looked cautiously down the river, but the steamboat was gone. I smiled at Kamia, and she put both of her hands on my cheeks and said, "You should show your teeth to me again, Mother, it makes you pretty." I strapped Little Brother to my back. I took Kamia by the hand and stepped from the place where we had passed the night in the grass. It looked like a deer rest, the way the grass flattened in a gentle circle of a bed.

The other Yellow Earth People were waking too. I could hear them making morning noises, yawning, speaking softly to one another. The grass was so beautiful, green and lush from the rain, sparkling under the morning sun.

Journal of Lt. Philip St. George Cooke, 2 August 1832

THE General marched us to the rocky pinnacle overlooking the Bad Axe River. With us were various brigades of volunteers, including Dodge's mule-mounted miners. The morning was beautiful, the grass stretched away and mist filled the swales. I carefully placed my journal into my pack with a letter of instruction in the event of my death addressed to Cousin Mary. I removed the last of the cinnamon candy and filled my mouth with it. I chewed it so hard my jaw hurt, and I nearly broke my teeth.

The General ordered the squads told off in sevens, the fourth man of every squad to guard the officers' horses. We dismounted, left our horses and knapsacks with the sentry, checked our priming and loaded our weapons. Though I was sick with dread, I did not show this to my men. We were on top of the bluff; the Sauk hid in the marsh grass along the river bottom, below us.

"Fix bayonets." I gave the command. My men were tense to every sound around us. There was a low hum down below us, whether human or animal or insect, I do not know.

"Shoulder arms."

The bluff dropped straight down. My men would have to slide down that incline on their backs to reach the marshes and the hostiles.

"Charge bayonet, at the quickstep."

The General put the field glass to his eye. There were flashes of powder in the woods north of us. To my right, I heard a light scattershot, but the General shook his head when we thought to move in that direction. "Diversion," he said. He squinted in the sharp light and made it clear to the regulars that we were to take all Sauk women and children to safety. Over the river, there was a long cloud, and in that cloud, I guessed the Sauk were hidden—probably as scared as we were.

As this seemed a good a time as any for praying, I tried it inside my head, then muttered to myself, "' . . . he goeth on to meet the armed men . . . He saith among the trumpets, Ha, ha; And he smelleth the battle afar off, the thunder of the captains and the shouting.'"

"Mister Cooke?" Russell said. "Hearing you declaim Job doesn't inspire my particular confidence."

I had not known that I was speaking aloud. I wiggled my brows up and down as I tried to redirect the sweat rivuleting down between my eyes.

Russell frowned up at the clearing sky and appeared to be thinking. "The worms can wait for their supper is what I allus' say, Mister Cooke. Let 'em wait!"

"Forward march." The drums snared up around us. "Double-quick time. March!"

The General directed the regiments down a sharply inclined sluice. In the brambles on the hillside, we met the Sauk snipers. Some of the snipers were women. Me and Johnston ducked at the sound of balls whistling past us. It didn't seem worth the effort to spend powder and ball upon them from a hopeless angle. Coming over the side of the sluice, we found Sauk snipers had positioned themselves precariously in hummocks all down the side of the scarp.

Our cannon smoked on the promontories. The General gave the order to begin firing into the tall grass below, and our artillery units went to work. Geysers of dirt shot up, and the air was brown with dust, and we could not see the field. I do not know how the General directed his forces. Our bugles signaled orders, company commanders shouted. I kept my men in a line behind me as we descended. The grass was up to my chest, concealing the Sauk combatants. My troops tripped over timber hidden in the undergrowth.

The General sent Johnston across the defile to order Dodge to keep to the left.

But Dodge shouted, "Tell Atkinson I'll not obey his orders." Dodge glanced down at the river bottom. Then, with a whoop, he spurred his horse, hollered at his two companies of militia to follow him and raced down the hill. Dodge's militiamen were off and sliding down the buggy sluices. They tumbled down the hill off to my left in the distance, pouring down without thought to formation or order. Many fell off their mounts. Even so, I envied that they were at a gentler incline. As they went, they shot one another and our Menominee scouts, who got ahead of them.

Reason Stillman, in his mustard-colored shirt, was close upon Dodge's heels.

Seeing Dodge run, the General lost his temper and elevated his rifle as if he were going to shoot him, but he didn't. I wish he had. Instead, he issued a fire-at-will order, then he hollered at me over the noise, "Get to her before the militia does!"

With my men lagging behind somewhat, we raced down the scarp, into alluvial gullies, hummock and hawthorn thickets, but two companies of Dodge's mounted militia were far in advance of us as they spilled onto the river bottom.

As I led my men through the marsh, the wet grass whipping at our faces, our boots sliding around in the mud, the air about us stinking of dead fish and rotting vegetation, we could discern nothing of our enemy. Nothing but the occasional flash of powder, sometimes the shine of a black head in the moment before they fired upon us.

Bright Sun's Story

KAMIA pointed at the hills above us, then turned to me and asked, "Mother? Who are they?" But I looked away from her because I saw Whirling Thunder running toward me, his eyes shifting back and forth over the camp. He grabbed me by my shoulders and said, "The militia are here. Listen to

me, Sister, this is what Black Hawk told me to say to you. Try to find the
bluecoat Zha'becka. But run from the militia. Black Hawk says Zha'becka
will not kill women and children. Give yourself up to him."

"Where are Black Hawk and Singing Bird?"

Whirling Thunder took me by the arms and said, "After dark, they left this
place. Black Hawk said you had a better chance of surviving if you gave
yourself to Zha'becka. If you and the children followed Black Hawk, you
would all surely die of hunger. And Black Hawk thought that if he were here
when Zha'becka came, the bluecoats would go rougher on us."

"Black Hawk has abandoned us here! He brought us here and now he
has left us!" I was so shocked I could not speak beyond this.

Whirling Thunder turned and began to walk away from me! In a panic, I
looked down at Kamia and Little Brother. "Whirling Thunder," I cried, "do
not leave us, let us all cross the river together now and run away to the safe
place before the bluecoats come. Why do you leave us too?"

Whirling Thunder's eyes shone dark and mournful. He put his hand upon
Kamia's head, then pointed silently through the lifting mists at the hills behind us. The militia were pouring down the scarps, coming for us. He
reached into his belt and gave me his knife.

Whirling Thunder ran from us, stooping low so as to stay beneath the tall
grass. I heard him sing his death song, *Mai'napano tukwunosa motcikano-
mokumi ki beha piyani*—I die on the surface of the ground, I will be under
the earth someday."

The many-rains had allowed the grass to grow tall enough to conceal our
warriors. Kamia jumped in surprise when loud horns blew from the hills,
when the drums began pounding. I could not see very far before me, for the
air was thick and heavy with dust and burning gunpowder.

We felt the ground stirring as the militia horses thundered down the hill
toward us.

I wanted to be brave, but I was not. Frantically, I dragged Kamia down
the hill to the river, and I looked downstream, then upstream. Our horse was
gone. Behind us, I heard the women and children wailing as the militia
moved through the grass. Yellow Earth People ran past me toward the river.
I saw little girls and boys climb into the trees and try to hide.

I pulled Kamia along the dunes of sand. As the mists lifted over the low
ground, our warriors could be seen fighting the militia. The sand flew up under my heels, I ran looking down at my feet, because women and children
had buried themselves in the dunes, and I did not want to step on them.
Women covered their children with sand, so that only their noses were
showing.

"Mother! The boat is here again!" Kamia cried. I jerked around and saw the soldiers on the boat loading their guns and their cannon. They fired at us.

As we ran, Kamia fell dangerously behind. "Daughter," I shouted, "you must help me. You must run as fast as you can!"

With Kamia struggling to keep up, I ran downstream under the trees where some children tried to hide themselves. I couldn't breathe because Little Brother's board was so heavy, and it banged against me. Women and children jumped into the Great River Mashisi'pu, screaming in fear as they tried to swim. Kamia was silent beside me, both of us breathing hard and running. She looked back over her shoulder at the women hiding in the sand.

On the grass side, the militia horsemen broke through our line of warriors. They charged past our braves to get to the Yellow Earth women and children. Behind them, I could see bluecoat foot soldiers racing to keep up with the militia. I turned, and there were militiamen everywhere. They leapt from their horses and loaded their guns. There must have been one hundred of them pointing guns up at the trees. Some of them paused to eat hard-bread from their knapsacks, or to drink from flasks, and I felt confused at the festival mood along the river.

The militia laughed and encouraged one another as they began shooting the children from the trees. The children dropped helplessly from limb to limb like ripe plums. The militia calmly reloaded their guns, took careful aim, then fired another round into the branches. A few of the militia ran to the riverbank where the women were trying to swim to safety, but coming upon the ones buried in the sand, they bayoneted them. They laughed at the quaking of the earth as they stabbed the women and children hiding under the sand.

The water was red as clay. Kamia and I had trouble running, because the red sand was slick and wet. I fell upon my hands, and I stared at my red, shining palms. A man with green eyes, brown hair and a bright-yellow shirt locked eyes with me. Seeing me fall, he came after me.

I grabbed Kamia by her thin wrist and ran as fast as I could.

The steamboat chugged up the river so that Kamia and I were running toward it. As I ran downstream, I saw the boatmen load the swivel gun and point it at me. Then I looked up at the boat itself, and I saw bluecoats crowd the decks. They leaned over the rails and shot the Sauk women and children in the water who were trying to swim to safety.

Behind me, the Yellow-Shirt Man chased after us, hollering terrible things. I could not think what to do. I turned around, looking in all directions, but I was trapped.

Kamia yelled and pointed, but I could not hear her over the guns and men shouting. There was dirt in my eyes and in my throat. I yanked Little Brother from my back and dropped him board-side down into the water. I tried to push him out into the current. I was shaking so badly. I thought he could float down the river, close to the sedges, to a safe place. I splashed into the cold water to shove him away.

I turned to look over my shoulder at Kamia, and she was screaming. The water lapped the sand, bringing the baby back to the shore. Little Brother cried as he disliked being in the water. I could see his hands waving to me; he wanted me to pick him up.

A cannonball landed in the sand before me. Sand flew up into the air like a snowstorm.

Over the top of the shimmering grass, beyond the line of battle, I saw Zha'becka on his horse. I saw Cooke and the other bluecoats too, running to us, shouting, Zha'becka raced to reach me. But first he had to fight through our warriors, and I saw Zha'becka cutting through one of our braves with his sword. Cooke clubbed a militiaman who turned on him.

I thought, perhaps Zha'becka will be here to help us . . . but the Yellow-Shirt Man struck the side of my head with the butt of his gun. As I fell onto my back, my eyes were wide open. I lay on the ground, shaking so hard that the land around me seemed to tremble.

Yellow-Shirt Man pointed his gun at me, but he did not shoot me.

He pointed his gun at Little Brother and shot him.

I held Kamia as tightly as I could, I rolled on top of her to hide her. I screamed so loudly that I could not hear the guns. Yellow-Shirt Man kicked me in the ribs. When I would not roll off of Kamia, he kicked me again. I tried to hold onto her, but I failed in this. He hit me with his gun again, and dragged her out from under me, lifted her by the back of her tunic clutched in his fist. She made small movements with her arms and hands, and she coughed because she was choking on the front of her tunic. She looked light as cornhusks, I thought I could see the light going through her.

Yellow-Shirt Man said, "Hold real still. I'm gonna pop you in the ear now. You won't feel a thing. Just a real loud sound, then nothing at all forever and ever. Ah-ah, don't move, little girl."

I drew Whirling Thunder's knife, I rose to my feet, I stumbled toward him. The Yellow-Shirt Man knocked me down with his gun hand. Kamia looked into my eyes. My daughter had eyes the color of the sky. She opened her mouth and began to ask something of me, but Yellow-Shirt Man fired his gun into her hair. Her head jerked violently to the side as if someone had hit her. Then he tossed her away roughly, like she was a clod of dirt. My daughter crumpled to the ground, small and still. I crawled to her and covered her and protected her from the rest of them. I lay over her and told her to wake, to get up and run with me away from this place. The Yellow-Shirt Man laughed at me and loaded his gun again.

"Lice breed nits, nits breed lice," he said, pointing the gun at my head.

I felt the cold barrel against my temple and lay still, hoping he would kill me so that I could be with my children.

Yellow-Shirt Man dropped his gun, he made a gurgling noise, and I saw a gout of blood come out of his mouth. He swayed, his knees bent and he fell onto his back. I heard Zha'becka's voice above me. When I opened my eyes, Zha'becka held me against him. He put his hand on the side of my face. He coughed so hard I felt his bones shake. He lifted me in his arms and began to carry me away from Kamia and Little Brother, but I kicked him to free myself. I ran back to the river's edge where my children lay sleeping. I pulled Little Brother's cradle board out of the water, and feeling him on my back once again, I knew I must have dreamed the Yellow-Shirt Man.

Zha'becka stood like he was frozen in ice. "Bright Sun, you can't . . ."

Someone fired a gun near me, the greased patch hit my face, and I felt it burn my cheek.

Zha'becka yelled at the bluecoats around him to stop firing.

I crouched and tried to lift Kamia, but with Little Brother's cradle board on my back, it was too much weight. I no longer had the strength to rise from the ground. I yelled, "Carry my daughter to the safe place." Zha'becka gathered Kamia up in his arms, brought her limbs tight against his body and shouted at me to follow him. Cooke ran up and down the beach with Johnston, both of them were screaming, "Cease fire! The General has ordered a cease-fire!" The bluecoats fought with the Chemokemon militia, and strangely, the militia shot their Menominee allies.

Zha'becka brought me to the steamboat in the river. I remember it was crowded with white ladies and men who watched and spoke of the battle as if it were a happy feast–story. Sometimes they applauded, their gloved hands making a soft sound. Zha'becka yelled at them to return to their cabins. He shoved aside the man who owned the boat and told him he was impressing it into service for prisoners and the wounded bluecoats.

The white people stared at Zha'becka as he put my children on blankets beside me. He wrapped me in a blanket, and I crouched against the wall. He put his hands upon my face and said, "Do not look at the river, Bright Sun."

Then Zha'becka ordered One-Eye Decorah and the Winnebago off the boat, he told them to stop shooting the Yellow Earth People. Zha'becka made two big-armed bluecoats guard me. They crouched beside me and rubbed their big hands over the bones of my shoulders. They tried to offer me food, but I said no. They tried to make me drink, but I would not.

"Mister Mahaffey, I fear this poor child has taken flight of her senses."

A Yellow Earth mother must tell her children how to find the Afterworld, for there are dangers in traveling over the death river. I told myself to be strong so that I could speak to Kamia and Little Brother of these things. I stood and looked at the red lines in the water. The deck of the boat was smooth beneath my feet, like a water-polished stone.

I said aloud, *"Makataimeshekiakiak,"* the Black Hawk, and his name was borne away by the four winds. I said aloud, *"Asshewqua,"* the name of Singing Bird, but the waters under the boat answered me not; I said the name of Little Brother, *"Naso'nomuk,"* and the rocks on the shore echoed my voice; I said the name of my beautiful daughter, *"Kamia,"* the rain, but the Thunderbirds did not descend from the sacred hills to avenge us.

I said my prayer, but the two men beside me mistook it for something else.

"Give us the knife, now, Miss Bright Sun. We would never harm you, give Mister Mahaffey the knife." I tried to put it into my heart, but Mister Mahaffey pulled it from my hand and threw it into the water. I am alone now, and my children are quiet.

23

BRIGHT Sun sat in a contemplative daze on the sand beside the Mississippi, silently gathering her sorrows, sorting them into sentences that cut every truth I knew into shreds. So there it was, plainly described. The General had presided over the massacre of women and children. I felt sick and weak and shaky. My throat was dry as smoke, and I stared at Bright Sun, waiting for her to yell at me, to blame the General, to cry out in anguish at the memory of her children. But she was very controlled and measured. She said matter-of-factly, "One hundred of our people escaped across the Great River Mashisi'pu. The Sioux were waiting. They killed nearly all of them. One-Eye and the Winnebago hunted down Black Hawk and Singing Bird and brought them alive to Zha'becka for a ransom of twenty horses . . ." Bright Sun stopped and dragged her fingertips over her eyes.

I poked about in the sand to avoid looking at her. "I watched the transport arrive at this very landing with Black Hawk. He's just up the hill in the guardhouse. Have you seen him? Do you wish to see him?"

"I have seen him there. I go to see him every day," she said.

I narrowed my eyes at her and paused, because I wanted to ask her how she felt about Black Hawk leaving her behind at Bad Axe, but I lacked the courage to ask the question. It was remarkable to me that despite Bright Sun's horrendous loss at Bad Axe, she had not uttered a derogatory word about either the General or Black Hawk. But I did not know her well enough to inquire further, and I felt it would have been cruel to quiz her about her emotions after what she had revealed. Bright Sun folded her memories of Bad Axe up tightly, but they had a form, a will, a presence that would shadow her the length of her days. After telling her tale, she said fiercely, "It is good to speak of my children again. People will not allow me to speak of them, because they worry how I will be. They act ashamed. Even so, I keep my children close, I will never stop dreaming of them . . . but what troubles me most is that I was unable . . . that I could not do the one thing a mother . . ."

"Bright Sun, you cannot criticize yourself for thinking you could have protected them. No woman can fight off an army." I felt sick when I considered it was my husband's army that did this. It astonished me that she was ready and willing to gather all the blame unto herself. She looked impassively at gray foam curling over the breaks in the river.

"I think of sinking to the bottom of that river sometimes," Bright Sun whispered.

"Don't think of it. The survivors will need you."

"All of my people are gone. All of the Yellow Earth People in Black Hawk's band." She sat up stiffly, wringing her hands and biting her lower lip. "Sometimes, I think the ravens, the laughers, the tricksters have chosen my future for me. To take away so many . . ."

"No, Bright Sun, you mustn't think you were chosen for suffering. It's all rotten chance."

Everything I said sounded wrong. She frowned. I have seen people grieving as she did; everything about them changed—the cadence of their speech, their comportment. She lay back in the sand, staring up at the gulls wheeling in the air. I saw, for the first time, freckles over her cheekbones. I studied her fine features, the rose color of her cheeks, her green eyes. She traced the arc of flight with her gaze, but her eyes seemed hollow to me; the mischief she had manifested that first day I met her outside of Uncle William's house had vanished.

She poked me gingerly with her forefinger. "Mrs. Atkinson?"

"Yes."

"I will tell you now what I would like? The General has something I would like for my own. Can you help me to find it?"

"I'll certainly try."

The light reflected sharply off the river, and I felt it burning my cheekbones. The wind tossed up a spray of sand that made a soft gritting noise against my skirts. She cupped her hands, then made a swirling motion with her finger. "I want the leather pouch—it would fit into my hand—worked with porcupine quills. Singing Bird told me of this thing, she said the General had it. I would like it."

I froze, washed over with guilt as I remembered how I had destroyed my husband's secret possession. I drew my knees up and wrapped my arms about my legs and lied to Bright Sun.

"Oh, I'm afraid that was destroyed in a fire."

"A fire? I did not hear of this fire. Was your house burned?"

"In a manner of speaking," I mumbled. "Is there something . . . anything else I can give to you?"

Bright Sun wiped the sand from her thin legs, made a whistling pucker, then stared off across the river. "No. I wanted that sacred bundle more than anything."

I took a deep breath and worked to keep my voice even. "Oh? Why?"

She crouched and gave me a hand up. "It was important to Singing Bird—Black Hawk's wife—that is why."

"Did you make this thing for the General?"

She shook her head, knit her brows, picked at the hem of her tunic. "No."

I felt contrite in the presence of her suffering, and embarrassed that I had not been able to keep my bargain. "What will you do now, Bright Sun?" I asked, brushing the dirt from my gown.

She tilted her head and closed her eyes as a humid wind circled around her. "I will go to see Black Hawk now, at the jail. Good-bye, Mrs. Atkinson."

Quick as thought, I realized I wanted to see Black Hawk too, that I wanted to look into the eyes of the man who had indirectly governed my destiny these six years passing. So I said, "I am coming with you, Bright Sun." She flashed a startled look at me, but it vanished just as quickly and she shrugged. I ran my tongue over my bottom lip, which felt dry and a little sun scorched. I touched her elbow lightly, and she halted, then turned to me.

I said, "I will meet you there."

I could feel her watching after me as I lifted my skirts and dashed up the steep, rickety staircase that curved up the bluff. I intended to ask Black Hawk a question, the one question that had plagued me for six years, but I thought a bit of a bribe might help.

An hour later, as I headed toward the guardhouse, the blue ribbons of my bonnet snapped in the wind, and glasses of plum and pie-plant preserves clinked in my basket. The dry grass under my feet sent up a brown cloud of dust into the harvest-dry air. I passed the living quarters where the wives of the troops were about their morning industry. When I arrived at the guard-house, I nodded hello to the sentries outside the door.

"If you please, ma'am, leave the door ajar. It gets a mite heavy in here," said the sergeant at arms, rising up from behind his desk.

It was a roughhewn place of punishments. There were three rooms linked by three open doorways. Light came through a narrow window behind the sergeant's desk. A prisoner sat over the beveled edge of a beam, also known as the horse, with his ankles and wrists bound, begging the sergeant to let him down, as his personals were swelling.

"That'll teach you to beat a laundress with the flat side of your sword, won't it? Say, Mrs. General! What can I do for you?"

"Sergeant, I must see the prisoner Black Hawk. Do you have any objection?"

"Mrs. General, it don't matter to me one bit that you care to see him. Seeing as how His Highness has entertained that scrawny painter feller with the hoity-toity attitude—what was his name?"

"George Catlin."

"All of them Eastern fellas come out here, poke their faces through the bars, like 'look at that monkey.' Say"—the sergeant lifted the cloth over my basket and laughed—"y'ain't got a gun in there what you're plannin' to give the old red, do you? No? Follow me this way, Mrs. General. Now, you want to have a look at any of the others? Whirling Thunder, say?"

"No. Just Black Hawk."

We ducked through a narrow doorway and stepped over into another small room. On my left were three oak boxes fronted by black iron lattice gates. Within each cell I could see four iron bunks, two to a side, one atop the other, suspended from the wall by chain link. In one of these cells sat an emaciated man, hunched over, covered up with a red blanket even though the day was warm. Bright Sun sat upon the opposite upper bunk, working a needle through a moccasin japanned black from use. She did not look up at me.

"That Bright Sun, she comes every day. Leaves before sundown. Sometimes she talks to him in Saukie, but usually he never does talk back to her. Liken' he was her baby or something. Here we are."

"Open the gate. I want to be let in."

The sergeant frowned, looked at Black Hawk and Bright Sun, then at me. "Uh. No. Pardon, ma'am, but no."

"Yes. I said open it."

"But, Mrs. General!"

"Sergeant, look at him, will you? His arms are thin as rye straw, what could he do to me?"

"But, ma'am!"

"Why is he so thin?"

"Dysentery, ma'am."

"Open it. Greggs will watch over us, I have no concern about that."

The sergeant sighed and shook his head, mumbling something about it being my throat and he supposed I could choose to let Black Hawk throttle me if it pleased me.

"Greggs. Take a chair right here. Shoot this old red if'n he does one thing wrong."

Black Hawk's hands were curled with rheumatism. He propped himself up and turned to look at me. His face was pinched, and his jaw looked small. I glanced over my shoulder at Bright Sun, who flicked her eyes over me, then resumed her needlework.

For a long, quiet while, Black Hawk and I studied one another. I could see that the memory of the war lived in him, insidious and lethal. I believed it was killing him even as I stood there—he was disappearing like an insect being desiccated by a spider. The cell gate clanked shut, and Sergeant Greggs grinned, "Mrs. General, you want out of there yet? Had about enough?"

I pointed at Black Hawk's ankles, which were ulcerated and raw from the manacles about them. "Sergeant, what is the justification for winding chains around an old man confined to a cell?"

"It's the General's orders, ma'am."

"Well, take them off."

"That order's got to come from the General."

I challenged the sergeant with a stare, but he was a veteran of staring down much tougher cases. Bright Sun lifted her green eyes to me, let them wander over me from my head to my toes. When I removed my bonnet, she studied my hair, a wave of curls and braid twined with ribbon. I allowed her to scrutinize me.

"You are wearing a different dress. You must have many," she commented.

"Miss Bright Sun, may I ask yet another favor of you?" I said. I assumed her silence to mean assent and I continued, "If you would translate for me, I would be most grateful."

"He will not speak to you."

"Please. I shall return the favor in any respect you like. All I ask is that you speak for me."

Bright Sun turned her head aside so that I could not see her expression. She set the moccasin neatly upon the pallet, then tucked the needle inside the moccasin and folded her small hands in her lap. "I know what I want you to give to me."

"And what would that be?"

"I will tell you after we leave here. What do you want to say to him?" She set her jaw, her demeanor having shifted to reticence tinged with disappointment at my not having the leather pouch worked with porcupine quills, or perhaps she felt regret for having confided in me earlier. I tipped my head aside and said, "Well, why don't we begin with: Hello, Chief Black Hawk, I am Mrs. Atkinson."

Bright Sun smirked at me and began speaking in Sauk. Black Hawk spoke then, and Bright Sun translated, "You are the General's woman?"

I nodded.

Black Hawk asked, "Why do you come here?"

"To see you."

Black Hawk clasped the blanket around his shoulders before his ribs. He passed a dark-eyed glance over the full skirt of my gown. "That is a big dress."

He pointed at the chatelaine that clinked from a ring upon my waistband and asked, "Is that a knife?" I lifted the top of the chatelaine and showed him the contents; scissors, a nail file, an earwax pick, my keys, ivory strips for writing myself notes. He motioned at the black lace mittens that covered the tops of my hands and half of my thumb, ending in a lace fringe about my knuckles so that my fingers were exposed. "You have wounds on your hands? Is that why you cover them?"

"To protect them from the sun."

His eyes revealed the smallest glimmer of amusement when he pointed to the cluster of green feathers on the side of my bonnet. "You wear those plumes to taunt me, heh? Only warriors wear feathers on their heads. Did you come to fight me, the General's woman?"

"No, sir, I save my fighting strength for the General."

"Heh." One corner of Black Hawk's mouth turned up.

I looked pointedly at the iron bracelets about Black Hawk's ankles. "Miss Bright Sun, ask him if the manacles pain him."

"He will not admit that they pain him. He would not complain or be weak," Bright Sun said.

"Please ask him."

Black Hawk drew his ankles back under the pallet, out of my sight. He razored the air with his hands. "No. There is no pain."

Putting my hand to the bunk behind me to steady myself, I opened the basket. I peeled an egg-dipped paper from a glass of plum preserves and offered the glass to him, along with a spoon.

Bright Sun said, "He will not take it."

But Black Hawk extended a trembling hand, and I guessed the cause of the trembling to be his illness, so I slid my hand about his as he gripped the glass. His eyes flashed up at me, wary, as if I were tricking him somehow. He frowned at the white bars of my fingers about his brown hand and made a disgruntled noise, so I withdrew my hand hastily and said, "This will make you feel stronger."

Black Hawk would not accept the spoon, but scooped the plums with the first two fingers of his hand into his mouth, hesitantly at first, then greedily. I offered another jar to Bright Sun, who was so thin that her cheekbones looked to poke right through her skin. She sniffed at the jar, jabbed her finger into the preserves, then licked it. I brought out biscuits and some of the ham I had kept packed in oats and ashes in the root cellar. Bright Sun and Black Hawk ate everything, then returned the preserve glasses to me.

"I know you and the General have been enemies for many years. Will you tell me why?" I asked this casually, as I arranged the glasses in an orderly fashion within the basket, then glanced over my shoulder at Black Hawk. Bright Sun did not translate but sat perfectly still and glared at me. I met her gaze and asked quietly, "Why will you not speak for me?"

Black Hawk covered himself with the blanket, rolled onto his side, facing the wall.

Bright Sun said, "He is tired. You should leave now."

"Will *you* tell me, then?"

"I don't understand what you want to know," Bright Sun answered firmly.

"What is your relationship to the General?"

She heard the tension in my voice, but she did not flinch when she said, "General Atkinson asks me to speak the words for him. I speak the words for him."

"That is all?" My voice wavered, and I cleared my throat to cover it.

Bright Sun lifted her brows. "That is all."

I wasn't sure I believed her, but there seemed to be no point in starting a fight, particularly since she had suffered so much in the telling of her story on that particular afternoon. I nodded graciously and gathered up the picnic basket, then held out my hand in the direction of the lattice gate. "Shall we let Black Hawk sleep?"

Sergeant Greggs paused at the open cell door, glancing about at the three of us. I slid the basket handles over one arm, and the wicker bucket banged against my hip as I tied my bonnet ribbons under my chin. Bright Sun narrowed her eyes at me, but then I heard Black Hawk speak.

Bright Sun's voice carried lightly over his as she translated. "The General's woman."

I turned hopefully at the sound of Black Hawk's voice.

"The Yellow Earth People, my people . . . we are a warring people. But we are also a sacred people. The white people hurt one another, they lie and steal, then say they are sorry for it and believe they have good hearts. They say they are forgiven. But the Yellow Earth People are taught to do right all of their lives, from the beginning to the end."

I looked uncertainly at him, but Black Hawk had covered his head with his blanket and appeared to sleep. The sergeant at arms motioned Bright Sun and me out the gate.

We paused outside the guardhouse, where a brilliant yellow light filtered down through the cottonwood trees. Bright Sun held the old moccasins against her breast, and seeing the ragged state of them made me wince. So I said, "I owe you some recompense, Bright Sun. I wish to make good on my promise to you. Can't I give you something? Food, clothing? Money, perhaps?"

She lifted her face to the sky. "I have no use for it."

"You are clearly hungry. And you need something to wear."

As Bright Sun gazed downriver, the sun reflected off the yellow sunbaked watercourse and the brown waves that thinned against the sandbars. She waved off a fly that was pestering the air about her. "If I dressed like a white woman, would I be protected from the things that are done to red people?"

"No." I cleared my throat. "But if this is what you wish I could—"

She startled me by pressing her flattened palms to my whalebone stays, listening carefully to the creaking noise they made. "How do these feel? These bones around your bones, squeezing you in?"

"It is hard to breathe," I admitted.

As I led her to our house, Bright Sun walked silently at my side, I could hear her feet scuffing over the floorboards as she trailed after me into the bedroom. She looked around with unabashed interest, bending to run a hand over the river rock of the hearth. I peered at her now and again from the corner of my eye as I filled a small valise for her with my things; a few plain and practical work dresses, stockings, boots that would be too big for her, and forty paper dollars issued by the Bank of New York, a currency always taken at full value in the territories.

And then, seeing her standing in the shadows of the room, her expression both childlike and despairing, I motioned her to one of the ladder-back chairs against the wall. She sat obediently, folding her hands in her lap, and looked up expectantly at me. Though I guessed her to be only about five years younger than me, I felt as though I were in the presence of a very young woman. "Where are your boys and girls?" she asked, bending at the waist and peering down the hallway.

"My children are visiting at Uncle William's house, with my mama."

"Oh." She nodded.

"Bright Sun, have you thought about what you wish to do now? I guess you could wait here all winter for Black Hawk, but you must understand that the United States government may try him for crimes."

She squinted, uncomprehending.

I began again. "What I am trying to say, is that Black Hawk may never be released."

Bright Sun gasped and straightened in the chair, her jaw dropped as if she was considering arguing with me, but then she said, "Whirling Thunder?"

"The same."

Her shoulders slumped, she propped her elbows on her knees and held her chin in her hand. Bright Sun's gaze drifted over to the window. Slowly, deliberately she said, "Then I know what I will do."

"And what is that?"

"I will go to Keokuk's village in the Iowa lands, to the safe place. And I will take Singing Bird. She lives in a *pukwe'gan*"—Bright Sun pointed vaguely in a westerly direction, and I knew her to be speaking of the Sauk refugee camp outside the barracks—"so Singing Bird can come with me. We will wait for Whirling Thunder and Black Hawk in the Iowa lands."

"But, Bright Sun, how will you get there?"

Once again, she shrugged, her brow furrowed and she pursed her lips.

I reached for her, then patted her hands reassuringly, "The steamers do not run the river when the water is this low, but the keelboats can navigate the channel. So there is our answer. It will be my gift to you for helping me this afternoon."

Bright Sun started, her eyes were full of worry, "But Singing Bird? I cannot leave . . ."

"I shall purchase passage to Keokuk's village for you both, Bright Sun. As I understand it, the Sauk people are camped very near the Des Moines Rapids, a few miles inland."

Bright Sun's eyes filled with cautious hope, as I directed Dahlia to pack a hamper with food, then sent Nicholas to secure the keelboat passage. At dawn the next morning, I saw them aboard an American Fur Company gaff-rigged keelboat that was headed up the Mississippi and would eventually pass the mouth of the Turkey River where Keokuk and the Peace Band had settled.

Selfishly, I admit, I had hurried her on her way, knowing that nothing provoked the General's chivalrous instincts like a despairing woman. Bright Sun, to my thinking, would surely lead him into temptation when he returned home from the Indian Territory. Besides, what would she do here? Sit around the barracks waiting for Black Hawk . . . waiting for the General? She was entitled to begin a new life, and in a way, so was I.

After bidding Black Hawk a tearful farewell, Bright Sun and Singing Bird departed aboard a keel crowded with homesteaders venturing to settle the newly opened territory of Michigan. Bright Sun stood primly in the bow, wearing a simple cotton dress and flax bonnet I had given her. She stared hopefully to the north with her arms folded about her waist, and I wished her well.

I wished her peace.

❧ THE General came home from the Black Hawk War on a cool autumn night, while I dozed with the household mending in my lap. The coal fire had cooled to white ash behind the grate. We had not had a wood fire since 1826, as wood had become scarce and coal was cheap, selling for 12½ cents a bushel. I heard footfalls outside and went to the door, pulling my wrap tight about my waist, then lifted the latchstring. The leaves had begun to turn, and a large orange moon floated over the trees. When I opened the door, gold cottonwood leaves skittered down the hallway. A strong, cold wind came up and blew my hair over my face, obscuring my vision. I tossed my head, then winced at the chill and peered through the darkness to see him standing at a polite distance, as if he were an acquaintance coming to pay a call.

"Henry," I called, "is that you?"

I crossed the porch and descended the stairs, but he did not respond or come close. I held the candle up before his face and was shocked by his appearance. His beard was fully grown in, almost completely gray, his skin was dark, but he looked rain worn and weary. And when his eyes met mine, he seemed not to recognize me, his brow furrowed as, for a blink, he searched his memory for a hint of who I might be. And in the instant when he remembered, he looked guilty, as if I had caught him in the act of committing a crime.

There was something so brittle and tentative about him. When I embraced him, he stood rigidly and did not return my kiss. I took his hand, but he hesitated and looked back over his shoulder at the lawn, as if he wasn't sure he wanted to come home at all. By a trick of the feeble taper light I thought I saw specters clustered in the river haze around him. But it was only the sharp strain of the months passing over him with no respite for his spirit or his body.

"Come inside," I said, guiding him over the threshold with a hand to his back.

"The house . . ." He stepped back from me, down the steps, and stood a goodly distance from the porch to survey it. "I remember it being larger." He seemed to be fighting his way home, struggling in his search, even as he stood before me. "I thought . . . I seemed to remember . . ."

I stepped from the porch and stood beside him, looking at the old log place. "What do you remember? Come inside, Henry. I'll draw a bath, and we'll wash the summer from you."

Though I urged him indoors, he curtly refused to look in on our children, whom he had not seen in months. He looked out of place in the house, paced in an agitated way in the library while his bath was being prepared and did not trouble himself with pleasantries or reacquainting himself with me. Rather, he behaved as a man in a hurry who is suffering the trivial rituals of living because he has been compelled to do so. All the while he was restless to move forward to a place where he truly belonged. The General wanted desperately to remove himself to a familiar landscape, to a fair field of honor where his army, his men, did as he directed, where he quartered a noble peace and the red people returned to their homes, unharmed. But there are times when the landscape betrays us and displays precisely what we do not wish to see. Such was the General's plight, to see in every shading and sun-baked field the apparitions that came into being during those eight hours at Bad Axe.

After bathing that first night, he pulled on a pair of clean trousers, but no shirt, and curled onto his side, sleeping in his clothes like a wounded stranger.

Time and again, in quiet tones, in contemplative moments or the intimate hours passed in our bed, I put forth gentle inquiries accompanied by reassurances of my unconditional affection for him. I pleaded without provoking, I smoothed out long, patient silences. I asked him to speak of the Trembling Lands, the Wisconsin River and Bad Axe, I asked nearly every day, but the General would not relent. He would not speak so much as a sentence about his war, and gradually, it mazed up between us thick and impenetrable, a barrier of secrets and unspoken resentments until I stopped asking him altogether.

At breakfast, the day after he arrived home from the war, the General said over his coffee, "I must visit that Sauk refugee camp and see that the people there are fed and adequately sheltered."

I pressed my lips together and cleared my throat. I held the coffee cup with both hands before my chin and said evenly, "Henry, while you were away upriver, Bright Sun came to speak to me. She told me she wanted to go to a safe place—in other words, Keokuk's village. She didn't see any point in staying here since Black Hawk might be jailed until he died. So she left with Singing Bird, and she went to the Iowa lands to start her new life."

He displayed no emotion at this, but I saw his jaw flexing, a sure sign that he was frustrated. I waited for a rebuke, a snide comment, perhaps even a word of regret. But the General raised his brows quickly, one shoulder flinched, it was the gesture of someone shrugging off an insult. I felt washed over with sympathy for him. I knew at that moment he believed that Bright Sun was angry with him and he had taken offense at her anger. He returned to reading the newspaper without saying anything further, and I did not mention her again. But I was overwhelmed with remorse in the years to come, because I realized that I had done something unpardonable. By urging Bright Sun to go forward with her life, I had destroyed the General's ability to go forward with his own. Having encouraged a safe distance between the two of them in the hope of bringing the General closer to me, I had inadvertently pushed him farther away than ever. Now that Bright Sun was gone, the General lost all hope of making amends with her, of benefiting from her mercy and forgiveness, of making his penance.

Such was my ruinous jealousy over my husband. I have always wanted to believe there was some aspect of him that was wholly mine, not shared with the government of the United States or the War Department, those forces that tore him away from me day after day, year after year. But it was not to be. In the months after Bad Axe, he separated completely from me. I did not understand what had happened, but I knew that in the General's heart, all was over between us. He no longer cared for me, if he had ever truly cared for me at all. Though I still served some useful purpose as keeper of his home and mother to his children, I was nothing more than a final consideration upon the General's list, a niggling detail to be dealt with at the close of a long day. Some evenings he strolled into the library after the children were abed and caught my eye as if he were surprised to discover that he had a wife.

24

⁂ O N that particular October morning in 1832, I had tacked mosquito netting over the open nursery windows, but the flies detoured through the chimney and the front door. The General had built a diminutive table-and-chairs set for the children, which Dahlia covered with blue-and-white oil-cloth. Elizabeth, Walker and Ned had left their breakfasts largely uneaten, and the flies rejoiced over the leavings of buttered bread with molasses. As I tied my bonnet ribbons under my chin, I could hear the children outside, shrieking delightedly at their father, who laughed and encouraged them to be wild.

Our carriage had been pulled round, rattling over the pebbled drive, while the General, armed with an elm branch and much flourish, pretended to fence with all three children simultaneously. Walker was much discontented with his playful younger siblings, urging his father to stab him seriously and ignore the others. I bent from the waist to retrieve the General's new hat, which Nicholas had taken great care to brush to a high sheen, with the nap all lying in one direction.

"Henry? You shouldn't leave your new hat on the porch."

"Hah!" The General laughed. "Walker, you're too slow on the parry. I've just taken your liver, and I shall fry it up with onions and eat it while you watch."

"Eat my liver too, Pa!" Elizabeth laughed, lifting her dress up to her chin.

"Elizabeth, drop your dress right now!" I scolded as I continued to brush the dust from the General's hat. "Henry, stop it."

"No." He tried to jump away from Walker, who was swinging his stick violently from side to side, while Ned hung on to the General's leg like a monkey climbing a palm tree. I startled when he tumbled over backward, laughing as the children piled on top of him. He covered his face with his arms and howled when Elizabeth knelt on his belly.

We were late, terribly late, and if we were too late, we would miss dinner and the race meeting. Impatiently, I tossed the beaver hat into the barouche and began plucking the children off of their father, ordering them to climb into the carriage. I offered him a hand up, but he lay there laughing. He pulled me down on top of him and put his mouth over mine. I tasted liquor on his lips and smelled it over him like a dangerous perfume.

"You've been drinking!"

"Oh now, Mary."

"It's only ten o'clock in the morning, and you're tight as tree bark?" I pulled away from him, but he held me and grinned. "Let go of me," I said. "You're acting like a fool."

"Don't be a shrew."

"How dare you call me names when you're drunk in the morning, before your children, before everybody." I stood up and felt my heart pounding fearfully.

He rose slowly, chagrined, and mumbled, "Well, Mrs. Atkinson, we can't all be useless and beautiful."

"What is that supposed to mean?"

"Mama! Let's go to the race meeting, c'mon!"

"What I mean is what I said." He wore civilian clothes and clumsily brushed the grass and dirt from his elbows. "Useless, but beautiful."

"You malicious bastard."

"The idol of my soul is profane."

I glanced back at the children, who sensed discord and watched us keenly.

"Just tell me why. Why this morning of all mornings? When you know we're supposed to dine with Senator Benton, Uncle William, all of our old friends, the other officers . . ."

"Listen to you harrowing us up. I don't need you to carp at me."

We splintered a look on one another, stilled by our mutual anger and disappointment. He swayed a little on his feet; it made me sick to see him so reduced. My throat felt dry. "Tell Billy we are not going. I will not be seen with you when you are like this."

He narrowed his eyes at me, then looked off in the distance.

"Mrs. Atkinson, I am going to the race meeting and I am taking my children. They've been looking forward to this for days . . ."

"You will not embarrass *my* children before their kin and the good families of St. Louis."

"Ah-ah-ah, that's the tone you use with the servants, Mary Bullitt. And I am not so drunk that I don't perceive the slight."

As we confronted one another on that golden October day under the black locust saplings we'd planted a scant two years before, I resented him for deliberately trying to destroy my affection for him, my pride in who he was and the expectations I had for the both of us. His sudden dislike for me was palpable and crudely offered. He knew exactly what he was doing, getting drunk the morning we were to dine at the St. Louis fairgrounds with the other families, with my family.

I turned away from him and struggled to keep my composure. I stared off at the barracks and observed a squad of troops marching alongside a wagon. "What are they doing down there?" I asked, grateful for a momentary diversion.

"Bringing in a few more prisoners to keep Black Hawk company."

"Who?"

"Winnebago Prophet, Grizzly Bear Skin, some others. When all of them are finally brought in, I'll have a dozen prisoners. Then next spring, when the rivers are running, they'll be sent on their way."

"Sent on their way? Where are they taking them?"

"Ah," the General wavered. "My recommendation." He touched the pockets of his vest, searching for his pipe, then tamped tobacco into the bowl.

"And what was your recommendation?"

He lit the tobacco and peered at me through the smoke as if gauging my mood. "I wrote Cass and President Jackson that Black Hawk needed to see the great cities of the Eastern Seaboard. He required humbling."

"Humbling?" I asked, incredulous. I felt my eyes sting as I recalled Bright Sun's account of the massacre at Bad Axe. "Humbling, you say?"

"If Black Hawk had had any idea of the size of our forces, he would not have—"

"He would not have dared defy you? So you're going to treat your enemy like a zoo exhibit?"

"Black Hawk isn't my enemy. He's my prisoner."

"Oh, yes, how could I forget the manacles? That was gracious of you."

The General smirked and drew on his pipe. "Do you know what Black Hawk said to Antoine Le Clair? Told him that if he had captured me, he would have killed me outright. You know what Black Hawk likes to do? Guts his victims while they're alive to see the expression on their faces, yanks their vitals out of their bodies; he takes their scalp while they can still feel the top of their head being torn off, and then"—the General exhaled a sickly sweet bourbon cloud over my face—"and then he pops the eyes out, pops 'em out like oysters out of their shell." I heard the silver stem of his pipe click against his teeth as he hissed, "So you might consider reserving your compassion for those closest to home."

"Have you been to see him, Henry? Have you gone into the guardhouse?"

The General's false good humor evaporated. "Why the hell would I do that?"

"He is a sick old man."

"Why the hell did you go to see him?"

I squared my shoulders. "It seemed the charitable thing to do. He is a war leader."

"Ha!" the General shouted, then gripped my chin and jaw with one broad hand. "You little idiot. Charitable? If Black Hawk chanced upon you up in the north woods he'd rape you in an instant, then give you over to his men for entertainment."

I yanked his hand away and said angrily, "Stop being vulgar. I won't listen to you."

But when he laughed again, his eyes were cruel, "You should know your loyalties. You are a delightful ornament, aren't you?"

"I would rather be frivolous than be the Butcher of Bad Axe."

The General's head tipped back slightly, as if I had struck him, but I was so angry that I could hardly bear to look at him. I began to march away from him, but he lunged at me, yanked me back to him by my arm and lowered his face near mine with an expression of icy malice.

He spoke through his teeth. "Don't you ever say that to me again."

"Do you consider that your mean-spirited attitude toward Black Hawk might be destroying you?" I lifted my face to show him I was not afraid of him.

"Have you considered that you know not of what you speak? Stupid woman."

Behind us, the children were perfectly silent, and doubtless frightened as they had never seen either of their parents behaving so. Both of us stubbornly held our ground, glaring at one another. Finally, he released my arm and strolled nonchalantly to the carriage. I followed him, my blood speeding through me, my head aching, my jaw tight. I was fearful of what he might do once we reached the fairgrounds.

As our barouche rolled onto the dusty road, the children sat rigidly on either side of us, looking from the General to me, wondering at the cause of our rancor. I did not look at any of them, but rested my elbow on the open hood, rested my chin in my hand and watched the landscape roll by. After the first few miles, the children relaxed and began to chatter at one another about the races, but the General and I held our resentful silence.

"Uncle Saint George can beat Lutie any day," Walker sniffed.

"Huh-uh, Lutie is faster and he has one of those Spanish horses, don't he, Pa?" Elizabeth countered, but the General did not answer her. My daughter's ringlets poked out from under her little straw bonnet budding with silk pansies, she smoothed her frock, tinkered with the fringe on the door handles of the barouche, poked her gloved finger into the buttoned tufts of the black morocco seat leather. The children made a game of swinging their plump little legs out, then thumping them against the bench boxes. All of them looked like their father, dark hair, fair and rosy complexions, blue eyes.

Elizabeth tried to cheer me up. "Mama, I got the fidgets, don't I?"

"Yes, you do, Elizabeth," I said smiling, pointedly ignoring my whittled husband.

Upon entering St. Louis, we heard the church bells ringing, which struck me odd. I thought back upon the calendar I had learned at the convent of the Ursulines, wondering if this were a Catholic feast day. I concluded it must be, as they occur so frequently. The carriage rolled onto Olive Street, which was becoming quite fashionable. There was a pall of vile smoke low over the old French quarter. As many of the Creoles burned refuse behind their kitchens, the haze did not concern me.

"Mama? Why are the church bells ringing?" Walker asked.

The General looked about suspiciously, then broke his silence. "Is this a feast day?"

"Or someone important has died? But we would know—" I began, as we turned onto the Rue des Granges. The narrow, winding street was deserted but for the tumbrels driven by men in veiled stovepipe hats—gatherers of the dead watching for the addresses exited by physicians.

"Henry?" I asked, alarmed at the sight of two local surgeons exiting a house. He put his finger to his lips. As we passed under the swinging signboard of The Golden Hat, the smoke rolled like huge, dark rain clouds down the rue.

"Henry, tell Billy to turn us about, there is a fire ahead, and we are driving into it."

The General half rose from the bench to get a bead on the road ahead. The children began choking in earnest, I pulled Elizabeth to me and removed one of my gloves and told her to hold it over her nose and mouth, I did the same with Walker, but Ned buried his face against me and casually blew his nose into my bodice. I tugged at the netting of my nose veil and tipped my parasol like a shield.

The town bellman, dressed in satin colonial smallclothes, strolled past us on the deserted street ringing his bell. "Cholera morbus! Cholera morbus has come for the profligate! Negro houses closed. Bordellos closed. Taverns closed. All by order of Mayor Lane. Race Meetings at the fairgrounds are still on. Cholera morbus!"

I wanted to quiz the General, but we passed smoking bonfires of tar, resin and coal on every corner, so conversation was impossible. Up on the hill overlooking the city, through the heavy old growth of persimmon trees, I glimpsed the stone battlements, towers and the bastion built by order of the French king nearly a century previous. The General removed his coat and wrapped it completely around Walker, who coughed convulsively, but at last we passed out of the city, into the country where the fairgrounds rolled out in grassy yellow spans.

"Cholera morbus?" I whispered to him, "I thought it had run its course in the East, and why the fires?"

The General blew air over his lower lip. All of us looked dingy, shaded in grays. He said quietly, "The local surgeons believe cholera is an aerial poison. We are in no danger. As the bell ringer said, cholera takes only the profligate."

"Perhaps we ought to turn back?"

"Everyone is at the fairgrounds; you don't want to miss Cooke and Lutie's heat."

"But if cholera is in the air, I worry . . ."

"The only people who die of cholera are prostitutes, Negroes and drunkards."

I stared pointedly at him. "Would the profligate include those who imbibe at breakfast?"

"Save your high words for the children."

I drew in a breath and considered goading him, but we had entered the fairgrounds and were in full view of a crowd of thousands from all over Missouri and Kentucky, who had come for the semiannual race meetings. I would gain nothing by provoking him now, and so I asked, "Do you see the Mullanphy tent? How will we ever find them in this crowd?"

"Mrs. Atkinson, they're under that banner." He motioned vaguely at the grandstands.

I tilted my parasol to deflect the glare from the dirt track. "What banner?"

"The Royal Kentucky Squirarchy of Pot-wallopers. And look, *all* the Bullitts are there."

"Pot-walloper! Pot-walloper!" Elizabeth and Walker chanted as they skipped down the pedal-up and dashed to the long table under the Mullanphys' canvas awning.

The General grinned hello to Mullanphy and Lucas, then turned an acid look on me. As there was no point in arguing with him when he was in this mood, I brushed past him and sidled through the crowd to reach our party.

A pair of fiddlers bowed "Yellow Barber" as I ushered the children to our table, where I found Mama, Eloise, Uncle and Cousin Philip discussing their wagers. The General cut away to join Mr. Mullanphy and Mayor Lane. I tried not to look in his direction and feigned a cheery mood as Philip made predictions about the horses. I kissed Mama hello. She had been invited to stay at the Kennerly house on Persimmon Hill, or Côte Plaquemine, as they referred to it. She chattered briefly about the large, lovely house, the graveled paths through the French gardens, while I tended overmuch to the children, feeling vaguely miserable.

Waiters entered the tent carrying silver trays of cold omelets doused in rum, lit so that blue flames triangled up. Mama helped me divide the children's portions and scraped away salad swimming in astregon vinegar. The fiddlers had taken up "Brown Button Shoes" at a manic tempo that grated on my nerves.

"Mama, what have you heard about this cholera?" I leaned aside and wiped Ned's mouth.

Mama said in a low voice, "Mary, the only people who die of cholera are strumpets, drunkards and Negroes."

"But, Mama, I saw surgeons coming out of the houses of respectable Creoles."

She raised a warning hand. "Don't eat fruits or vegetables, wear flannel next to the skin, avoid alcohol, that's the most important thing."

"But if that is true, why the bonfires?"

"To cleanse the air, of course. Everyone knows cholera is an aerial poison."

"But if it's aerial, why can't I eat fruit?"

"Because the air-poison alights on the fruit. And flannel, don't forget to wear flannel. Ah, here is the General, how does the day find you, sir?"

"Quite thrown away, Mrs. Bullitt," the General retorted sharply, opening a bag of gold dollars and ostentatiously emptying them into his hand. Mama pretended to smile, but I could see the strain about her eyes. "Who is your favorite, General?"

"Any horse Cooke isn't riding."

I rose, cleared my throat and whispered to the General, "How much have you wagered?"

I shifted my gaze from the General to Mullanphy and felt gripped by a cold fear. Mullanphy was the sort of ostentatious millionaire who gambled and lost thousands in a night and thought nothing of it. But the General avoided me and greeted a stranger who congratulated him on "crowding Black Hawk mighty hard."

A roar went up, and I knew the horses were at the gates. I heard the bugle, and Mama waved at us to take our seats in the grandstand on the speed ring.

"I'll tend to my grandchildren," she said and smiled.

I put my arm through the General's as we worked our way through the crowd. The benches were crowded with Creole ladies in expensive new dresses with flaring skirts and huge "imbecile" sleeves. The Negroes congregated along the track, hollering like everyone else. Mullanphy rustled to a seat in the row behind us. He tapped the General on the shoulder and bellowed, "Sir, you are admirably sanguine for someone who's wagered so much on so poor a horse."

"How much have you wagered?" I asked again, catching his wrist. His eyes were black with emotion as he pulled my fingers, one by one from the sleeve of his coat. He ignored my question, leaning to his left to speak to Abigail Churchill Clark.

After the Kearny wedding-day fiasco, Lutie had married one of my Bullitt cousins, Abigail Churchill, a girl overly fond of horses and horse racing. She sat on the General's left side and provided ongoing commentary that seemed to amuse him. As Lutie is an architect and Abigail is a horse fanatic, they have grand plans for building a horse-racing track in Louisville. Lutie sends us sketches of grandstands and cupolas and lists of names he favors, like "Churchill Downs" in Abigail's honor.

I paid the race no mind until its conclusion, when the crowd roared its astonishment.

The General, exuberant at his gambling victory, forgot our earlier disagreement, embraced me, then kissed me on both cheeks. Lutie trotted by, waving the trophy, a silver cream pitcher, presented to him by Jaccard's Jewelers.

⟡Ꭵ ANOTHER morning in October of 1832, a few days after the St. Louis Fair had closed for the season, Uncle appeared at our door with a small party of guests, including an elegant older man named Washington Irving. Irving had come West to write of his adventures in the buffalo country, and like everyone else, he wanted to see the great villain Black Hawk. Every day, scores of people arrived from St. Louis to have a look at Black Hawk, the Prophet and the other prisoners. This was so disruptive to the daily routine of the post that the General curtailed visiting hours. I thought these sightseers, including Mister Irving, despicable, but Uncle insisted I accompany the little party to the guardhouse.

I said hello to Russell and Mahaffey, whom I found intent upon the curious occupation of prying apart paper musket cartridges, piling the priming charge neatly in one soft pyramid and reserving the lead balls in a mint dish, all of this, whilst smoking pipes, of course.

"Yah!" Uncle William cried out, tossing his hands up. "What the hell are you two doing?"

"A stroke of inventiveness has come upon us. We are devising a plan . . ." Mahaffey began. But Russell lifted his watery eyes to us and added, "Slugging our balls, as it were. Mister Mahaffey here was curious as to how much powder and ball our 1816 Springfield musket barrel could fire all at once. Thus far, we have tested four times the ordinary priming charge and four times the balls, and the old girl has held up admirably."

"Let me make sure I understand this. You're overfilling your guns with four times the powder and balls of an ordinary cartridge, and then what?"

"Then we fires it," said Mister Russell.

"Then we sees what happens," said Mister Mahaffey.

"And if you were to hypothesize a scenario, Mister Russell, what might you think would happen?"

"The musket barrel explodes in a most epiphanous way. Shards of metal make egregiously creative tracks over my vitals."

"I see Gabriel and wheels within wheels within . . ." Mister Mahaffey sang.

Mister Irving was decidedly an effete drawing room hybrid. He raised a monocle above his aquiline nose and sniffed at Mister Russell as if he were a gangling hollyhock. Seeing a book on Russell's lap, he asked, "What are you reading there, sir?"

"That would be *The Libertine Enchantress,* a dour coming-of-age tale of what a tender lass saw done to her lonely aunt. With pardons, Madam General, but the gentleman asked."

Out of the blue, Uncle William blurted, "Mrs. Atkinson once told me she would rather be a horse than an Irishman. What do you think of that, Private Russell?"

Russell tipped his head so severely he looked to be listening to his right shoulder. "I say that would depend on the horse, Mister Clark. Now, have you fine people come to pay a call upon our resident sons of the forest?"

Without waiting for our response, Russell motioned us through to the cells.

Irving hunched near the cage as if he were examining a specimen. "But he's so old. And emaciated. Mrs. General, have any of our phrenologists from the East issued opinions about Black Hawk's skull?"

"He is a human being, Mister Irving. A prisoner of war. I don't think he should be subject to that sort of scrutiny. Would you stare at a white man and comment on his attributes?"

"If he was an interesting specimen of a white man."

Black Hawk wore a sly look. He gazed at me, then at Irving.

"This particular savage seems to have . . . yes, yes, a large area of the skull denoting benevolence."

Irving reached for Russell's inkwell, dipped his quill and scratched a note in his journal.

"You, Mister Irving, seem to have a highly developed cranial area for buggery," Russell said.

Black Hawk tensed, his brilliant eyes locked on Mister Irving.

"I'd rather not converse with Irishmen," Irving said, leaning close to the latticed iron gate and staring at Black Hawk.

Black Hawk jumped at the gate, screeching an ear-splitting war cry.

Irving leapt into the air, knocking me to the ground as he scrambled out the door.

"Mister Irving looks precisely like Ichabod Crane, to my thinking, only Ichabod had more spine," Russell drawled, giving me a hand up.

"I hate these crowds of people," I said. "I shall speak to the General and tell him that Black Hawk isn't some ethnological curiosity. He shouldn't be demeaned like this."

Russell tipped his hand to me, "Ah, Madam General, were that things could be so easy."

"What do you mean, Mister Russell?"

"If I know anything, I know Black Hawk and the General. This is how they go through the years. They're still fighting their war. They'll fight it until one of them dies."

❧ I COUNTED them. There were forty women in our dining room. The officers stopped in after morning roll; all of them kissed me. People seemed to wash in and out of the house like a tide-pulled wave. Mrs. Ewing removed a fan from her pocket and relieved Mrs. Benton, who gratefully took a seat. After opening the fan so it would not snap rakishly, Mrs. Ewing made smooth sweeping motions above my table to keep the flies away.

"I can think of very few flowers still in bloom," Mrs. Ewing said, swishing her fan over the table. I thought she resembled a curlew with a broken wing. Her hair was violet red, and I wanted to say, Yes, but there is your hair, and it is either abloom or afire, I don't know which.

Mrs. Benton slid a cool hand atop mine. "There are three flowers that bloom after a frost. There is the gentian, a very pretty blue, ladies' tresses and the silky aster. So we shall have small bouquets of lavender, blue and white, very lovely."

"Very lovely," Mrs. Ewing parroted. Mrs. Benton cleared her throat and whispered, "When does the General return from Fort Leavenworth? Has an express been sent for him?"

"Yes. Tomorrow morning. First thing."

"And her mother?"

"Four days at the outside. If she leaves Louisville today."

My brain felt dry as my throat. I said, "I can hear you. My faculties have not left me."

"Oh," said Mrs. Benton.

"Oh," said Mrs. Ewing. "And where is your Uncle William?"

"Philadelphia," I said.

"Oh," said Mrs. Ewing.

I bit the insides of my cheeks, slid my hand away from Mrs. Benton and forced myself to sit primly erect in the center of the circle of borrowed chairs. I did not look at Mrs. Ewing, still chasing the flies from the table.

She said, "The ice will not last past noon tomorrow."

The conversation troughed, and the women looked down their black skirts at their shoes, or pretended to study their hands.

"Look at how slow and clumsy the flies are this time of year. Why, they thud-thud on the sill as if they each weighed five pounds, don't they? Hear that? Thud-*thud*."

A chorus murmured, "Mister Cooke, come in." Philip twisted his gloves in his hands and avoided the table. He went about the circle, solemnly and respectfully greeting each officer's wife, and all of them instinctively made pigeon noises—noises of comfort and solace.

"When is the General coming?" he asked.

"Tomorrow." All of the women nodded in unison.

Elizabeth and Walker lay upon a mound of chipped ice, with their heads resting on their bed pillows covered over with polished cotton that absorbed water. It bothered me that Elizabeth's dark ringlets floated in ice water. A steady drip sounded under their coffins as the ice melted onto the floor. Mrs. Ewing told Dahlia to get a dish towel. Mrs. Kennerly mopped up the leaking water under the table.

"Mary," Philip said, squatting before me, taking my hands in his. I noticed he took great care not to look into their boxes.

"Yes."

"Mary, let's go for a walk."

"But the children," I pointed at the table, and Mrs. Benton said, "I will watch the children for you."

"Even after the frost, ladies' tresses keeps its pretty scent," said Mrs. Ewing. This prompted a buoyant chorus of agreement from the women.

Someone added brightly, "Elizabeth looks lovely in her coffin."

"Like a little angel."

Philip put his arm around me and led me out the back door. I smelled a grass fire somewhere in the distance. The sunlight was clear and sweet, the air so warm, and all the leaves sparkled—the cottonwood foliage looked like gold coins. We passed onto the bluff overlooking the river. The pin oak leaves were brown and dry as paper. The river was crowded with flatboats going downstream and keelboats going upstream, shallops, canoes and steamers. I had been leaning on Philip's arm, but when we paused on the promontory, I felt too weak and sank to the ground. "Oh God, if you're here, it's really true. Oh God, Philip. Go back and wake them up." He tugged at my arms, trying to pull me to standing as if that would help, but I refused to stand. Suddenly I could not breathe. The grief came hammering at me so that I put my hands in the dirt and heaved out breaths as if I wanted to empty my insides. "He doesn't know. He wasn't here. He doesn't even know they're gone. Oh God, what will I tell him? How do I let him know?" Philip groaned and looked up at the brilliant blue sky. The tip of his nose and chin, the ends of his fingers were still black from the cholera. I said, "Surgeon Mower bled Elizabeth and Walker with a fleam. I held the basin to collect the small rills that trickled over their ribs onto the sheets until the linens looked like a meadow blooming with tall wine cups. But you know, Philip, I talked to them the whole while. I thought if I reminded them of all they loved on this earth they would not leave it. Go back to the house, Philip, and wake them. From the time they fell sick until they left me, it was six hours. Then I opened the window for them so that they could find their way . . . I said to them . . . I said, 'How can you go away from me? You've been with me for so short a season, don't go yet, not yet.'"

THERE were horns on the moon, so I knew it would rain. The General came home in the middle of the night to find me keeping a vigil over them. I extended my arms around both coffins, as if to embrace them both, I listened to the rainfall, a slight sound like distant applause. I had not moved for any reason for a whole day. I could not. When he came into the room and saw his children, the General gasped, and then he moaned. I pressed a palm to my forehead. I could not look at him. I wish I could remember that I had been tender to him, perhaps greeted him with an embrace. I did not. I had not the strength, nor the courage, nor the will to console my husband. He walked to the table, I could hear his breath drawn in harshly, as very gently, he cupped his palm first around Walker's face and then Elizabeth's. "Jesus," he said, then pulled a chair from the table, sat before Walker's coffin, crossed his arms and hid his face. He shook with anguish, and a rough aching sound came from him. I pulled him up, I held him to me as if he were my own child as he sobbed into my shoulder.

On the morning of their funeral, I thought I would lose my mind from grieving, so I took laudanum. I poured it a finger deep into a glass, added water and swallowed. I nearly threw up, but held onto the side of the chest of drawers until the nausea passed. The General did not see this as he was on the porch. I dressed in black bombazine, fastened the long, heavy veil to my hair with tortoise combs. I slid gloves over my knuckles, entered the hallway, took Ned by the hand and walked onto the front porch. The General took Ned's other hand and we proceeded together, stiffly, rigid with grief, to the grave site, where soldiers bent over the two small coffins holding Walker and Elizabeth. The soldiers pulled nails from their knapsacks. It was seeing the nails.

All morning, it had rained, the clouds were dark and low, the river was fogged in. But at that moment when the soldiers removed the nails, a light broke from the clouds and fell over Elizabeth's face. I remember, I put my hand to the arm of the man nearest me to stop him and I pointed at the light and I said, "Look, there is a bit of sun on my daughter's face. Let her be a moment, she won't feel this again." And that was when my reason slipped under a cloud. How could I let anyone put my children in a place where they could not breathe? What kind of mother would allow such a thing?

I bent protectively over both Elizabeth and Walker, and I pushed the men away who had come with the caissons that carried their caskets. I said, "No. When they came into this world, Mama put them into my arms, and it is from my arms that my children shall leave it. Not the arms of men who do not know them or care for them other than the trouble their passing has caused this morning."

The General came up behind me. "Please."

I pushed him away and huddled over my daughter. "You go away too. Everyone leave us alone." The mourners shuffled uneasily at the spectacle I was making of myself. I could hear the General inhale sharply as Mrs. Ewing knelt beside me. "She is in a better place now, Mary."

"How dare you say that to me," I retorted, wiping my eyes with the back of my hand. I felt the General kneel too, then he urged Mrs. Ewing away. "Mary," he said softly, "we will not close the lid if you do not wish it."

I nodded, feeling stupid and wounded and numb from the laudanum. "I do not wish it, Henry. Don't let them."

"Come with me, my girl. There is no hurry for us. Let's take a walk in the woods along the river. Do you remember how much the children loved to walk along the river? So let's go now, and the children will come with us in spirit. One last walk together, all of us."

"Yes," I said, "all of us."

We walked into the cloud-darkened forest where the leaves shuddered under the rain and the moss grew thick on the bark. I felt ghostly and frail under the sweep of drops. There was a dense white mist, and the damp leaves gave way softly underfoot. It seemed to me that the woods and the heavens lamented with us for what we had lost. The viburnum bushes were heavy with velvet leaves and purple clusters of fruit. We stood arm in arm on the strand and gazed upon the river as the mist rose in clouds. "The clouds look as if they conceal restless angels," I said. The river flowed on, carrying away the summer. I needed to feel the water over my skin, craved the feeling of being cleansed. I waded into the river and imagined myself floating southward to the warm air of the gulf, to the clear waters of redemption and hope and eternity, but the cold of it sliding over my skin shocked me. I heard the General cry out in alarm after me. Still, I sank into shallows, my skirts billowed about me as if I were a dark aquatic plant. I felt the cold water rushing to me, felt salvation in its buoyancy as it lifted me, cooling to the waist, to the chest, and I sank until my face disappeared under the Mississippi. I believed the river was my kindred spirit in sorrow as I felt the creeping tendrils of cold in my hair suffered the weight of the penitent's sorrows and grief. I kicked my shoes into the darkening current and allowed the silt to move under me. The thought came to me that I should join the children, that I should breathe this redemption into my soul, I opened my mouth and took the water into my lungs.

He pulled me from the water with a swift motion of his arm, I saw a glittering arc of the river above me, then his face close to mine. I lashed out at him, futilely, I tried to strike him with both hands, but he held them off easily, then carried me to the riverbank and laid me beneath the trees, pushing the wet hair away from my face. I stared past him, up at the trees, and I listened for the approach of autumn.

Every twilight thereafter, we walked along the precipice of the bluff, through the woods, listening to the river make noises of accretion and reclamation. When my children died, I did not weep for them at first. My eyes went wide open, and sleeping forgot me. I sat up straight through the nights and stared into the darkness, believing I saw them. I felt like an amputee. And though I dislike the morbid idea of being bound to another in sorrow, still it was true for us. Every night, we spent long hours confiding our grief to one another, a thing best done silently at times. After our walks, we'd sit beside the enormous banks of bridal veil and stare off at the opposite shore.

Sometimes finches settled in the elm.

On one such evening, in the spring of 1833, I pulled my knees up and looked at him, resting my head against the cup of my hand. His eyes were dark and his face deeply lined. "I have something for you," he said, removing a package from his breast pocket. He placed it in my hand, and I untied the thread. It was a soft leather book no broader than my palm, the blank pages inside gilt edged, the endpaper opulent with color. On the first page he had written,

The retelling of memory, a thread not to be broken.
For Mary, 1832.

I traced the gilded spine of the journal and watched a steamer chugging north under a wind-tossed flag of smoke. "I feel as if I've diminished to a companionable ghost. I can't quite grasp the days. People expect me to pack my sorrow neatly away into boxes, tuck them in the attic, another inconvenience disposed of . . ."

He understood and nodded. "Will you write in this . . . everything you remember of our children? For me. I did not know them as you did, but I
should like to."

He sheltered his eyes with his hand as I looked away from him . . . up at
a new moon that seemed to cast nets over the paths cut by soldiers through
the tall grass.

25

Jefferson Barracks, Missouri, Spring of 1833

✼ THE ice broke on the Mississippi in late February, dirty floes bobbed atop the glassy currents, and the geese returned in the midst of a spring snowfall that lasted for a morning only. The crocuses and jonquils poked out from between the roots of the General's beloved black locust trees on the day the transport arrived to take Black Hawk on his great journey. Black Hawk, ten others and the Prophet were being sent to Washington City to meet with President Jackson. Then they would travel to New York City where, presumably, they would be humbled by the sight of our great American slum tenements and herds of fashionable white people crowded together in ludicrously small spaces.

I stood alone on the boardwalk as Black Hawk emerged from the guardhouse wearing a completely new suit of white elkskin clothing, a magnificent ensemble that Singing Bird had carefully worked with porcupine quills and elk teeth. He lifted his face to the sun and nodded as if he were having a conversation with himself. Then, lowering his gaze to me, he said something in Sauk. The Prophet droned, "Mrs. General, Black Hawk has something to say to you."

I approached Black Hawk tentatively. He was thin and weakened from prolonged illness, he seemed to have withered during his imprisonment, and though he must have been only nearing sixty years old, he looked like a man of eighty. As I came near, Black Hawk said, "The General's woman, it is difficult to know peace when your children have gone before you. I know this."

His comment took me off guard, and I looked away quickly to hide the tears stinging my eyes. Black Hawk stared pointedly at the doll in my arms as he spoke. After Walker and Elizabeth passed, my arms felt as empty as my heart. For six years, I filled my days and nights with tending to them, loving them and nurturing them, so now that they were gone, my arms felt empty. I craved to fill them, in the way the hungry long to eat and the thirsty must drink.

One morning, while tidying the nursery, I found Elizabeth's old doll. It had fallen between her bed and the wall. I dusted it, wrapped it in one of her old baby blankets and held it against me. And I felt better. So much better, I did not put it down for any reason whatsoever.

Black Hawk reached his brown hand toward the doll, tapped its porcelain head with his forefinger and said, "I have a small gift for you."

He reached into a waist pouch and removed a small deerskin envelope, placed it into my palm, then embraced my hand with both of his. "This small thing I carved for you. I think of it as the good that might be possible between the Chemokemon and the Yellow Earth People. Good-bye, General's woman."

I pulled my shawl tightly around me and blinked against the cold spring wind. Black Hawk was boarded onto the main deck of the steamer under armed guard. As the engines groaned to life, I opened the deerskin package with one finger to my palm. I drew in my breath at the sight of Black Hawk's delicate gift. In white soapstone, Black Hawk had carved, with graceful arc of wing and an ethereal expression of hope, the white spirit bird of Sauk legend that the General had told me about on our wedding night.

And so Black Hawk began his journey, traveling first by steamer, then by coach upon the National Road, then in a car pulled by the newly invented railroad steam engine. The farther east Black Hawk traveled, the more ludicrous the stories fabricated by the newspapermen. American readers were told that Black Hawk surveyed every crowd for prime specimens of white scalps. We learned that fashionable city ladies showered him with kisses and praise of his noble nature. When Black Hawk finally arrived in Washington City, President Jackson received the Sauk prisoners in a manner predictably surly and bellicose. Having determined that the old chief's time served at Jefferson Barracks was insufficient, Jackson ordered Black Hawk imprisoned for another six weeks at Fort Monroe in New York for good measure.

The General read these accounts aloud in the evenings, from the *Niles Weekly Register,* the *National Intelligencer,* the *New York Mirror.* When the weather was warm, we'd sit on the porch and light the hurricane lamps and read to one another while Ned toddled about the yard. After an hour or so of this, the General kissed me on my temple. Then he would excuse himself and return to his office at the barracks, where he would remain until reveille. He did this to conceal his drinking from me, but I wasn't fooled. He drank himself into an hour or so of sleep in his quarters at the barracks, he rose at reveille, and both of us pretended nothing untoward was happening. It seemed to me the farther Black Hawk went east, the sicker the General became.

One beautiful summer evening in July, while indulging our miserable little routine of pretending, the General kissed me on the temple, excused himself, then entered the house. I heard his footsteps down the hall. I shook my head, clasping my hand to my cheek as I watched Ned chase the cats across the lawn. The truth was, I had given up hoping for us. I had become expert at avoiding my husband's gaze and at smelling his breath. I no longer wanted him near me, yet, I was unfailingly polite to him. I did not challenge him. We did not banter or bicker or make love or dance together at the cotillions we attended. I knew we were edging into the dangerous waters of indifference and contempt.

I listened to him enter the library and guessed he was searching for paperwork he would review while he drank himself to sleep. The drawer of his desk slid open, then closed. The other drawer opened, and closed. A third drawer opened, more quickly, and the General slammed it shut. I heard this sliding and slamming repeated two or three times and then he bellowed in a way that made me leap to my feet, "Mary. MARY!"

I ran into the yard, picked Ned up, then dashed down the hallway, with Ned riding my hip and one hand holding up my skirts. I rounded the corner into the library, "What is it?"

"What the hell did you do with it?"

I set Ned down and told him to go to the nursery, but he stuck his finger in his mouth, hid behind my skirts and stared at the General with frightened eyes. I smoothed my hands over my waist and lifted my chin, "I don't know what you are speaking of. And you will calm yourself."

He slammed a hand on the desktop.

"Don't you dare correct me. What the hell did you do with it?"

"With what?" I stepped back, feeling terribly afraid of him.

"You know what." He pointed at the desk, his face so flushed with rage that he shook with emotion. "You know what. You opened a private drawer and you took it. It belonged to me. It was mine, damn you."

I inhaled, bent to lift Ned and took him into the nursery. I looked about for Dahlia, trembling with fear. I had never seen him like this. I stepped out the back door, and called for her. In the twilight, I saw her narrow form hurrying toward me. "Dahlia, would you mind awfully taking Ned to your quarters for a few minutes? I will fetch him up as soon as—"

"Mistus Mary, say no more. I hear'd him all the way from my house. That's why I come." I felt the General behind me as I put Ned into Dahlia's arms. I heard his heavy footfalls on the floor; I could hear him breathing heavily. The back door slammed, and seeing Ned off, I turned quickly. The General gripped my arm and pulled me along behind him into the library. I tried to pry his fingers off of me, but he held me so tightly that he was hurting me. He put his face down close to mine and he said, "Where the hell is it?"

"I told you, I don't—"

"Goddamn you, don't lie to me. Don't you dare lie to me."

"You of all people should talk of lying. You live your lies, my only crime is speaking them."

"You destroyed it, didn't you, Mary?"

"Yes. I did."

He paused and regarded me. I had never thought him ugly until this moment. His nostrils flared, his eyes looked bloodshot, his face radiated contempt for me. "You destroy everything you touch." My eyes flicked up at him, and I knew he was speaking of our children. Cruelly, knowing the impact his words would have, he said, "You destroyed them too. I have no doubt."

I winced, clapped my hands over my ears, then turned my back on him. "Oh God, Henry, don't say that."

"Get out of my sight."

"Stop it. Why would you say that to me?"

"Because I mean it, damn you." He narrowed his eyes at me, and his fury seemed to increase even as I withdrew from him.

"Maybe I am damned. Just like you. You damned us long ago, the first year we were married, with your talk of curses on our children, you damned them before they were born."

"For once in your life, shut your goddamned mouth, woman."

But I couldn't. I shouted, "Why are you treating me like this, as if I were your enemy? What have I done . . . ?"

"Get out. Goddamn you, get out."

I glanced over at the gun case. He snarled, "I wouldn't waste the powder on you." Then he shoved me roughly toward the door. "Get out of my sight." I hugged myself miserably. "I can't, there is nowhere out of your sight . . . out of your reach or responsibility. All of this ruin and hatred and suffering is yours and now it's mine. You're the one who said it."

"You selfish bitch. I told you what I was afraid of . . . about our children . . . and what do you do? You throw it back in my face."

"You're the one who said it," I repeated, numbly. "You want to blame me, but it's all your doing, all of it. How can you say such horrible things to me?"

"Because you kill everything, you probably killed my children too."

Panic and anger raced through me so fiercely that my vision clouded. "I am *not* the Butcher of Bad Axe, *you* are. That's what they call *you*."

His face contorted with fury as he hooked his hands over my shoulders and shook me.

"I hate you," I screamed, wrenching free of him. "I hate you, and it seems to me that is exactly what you want of me. Now you can go off to your dirty void of a room and feel sorry for yourself and drink yourself senseless."

In that instant he turned viciously on me, his arm shot out and I felt myself hurtling against the wall. As I fell, I knew only disbelief, there was no immediate pain, just a faint buzzing noise and a vague grayness obscuring my vision. I put my hand to my head and closed my eyes against the dizziness and nausea. I heard him breathing hard as he stood over me. "It is mighty clear to me, Mary Bullitt, that I don't measure up to your standards. So how about this." He removed the small knife he wore on his waistband. He strode across the room so swiftly that I did not trust what I saw. He gripped the middle strings of the rosewood harp with his fist. "Let's you and I agree to disagree." With an easy and vicious motion, he cut them so they jangled out like silvery broken limbs. He jammed the knife into the rosewood, leaving it there as he brushed past me, bumping me roughly. As he passed by, I cried, "I suppose you'll go after her. I suppose you'll make a jackass of yourself chasing after that young girl."

He crossed over to the bedroom, I heard him open the wardrobe and haphazardly toss his boots and his uniforms onto the bed. "I did that once. I have paid for my mistake in trumps, haven't I?"

I shivered, and muttered to myself, "I will go home to Louisville."

"Good," he said, and knotted the blanket like an enormous knapsack and threw it over his shoulder, "good riddance to you. I never want to see you again."

I struggled to push myself up, I stumbled after him as he stepped onto the porch. The General did not turn to retort. He walked off into the darkness with his meager belongings, his hurt pride and his seething resentment, leaving me convinced that the past seven years had been a hollow and terrible mistake.

❧ I MOVED into my old room at Mama's house, which was considerably less crowded than it had been seven years previous. My twin brother Aleck was now part owner and editor of the *New Orleans Picayune;* my brother Washington, a botanist, had set sail for South America to collect specimens; sixteen-year-old Nannie was being courted by a handsome young lieutenant; Eloise was torturing the earnest heart of the Baron Frederick von Ripa; Diana—or the "Glorious Diana," as she was known in certain social circles—enrolled at the prestigious Madame Sigoigne's Academy for Young Ladies in Philadelphia, where she cultivated both her French and her superior attitude toward everyone else.

When Ned and I arrived by steamer, I told Mama the truth. She gazed off at the misty falls of the Ohio and sighed. "It is our churlish blood: we are incapable of making a happy marriage." Whereupon she threw her arms about me and sobbed that people knew a strange madness after suffering calamity and that I was not to blame, for calamity adored me. Poor Mama. I did not wish to cause her any more heartache or social disgrace than I already had. But I need not have worried, as Mama concocted a series of lies about why I was living with her. It went something like this: The General was off so often on frontier duty, patrolling the trails frequented by the red Indians—which was true. And I was in perilous health—I was robust as a haying peasant—and thus required Mama's tender attentions.

We sank into a docile routine, and Mama found purpose for me. Every evening from August through December of 1833, when I wasn't attending a concert, dinner party or cotillion, I sat by the fire with Ned at my feet and a basket of knitting in my lap. In the first week of exile, I fumed over the wrong that had been done me; in the second week, I regretted my temper and vicious words; by the third week I wanted to go home, but I feared the General would turn me out. I whipsawed between yearning for him and my home, and seething over having been mistreated. In my memory, 1833 reigns as the year of the stocking. Whilst Eloise read chastising passages from *A Vindication of the Rights of Women,* I knitted stockings for our forty servants, an appropriately dreary task for a woman who imagined herself scorned.

"'Soldiers, as well as women, practice the minor virtues with punctilious politeness,'" Eloise recited as I pearled and knitted 150 rows a day. "I told you marrying a military man was a bad idea. Didn't I tell you the first moment you saw him at church? Oh now, here Miss Wollstonecraft says, 'Soldiers acquire a little superficial knowledge, snatched from the muddy current of conversation.'" Eloise arched a knowing brow at me as I finished one stocking every six days, a pair every fortnight.

"Oh, Eloise, there's never any middle ground with you."

"Middle ground is for those who haven't the courage to seek the high ground."

"No, Eloise, there are times when you can't find the high ground because the children have the croup, the cook is sick, you haven't taken a bath in a week and your husband is out on frontier duty getting himself shot at, and by the end of the day, the only ground you can find is covered with toys and dog hair and baby throw-up."

"Meaning what, Sister?" Eloise said coolly, knowing she had the best of me.

"I don't know exactly, except you're bothering me." I sighed and walked to the window with a hand to my back, feeling trapped and tired and frustrated. Ned snored contentedly on the chaise. Eloise bobbed after me like a june bug about to eat a mayfly. "You remind me too much of myself," I snapped, and touched my hand to my hair.

"I don't mean to be cruel to you, Mary. All of my experiences have been through books. I guess I really hoped Miss Wollstonecraft could tell us what to do about the General." Eloise sniffed. "Mary, I have to confess, I have never liked him . . . the General, that is."

"But, Eloise, why?"

Eloise swayed side to side, hugging herself. "I never feel as though I am meeting a real person when I talk to him, almost as though the real man is deep inside that hard shell. I can see his attractions. He is handsome and he is accomplished and charming. But for myself, I never want to marry a man who is that worldly-wise. He is too far ahead of us. I want someone I can grow up with. A boy. I want a boy who is my age and of like temperament."

One of the cats leapt onto the windowsill and mewed at us. Eloise slipped her arm about my waist and put her head to my shoulder. "And I'm jealous of him; I like having you at home, all to myself, even if we do argue. I like arguing with you, Mary. No one else understands my penchant for Wollstonecraft."

Mama and my sisters thought to celebrate my thirtieth birthday on December 3 by surprising me with tickets to Mozart's *Così fan tutte*. "Are you trying to be funny?" I asked as they danced about me, slithering into their evening gowns and twining strands of pearls into their hair. "Do you really think I want to sit through an opera about mistrustful lovers?" And so on it went until the day after Christmas 1833.

On Christmas Eve, the house was crowded with guests who rent the air with merriment and warmed the old music room with carols. I stayed in my room alone before the fire and wept over Walker and Elizabeth. Thinking the General was probably doing the same in his lonely office while everyone around him celebrated, I buried my face in my pillow and sobbed until my nose was swollen. I wanted to go home, I hated the idea of my children resting under the snow, so far away. Ned, however, loved my family's holiday excess; he adored being the center of attention with so many aunts and uncles. He never spoke of home, but being only three, how could he remember it? I wasn't sure he'd even remember the General.

When the servants came to wake me the next day, my eyelids looked as fat and shiny as Jamaican bananas. Mama whisked into my bedroom to find me lying on the rug before the fire with one arm outflung, the other hooked around Elizabeth's doll as I looked out the window, staring at the snowfall, staring at nothing.

"Mary?" Mama hunched down. "Mary, are you having visions?"

"No, Mama."

"Why are you on the floor? You look like a starfish, absent a point."

"I have made a ruin of my marriage, Mama."

"Oh." She sighed, sitting beside me, cupping her hand over my forehead as if testing for fever. "My darling girl, everyone does that."

"You endured. Why can't I endure?"

Mama was beautifully dressed in a midnight-blue velvet morning-rounds gown and matching ribbons braided through her hair. She scented her hands and throat with neroli oil. I was disheveled, still in my nightgown. Next to Mama, I felt like a dishrag. I could hear the children running and laughing through the house.

"Mary, every Saturday and Sunday, your father visited his . . . diversions. He'd come home smelling of them. Every Monday, I packed my valise and prepared to leave him."

"Why didn't you? I think you should have left him. On principle."

Mama nodded at this remark and laced her fingers. Her skirts poufed and swirled around her as she sat beside me. "Oh, yes, you are quite right; on principle, I should have left him. But"—she paused to sigh—"the dramatic effect of my leaving would have been blunted."

"By?"

"By the thirteen children I'd have to drag along with me. There is no way to make a dramatic, graceful, *you'll be-sorry-for-what-you've-done* sort of exit with thirteen children. It would have been farce. I'm too proud for farce."

"You should have left us."

"I could never leave my children. But in the last years, Mary, I despised him. Loathed him. Didn't care to be in the room with him. I didn't cry when he died."

A harsh suspicion stole over me. I propped myself on my elbows. "Mama, please tell me that you didn't . . ."

"Lord, Mary, no. I did not poison your father." But she whipped out a handkerchief and startled me by giggling into it. "No. I most assuredly did not poison him."

I frowned at her. "Mama, what do you think I should do?"

The hickory in the fireplace snapped, and the myrtle-berry candles wafted a sweet scent through the room. A servant changed the water in the pitcher, brought in warmed towels, placed soap in its paper atop the towels, silently stripped the bed linens, fluffed the pillows. Another swept the floor, another polished the baseboards with beeswax, a third wiped the windowsills. The luxury of the house was intoxicating; it was so easy to fall into the routine of being looked after, catered to and fussed over. I watched the snowfall and scooted about on the floor until my head was in Mama's lap. She put her fingers to my temples.

"Every marriage is a small tragedy, you know, Mary," Mama said, her Virginia voice low and, as always, rhythmic like a hymn. "Men and women can't help but wound each other. They have to be careful, to restrain themselves so that the wounds are only of the flesh. If they go too deep, they do not heal. Our wounds—mine and your father's—they were too deep. They were mortal. But you and the General . . ." She narrowed her eyes and tipped her head as if she were considering our marriage.

"Mama, I'm not sure we haven't hurt each other beyond healing. We were terrible to one another."

"What do *you* think you ought to do, Mary?"

"I miss him. I want to be with him. But Mama, when he is angry, he is so cold. He cannot be reached. And he does provoke my temper, in the worst way. I am afraid if I were to go back to him, he'd enjoy being cruel to me."

"I don't think he is like that."

"You aren't married to him, Mama."

"What did you fight about?"

"I destroyed something of his—he destroyed something of ours. We accused one another of horrible things. Sometimes I think I am so wrong for him."

Mama laughed and combed her fingers through my hair. "And who would be right for the General, Mary?"

"One of those fatally nice girls, the uncomplaining type with divinely plain faces, the sort who can sit in church and be reverent for hours on end, a woman who could give herself wholly to him, someone who could extract the General's secrets like shot from a wound, then make use of the shot, sew it up into something useful, like the hem of her riding habit. That sort of woman—Mama, why are you laughing at me?"

"You don't think the General met those women in Louisville?"

I held Elizabeth's doll up above my head. I overheard one of the servants say, "Yaz, it is crazy, Mistus Mary carryin' that doll around, but at least she don't ax me to make it porridge. So I cain't complain."

"Mama, I don't inspire him to share confidences with me. He doesn't trust me to keep his heart. I am too prickly."

"And the General likes that. He too is awfully prickly you know. He'd perforate one of those divinely plain girls and have her dissolved like saleratus in water before one day was out."

"Still, one of us . . . shouldn't one of us be . . . well, of a more yielding nature?"

Mama made circles on my temples with her fingers. "Mary, I fear the one who surrenders first would be trampled underfoot. What each of you loves in the other is the unattainable. You're both so proud."

✣ ANOTHER winter's sewing day.

Eloise said brightly, "Miss Wollstonecraft says that the most accomplished women are usually not the most beautiful . . . Why, Mary, that means hope for you. As you have lost your beauty, you can now anticipate being accomplished." I threw the ball of yarn at her, but glanced up at the butler, who announced that I had two callers who refused to go away. I motioned him to show them into the library. He bowed his dark head beside mine and whispered, "Mistus Mary, they is a couple of rapscallions if'n I ever saw'd one. Worse, they *Irish*."

The butler made a face.

I tossed aside my knitting and scrambled into the hallway.

Russell and Mahaffey, dressed in civilian clothes, stood hat in hand, star-

ing at their surroundings, dripping snow puddles onto the carpet. Seeing me
slide toward them, they brightened and exclaimed, "Madam General!"

In a burst of homesickness, I greeted them both with awkward embraces.
I led them down the hall to the back of the house, into the winter
kitchen.

Mama's winter kitchen was a place of marvels. The wine cellar was
stocked to capacity for the holidays with Möet et Chandon Grand Crémant
Impérial. The pantry held a spice cabinet with sixty drawers, in them, every
condiment and jarred delicacy a guest could desire. In the winter kitchen,
the floor and the walls were brick as was the hearth, which was six feet
wide and just as high. There were four Negro women hard at work when
we entered, and two youths. The air smelled of oranges being peeled and
cinnamon, mulled wine and berries.

One of Cook's assistants sliced apples and eyed the Irishmen with open
disdain. The other peered into an enormous copper bucket filled with snow
and oysters in the shell. One youth brought water for Cook, the other
stacked wood neatly in three piles; big back logs, middling front logs and
kindling. As we entered the room, Cook was warming a Dutch oven in the
coals.

Russell and Mahaffey sat at the enormous old refectory table my ancestors brought with them when they arrived in Port Tobacco, Maryland, from
Languedoc in 1634. They brushed the snow from their coats as the servants
bustled around us, and they sniffed the courses Cook was preparing for a
dinner in honor of Daniel Webster that Mama was hosting that evening.
Cook brought each of them a heaping plate of leftover mutton, batter bread,
lima beans and sweet potatoes. They each drank two cups of coffee with
cream and sugar while I waited impatiently.

"Raspberry pie, Madam General?" Mahaffey salivated. I cut each of them
a slice.

Russell dabbed the corners of his mouth with exaggerated delicacy and
coughed. Mahaffey hunched over the table so that I could see him only from
the shoulders up. He stared at Russell, then prompted him, "Well? Go on
then. Tell the Madam General why we've come all this way."

Russell blew air out his nose and gazed at the ceiling with a hand under
his chin.

"You see, Madam General, Mahaffey and me have been with the General
since '08."

"Aye, and never once have we taken a leave. Not once," Mahaffey added
proudly.

"And after all that time, we flatter ourselves that perhaps we know him better than anyone else."

"Aye," Mahaffey concurred. "Being as we have followed him from the tropicals of Pass Christian, to the arctic-als of Plattsburgh, that being in New York, where the goddamned British tried their best to—"

"Mister Mahaffey, now you would be fuzzling your narrative to a degree that might confuse Madam General, you are off the road and in the ditch, as it were," Russell said curtly

"Aye. We're trying to say, that we are in some ways the General's messengers. Think of us as being Saint Michael . . ." Mahaffey said dreamily.

"With chicken wings."

Russell cut in. "And not nearly as beautiful of form, Saint Michael being the most lovely of all the angels."

I tapped the table. "Gentlemen, your point would be . . . ?"

"We are here on the General's behalf," Russell began, and Mahaffey continued, "only he wouldn't know that, he thinks we are on leave, reveling in gluttony, going about corn-raddled . . ."

"Perhaps exploring the quaint local cemeteries—my private zenana," said Russell, sighing.

"Your private *what?*" I squinted.

"Or maybe building a rocket, experimenting with some of the newer flammables in our spare time. Mahaffey and me are Renaissance men." Russell licked the tines of the fork. "Madam General, have you perchance read *Lady Holland's Memoir, Volume One?*"

"No, Mister Russell, I have not."

Mister Russell removed from his coat pocket an inexpensive edition, printed in the brown-paper version, and the book fell open to a page he had marked with a rosary card. He cleared his throat, held the book aloft and read: "'Marriage resembles a pair of shears, so joined that they cannot be separated; often moving in opposite directions, yet always punishing anyone who comes between them.'" He snapped the book shut.

Mahaffey nodded, smiling. "Well done, Mister Russell."

"Quite." Russell lofted his brows at me, then took a prim sip of his coffee.

"Meaning what, Mister Russell?" I asked.

"You must concur, Madam General, that I have just described you and the General most efficaciously?" Russell insisted, leaning over the table.

Mahaffey nodded. "Most efficaciously indeed, you being one side of the shear, the General being the other side of the shear . . ." Mahaffey attempted to portray scissors with his wide palms and short, thick fingers.

"I am baffled as to why the two of you, at great expense and trouble to yourselves, have come to Louisville to tell me this."

"We are aware of your estrangement, Madam General."

"Aye, keenly aware."

"And, at the risk of intruding into the sanctity of your marriage, which is in tatters, if I may say so . . ." Russell whispered, casting a covert glance around at the servants, who were suddenly about their work with very little noise.

"The General sent you to tell me this?" I sat back in the chair, suspicious of their motivation, but my heart was thumping with hope, and I blushed with expectation.

"Ah, not exactly, but he would if he could . . ." Russell began, and Mahaffey cut in once more, ". . . if he could stay sober long enough. He's in a bad way, Madam General. A very bad way indeed. Despairing, as it were."

"Deepest despair. Of the biblical sort, Old Testament of course."

Russell tore his fingernail with his teeth, then spit it onto his plate.

"He despairs over you when he drinks. And the children—Walker, Elizabeth. He talks of you when we go in there every night to blow out his candles . . . Mary, oh my Mary!" Mahaffey crooned sotto voce with a hand over his heart.

"Because, Madam General, to my thinking, the General isn't a drunkard by lapse of character or force of nature. I have known *born* drunkards, for example Lawrence Fitzhunt, whom we called 'Liquefied Larry.' Now, he was a born drunkard."

Russell lowered his voice and mumbled into his handkerchief, "You know, Mister Mahaffey, I could swear a single-malt scotch come out of his mother's teats."

"But the General drinks only after all the day's work is done, because he's hopeless. You could save his life, you know," Mahaffey said.

"Come back, won't you, Madam General? You don't belong here amongst this sybaritic luxury, this mind-boggling opulence, in this palatial pleasure house. You'll rot of contentment. Such happiness will kill the likes of you," Russell scolded.

"Right. You belong in the honest and humble dwelling the General built for the two of you. Besides, it's coming up on *le jour de l'an* 1834, the New Year, a new life, a time for forgiveness." Mahaffey tucked a whole piece of bread into his mouth and smiled with bulging cheeks. He leaned back in his chair and admired the swags of tarragon, rosemary, onions, garlic, peppers and leeks hanging to dry from the high ceiling.

"If I may be so bold as to theologicalize," Russell said, "atonement is more an act than words. Confession aside, it takes a body doing right, to make right."

"Atonement is an act." Mahaffey tapped a finger against his lips. Russell pushed his chair away from the table. "You cogitate upon it, Madam General. We aren't here to gather up your answers. We're just the General's messengers is all. With chicken wings or some such other." They took their leave, linked arm and arm, humming and jovial, certain of having done a very good deed.

I packed my belongings that afternoon. The winter light slanted across the floor as I folded my things over the bed where I had given birth to my children. Somehow, I knew I was doing the right thing, even though I bristled whenever I thought of our last fight. After nearly eight years of marriage, I was still divided between the urge to bite him and the desire to feel his body up against mine. Well, perhaps my sentiments weren't so divided after all. If there had been one positive constant over the years it was bedtime. But I was anxious about how he might react when I met him once again. The worst possible thing would be if he was utterly cold to me, if he refused to forgive me, or worse, if he would not allow me to forgive him. What was I thinking? The man shoved me into a wall for burning his memento. I stopped packing and reconsidered. Then again, that was an awful thing for me to do. I put my hand atop my valise, tempted to toss everything on the floor and forget this impetuousness. It was foolhardy. He had said as plainly as possible, *Let us agree to disagree.* Worse, I was dragging Ned into a bad situation. I huffed and stared off out the window, paralyzed with indecision.

"Ahem, cough cough," Eloise said, leaning against the door with her hands behind her back. "Sister, I'm sorry I've been so hard on you."

"You haven't been hard on me, Eloise. You're just dogmatic." I grinned at her. She came up behind me, pressed her cheek to my back and wrapped her arms about my waist. "Write to me when you get there. And come straight home if he's wicked to you. Don't tolerate it. You don't have to. You have a home and a family who love you."

Eloise smelled like geraniums, her gown rustled whenever she moved. I looked at our joined reflections in the mirror. Same dark hair, same shape to the eye.

"Lord, Eloise, we both look like Mama."

26

❧ THE old forests around Carondelet and Vide Poche were gemmed with frost, and the snow drifted against the wattle fences favored by the Creoles. Whiskey vendors set up tents upon the frozen Mississippi to warm ice skaters and recreational sleigh riders who happened along the towpath. The laughing challenges from one skating party to another floated up in the winter-still air. A few children rolled down the snowy hills, chased by barking dogs all the way. I sank into the buffalo robes and smiled at the sight. In the distance, the church bells rang in the Catholic cathedrals, though none of the Creoles went to Mass on this day. They were too busy flitting from house to house, making a round of social calls that began before dawn on this first day of 1834. It was a day for dancing parties and *croquignoles*.

I guessed it to be before noon. The bells woke Ned. He rubbed his eyes drowsily in the corner of the sleigh. "Happy *jour de l'an*, Ned." I smiled at him. He scowled and went back to sleep. I was overwhelmed with apprehension when the sleigh neared Jefferson Barracks. I laced my fingers and held my own hand and told myself to have courage. After all, *le jour de l'an* was a day of peace, a day to revive friendships, to atone for past wrongs, to draw loved ones near and begin anew. I hoped the General remembered it was *le jour de l'an*.

The sleigh hissed over the rutted snow between the stone posts of the barracks. The sky was evenly iron gray, the trees held a layer of snow on every branch and twig. I strained to see the barracks; a curl of white smoke issued from every chimney. It was a holiday, and the ordinary bustle and noises of the barracks were stilled as families slept late, or departed in groups to pay calls in town. Our house looked dark, empty and very small. It was so peculiar to see it again, ringed by the black locust trees, the foundation tucked neatly into the snowdrifts. The sleigh pulled up, I took a deep breath and tried to calm my stomach. The driver offered his hand. I set the buffalo robes aside and said, "Take Ned around back to see Dahlia. I shall come and fetch him in a moment."

The snow crunched under my boots. I gathered my fur-lined cape around my throat along with my courage and stepped onto the porch. Then I stopped. I didn't know whether I should knock or not. I glanced over my shoulder at Ned and smiled weakly. He stared impassively at me. My stomach fluttered, my mouth felt dry. I considered running back to the sleigh when I thought I heard someone inside. I pushed my hood back, put my hand to the door latch and lifted it. The door creaked and seemed to sag unevenly, it dragged over the floor in an arc as I stepped over the threshold.

I looked down at the floorboards. They had not been thoroughly cleaned in a long while, and there was an edging of dust along the baseboard. I sniffed. A fire burned in one of the rooms, but none of the candles in the hallway cressets was lit. I felt a pang under my ribs as I passed the bedroom. The hearth was cold, the mattress had been stripped of linens and a cottony layer of dust muffled the furniture.

The door of the library was slightly ajar. I put my fingertips to it and pushed. It groaned on its hinges. The room was dark, but there was a coal fire burning in the grate, and all of the books were where I had left them on the day we parted. Small stacks of them pillared on the floor.

I saw him in his chair.

He wore uniform trousers and a white shirt, and his boots were up on the ottoman, even though it looked as though he had just come from the stables. He sensed my presence, but he did not look up from his newspaper when the door creaked. The General wasn't really reading. I had never seen his eyes stay in one place that long while reading the newspaper; he didn't turn the pages, and he didn't look up. Besides, the room was almost dark. His spectacles were folded in the center of his desk, next to a stack of letters and his redware ink jar. The General couldn't read a word without his spectacles.

I couldn't think of what to say, and he didn't seem to want to acknowledge me. So I passed by him, went to the desk, collected the glasses. I removed my cape, and dropped it over the desk. As I came near him, I studied him. He looked awful. There were dark crescents under his eyes, and he had gone very thin. I took a deep breath, bent and put my forearm under his knees and slid his feet aside to make space for myself on the ottoman.

The General kept the paper up in front of him. I pulled it from his hands.

"These might help." I reached close, felt the warmth from him as I slid them over his nose. I stubbornly refused to give him any quarter until he looked at me. When finally he did, his eyes betrayed him. They were intense with emotion, yet he wore his stern council face. I wasn't fooled.

I said, "You look terrible."

"So do you. Give me my newspaper."

"No."

He challenged me with a look. I tilted my head back and stared at the ceiling, considering whether I wanted to resume anything at all. "Do you live here still, Henry?"

It didn't look to me as if anyone lived here.

"I visit this room. It's a museum of sorts," he said bitterly, and I detected a hint of fear in his countenance, as with someone waiting for a surprise attack. The room made me sad; it brought to mind diminished hopes and dreams extinguished.

Both of us tried very hard not to look at the harp.

"This room was always my favorite . . . from the very beginning," I said.

If I waited for his welcome, I would be sitting on this ottoman until one of us passed over.

"Why?" he asked, but in that small word, his voice broke a little, he pursed his mouth and looked away from me.

"It spoke of you," I said, clasping my hands under my chin, tucking my knees up protectively.

He could not look at me, and I guess I felt despair for the two of us. I didn't want to feel that, it seemed a wasted emotion when both of us were clearly miserable at the separation—at least I hoped he had been as miserable as his messengers had claimed. I put my fingers to my lips and said, "Henry. Ned is with Dahlia right now. I have brought him with me."

He looked surprised at this. He hadn't given Ned a thought. The General's heart had been all filled up with Walker and then Elizabeth. I knew he unfairly thought of Ned as the child who almost killed his wife. The General cleared his throat and spoke slowly, but again his voice gave way. "How is Ned?"

"Fat. Thriving. He is an excellent horseman. He hangs a little high on his post, but he's coming along."

"Ah." He nodded, and his eyes were sharp with anguish. "I suppose you came to collect your mother's furniture."

"No. I did not come for the furniture."

"Have you seen a lawyer, then?"

"No. I hadn't given that a thought. Have you . . . seen a lawyer?"

"No," he said, but he exhaled, and I saw him straighten a bit, with hope. Gingerly, he put his hands to my shoulders and said, "I can build up the fire. It's gone low." I nodded, put my hands atop his until he looked at me. "Yes," he said, then rose and motioned for me to follow him through the back door to where the wood was stacked. The steps were iced, and seeing me balance there, holding the door open, he cautioned, "Do not come any farther. I shall hand you kindling."

I extended my arms, and he filled them with pine and ash. The bark flaked over my sleeves, and I kept the door ajar for him and followed after him, back to the library. This distant courtesy and the hope both of us dared not express made us both reluctant to say too much for fear of spoiling our chances. He liked having something to do and balled the newspaper under the grate, made a sort of tent from tinder, then fanned the sparks.

When I moved away from the hearth, he turned and asked too sharply, as if he were panicked, "Mary, where are you going?"

I pointed silently at the pine and ash kindling, then handed him more twigs. When he took them from me, he grasped too high, attempting to take my hand in his, we both looked at his fingers around my wrist.

"What is it that you want from me, Henry?"

"What was, Mary. Before."

I wasn't sure what to say to him. I didn't want to begin with a lie. I couldn't reassure him that things could be as they once were as I didn't believe that anymore. I couldn't be twenty-two and naïve again, just as he couldn't be assured that he would always prevail and bring peace to an impossible situation. But I didn't want to go back to Mama's house and leave my husband—a living, breathing exhibit in his own "museum." For a moment, I was so daunted by the idea of reconciliation that I lost my composure. I bent over and buried my face over my knees and looped my arms protectively around the top of my head.

"Tell me," he said in an unfamiliar tone.

"The thing is, Henry, I just remember being happy . . . first because everything was new, and I thought you might one day love me, and second because of the children. I've grown up since then. Now I know . . . certain things . . . aren't possible."

"That isn't true, Mary."

"Oh but it is. I'm not sure that you and I can change, and I don't want to force promises from you that you will. It doesn't seem right."

He was silent, as if he had turned to stone; I felt the tension from him. He wanted to fix us right then, design us into happiness, construct the good marriage for us. I stepped away from him, slumped on the ottoman, then felt his hands on my back. He crouched down beside me, lifted my chin so that my eyes met his and kissed me. I wish he hadn't done that. His kisses always unsettled me in the best of ways. I felt my stomach flutter and my heart race. I touched the bones at the back of his neck, allowed my fingers to linger there, closed my eyes and relented. I sank against him, buried my face against his neck and drew the smell of him in. He smelled like artemisia and laundry soap. He smoothed a hand over my hair and said, "Do you know what today is? It's *le jour de l'an.*"

He slid his hands around my face and smiled at me, but his eyes filled. All the memories of the children and our happiness crowded over me. I snuffled, my throat ached, I tocked my ankles together to kick the melting snow off my feet. It scattered over the carpet and some of it sprayed on him. He frowned, looking down at my feet, and I could see very plainly what he was thinking. His whole demeanor changed as a strategy formed in his mind. Gruffly, he said, "Mary Bullitt, you wear the most ridiculous shoes, given the rough country you're traveling over."

Quickly, before I could protest, he reached a hand about my ankle.

"Stop it," I said, trying to push his hand away, but his grip was too strong.

"No, these shoes are impractical in the extreme." He whipped off my wet slipper.

"Give that back."

"Not until it's dry. And this too." He reached one hand up my skirts and yanked my stocking down to my ankle.

"Oh! You give that back too!" I reached for my things. "You are not going to keep me here by keeping me barefoot. Of all the ridiculous things . . ." When I tried to kick him with my shod foot, he grabbed that ankle and I was quickly divested of both my wet slippers and stockings.

"Ha!" He tossed a stocking over the spark-burnt fender. "Try walking home without them."

"I may do just that," I huffed. He came up behind me, trying to be charming . . . and succeeding against my resolve. "Your skirt is snowy, and the hem is muddy."

"I am not taking off my skirt."

I wanted to take off my skirt in the worst way.

He said, "I know that. I'm taking it off for you." He regarded me until I could no longer ignore him.

"Why are you staring at me?" I asked, blushing.

"I don't want you to leave," he said, then hesitated, his mouth slightly open. The breath came out of him, a bittersweet sound, and he said almost shyly, "While you were gone, I went to Turnbull's bookstore. I bought you Hannah Moore."

"Who?"

"One of those women who write books about how things ought to be for other women."

I grinned at him, "You bought *that* for me?"

"Among others. I would go into Turnbull's while you were gone, and I found myself picking out books for you, and I'd buy them and bring them home, hoping you'd be there to read them."

I looked down at my hands.

"Unless you decide to burn my clothing with me in it, I will hold my temper," he said.

I looked off at the windows; it was snowing again. "What I missed most, was the weight of you sinking the mattress down beside me. At night, to make myself sleep, I would imagine that you were next to me, making the mattress cave in. Sometimes, when I was alone in my room at Mama's, I pretended to tell you about my day. I guess what I am saying is that I missed you just about constantly.

"Mama has a clock, you know. It's a Scottish clock, faced with pictures of poets, winged by a pediment. I hated that clock. I could hear it chiding, a minute-gone, a minute-gone, paring my days into insensibility. Nothing made sense to me when I was away from you."

I pointed my slipper at him. "I wear the most ridiculous shoes, given the rough country I travel over."

He slid his hands around my waist, and I felt the rough stubble of his cheek as he nuzzled at my throat. His palms were rough when he held my face in his hands as if it were a chalice; he put his lips against mine and paused as if fearing he might drink up the last of his hope and his vitality. I undressed him slowly in that icehouse of a bedroom, it had been so long since we had been together that I had to learn about him all over again. And somehow it was better now that we knew the faults of the other and had come to understand how fragile were the hours left to us.

✢ "THE stone carver in St. Louis made these. I found the granite this summer, while I was away in the Indian country," he said. The General's nose and ears were red from the cold. He sniffed, and I noticed the lines over his brow were deeper. The wind sharpened as the day tapered to a close and tossed his great cape. I leaned against him, lifted his forearms and brought them around me.

He continued, "I come here every morning to look in on them . . . to see that they're not disturbed. After you left, I put a little sod down over the dirt, I didn't like the look of that dirt mounded up, but the sod took. I was thinking, in the spring, we could put in a small tree or two—there and there." The wind blew the snow up in a plume that made a whispering noise. He sniffed again. I thought he looked pale. "One morning in November, I was here at sunrise, my usual time, and . . . ah, the funniest thing, there were fox kits tumbling and rolling . . . they reminded me . . . I thought." He put his head down, pressed his lips together and looked away. His voice broke, "I can't think of them being under the snow."

I hid my face in his cape and pulled his arms about my waist. "They aren't under the snow, Henry."

27

The Sauk Village on the Iowa River, Summer of 1838

✣ THE morning of May Day 1838 was cool and sunny. I had opened the windows to let the breeze circulate through the rooms, so I heard the General coming up the front steps with Uncle William and an engineer newly arrived from Virginia, who was apparently quite good with puns and anecdotes, because Uncle and the General delayed on the porch, belly laughing at one of his off-color quips. The house was a mess, the hallway littered with lilac and anemone that my sisters had dropped on their way to the dining room. In our bedroom, Mama fussed over the three open trunks. "You didn't pack a single decent tea gown. Now why is that?"

"Mama, what am I going to do with a tea gown in the Indian country?"

"You need a walking-out gown, a tea dress and a ball gown . . ."

"Mama! I am taking one trunk, and I am packing practical things only, so empty those."

My May basket–building sisters Eloise and Diana screeched with laughter in the dining room. Ned flew out the back door, tearing flowers out of his hair and shouting, "Aunt Di, you ain't gonna make me look like a gal." The General poked his head through the door and said, "Mrs. Atkinson, Mrs. Bullitt, there is someone I would like you to meet."

Mama and I were too busy arguing to be civil to an unannounced caller, so the men came into the bedroom. The General motioned to me. "Mrs. Atkinson, this is Major John Lee's cousin from Virginia. Lieutenant Robert E. Lee is with the engineer corps. He is here to do the blasting work on the Des Moines rapids and build the pier to redirect the current of the Mississippi."

"Good for you, Lieutenant Lee, blast the daylights out of that river," I said, laughing when he took my hand.

Uncle William said, "And Mrs. Lee and all the little Lees are staying at my house while I'm gone." Mama was cordial when she remembered Lieutenant Lee was related to Martha Custis Washington by marriage, and that he was the son of Lighthorse Harry Lee of Revolutionary fame. Mostly I remember Lieutenant Lee had eyes dark as chocolate truffles. A very pretty man. I mention him because his visit was one more nuisance amongst many that day, and sometimes I think of new people I meet as signposts through time marking a new direction in my life. Lieutenant Robert E. Lee was one such signpost, marking a turn in the road that I hadn't anticipated at all. That morning, I had casually suggested to the General that I might accompany him to the Sauk village on the Iowa River, and he said, "I have no objection to that."

There was much to do before the General, Uncle and I departed for the council. Surgeon Beaumont had not sent over the calomel or tartar emetic, and the General was often sick with violent colds and bouts of fever, so I would not leave Jefferson Barracks without a well-stocked medicine box. I remember thinking that the General did not look well enough to make the trip to the Sauk village. And Ned reached an interlude in one of his fever-and-chills episodes, from the *mala aria*. Like me, he had his seasoning off at a young age, turned yellow as a jonquil for a few months, then intermittently suffered fevers and chills.

"Have you heard the latest news from Florida?" I asked Lieutenant Lee.

Uncle and Lieutenant Lee answered at the same time, rattling off the names of soldiers who had fallen under Seminole guns. The General sidled out the door, leaving them behind. I rose and peered out the window. He walked down the hill to the deserted barracks that now housed only three officers and thirty-five enlisted men.

⁂ THE Sauk village was situated in an oak grove alongside the Iowa River. The Sauk trampled the grass until it resembled polished clay. Their wickiups clustered under the large old trees. There didn't appear to be form or reason to the organization of the village. Women built fires in bough arbors adjacent to their homes, and the heat from them mirrored upward. Forty rods to my left, two women planted tobacco seeds in a cold, ashy fire ring. Beside me, an elderly Sauk woman scraped green corn from the cob with a deer jawbone, preserving the milk. A little girl picked flies from the liquid. It looked like a temporary campground of twelve hundred, rather than a permanent settlement.

The few men left in the village gathered on the northern edge of the settlement around the makeshift corral that the company of army regulars had built to hold sixty beef cattle. The Sauk warriors had never seen longhorns before and thought cattle dumb and comical. They laughed and mimicked their lowing and bawling noises until one of the hungry Sauk grew impatient and shot a steer dead. They commenced to debate how to butcher the strange animal.

I cupped my hand over my nose when I breathed in; the gnats were thick in the air and I wasn't eager to taste them. The General sat cross-legged between Uncle William and Dodge, the new governor of the Wisconsin Territory. The purpose of this council was to persuade the Sauk to leave the Iowa lands and move to the Red River, a new and arid country north of the Texas Republic.

King Keokuk the First brushed away the mosquitoes alighting on his face and stretched his legs. One of his six wives tried to discourage the bloodsuckers by waving a pin oak branch above his head. Thunderheads bulked on the horizon, flourishing in the swelter. I felt perspiration trickle between my breasts. Dogs barked without provocation, grinning and snapping at the loose horses. A few Sauk women screeched at the ponies, which tried to eat the trumpet-shaped pumpkin blossoms from the vines.

Dodge had lost most of his lower front teeth, so his bottom lip caved in when he spoke. "Ah, now here, I've calculated you would sell us 256,000 acres at seventy-five cents an acre . . ."

Keokuk straightened, brushed the dirt from his white deerskin leggings. Gnats worried at a poulticed-with-mud-and-spiderwebs knife wound on his belly. "No. One dollar twenty-five cents per acre. Payable to me and only me."

The General ran his hand over his face. "One of the stipulations that I will insist on here, is that individual payouts be made. I would like to recognize a few of the tribal chiefs and ask them if they agree that each member of the Sauk Nation should be paid on an individual basis."

Bright Sun's upper lip beaded with perspiration. Her eyes shifted around the ring of tribal leaders. Keokuk's face flushed darkly, but he was too wily to show anger. Rather, I suspected, he would bide his time and connive his way into controlling the disbursement of tribal annuities.

A still, hot afternoon, humming with insects, the air heavy with the scent of trees and standing water under the sun. I reposed against an enormous old oak, closed my eyes and wondered what Mama, Eloise and Ned were doing at this moment in Louisville. Ten rods to my left, a young woman, having gutted a white mongrel, stood on a three-legged stool to rope him by his hind legs to a branch. Her small daughter tied a carrot twist of tobacco to the dog's tail.

The General studied documents and maps spread on the clay in front of him. "The nation's foremost expert on Indians," is what the President called the General when his regiment, the Sixth Infantry, was ordered to Florida. "The frontier can't spare you," the President wrote when he ordered the General to surrender command of his troops in March of 1836.

Keokuk said, "I know you will sell the land to white people for three dollars an acre. That is a very good profit for you. One dollar twenty-five cents."

Dodge said, "You're getting trade goods besides. Services of a blacksmith for thirty years."

"Difficult to work with," the Secretary of War said of the General when he insisted the Potawatami be paid two hundred thousand dollars in annuities owed to them by the U.S. Government. "The General prefers to make policy rather than obey orders," the Indian Affairs agents had complained.

The General and Uncle William traced a pattern over a map of the lands west of the Mississippi. Together, they determined the extent of the cession requested and then checked their figures.

"Hesitant to go after Indians," the Missouri militia charged when the General refused to imprison six Potawatami for pursuing the outlaw Heatherly brothers, who had stolen Potawatami horses.

Bright Sun and Whirling Thunder asked to be recognized.

Dodge nodded at them.

"The provisions regarding a Christian mission on the new lands . . ." Bright Sun hesitated. "The Sauk people do not want it."

"Too sympathetic to the Indians," Cass had written of the General when the Winnebago refused to sign a new treaty with the United States until they had a chance to meet first with Zha'becka. "He is the only white man who has never lied to us," the Winnebago leaders said.

The General and Uncle conferred, a vote was taken, the provision requiring a Christian mission was eliminated. "And the manual-labor school, to change our children into make-believe white men and women, we will not send our children to such a school," Bright Sun continued.

Dodge wagged a finger at her, "Now see here, missy, if you don't teach your children to get along in the white world, they will be lost and at a disadvantage."

"You change our children into strangers, the young men ridicule them for being make-believe."

The General interjected, "Superintendent Clark and I agree that the mandatory attendance at a white school provision shall be eliminated." For a few moments, the assembly was quiet.

Well, that was easy enough, I thought as I dabbed my sleeve at my hairline and considered that Uncle and the General were being awfully amenable to the Sauk demands. I knew why. They'd eliminate minor points of contention and focus on the land-cession issue.

Uncle William reviewed the treaty provisions agreed upon thus far and held an accounting of the rations. The General cleared his throat and stood. "I would propose that an additional clause be added, granting Miss Me'um'bane the Bright Sun a parcel of land equal to fifteen acres, a modest frame home and one thousand dollars in payment for services rendered the Sauk People as a translator during the Winnebago and Black Hawk Wars."

Keokuk leapt to his feet and began to protest. How nice, I thought, full up with pettiness—Bright Sun was going to be landed gentry. She dipped her chin and blushed with gratitude and a pretty, *Who me?* manner that brought out my throttling instincts. Given her labors on behalf of her people and her struggles, I did not begrudge Bright Sun happiness. But I scowled at the General—using government funds to pension off his mistress.

Whirling Thunder was the first to approve the land grant to Bright Sun as a gift from the Sauk People. Keokuk extended his arm like a pompous brown version of Henry Clay, but the other chiefs shouted him down. The General scanned the crowd, waiting for the verdict. An old chief named Dark Antler scoffed at Keokuk: "We are tired of your voice. Sit down and be quiet. You no longer speak for us."

A cloud passed over the sun, and a wind came up. I looked up through the branches and watched a pair of rough-legged hawks tracking something along the river. Since the last war, the General rode out every few weeks with the small units of dragoons that crisscrossed old Indian game trails all over the river country—his idea—alerting all the tribesmen that the army would clip their lines of communication in an instant if they started a war. And that was the real danger in the late thirties, Indians didn't attack whites, Indians fought Indians over hunt lands, and sometimes whites accidentally fell under their guns. The General's preventative, with only fifty men, created the illusion of numbers in the minds of native peoples.

Did the General still drink to excess? On occasion, in the seclusion of his office, every few months or so. I could sense when the mood was coming over him, and I knew it was melancholy over Walker and Elizabeth along with his shame over Bad Axe. In the five years since our separation ended, had he ever been cruel to me? No. At worst, I suffered his paternal condescension, at best, he was warmly attentive with a gentle humor. I wanted more from my marriage, but by 1838 I was thirty-four years old and I had come to accept that my husband preferred to lavish his energies on his larger view of the world—on his abstractions and ideals. Even so, I had become rather proud of his ideals, as time and again he stood firm in his convictions and suffered for it. Though most native tribes viewed him as the one honest white man in the army, the army and the War Department watched the General's every action with skepticism and distrust, whispering that he was an Indian lover.

I separated myself from my musings and watched the council proceedings.

Uncle William ran his hand over his pink, sunburned scalp. "Ah, the village crier should announce that we will begin distributing rations by our tents along the river when the sun is—" Uncle paused as he squinted up at the sky, raised his arm a small distance to the west of the sun's position: "Ah, about there, yes. Tell the women to come with many bowls. Let's stop for the day, we'll resume talks tomorrow over the land-price issue."

As the Sauk adjourned to return to their homes, Uncle, the General, Bright Sun and I walked to the provender wagon where the rations were stored. Bright Sun's pretty face was still flushed over the idea of her new home. She wore one of the simple muslin gowns I had given her years ago, in perfect repair. She had hemmed it, but it was a bit baggy for her slender frame. Her hair was plaited down her back, making her look too young and too fresh.

The General did not gaze upon Bright Sun, but conferred over a contract with Uncle.

I glanced sidelong at her and made a rattling noise with my lips—which I tried to stop, but too late; it came out anyway. "Congratulations, Miss Bright Sun," I said. She turned her green eyes on me and smiled in such a heartfelt way that I felt myself a small and peevish creature.

"Yes, well." I patted her hand. "Let me know if I can help you with anything."

Bright Sun erupted in the giddiest mood I had ever seen her wear. "I am twenty-nine winters, Mrs. Atkinson, and I have never had my own wickiup!"

I looked off at the enlisted men as they rolled barrels of salt, flour, sugar, coffee, salt pork and corn out of the wagon. Bright Sun told the Sauk women to form queues. They carried birch bags, buffalo bladders and bowls. Many of them were sick, maimed or ailing, as were the children.

Uncle and the General looked tired. I saw them pass a flask, take a nip, then wearily remove their tobacco bags and their pipes. Overhead, the hawks lofted under the storm clouds.

"Where is Black Hawk?" the General asked as the birds wheeled to the south.

Bright Sun dipped a tin cup into the open barrel of salt and smiled to herself. "He is hunting blackhorns to the west with his young men. Black Hawk is sixty-five winters, but he is still the best hunter. The young men follow him to learn how he trains his buffalo-runners." Bright Sun looked at the clouds bunching in the western sky. "He will not come into the village when Keokuk is here. They hate one another more than ever."

Uncle William mumbled, "Speak of the devil."

Keokuk had a lumbering, low-centered gait. He crossed through the lines of patient Sauk women. "Red Hair," he bellowed to Uncle William, "the Great Father in Washington said *I* was the One-Chief of the Yellow Earth People. . . ."

The General smirked. "Yeah, Ol' Red Thunder, didn't you know that? Keokuk is the One-Chief."

Bright Sun dipped her cup into the flour, carefully measured out her allotment and said to no one in particular, "All the Yellow Earth People know Keokuk is the One-Chief of the Poker Players."

The General laughed at that, "Well, I didn't know you played poker, Keokuk. What say you come on over tonight and brag your pile; you'll be on your own hook."

This seemed to settle Keokuk, who nodded with his whole body: "*Henekohe.* All right."

I pushed up my sleeves, undid the top few buttons of my bodice and grumbled, "You're having a poker game in our tent tonight?" The General pinched my cheek then pretended to peek down my bodice, "Not our tent, Clark's tent."

"Well, I should certainly hope——" I began. But he whispered in my ear, "In our tent we're going to have a hunt for the sassafras root." I smacked him on the chest with both hands. "I've seen plenty of that root, and I have no interest in hunting for it out here." But he only looked smug and said, "Why do you lie to me so often, Mary Bullitt? Nobody likes sassafras like you."

The hot weather foddered the storm clouds that seemed to billow up even as I gazed upon them. The enlisted men charged with distributing rations looked up at the darkening sky and slid the lids as far over the barrels as possible. Bright Sun put her finger to her lip, then counted her rations by bobbing her forefinger. Uncle stared drowsily at the long lines of Sauk women.

The General tensed, turned his back to us and began loading one pistol, then the other. I grew alarmed when he loaded his rifle, and the enlisted men, even those at the barrels, did the same, but quietly. A few big fat drops of rain fell onto the clay, each sending up a tiny red poof. Seeing the heavy weather, the Sauk women in line wavered, debated with one another whether they should come back after the rain. Two regulars pulled canvas over the barrels.

Governor Dodge walked briskly over to the wagons, glancing rapidly right to left. Uncle William followed the General's gaze along the opposite bank of the Iowa River where the currant bushes and nettles seemed to shiver in the breeze.

Except there was no breeze.

"Ghosts bring a wind that scatters the blackhorns, and the people go hungry," Bright Sun said, lifting her nose in the still air. "Black Hawk shaves his head so that his hair does not move and cause the wind to blow. When a Sauk warrior's hair moves, the wind blows over the blackhorns and the blackhorns scatter."

I was about to inquire of Bright Sun, Meaning what exactly? Then I saw him.

Black Hawk and his warriors emerged silently from the green curtain of vines, wearing nothing but their breechclouts. Though his scalp lock fell down his back in one neat drift of gray, Black Hawk looked as he had the day in 1826 when he burst into Uncle William's council house. The rigor of his life had revitalized him, and he appeared ageless.

I sensed a fight coming on. Even so, I felt a racing excitement at seeing Black Hawk again. Bright Sun turned beseechingly to the General and said, "He has not come to make war. Black Hawk and his men wear the symbols of forlorn hope—look and you will see that each man is wearing his sacred talisman. He wishes to speak to you, Zha'becka. Will you hear him?"

"Probably some self-serving drivel," the General said with a scowl, and ordered the regulars to form ranks. Having loaded their muskets, the troops held the ready position. Black Hawk and his men stood of a line along the river shore, seemingly unafraid of the guns. Dodge called, "If you intend to return to your home, Black Hawk, you will answer to Keokuk."

Bright Sun shouted this to Black Hawk, then translated his reply. "I do not talk to you, Hairy Face," Black Hawk retorted. "I come to speak to Zha'becka."

Once again, I saw evidence of Black Hawk's difficulty with speaking under pressure. After a false start, he stammered, paused to collect his thoughts, then began again, "I am a gray-hair and I will act for myself. I do not care for Keokuk's counsel, and I do not care for his opinion of me. I have come today for one reason, Zha'becka, and that is to ask you a question. But I will only do this if Zha'becka will speak to me without his bluecoats, without guns."

All eyes turned to the General, who weighed Black Hawk's challenge and hesitated. Then he nodded his assent. One of the regulars muttered, "What is this gonna be? Two old men what ain't got no wind in the pipes, what ain't got no muscle on the bone pitching a fight? It'll be a dog fall."

Black Hawk gave Whirling Thunder his club, his knife and his rifle. The General divested himself of firearms too. I wanted to hear what was said; I felt I was entitled and I would not be deterred. I stepped out from behind my safe tree and clenched my hands together to keep them from trembling. I scampered up behind the General. Bright Sun marched after him authoritatively, knowing she was needed to translate.

On the northeast bank, Black Hawk strode out with a long gait, keeping his sights on the General and looking as though he was about to break into a run. The air was humid, heat lightning sheeted overhead, the discontented sky grumbled. Black Hawk leapt into the shallow river at a point ahead of us. I thought it thrilling to see him swim the current, then allow himself to be brought downstream on the southwest shore. He walked from the shoals, swiping his forearm across his face.

He put himself directly in the General's path. Black Hawk spoke in the forceful and virile Sauk cadence. He greeted the General, then I think he attempted to make a joke, but the humor was lost upon us. Black Hawk sniffed and looked up at the stormy skies. "In a few moons it will be autumn; in the first snow we hunt the bear. Upon finding him slumbering, I tie a rope around his paw, I drag him from his den. I club his head."

Oh, that was a bad idea. It put the General in a fighting mood: His expression hardened and he bunched up and poked Black Hawk hard in the chest. "Where I come from, it's hawk season every goddamned day. Shoot 'em right out of the sky."

I really think Bright Sun smoothed and tweaked this statement, because Black Hawk seemed not at all offended. For a long, uncomfortable interval, no one spoke. Black Hawk breathed from his mouth, his eyes worked the landscape and the General's demeanor for clues. Finally he began to speak. Bright Sun paused at length between each sentence as if being meticulous in her translation.

"You know, Zha'becka, that I have killed many men. I have eighty scalps on my lodge pole. When I lead a war party, we have customs that must be followed. I will not lie to you, though I would rather not kill women and children, there are times when it is necessary."

The General snorted derisively at this. "There is never a time when it is necessary, you sonofabitch."

As Bright Sun did not translate this, Black Hawk drew a breath and continued. "Long ago, more than twenty years, my war party rode up on four women and four children. All of the women allowed themselves to be captured by my warriors. Except her. She looked at me defiantly, she had eyes like the long-tail tree-walker and she was strong. I tried to bind her elbows together behind her back. She fought me, she took the knife from my belt. I took it back and cut her throat."

Black Hawk dragged his finger from ear to ear. I felt cold and terrified. I riveted on the General's face, searching his countenance for some clue as to who Black Hawk was speaking of. But Black Hawk was mercilessly precise in his account. "The woman—she bled to death quickly, because her heart was beating fast with fear. I did those things I had been taught to protect myself from the spirit of a murdered woman. With my knife, I slit the soles of her feet lengthwise to stop her spirit from walking the long way to Saukenuk and finding me and my children."

I put my hand to the General's sleeve and asked, "Henry? Who is he talking about? Who is this woman that he killed?"

The General glared at Black Hawk and answered me without averting his glance from his enemy. "He's talking about someone I knew a long time ago, when I was a young captain in Pass Christian, Mississippi. Black Hawk was down there raiding the Cherokee. He did so every spring, now he's bragging about one of his murders."

Black Hawk did not meet the General's eye. His shoulders were rigid, his stance official and uncomprehending. Finally he said, "But then, I looked up at the crest of the hill. I saw you riding down after me. In my haste to escape, I forgot to turn her face downward, so the woman looked up at Fire-Keeper. He told her how to find me and the Yellow Earth People. I did not have time to put a piece of blackhorn fat in her right hand, the symbol of plenty, so her spirit found me and brought famine to the Yellow Earth People. So I have suffered, and the Yellow Earth People have suffered because of my one act—in a winter more than twenty years ago. Her spirit has been avenged as she has destroyed us. But my people have lost their homes, their children and their hope."

As the General put his hands on his hips, his expression was anguished. He stared down at his boots, unable to look at Black Hawk anymore.

Black Hawk inhaled sharply. "Zha'becka, will you join me in the Night Feast to send away this spirit? We must allow this woman to cross the river to the Afterworld and to know peace."

Without looking at him, Bright Sun put her hand to the General's sleeve and said in voice barely above a whisper, "Black Hawk is seeking forgiveness for the Yellow Earth People."

My stomach churned and my heart beat fast as I waited to hear the General's answer. I was wracked with many conflicting thoughts. Black Hawk was selfishly concerned with his own fate, and I did not condone his past bad acts. I wondered how well the General knew the murdered woman, and why Black Hawk would come to my husband seeking forgiveness. It made no sense to me. As for the General, he was silent and immobile.

It had begun to drizzle. Rain glistened in his thick hair as the General leveled his gaze on Black Hawk. "At Pass Christian, you took an innocent woman's life because she defied you. Then you abandoned your people at Bad Axe—left them to die." The General said matter-of-factly, "I will never forgive you, Black Hawk. I told you that once. I told you when I took you hostage aboard my keel during the Winnebago War—that's our bargain in this world. I live with your sins. You live with mine."

The General turned on his heel and left the river shore, then. I followed after him as he cut through the old oak forest, and as I did, I imagined I heard the sound of wings brushing up against a gate that would never open for him. My husband was transformed in that instant, eternally forsaking the lineaments of mercy if he ever possessed them at all. The General could not forgive Black Hawk and thus could never forgive himself, a man beyond redemption because he believed himself to be so.

That night, in our tent, he snuffed the candle and lifted the blanket to join me on the bed.

I asked, "Who is the woman Black Hawk spoke of? Who was she to you?"

The General reclined, shifted his weight and exhaled in the sooty darkness.

"An acquaintance."

A lie.

"An acquaintance?" I repeated, touching my fingertips to his chest. "Black Hawk seemed awfully concerned over your response, given she was nothing more than an acquaintance."

He slid his hand over my hip. "I don't clearly remember." He lied again.

"Then tell me her name," I said.

He was quiet, as if weighing the cost to himself of revealing this one tiny fact. I imagined him measuring out the risk to himself of sharing one glimpse of his past with me; considering his possible relief in the telling versus the strain of having to explain himself to another living being.

"Nicomi," he said.

"Nicomi," I whispered. "That sounds like an Indian name."

"It is Cherokee. It means voice of the waters."

"Did you love her?" I asked, intuiting the answer as clearly as if he had said it.

The General pulled his arms away, rolled on his side, presenting his back to me, allowing me to know what he thought of my questions and my curiosity. He closed himself off from me, ending the conversation in his familiar manner.

I lay in the darkness, listening to the rain, but I could tell from his breathing he was not asleep. "Yes, you loved her." I said aloud, as I thought it warranted saying. "And your silence tells me you loved her deeply. So you see, there are some things I am beginning to understand all by myself, Henry."

He tensed, and so I knew he was listening to me.

"Do you imagine that I will think less of you because of it?" I asked. "Because I won't." I was talking to myself now, staring up at the blackness of the pitched canvas roof. I knew he wouldn't answer me. "Or perhaps you think less of me for caring about who you are, for trying to know the secrets you keep locked away inside you."

I could smell wet clay, rain and moldy canvas. The horses nickered at one another.

"I am not your enemy, Henry. I ask because I love you."

For the first time in our marriage, the General slept embracing me. The unromantic truth is that it is very uncomfortable sleeping in someone's arms. But he held me to him, and as he did so, I believed that it wasn't me he was holding—it was the memory of Nicomi that he wished to gather close to his heart. The tent shuddered as the wind lashed around us. I tried to see his face in the darkness—I knew he was still awake—but the General did not answer my questions that night, or any night that followed after.

We departed the Sauk village the next day, and the tribal chiefs—with

Bright Sun's fierce advocacy to credit—refused to cede the Iowa lands to the U.S. Government. I did not speak to Bright Sun until four years later. She was not my friend, and though we recognized in one another a woman who had come to know sorrow, to borrow her words, it did not shape us into kindred spirits. I refused to dishonor either of us by pretending otherwise. We simply were two women from very different places who kept bumping into one another as we were tossed along by the unforgiving drift of time.

28

Jefferson Barracks, Missouri, June 1842

FOUR years after I attended the Sauk council on the Iowa River, on the morning of June 12, 1842, the bugles sounded reveille and I rose in the predawn quiet, but the General lay abed—something he had never done before. I lit the taper with one of those newly invented "matches" and let my nightdress slip down around my ankles, expecting that he would prop himself up on his elbows and rub his eyes. But he did not. I stepped into a day dress and tied the laces up the back. I remember holding the candle aloft and bending over him. The promise of summer filled me with energy and good spirits; though there was as yet no light, an early breeze had come up off the river, and I smiled into it. I could smell the briar roses in bloom.

When the General slept on, I watched the taper light flickering over his sleeping face and I said his name. He was a light sleeper. Ordinarily, he would wake easily. When he did not, I set the candle upon the dresser, then put my hand to his shoulder.

"Husband. It is reveille."

I laid my hand upon his forehead and winced. He was hot to the touch, feverish in an alarming way. I drew a breath and calmed myself. People caught fevers all of the time, particularly in the sick months of late spring and early summer. The General suffered the yellow fever in Pass Christian, but he had recovered, hadn't he? This must be a rare fit that has come upon him, I reasoned. I pressed my lips together and regarded him, then sat beside him on the bed and felt his forehead again.

I whispered urgently, "Henry? Can you wake yourself?"

But he didn't stir.

I touched his shoulder and gently tried to shake him. "Henry, it's time to get up." With the first three fingers of my right hand, I touched his throat, hoping that my senses were deceiving me, but it too was dry and hot. I clutched at a yellow cotton cloth in the basin upon the chest of drawers, dipped it in the water, squeezed out the excess, then folded it over his forehead.

"I'm going to get help for us," I said to him as if he could hear me, then hurriedly stepped into my slippers. "You don't worry a bit about this, I will find someone who can make you well," I promised. Though I was fearful of leaving him alone, I dashed from the house, down the back stairs and ran across the cold, wet grass to Dahlia's cabin. I did not knock but opened the door to find her tugging her boots over her ankles.

"Mistus?" Dahlia lifted her face questioningly as she tied the lashings.

"Please, Dahlia. It's the General. He's very sick, more sick than I've ever seen him."

She tucked the ends of her head scarf up under her hair and asked, "What's wrong with him?"

"I don't know, he's feverish-hot and he won't wake. I can't get him to wake."

"Oh, that ain't good, that ain't like him at all." She straightened slowly, reading the fear on my countenance. "I'll fetch up Surgeon Mower. Don't you worry, now. I'll wake Nicholas too. We'll all be with you real quick, mistus."

As I ran back to our house, the dew over the lawn soaked my slippers. The old trees along the crest of the bluff shivered under the cool breeze. I could hear the boats navigating the river, and the familiar five-tone chime of the *Annie Laurie* sounding in the channel. The camp dogs set up a chorus of barking that faded off in the distance. Though it was still dark, a few men arrived at the regimental stables, and the horses whickered at them for their oats and hay. I remember wondering how the people at this post could go about their daily routines when the General was sick—such was the scattered nature of my thinking that morning. I let the back door slam behind me and dashed down the hall to the bedroom where I expected to find my husband up and dressing, but he lay still, breathing silently.

Gingerly, I touched the cloth over his forehead, and feeling his heat come through it, I peeled it away and dipped it once again in the basin. I turned the blanket back until it was folded at his waist. I could see his eyes shifting under the lids as he dreamed. Now and again, he frowned in his sleep, a deep line creasing his brow. His lips parted slightly, but he issued no sound. I didn't know what to do, so I lifted his hand and pressed his palm to my cheek, then observed a dried fleck of ink on the quill-callus of his middle finger. I removed the cloth from his forehead and scrubbed at the ink on his hand.

As I did so, I allowed that Surgeon Mower would soon arrive with patient assurances that I was overreacting to a common bout of the summer troubles. After all, a man cannot sleep summer after summer on the prairies without benefit of tent cover, nor drink from the Western rivers, and not expect to feel the consequences. The General had jeopardized his health, and now a minor illness had come over him, but he would be in fine form within the week. I just knew it to be true.

I heard brisk footfalls on the porch, and someone opened the front door. Surgeon Mower entered the room to find me sitting on the bed with my legs crossed under me. I bit my thumbnail when I saw the surgeon cross the threshold of our bedroom in his all-black uniform. As it was still before dawn, the light was scant in the bedroom, and seeing the surgeon caused my stomach to knot. It all reminded me too much of the day I lost Walker and Elizabeth.

He nodded crisply at me. "Good morning, Mrs. Atkinson," he said, and with the chilly practicality of manner common to medical men, he held the taper over the General's face. Then he looped the General's wrist between his thumb and forefinger and felt his pulse whilst staring blankly at the ceiling. Surgeon Mower opened his case, removing a bleeding pan, thumb lancets, a bone-handled fleam and dry cups. He kneaded the General's abdomen and made a clicking noise with his tongue to show his dismay.

"Mrs. Atkinson, you'll please leave the room while I examine the General."

I startled and blinked at the doctor, "No. No, I won't leave the room."

The surgeon turned the fleam over the flickering taper light, watched the flame fold over the blade, then put his hand on my arm and tried to gently push me aside. In that instant, I knew I couldn't allow him to cut into my husband. Seeing the fleam glitter in the poor light, I recalled how he had bled my children—and panic swept over me. I pushed the surgeon away, albeit with a lesser measure of gentleness than he had pushed me, and I sheltered the General protectively with my arms.

"You are not going to bleed my husband," I said.

Surgeon Mower cut circles in the dark air with a thumb lancet as he spoke. "The General has a fever. I can see even in this darkness that his liver is distended. He has a bilious fever, ergo, I must bleed the bilious humors out of him."

"No." I laid my cheek on the General's chest and extended my arm down his body.

"Mrs. Atkinson, this is womanly folly."

"You bled my children to death. I won't let you do it to my husband."

"Madam . . ." The doctor gasped at my rudeness, but I glared at him and would not move from the General's side.

"Go away," I said miserably.

"Mrs. Atkinson . . ." He menaced me with the fleam.

"I said, go away. Now leave!"

For a long moment, we glared at one another, until Surgeon Mower hissed, "If this man dies, it is your doing. You remember that." And he left muttering about how I reminded him of a mean old dog left guarding the corpse of its master. I stared after him, hearing his words echoing in my head—*If this man dies*—but I refused to think of it. He was wrong, plain wrong.

I called after Dahlia, who was greeting yet another arrival at our front door, and told her to bring me a bottle of rum and a fresh cloth. I had to keep my composure and my wits about me, and I did so by fussing over my husband as he slept. Dahlia brought in the rum with a rebuking look, and I said, "It's not for me, it's for him." Then I sponged it over his skin; it was the only fever cure I knew: Mama had once recommended it to me for the children. I wrinkled my nose at the sharp odor of alcohol in the humid morning air.

The news of the General's illness quickly spread through the camp, and by midmorning, our library was crowded with soldiers keeping a vigil. I have come to associate the smell of coffee with waiting and sorrow, it seems to be on the air when people gather to reassure one another that what is happening couldn't possibly be as bad as it appears. Notwithstanding the people filling up my house, I felt more lonely than I have ever been in my life. My mother and sisters were in Europe. Cousin Philip was on frontier duty at Fort Leavenworth. Our eleven-year-old son, Ned, was at the Catholic boarding school in St. Louis.

I sat up abruptly, keeping a hand upon the General's chest.

"Nicholas!" I called.

Nicholas poked his head in the room. "House is real full, ma'am," he said nodding. I saw Dahlia rush down the hall, serving refreshments to the crowd in the library.

"Nicholas, someone has to fetch Ned up from school."

Nicholas nodded, "I done that aw'ready. And sent an express man after your Cousin Philip St. George Cooke. One to Louisville too, for whatever of your kin ain't in Europe, ma'am."

I tried to thank him, but my voice caught in my throat and I merely nodded. As I stretched out beside the General, I slid my arms over the bed linens and felt the fever-heat radiating from him. I lifted my head aside to admire the quality of the light breaking through the elm trees.

In June, the light angles into our bedroom with a sublime power, and I watched it move over him, wondering if the General was fighting his way to peace. Hours passed, and through all of them, I talked to him as if he were reading the paper and drinking his coffee; I spoke to him of all the simple matters that concerned us daily. Under the morning sun, his face looked drawn, the skin appeared tight, almost translucent. I touched the flat spot in the center of his lower lip with my small finger, and I told him he had to wake as our house was full of people who wished to see him. Late in the afternoon, I heard the familiar and comforting sounds of the laundresses laughing over their kettles until the steady June breeze and the closed warmth of the room lulled me to sleep. Dahlia brought in a vase of briar roses, butterfly weed and artemisia and set it upon the chiffonier.

And I dreamt of the two of us working in the garden together, the General and I. The sun was hot, and my skin damp, but I was perplexed because this was a winter garden and there was a hard frost over the soil. I turned questioningly to the General. He was standing over me, I couldn't see his face for the sunlight behind him. I was shadowed by the outline of his form and his broad-brimmed hat. I said to him, "I do not recall what we have planted here."

I awoke because the General had begun shuddering violently. I called out for Nicholas, who helped me restrain him. "It's the fever that's causing him to seize," I cried out, as Nicholas stripped the blankets from the bed, then helped me lift the General's nightshirt from him.

About then, my eleven-year-old son, Ned, arrived home. He stood in the doorway, rigid with fear, and refused to enter the room. I remember that I leaned over the General with all of my weight and strength, shoving his shoulders into the mattress, but upon hearing Ned, I looked around wildly. Poor Ned had reached our room just in time to witness something akin to a sordid asylum tableau—a straggle-haired woman of middle years and a Negro man pinning a convulsing patient to the bed. Ned's eyes grew big and he paled. I could not fault him for being frightened. He had always been in awe of his father, yet distant from him. Now, he could not reconcile the General's apparent invalidism with all of those years of hero worship. I

wanted to comfort my son, to reassure him, but I could not so much as leave
the bed for fear the General would injure himself. Thankfully, Dahlia came
to our rescue. She pulled Ned away from the threshold, saying, "Why don't
you come visit with Colonel Kearny? Come on, I'll get you something to eat."
Ned was so grateful to escape, he fairly ran down the hall in advance of her.

I sent Nicholas to help Dahlia when the General gradually stilled. His
fever abated somewhat, but then he became delirious. He tossed from side
to side and spoke aloud to his ghosts. I tried to understand what he said but
could not. I heard the guests asking after me, in pitying tones, as if they'd
decided for themselves that the General would never wake from his fever
sleep. At twilight, the officers, their wives and the soldiers politely departed,
all except for Russell and Mahaffey, who served sentry. I could hear them
talking mournfully on the porch. My lower back ached, I put my hand to it
and bent close to the General to listen to his breathing. It came steady and
tickled my ear. At that moment, I fought the urge to break down and weep,
I forced myself to be calm, knowing Ned was in the next room.

"Mama?"

I turned to see Ned shuffling in the doorway. He peered around me at the
bed. "Is he goin' to die?"

"No." I shook my head. "He's just tired. He's worked so hard for so long
that all of it is catching up with him."

"But if it's only a fever, why have all those people been coming to visit?
Colonel Kearny? He was here all the day long, Mama. So was Mrs. Kearny.
And the Kennerlys and all Pa's officers, they came down . . . a whole lot of
St. Louis people too. Cousin Philip is on his way, but he ain't here yet. I
heard a passel of ladies saying they was coming back to keep watch over
you and Pa all night, but Dahlia told 'em not to. Dahlia sent everyone home.
She told 'em you required your rest."

"Don't you worry, Ned, he'll get better, I know it. But right now, he needs
to sleep." Ned followed me into the dining room, watching me forlornly for
signs that I might not be telling him the truth. I surveyed the mountain of
food that visitors had left as a cordial offering on the table. Trying to lift
Ned's mood, I plucked a raisin cookie from a plate and tucked it into his
pocket. He scuffled dejectedly in my wake as I lifted one of the chairs and
carried it back into the bedroom. He bit his bottom lip, then said, "Mama,
what will we do if Pa dies?"

I quickly glanced away. The truth was, I hadn't thought of it—wouldn't
allow myself to think of it. "He's not going to die. Why don't you sit here
with me, Ned? Tell me about school."

Ned frowned, looked at the chair I'd brought in, then at his father. He stuffed his hands into his pockets and shook his head. "I'm tired." He padded away. I heard his bed creak when he sank into it. I sat on the hard old chair and propped my feet up on the mattress.

It was after midnight when I allowed myself to reminisce. A jumble of memories came over me all at once, and I cupped the palms of my hands over my eyes. Then I stretched out beside him on the bed, and I must have slept again.

"Mary," he said.

I opened my eyes to find the room still and dark. I rolled over onto my side, pushed myself up and looked down at him. I could barely make out his features.

"I'm thirsty," he whispered.

"Henry, you're awake!"

"And thirsty," he rasped.

My heart soared with hope. I leapt up, lit the candle, poured a glass for him from the pitcher on the chest of drawers, then held the glass to his lips. His eyes glittered at me, but he was too weak to lift himself, so I slipped my arm under the bones of his shoulders, then dabbed his chin with my handkerchief.

"You've had a fever," I said. "You've slept a whole day through and scared me silly."

He stared at me as if he were memorizing me. I rejoined him on the bed, and I said to him, "I've been so worried over you." He closed his eyes and tried to swallow, but finding he could not, gave a small gasp. He shivered like one afflicted with violent chills, "I am cold, Mary."

"Here, then. I'll get you a blanket"

"No. That's not what I want. Help me . . . dress."

"But, Henry, it is the middle of the night."

He raised his forefinger and brushed a wisp of hair from my cheek, pushed it behind my ear and said simply, "Please."

"No, Henry, it is only shortly after midnight, and in any case, I'll not allow you to go to your office today, you must recover."

He exhaled heavily, then closed his eyes and tried to wet his lips. He said in a voice that allowed me no quarter for argument, "Mary. Do as I say."

I was overcome with dread as I met his eyes; something in them told me to forgo my arguing habit. I wondered if he knew the moment he awoke, if he could feel the difference in himself, of being on the verge of something. When I spoke, my voice sounded small.

"What do you wish to wear?"

"What I've worn every day," he said.

I opened the wardrobe doors and gathered his shirt, his blue uniform coat and his trousers. I folded them and sat on the bed, watchful of him. He glanced first at the clothing in my arms, then out the window at a faint cloud of light drifting up into the darkness from the barracks. He said thoughtfully, "I don't like the gaslights they've installed around the parade grounds."

I smoothed a hand over the crease in the sleeve of his coat. "And why is that?"

"It's a vanity, that's why."

"Oh, now." I smiled, relieved to hear him about his familiar pattern of grousing. I fingered the buttons on his coat, pretending to examine the eagle with shield and stars all around. "This one is loose," I murmured.

He narrowed his eyes critically at the night sky. "The gaslight obscures the moon and stars." I bent and touched my lips to his chin and teased, "A river of light. I think it's wonderful."

"I don't. How can a man find his way over the plains at night if he can't see the stars?"

I lifted his left hand, slid the crisp white broadcloth sleeve over his forearm. He winced in discomfort as I lifted him to get the shirt around his back. I tried not to show my concern over his shockingly weak condition, but I murmured, "Do not try to help me, Henry. Let me do the work." He held onto my forearm as I buttoned his shirt. His expression was solemn, his gaze keenly attentive upon my hands as slowly, and with great care, I poked each button through its grommet. He shuddered and whispered, "Why is it so cold in here, Mary?"

His question startled me, because the room was stiflingly warm—warm enough to provoke a dampness about my temples as I struggled to lift him and dress him. But I did not say this. Instead, I sighed and told him a gentle lie. I said, "Sometimes in June we get these cold nights, Henry, when I do believe we will wake to see snow on the briar roses."

He shivered again and said, "This is certainly one of those nights."

"Yes, it is, it's very cold. Take a deep breath now and relax. Let me lift you. I have to get this coat around you," I murmured, and he closed his eyes as he felt the familiar blue uniform wool over his shoulders. Then we both paused to rest as this small effort of dressing had stolen a large measure of his strength. His brow creased, and he reflexively touched his fingers to the buttons. He had always been proud of his appearance.

"You look very fine this morning, Henry," I said, covering his hand with mine. I teased him, brushing my lips against his cheek, I said, "I think I even love your clothes." He jutted out his lower lip a little doubtfully and said, "With good reason, Mary Bullitt. My clothes are magnificent."

I tugged the trousers over his knees, then his hips, and knotted the waist strap. He lifted an eyebrow at me and cast a critical glance down at his feet. "Socks?" He asked. "Socks," I said, as I crawled to the end of the bed and lifted his foot onto my lap. He stared at my face as I bunched the socks up, then slid them over his toes. Then the General closed his eyes. For a long time he was still—so still, he frightened me.

"Henry?" I asked, with fear edging my voice. "Henry!" I clapped my hands over his cheeks.

He opened one eye and peered at me. "What?"

"Oh." I turned quickly away, fluttering a hand at my waist. "Please don't do that again," I said, swallowing hard and shaking my head so he wouldn't see the moisture in my eyes. I covered them with my hand and felt my shoulders quiver. I didn't want him to see me weeping. I didn't want him to be frightened for me or for himself. He stared out the window at the night sky as the wind tossed the curtains.

"Mary."

"Yes."

"Stop fussing. Come lie beside me."

I think I knew. And felt a wild compulsion to speak it, and another compulsion equally strong that told me speaking was unnecessary. I tucked my hand under my chin, curled up against him, and we regarded one another silently. I wanted him to make promises to me that he could never keep. I pressed the side of my face against his chest and listened to his voice. He sounded dry and raspy—almost hollow, as if he had begun to distance himself from the room. It alarmed me, until he covered my hands with his own.

"When you came to me at the table that night, when I removed your hairpins . . . I loved you then. From then on."

"From then on?" I lifted my face to him.

"I could have stayed in Caswell County, I could have been a planter in a quiet corner of the world, but then I never would have met you, Mary Bullitt. Would I? We've had a good journey together, haven't we?" The General fell silent and looked past me, out the window. I was suddenly very frightened by his mood. I wanted him to reassure me that he wasn't leaving me.

So I blurted, "It's summer, Henry. Tell me how it will be for us this summer."

He thought about this for a while, drawing his breath with great effort.

Then he said, "You will put your hand over my arm, drawing me near to whisper some secret. That is my ideal for heaven in all its perfection—your face next to mine as you look in advance of the years and laugh at the angels."

"Oh, what are you saying?"

"That I shall watch you in your garden."

I felt my face contorting with grief and my breath heaving out of me, but he continued. "You have always whispered your secrets to me, Mary. Come close now. You have been diligent in the asking, and I won't deny you. Not now. I shall tell you whatever it is you wish to know." I listened to him breathing, the hoarse sound coming from his lungs; I have seen the dying and I recognized the signs. His vision dimmed.

With his eyes only half open, he stared directly ahead, but I had a feeling he was not seeing the things I saw. I tensed and listened as if for my life.

He said, "What I have done is beyond forgiveness . . ."

"No, Henry. No one is beyond forgiveness."

His breathing changed again, coming in harsh as if it pained him. It anguished me, this struggle of his, as if he knew he could not slip away into a safe place because more trials awaited him before he could rest. He shook his head, muttered to himself.

"Calm now," I said, with my lips to his ear and my hand to the side of his face. I knew he was thinking of Bad Axe, straining against a distant memory. In a lucid instant, he gripped my hand and searched my face. I felt him fighting to hold to this life, at great sufferance to himself.

I whispered, "Don't struggle for me, Henry, not if you are tired and wish to go."

I pressed my lips to his cheek, touched my finger to the corners of his eyes to brush away the moisture there.

"Husband?" I asked, searching his face, wondering why, suddenly, it had changed so.

All that night, I kept watch over him.

Even though he had gone, I did not want him to believe that such a small thing as the end of living could ever separate the two of us.

29

Jefferson Barracks, Missouri, June 16, 1842

W E buried him this morning. I couldn't reconcile myself to his absence, because the things he used every day of his life were still in the house with me. With a widow's logic, I considered that if the hair receiver still held his dark and gray curls, and the wardrobe his clothing, if his pipe remained in its stand, surely he would return home to me. I did not remove the linens from his pillow, but clutched it against me, inhaled the scent of him, then lied to myself that he must be somewhere near. It occurred to me that perhaps I had not looked in the right places for him. He might very well be working late in his office in the barracks quadrangle. I convinced myself that this must be so. I gathered up my shawl, then walked to the door. The cold of the iron handle under my fingers should have brought me back to the truth. My husband wasn't in his office, he wasn't working late; the only aspect of him that was left to me was the portrait in the library, and the painter didn't even get his eyes right. Everything was all mixed up in my head. I said aloud, "Henry, I need to know if you are . . ."

And I stopped, wondering what I needed to know of him. I needed to know that he was in a safe place, to steal Bright Sun's turn of phrase. I was frightened for him—and for myself, I suppose. The idea of spirit appealed to me in a primitive way, as I battled the old fear that my beloved was confined under the earth. The General should be in a country gold as a hawk's eye, cut through by old cedar trees, or returning from campaign, his skin brown as a Spaniard's, his beard full, his hair long over his collar. I paused on the threshold, pressed my forehead to the door, turned my head side to side. An impulse seized me. I opened the door, expecting to see him . . . but no.

Why does memory love familiar faces with a desire that cannot be satisfied? Perhaps it was this more than anything else that prompted me to seek the General in his office, to walk out that night with foolish hopes, leaving my child sleeping in the house. The dark was broken by Bright Sun's vigil fire burning on the sloping uplands. Out onto the promontory I ventured, believing I would find the General detained in his office. In the distance, in the hollow of the barracks quadrangle, I heard the night voices of the sentries. Men greeted one another in passing. Someone lit a match against the stone powder magazine in the elbow of the hill. A pinpoint light flared from the match and died. Down the hill I ventured, believing I would find the General detained at work. My steps fell over the spring grass. As I approached the buildings, I studied the sentries' shadowy focus, hoping to see his familiar gait, hoping one of the shadows had a bad left leg. I heard an iron kettle slide over a brick hearth, the soft crinkling noise of someone turning the pages of a newspaper, nocturnal coughing, men conversing in low tones.

The General's office, a narrow suite of two rooms, was located between the surgeon's and the cooper's quarters. Inside the barracks square, the yellow stone walls retained the heat of the day. I passed onto the wooden boardwalk, dreading the disappointment due me as I neared his workplace until I espied tapers burning within his rooms, causing my heart to spasm. I paused before the door, then pushed it aside. The anteroom was dim, the light came from the General's interior room. The adjutant's desk was piled high with documents. A warm draught of summer air fluttered the uppermost papers on the stack.

The General's office was centered by a large desk, fronted by two old ladder-back chairs he purchased in Plattsburgh decades ago. Three windows filled the wall behind the desk, and bookshelves lined the east and west sides of the room. A quill stained with ink angled near a clay jar. Next to this, my husband had preserved our Walker's slate, which bore a fading childish drawing of the General on his horse. I touched a fingertip to my eyelid to stop it from twitching, then observed the intruders as I gathered my wits.

Two open decanters sat in the center of the General's desk and Russell and Mahaffey stood reverently beside it, as if it were an altar of sorts, each cradling a different drink. Both had consumed more of the ingredient than was good for either of them. Russell's hairless scalp gleamed in the candle-light. Mahaffey was the shorter figure, his blond hair faded with gray. Both of them were around sixty years old, gone portly. They wore their uniforms, complete with white webbing crisscrossing their chests. Each had solemnly put his shako atop the General's desk by way of offering tribute.

For a long while, neither man spoke, each lost in his thoughts until Russell released a mournful sigh, then lifted one of the decanters. Mahaffey winced at the ruby-colored bottle of brandy as Russell poured himself a dram.

"Mister Russell, I didn't know you cared for cherry bounce."

"I am partial to it, Mister Mahaffey."

"Well, there you be. Live with a man for twenty years and only then learn the most disappointing aspect of his personality, that being, his palate lacks refinement. I am sorry to say, I cannot adequately express my disappointment."

"When did you become a connoisseur of ardent spirits, I'd like to know?"

"I know better than to swallow cherry bounce, now that's for sure. A poor way of entertaining the time until Satan comes for you. If you had common sense, you'd be blanching with self-disgust at this very minute."

Disgruntled silence.

"Aw, blow it out your nostril, you morphidite."

"Now, that's damned disrespectful, Mister Russell."

"Mister Mahaffey, if there were a particle of dust in the sky you'd complain about it. Here I am, at your behest. Didn't I join you in this endeavor? Breaking into and then trespassing in the General's office at the risk of court-martial? If Colonel Kearny finds us, he'll slip a noose around our chins, jerk us to Jaysus sure as we live, all because you had to visit this shrine one last time."

"Why will you serve me thus, Mister Russell? You know you're as distraught as I am. How can you pretend to be the most indifferent being in this indifferent world?"

"I am not indifferent. I have an aversion to dust and molds. Makes my eyes leak."

"There, there, Mister Russell."

"Aw, shut your gob."

"Well, pardon me gallantry, you insipid thing. I thought you was weeping and I thought to condole you."

"*Console,* Mister Malaprop Mahaffey."

Standing in the shadows of the anteroom, I said quietly, "Gentlemen."

Mahaffey snapped around, dropping the cherry bounce, wide-eyed with alarm.

"Holy Chroist, if it ain't the culprit-in-chief."

Russell wiped his eyes and bowed his head. "Madam General?"

"What are the two of you doing here?"

"We're keeping vigil here at this old . . . landmark. And why not?" Russell challenged, but his voice hoarsened with grief, causing me to feel so sorry for him I nearly forgot I was the primary bereaved. Defiant, yet uncertain why, both men slumped resignedly into the two ladder-back chairs. I sat in the General's seat and looked first at Russell, then at Mahaffey, peering between the twin pillars of their shakos at the corners of the General's desk.

They exchanged dubious glances. Russell pursed his mouth and scanned the ceiling.

"The deserted bride," Mahaffey muttered, leaning over his knees, cradling an empty tumbler.

Russell sighed, shoved the chair back, crossed his ankles, tipped back with his fingers laced at his nape, his elbows pointing both east and west. Peace came over his old countenance, rivaling the traces of anguish there as he appeared to study every fixture in the room but me. He said, "When they marry, man and woman become one being—the man."

Mahaffey sputtered a noise, furrowed his brow.

"If that be true, Mister Russell, what happens when the man dies?"

Russell exhaled soulfully, flatted the palms of his hands against his barren temples and squinted as if in mortal pain. "Do you imagine that I know the answer to every Socratic proposition you put before me! There are many conflicting claims on my daylight hours, do you think I spend my days in contemplation of flotsam and jetsam for your enlightenment? I am speaking aloud of the soul we have lost and you make me feel dragged upon—"

Mahaffey interrupted him with a fierce grip on his upper arm and pointed a look at me.

"His widow has come looking for answers, Mister Russell."

"Mister Mahaffey is right about that. I should like to know the truth. I believe I am entitled to it."

A silence engulfed us as the soldiers pondered their distorted reflections in the window glass. The promise of answers kept me leaden in my seat, and my heart pounded at the realization that the guardians of the General's secrets were sitting across the desk from me. Clearly, they wished me gone. As it was, I felt myself an unwelcome tenant in a place where I no longer belonged. In the spring of the year I had seen a nuthatch sit tenaciously on a nest that had been ravaged, all of the eggs broken by crows. That bird kept to her place, as if hope would bring back to her the fulfillment of every dream that had been fragmented. So it was with me. There were practical things that required looking after, the idea of surmounting those tasks was something I found most difficult. Suddenly, there was a hard edge to my life, the tack in the pad of the thumb that woke me to reason and said, pay attention to the business of living. And my eagerness to hear Russell and Mahaffey give accounting seemed a required element if I were ever to heal myself. I rested my elbows on the bevel of the desk, cooled the lids of my gritty eyes with my fingertips.

We let the quiet fill the room until Russell spoke.

"Mister Mahaffey, I'm afraid our moment of mendacious reckoning has come at last." Russell leveled a critical squint on me.

"Don't lie to me about anything. After all of these years, Mister Russell, I deserve better than soft falsehoods from you," I said.

Russell licked his bottom lip and studied me.

"There were some who said the General was born with a river around his heart."

Mahaffey shook his head. "But those would be the sort who couldn't comprehend an affair of rivers, Mister Russell."

"Aye, but all the same, it's a dark swim, this one."

I allowed myself to glint at Walker's slate drawing. With a wary look at me, Mahaffey muttered, "If I may suggest, Mister Russell, keep it short and sweet like the old woman's dance."

Russell drained his tumbler, set it to rest on the edge of the desk so that I smelled the acrid-sweet of the liquor. He drew a breath, then began. "The General was born into disappointed circumstances. His father, at one time owning the largest parcel of land in Caswell County, had long since fallen into poverty over taxes and too many children and tobacco having depleted the soil." In the flickering light, Russell looked scraggy and ruined, his massive shoulders set in a defeated hunch. "We came to know him in '08, in Norfolk, the General then nearing twenty-six years of age."

Mahaffey nodded, folded his arms over his chest.

"You see, when he earned his captain's commission, the War Department required him to recruit his own company of men before reporting for duty. And though he was monstrous poor, he had to purchase his own uniform, have it tailor-made for himself. So having the itchy new suit of clothes, our boy goes to Norfolk to enlist his company. And there we met him. In Norfolk, in a tavern."

"A tavern, being a locationally injudicious spot to organize a corps of troops. We were taking refreshment one evening, dredging our cups, worrying that the two of us would live out our days as impoverished hod carriers. We've been told by men of property that the Irish shoulder bore a hereditary indentation that suited us to burden."

Russell removed his uniform coat, folded it carefully over the back of the chair. His coarse shirt was ringed with perspiration. He stood and opened each of the three windows behind me, bringing in with the night the sound of the riverboats signaling one another and the steady murmur of the low June breeze through the cottonwoods.

Mahaffey grinned wistfully. "So one spring night, into the tavern walks this boy, this Captain Henry Atkinson. He ducks under the beamed lintel of the door, surveys the room uncertainly, then stands on the threshold in his newly sewn uniform. Looks about the place. He was red faced, not the loud sort, polite to a fault, which was getting him nowhere with the patrons. He had leaflets in one hand. Quite a poetical appearance, he lent the room."

Russell smoothed his palm along the chair arm and gazed at his shako on the desk as he continued.

"He was skinny, shamefully earnest. The only sober one in the place, and there he is with his leaflets and his modestly patriotic little speech, on the approach to each table in the room. Everyone he goes up to tells him to go fug himself. Either that, or he got calcified layers of silence and mean looks for his efforts."

Russell paused, cleared his throat and stared at his hands. Mahaffey mused, "So I says to Russell, how much bruising can a man's dignity take? And having finished our pints, we motion the captain over. Not out of pity so much, mind you, but because we were bloody bored with each other and sick of our lot as hod carriers, the grit under the heel of every propertied bastard in Norfolk. The captain promised us a half-gill of whiskey, our own firelocks, a daily ration of salt beef and seven dollars a month pay."

"So we signed up with him. He hadn't the first idea of military protocol."

"Marched us in formation, while reading aloud the directives from Baron von Steuben, prefacing every order with, 'If you prefer . . .'"

Mahaffey smiled, croaked a small laugh.

"Aye, Mister Russell, we were fine specimens in our youth, weren't we? Both of us stoic as the Spartan lad on picket duty who suffered the fox eating out his entrails without a word of protest."

"Mister Mahaffey, in the tender season of our lives, stoic *we were not*. If you're going to tell the story, you had best go straight with it, else why bother in the telling?"

"I for one," Mahaffey jabbed a finger at his own chest, "was stoic."

"You torment me, Terrence." Russell glowered. They glared at one another until Mahaffey looked away. Russell cupped a hand aside his mouth and mocked in a loud whisper, "I never did much like people who were not brighter than myself."

I said, "You enlisted with Captain Atkinson and then what happened?"

Russell said in a low voice, "Captain Atkinson marched us onto a clipper, and we sailed along the coast south to the gulf. You must remember, this being before the second war, British ships were harassing the coast, namely New Orleans."

"We came to the garrison at Pass Christian, and three-quarters of the troops instantly deserted. Another quantity very rudely died of dysentery," Mahaffey recalled, gazing through the open window at the night.

"Captain Atkinson nearly died of yellow fever. Me and Mahaffey turned nurses to relieve a fellow sufferer, and after a month, he gets to his feet to find he has only two platoons left. We had troubles with the Indians to contain, we had the Spanish harrying the borders of Louisiana and the British limey-juicers firing up and down the coast. Surely, we says to one another, our canonization will come quick as we've been put up for martyrs by the War Department."

Mahaffey ran a hand over the side of his face. "I says to Russell, when they strike my saint's medal, I trust they'll do it in profile, then I'll hang for all eternity between the snowy breasts of some pious schoolgirl."

"Terrence Mahaffey—Patron Saint of Snivelers and Dooflickers."

Mahaffey kicked at the leg of Russell's chair. "I'm wearing a hair shirt thirty years in the making, Mister Russell."

Russell extended his arms above his head, yawned, then resumed his tale. "At Pass Christian and parts north, we encountered the Cherokee Indians who came to the garrison to trade with us for steel needles, iron kettles, anything they could use. Now, Madam General, what do you know of the Cherokee People?"

I eyed him skeptically. "Very little aside from the politics of recent years, Mister Russell."

"They are foremost, a handsome people, an agricultural people," Mahaffey said, then nodded deferentially to Russell, who continued. "And amongst them, in this trading party, was a girl named Nicomi, of about twenty winters when we first made her acquaintance. We were dining, Captain Atkinson, me and Mahaffey and the others, in our company mess room. It was one of the finest meals we'd had, and I remember it most clearly. Cutlets, fried mush, butter and real coffee."

Mahaffey smiled, tapped the desk definitively.

"And buffalo tongue, sliced and roasted, on good bread with mustard. I remember that too. All of us eating in silence, the fireplace behind us so large three men could fit into it comfortably, a steady cold rain pouring down and us feeling smug, being well fed and warm and inside the quarters. The windows fogged up with all of us breathing, the smoke from the wood fire escaping into the room now and again. We were a contented lot until the door blew open."

Here Russell took up the tale: "And in strides Nicomi, this Cherokee girl, wearing a dress loomed in scarlet, soaking wet, mad as can be, shouting at us in French . . . which language I do not speak. She harangued the lot of us with obscure complaints, holding the hand of her sister, Singing Bird, no more than seven years old then, I'd guess. Mahaffey and me and Captain Atkinson stopped in mid-chew and stared at the both of them, more than a little resentful at having our repast interrupted."

I hooked my hands over my tense shoulders and frowned at them as I re-called the General revealing Nicomi's name, but nothing more, that night we camped at the Sauk settlement.

"Why was this Nicomi so angry?"

"Oh, some small matter, it was the treacherous sutler who did the trading. The Cherokee had come to trade, and Nicomi believed herself to have been cheated."

Mahaffey scratched at his jaw. "She was tall, narrow of face, up-slanting black eyes, long black hair, fine cheekbones. Beautiful girl."

"Upon seeing her, Captain Atkinson surrendered his fork, got up from the bench, walked out into the rain with Nicomi and that was both the prologue and the index to the whole matter."

"Meaning what, Mister Russell?"

"The next day, Captain Atkinson and Nicomi moved into married quarters. Neither spoke the language of the other, which greatly enhanced their romantic prospects. Syntax can obscure a romance quicker than anything, wouldn't you agree, Mister Mahaffey?"

"That I would, Mister Russell, and I am speaking now, as one dooflicker to another."

I balled both fists against my jumping stomach, then blurted, "He *married* her?"

"No, I didn't say that. I said they lived in married housing."

Now, upon hearing this news that shocked me in no little measure, I kept thinking, my God, he was in fact, if not in law, living as a married man with this Nicomi, and yet, that night in the tent in the Sauk camp, the General described her as a mere acquaintance. Russell and Mahaffey spoke on for a while, more to one another than to me, for I had gone pale, caught up as I was in my own speculations. Russell was describing how Black Hawk and his Sauk warriors raided down the Mississippi every spring, attacking isolated settlements on the river. But I was preoccupied with simpler thoughts, such as, how long were they together? The last question I asked aloud, interrupting Russell's monologue.

He replied, "The General was with Nicomi one year and a month."

Mahaffey objected, tugging at his ear, "No, now Mister Russell, I believe they were together a much shorter time, Nicomi was only recently out of childbed, and she conceived not long after meeting the General."

"A *child?*" I gasped.

"Aye," Russell answered blithely, then continued reminiscing. "Late that summer, we received orders to roust the Spanish from Mobile. Off we went, leaving Nicomi, her infant child and Singing Bird alone. After putting the Spanish troops on a transport, we sent them on their way and marched back to the post, weary, sore footed and eager for sleep. As we came down the hill overlooking the garrison, we saw it, though at a futile distance—the Sauk were attacking the Cherokee women, children, a few men. The Sauk killed the Cherokee warriors first. Then they took hostages, riding off with them, starting first with Singing Bird—who later became Black Hawk's bride. Black Hawk tried to take Nicomi captive, but she resisted him. Seeing our troops coming over the hill, Black Hawk killed Nicomi and stole her infant. Black Hawk and his band rode off far in advance of us. And though the captain and a few mounted officers pursued Black Hawk, they could not catch him."

"The captain was so distraught over Nicomi's murder, he kept vigil over her grave every night. Under his uniform, against his chest, he wore a small quill-worked bag that Nicomi made for him, a sacred bundle as she called it, with talismans to protect him. It was all he had left of her. But her death was a poison to him, from that time forward, he could not rest without thinking of how he would exact his revenge from Black Hawk."

I murmured, "It was the General who sought out Black Hawk at Plattsburgh, wasn't it? He killed Black Hawk's adopted son to get revenge for Nicomi."

"Aye."

I sat up rigidly, dropped my words one by one.

"Mister Russell, what happened to that baby?"

Russell motioned in the direction of the General's grave.

"She's up on the hill as we speak."

I gripped the edge of the desk, my heart pounding up around my ears. "Does she know?"

Mahaffey shrugged. "I don't believe she does. When the Sauk take an infant into the tribe, that child becomes Sauk. To speak of a former life dishonors the tribe. The General became reacquainted with Bright Sun again at Prairie du Chien when she was fifteen. He asked her to translate for him at councils . . . I suppose it was his mute way of trying to preserve some aspect of family. Not a very good one if you ask me. A girl as sensible as Bright Sun, he could have told her. Then again, he never told you, either."

Russell and Mahaffey nodded like the sages they perceived themselves to be. If I had slept at all in the past two days, I would have exerted myself by reeling with shock, or perhaps hurling invectives at the General's memory, but I was too tired for all of that. Even my limbs felt somewhat out of kilter. The men accorded me respectful silence while my brain whirled and I considered what should be done.

"Mister Russell, Mister Mahaffey, I think we must tell Bright Sun, don't you?"

But both men raised their hands in protest, shoved their chairs backward with a scraping noise, snatched up their shakos, slammed down their drink glasses, then hastily retreated.

Mahaffey called from the threshold, "Madam General, we'll cordially invite ourselves to leave now. And thank you for your courtesy."

"Oh no you don't." I scrambled around the desk after them. "Where do you think you're going?"

Russell affixed his shako's strap under his chin and muttered as he backed out of the room, "Now, Madam General, there are some matters what require the feminine touch, so if you don't mind . . . me and Mahaffey will go now. We have an early appointment tomorrow to have our beautiful phizzes daguerreotyped."

"You cowards!" I called after them, hearing them scuffle away.

Sitting alone in the General's office, the candles flickering fanciful shadows on the walls, I heard a small creature scratching about in the chimney flue. The solitude of the room made me feel lonely and disoriented, but then I heard footfalls in the anteroom.

"Madam General?" Russell placed his hands one on each side of the door frame and leaned forward, fixing his vision on some distant point behind my head. "We'll be at the house before eleven in the morning to assist you with packing your things . . . perhaps an aspidistra stand . . . or crating up the General's books or . . ."

His voice trailed off when he saw my chin quiver and my eyes fill, but I quickly looked away. I wiped my eyes with the heels of my hands. Russell came forward and reached across the desk, thrust a damp black handkerchief into my hand, saying, "I used it earlier, but it's still got a lot of dry in it." While I composed myself, Russell winced and eyed the exit with great longing.

"Mister Russell, I fear I unwittingly married a widower."

"If I may be so bold, Madam General, now that you are no longer in your first youth, extracting an idea from your head is akin to pulling a rusty nail out of a green hickory beam."

I sniffed, then glared at him with moist, red eyes. "How dare you?"

"Because you're the General's coconspirator. Haven't I just recited a parable of vengeance for you, thirty years in the making? And what have you done over the course of your days, you might ask yourself? I am speaking of Bright Sun."

He bored a stern look at me, hands on his hips.

I drew a breath, flashed a look out the window at Bright Sun's vigil fire. By being preoccupied with uncovering the General's secrets all those sixteen years, I never once realized how closely I had patterned myself after him. Our enemies inspired feelings of virtue and righteousness and granted purpose to our days. Hadn't I seen in Bright Sun an opponent whom I believed threatened everything I held dear?

"Madam General?" Russell said softly.

I returned the wet handkerchief to him, but he tossed it delicately into the waste can.

"I must say good night to you, Mister Russell."

I snuffed the candles, took up Walker's slate and allowed Russell to usher me out of the General's office. With a last look, we shut the door behind us, turning the handle until the latch clicked, then left the quarters in good repair, as if ready for the General to begin work in the morning. On the parade ground, Mahaffey waited for us, and seeing my tentative glance at Bright Sun, huddled before her fire on the hill, Russell slipped his hand under my elbow and searched my face with his watery gaze. The hillside flowered with wild orchids and the sweet white licorice blossoms on burred stalks. I crouched and plucked a spiked cluster from the hem of my skirt. And when I glanced up at Bright Sun's fire fading to a feeble glow on the ridge, Russell stepped before me, his face close to mine, his tone gentle and pleading.

"Woman? Is there no compromise in that soul of yours?"

Epilogue

❧ S O M E people say we fall in love with the shadow spirits of ourselves, the opposite within that never came to be, and others say we love only those whom we recognize, our familiars as it were . . . so I have often wondered, Henry, what do they say of us? Certainly not that we have finally found some little peace, or if we have, your version is sun filled, while I create a blurry shadow, exiled to quiet places where you have not ventured. I ask because your perception must be far more keen than mine. How have we come to this long separation, I ask you, look at us. Look through the snowfall at the two of us climbing into that carriage on our wedding night, going brightly into our lives. Have those exquisite hours vanished? Or have they been absorbed into the place and made part of its nature, preserved forever in the whisper of alder leaves? Passing strange, isn't it, and difficult to regard when we think of what might have been if only we hadn't been ruled by our impulses.

It is twenty years since you left me, but now you abridge my sleep, and I wake to find you standing beside the window. Seeing you here causes me a distinct unease, as if I had gone in search of a midnight disturbance, only to succeed in finding an intruder, then having no idea how to proceed. I dread knowing why you have come, but then again, this new time of war and rebellion evokes in me a long remorse. You know me, Henry. I have never quite grasped how time flows on and changes people within its current, leaving me to delude myself that while I am eternally twenty-two, the years are cruelly aging all around me. Though you keep to the curtain shadows, I see you clearly, and your uniform dates you. Men no longer present such a gentlemanly aspect. You clasp your gloves in that familiar way, then look about as if you are discomfited, and I want to cross the room and embrace you. But your countenance lengthens at the sight of me, and your expression makes me wish I could turn my face to the wall. I know the seasons have broken heavily over me; my hands are spotted by the sun, and I have been wasted by this blood fever.

What do they say of us? Still, you do not answer. Yet what I ask is a very little matter given everything you have conquered. I read the histories written about you and Black Hawk. Why, the *Republican* said you could make it rain on the Rock River, that your army fired smoke at the northern sun and the warriors told of great storms that washed the ash from the sky. Their words made me feel all the lonelier, because none of them captured you. You can imagine my surprise to find that you have come in search of me, but you've been away too long, there is so much I have to tell you, so much I learned after your passing.

Bright Sun is here with me. She teaches history at the Florrissant Indian School near my home. After you left us, I was doggedly persistent in seeking her company, asking her to tell me all she knew. At first I feared she would regard me as the widow unwelcome. But she was lonely too and relented, saying I was in no condition to view the world without escort. Thereafter, she let a room in my home, then a floor, and then it didn't matter, and why collect rent from family? We are quite a pair of cranky old ladies. She sits beside my bed, peers at me occasionally through the little oval spectacles she wears low on her nose.

This morning, she determined I had too little body left to hold my soul. She lifted my head gently, then combed out my hair over my shoulders. Bright Sun removed a vial from her tapestry bag, uncorked it with great authority, then flicked holy water on my face. I was not too sick to protest as I wiped it off my brow. "I would prefer dying unsprinkled, thank you," I said, but she ignored me and replied, "The rain falls on the just and the unjust."

"Well, which am I, in your opinion?" I asked.

Then Bright Sun opened my hand and placed Black Hawk's gift of the white bird in my palm, closed my fingers and gripped them as she whispered to me, "This is to mark the beginning of the good journey." She told me to cross the river quickly, not to hesitate, but to follow the stars. You should have told me about her, Henry, but if you have watched me as you promised, you know that I have come to love her.

I hope you see that I have kept your trust, that I have looked after her all of these years. Between the two of us, Bright Sun and I agreed we would not live by the mutual interchange of lies. Had I known she was your daughter by the Cherokee woman Nicomi, we all could have been spared so much anguish over the years. You should have been the one to tell me that Black Hawk killed Nicomi when Bright Sun was an infant, that he raised your daughter as if she were his own. How sorrowful to know that is how it began for you . . . for all of us . . . with you and Black Hawk caught up in your blind vengeance. I cannot draw a bead on Black Hawk. Was he a zealot, a murderer, or a visionary the times hatched into being? In truth he was only desperate to save something of the world he knew. Ah, Henry, you frown me down at the mention of his name. I should like to think that the better angels of your nature would have coaxed forgiveness from you, but who am I to chastise?

Like you, I wasted those hours, and I saw in Bright Sun an enemy of everything I held dear. Even thinking of it makes me shiver with my own wickedness. But when I look about in a suspicious way, waiting for retribution to appear in divine form, it never comes, because there is no such thing, is there? No tally of our transgressions is being kept in any quarter of the firmament these days. The God we know is too busy inspiring men to war.

The light in this room looks as weary as I feel; the chambermaid draws the curtains against the light, as if the light were something I should find troublesome. I wish she would open the windows and let me see the sky. Why do you keep your distance, Henry? Come close and have a seat beside me. My hand looks so old and feathery clasped in yours, but I am not at all afraid, now that you are here. There is white in your hair, but your face exudes a confidence that is pure as prayer. Let us both go home now, take a walk along the river, see the Mississippi one more time.

Take up your place on the bench where the forsythia plumes bright as a candle and draws the bees, where the ground is gray and wet from the afternoon rains and the black locust trees you planted for our children flourish. You seem in such a hurry, but this has always been your way. I wonder, are you covetous of me, or is it time itself you covet? Are you eager to bring me along because you desire my company, or will you tuck me away so that I do not interfere with your pursuits? Understand, this evening I may resist you. No, no, this time I *shall* resist you and make you wait until you have answered the question I put to you. Before you ask me once again to subjugate my will to yours, Henry, tell me, what do they say of us?

Acknowledgments

✻ I COULD not have written this novel without Dr. Liza Nelligan of Nelligan Editing, who guided me through the revision process. Victoria McGuire critiqued a dozen early drafts of the manuscript and still invites me over for dinner, which is really saying something about her good nature. I am grateful to Linda Chester at the Linda Chester Agency, also to Michael Korda, Cherise Grant, Chuck Adams, Cheryl Weinstein and publicist Rebecca J. Davis at Simon & Schuster.

Dr. Roger Nichols at the University of Arizona at Tucson generously allowed me to examine Mary Bullitt Atkinson's letters written from 1834 to 1860. His military study, *General Atkinson: A Western Military Career,* was an invaluable resource.

Dennis Northcott, Associate Archivist for Reference at the Missouri Historical Society in St. Louis, helped me to locate the General's personal papers and journals and gave me a tour of historic districts in St. Louis.

I thank Stimson Bullitt of Seattle for his friendship and for patiently responding to my questions with a keen wit and infinite kindness. A number of friends lent their professional expertise and encouragement in support of this project, including Robert E. O'Connor Jr., Jeffrey and Jodi Yonek, Charles and Cheryl Polk, Sandra L. Maass, Roxane Adams, Janet Grosjean and Charles Allgood. Lt. Col. William Gilchrist (USAF ret'd.) advised me on numerous matters. As always, Mary Patton's gentle wisdom was a guiding inspiration to me.

Elizabeth Bullitt Godfrey and Henry "Hank" Bullitt of Louisville, Kentucky, kindly gave me a tour of the Oxmoor grounds. Thanks also to Marc Kollbaum, Curator of Jefferson Barracks, and The Friends of Jefferson Barracks for their persistent efforts to preserve the hallowed ground Mary Bullitt Atkinson referred to as "that beautiful place" along the Mississippi River. I received research assistance from the Newberry Library of Chicago, the Illinois Historical Society; the Filson Club, the Kentucky Historical Society at Frankfurt; the Wisconsin Historical Society; the New Jersey Historical Society; the New York Historical Society; the Southern Historical Collection at the University of North Carolina, Chapel Hill; the Library of Virginia; the National Archives and the Library of Congress. As I wrote this book, I relied upon Ellen M. Whitney's remarkable three-volume set of The Black Hawk War Papers published in the Illinois Historical Collections. Thanks also to the divinities at the Evergreen Public Library, particularly Sally Angell, Pam Schwengler, Michelle Godden, Pat Warren and Sandy Wipf.

My son, Ian Gilchrist, enthusiastically illustrated this novel with lasers and exploding space ships, but as his art is currently being exhibited exclusively on our refrigerator, his ingenious sketches were unavailable to Scribner at the time this book went to press.

But most of all, my love to Scott, who made welcome in our home a score of invisible lodgers from another time and place.

The Good Journey

Discussion Points

1. In the prologue, Mary finds a note in the General's pocket, written by the General to an anonymous person. Whom do you believe was meant to receive this note?

2. Mary Bullitt and Henry Atkinson were married for sixteen years. In your opinion, was this a happy marriage? Why or why not? In your opinion, would Mary have been better off as an unmarried woman in Louisville? Did she sacrifice too much in this union?

3. The Black Hawk War was a small event in the scope of U.S. history. Given that this scenario with Native Americans seemed to be on instant replay countless times throughout the nineteenth century, is there anything we can learn from the Battle at Bad Axe?

4. Mary Bullitt publicly defended her husband, General Henry Atkinson, against his adversaries. But privately, she admitted that her husband was a difficult man to know. Even the General's closest friends in St. Louis murmured that he was inscrutable. What did you think of the General?

5. Why did William Clark (as evidenced by his callous treatment of York, a key member of the Corps of Discovery), Mary Bullitt Atkinson and General Henry Atkinson profess sympathy for Native Americans, yet seem utterly unmoved by the plight of enslaved African-Americans?

6. Black Hawk left the Sauk people the night before U.S. troops came upon them at Bad Axe. Should Black Hawk have stayed with the 150 members of his tribe on the river bottom until the end? Or do you believe his leaving in the night was a compassionate act, that he was deflecting vengeance away from the tribe by departing?

7. Do you believe Bright Sun's decision to follow Black Hawk was a wise one? If you had been in her position, what would you have done? Do you believe her decision would have been different if she had known the truth about Black Hawk and General Atkinson's history with Nicomi?

8. Did you feel that Mary's mother, Mrs. Diana Gwathmey Bullitt, was

or did she misguide her daughter? If you were Mrs. ⸺ have advised Mary to leave the General?

⸺ General Henry Atkinson's refusal to divulge secrets ⸺ to his wife? Do you believe that communication ⸺ usband and wife within the bounds of nineteenth-⸺ narriage was much different than it is today?

⸺ al Henry Atkinson and Mary Bullitt Atkinson had three ⸺ dren, all of whom predeceased their parents. Do you believe that ⸺ neteeth-century parents maintained greater emotional distance from their children because of high infant mortality rates?

Discover more reading group guides online
and download them for free at www.simonsays.com.